THE DROWNING HOUR

S. K. Tremayne is a bestselling novelist and award-winning travel writer, and a regular contributor to newspapers and magazines around the world. The author's debut psychological thriller, *The Ice Twins*, was picked for the Richard and Judy Autumn Book Club and was a *Sunday Times* No.1 bestseller.

Born in Devon, S. K. Tremayne now lives in London and has two daughters.

Also by S. K. Tremayne

The Ice Twins
The Fire Child
Just Before I Died
The Assistant

THE DROWNING HOUR

S. K. TREMAYNE

HarperCollins*Publishers*

HarperCollins*Publishers*
1 London Bridge Street,
London SE1 9GF

www.harpercollins.co.uk

HarperCollins*Publishers*
1st Floor, Watermarque Building, Ringsend Road
Dublin 4, Ireland

Published by HarperCollins*Publishers* Ltd 2022
1

Tarot images are from the 1909 Rider–Waite tarot deck,
illustrated by Pamela Colman Smith.

A catalogue copy of this book is available from the British Library.

ISBN: 978-0-00-830956-5 (HB)
ISBN: 978-0-00-830957-2 (TPB)

Typeset in Sabon LT by Palimpsest Book Production Limited, Falkirk, Stirlingshire

Printed and Bound in the UK using 100% Renewable Electricity
at CPI Group (UK) Ltd

MIX
Paper from
responsible sources
FSC
www.fsc.org   FSC C007454

This book is produced from independently certified FSC™ paper to ensure
responsible forest management.

For more information visit: www.harpercollins.co.uk/green

Author's Note

Dawzy Island is a creation of fiction: an amalgam of several islands on the lonely, beautiful, riverine coastlines of Essex, Suffolk and Norfolk. The River Blackwater is clearly not fictitious; it certainly exists: with its oyster beds and marinas, power stations and bird reserves. I have, however, taken some licence with its precise geography: moving villages, changing names, borrowing features, altering exact locations. I hope those who are fortunate enough to know this unique and poetic corner of England will forgive me.

As ever I want to thank my brilliant editors, Jane Johnson and Phoebe Morgan, and also my agent Eugenie Furniss – for seeing this book through to its birth, but also for being there during the trials of lockdown.

For Star, still

THE MOON.

1

Hannah, Now

Water. Just water.

That's all it is.

Get over it.

Even as I say this to myself, gazing at the darkness of the white-painted ceiling, I can hear another voice in my head. *Just* water? *Just?*

Water is *everything*. Water is my body, water is the womb and water was the dream. I grew up looking at water, the river that leads to the sea; I was a yearning little girl, hoping to travel the planet and sail across the waters.

Just water? We seek it out every day, to wash, to drink, to cook; we dive in it, we swim in, we run to it, we hunger to live by it.

We sink in it—

I turn over on the pillow, crushing my eyes shut.

We sail in it, we play in it, splash and plash, trickle, squirt, flush, sprinkle. Sex is mainly water: the moistness, the wetness, the flush of wet blood in the tingling skin, a soft wet kiss drying on the cheek.

Get up, Hannybobs.

Lifting my eyes, I check my little clock, the friendly, glowy green digits: *5.36 a.m.*

Why do I keep waking up at this merciless time? It has become the Waking Hour. Between five and six most days, ever since IT happened. Sometimes if I lie really still and shut my eyes hard and mummify myself in the duvet and banish nasty thoughts, I can get back to a kind-of sleep, which then becomes a gaudy parade of dreams, like an unwanted circus arriving in town: a cavalcade of zombie clowns, leering acrobats, tumbling freaks, huge trumpeting elephants, me.

Often, I just lie here, wondering if I should simply get the hell up, given that I probably won't be able to go back to sleep; knowing, however, that if I do get up, my best time, when my mind is most fertile, will be spent sitting around, eyes open, brain whirring fruit-lessly: filing memories away, taking them out again. And then in an hour, the great building will begin to stir around me: a whistling sous-chef, the clatter of the kitchens, hurrying maids laughing in whispers, and I will smell the first bacony breakfast smells, and I will likely hear the guests having vigorous morning sex down the corridor in Room 14, and then I know I will really have to *get up*.

Shower, in water. Make tea, with water. Drink coffee, made with as little water as possible. Short and black and multiple, because I will need endless coffees in the main office above reception to fight the yawns that are the daily wages of rising this early.

Get up.

This time, I obey. Pushing away the duvet, I consider turning on the lamp, but I decide not to. I like the dark. It hides things. And besides, it is not a total dark: there

2

is a near-full moon, and its fragile silveriness floods around the half-closed curtains. Which are means to hide me from that tormenting view onto the Blackwater River.

Stretching my hand out towards the door, I find my soft blue dressing gown, lovely and warm and fluffy, and definitely not a witch hanging from a hook.

That's a sharp memory, returning unprompted.

I am seven or eight years old waking up in my little bedroom and in the chilly gloom I see my long winter coat hanging from the door, but it looks like a crook-necked witch executed on a gallows in that book about witches, and I scream until Mummy rushes in and takes me in her arms, surrounds me, like warm water embracing soft coral. She soothes and cuddles me, kisses my forehead, with wine on her breath from last night mixed with minty toothpaste. But with so much love. The scent of faintly sour wine can mean love to me, even now.

On the best nights, if Dad was away, Mum would say, *OK, Hannybobs, you can*, and I would gleefully rise, all witches forgotten, and pick up Toffee the Bear by a ragged arm and follow her down the cold landing to her warm bed and she would let me sleep the rest of the sweet, perfectly dreamless night beside her, my heart slowing, fears dispelled, breathing deep and calm, like the sea in the summer, and me inhaling her scent, home-made perfume, home-made soap, Mummy smell.

The dressing gown enfolds me, warms me. My bare feet find my slippers in the moonlit dark. I can see the kettle and teapot . . . but I am, inevitably, drawn to the View Out There. I am going to do it. I am going to look at the Blackwater.

It is always like this. Some days I cannot bear to look

at the Blackwater. I close the curtains for twenty-four hours; I hide away. On the worst days I physically avert myself from, say, the famous, bay-windowed view in the heart of the hotel, as I walk through the brasserie to get breakfast. When I do this, I can sense guests peering at me: *Why is she looking to the side like that?*

At other times, like today, I yield, and stare at it. My enemy. My life. My home. My walls. The flowing Blackwater, part-sea, part-river, part-salty, part-coffin. Four parts making one pure terror.

Quickly, as if I am tearing off a plaster, I rip open the curtains. There she is. The Blackwater hasn't gone away. She runs past the hotel: a deep throb of lateral darkness, west to east. The reflection of the late September moon is a lane of silver cobbles. The night is cloudless. The miniature orange and scarlet lights of Goldhanger sparkle wetly at the far edge of the black.

I want to smell it. I need to breathe it in. Otherwise, I might get the fears again.

This is my allotted therapy, to expose myself.

My room has a handsome sash window, in keeping with the Regency core of the hotel. It's also old, stiff and takes an effort to lift, but when I manage, I am rewarded: the tide must be in because the air smells gorgeous, sweet and salt and ozoney, rather than of mudflats and fermenting brineweed.

As I breathe deep, I can hear the endless cries of the waterbirds in the dark before dawn. Wigeons, shelduck, turnstones? I'm never entirely sure. There are many species on the island; they sing most of the day, and often all night. If I look hard, I can see them, maybe alerted by the sound of the window opening. They are flittering away in the night, like tiny, frightened ghosts.

And what is that?

There is a small but elegant speedboat, moored up to the jetty. I don't recognize it. It could be anyone's. Freddy's spare? But it looks too sleek. Pricey. A guest's maybe? Some come privately. I often see boats, if I am brave enough to look out across the Blackwater.

The fears churn.

I will. I can. Why not? Right now? Jump in that handy little boat, pull the ripcord, and go. Because there has to come a day, an hour, a moment, when the rushing tides in my head will turn. I've been told this will happen, so maybe this could be that time: unexpected, but desired. The door is opening.

Could it be now?

NOW.

I must not waste this unique feeling of sudden fearlessness.

I will be stealing the boat but who cares? I'll give it back at the other side.

The tingling hope is almost unbearable.

Dressed. Ready. Pushing the door open, I peer out as if I am committing a crime. I suppose I am.

The corridor is silent, the smoke alarm regarding me with a singular, insectoid red eye. The guests in Room 14 are still silent. The maids are asleep.

There is no one, and nothing, to stop me.

Jogging down the corridor, I take a left. I don't want to storm through the building even if it is the quickest way. I might be seen. I've caused enough *trouble*.

Another left brings me to the external fire escape. Metal bar across it. I know it is not alarmed. I can just push. And I know that beyond this door the steep shingle beach begins; I'll run down it, crunching pebbles under boots, climb onto the jetty, untie the boat, trigger the motor – and steer away. Escaping my prison.

5

Sweating with excitement, nerves, the impossibility of this, I shunt the metal bar and the door swings open with a creeeeak like a bird. And as soon as I step onto the clanking shingle it happens.

Of course. I knew it would happen. Who was I kidding? What was I thinking? What was the point?

The fear breeds the fear.

The brent geese are honking, mocking. Catcalling the silly woman on the darkened beach, the scared young woman standing perfectly still in the moonlight as her brain fizzes like bad electrics, like the wiring in the east wing, the one we haven't finished yet.

First my throat closes, as if someone is choking me. What did the therapist tell me? The word *anxiety* comes from Latin *angere*: to choke.

Now comes the horrible dizziness, water in my brain, blurring vision: sometimes I can go blind. Next, I feel my heart: pounding like a baboon with a drum – *bang bang bang* – painful, angry, dangerous. I know how bad this can get: sometimes it is so bad I faint. I've read that it could possibly kill me – it is rare, but it happens – extreme tachycardia, panic so bad you die. And just the thought of that makes it all worse.

The fear breeds the fear breeds the fear. My heart is hurting, and it is way too much. Too frighteningly painful. As if it will burst through my ribs.

Retreat, retreat. Quickly, shudderingly, I step back into the building, turning my back on the river. I won't look again, today.

The door swings shut, and the silence imprisons me. I am defeated. As usual.

Ashamed of my cowardice, I lean back against the wall, and slide to the floor.

My heart is slowing, the panic receding – but now

comes the sadness. Tears roll. Hot salty water. Why do we make hot salty water when we are sad?

It is just water. And I am making lots of it. It dribbles down my chin and runs through my pale fingers.

Oh Hannah, little Hannybobs, you can't get over it.

2

My jeans are clean, my tears are dried, my shirt is crisp, white and pressed, and my pink cashmere jumper gives a necessary hint of luxury for someone working, even if it is in the back offices, at a high-end hotel. I don't have to suit up like Leon, the concierge, or Alistair the manager, but I am still expected to look 'respectable' when passing through common areas.

I am not expected to go out on the beach at dawn to steal boats. That is not 'respectable'; neither is it desired that I should slump to the floor, sobbing with panic and grief just as Elena the Polish maid comes down the corridor carrying clean pillowslips.

Luckily, I managed to crawl back, unseen, into the shadows.

Now Elena *is* here: she waves as I head for reception. She is pushing her trolley filled with mops and cloths and cleaning kit, and chic little soaps, Earl Grey teabags, tiny White Company shampoo bottles, Nespresso pods. She is much prized by management: she can turn a room, perfectly, in eighteen minutes.

'Lovely day!' I say, brightly, happily faking it all.

Elena gives me her crooked smile. Then she gestures, as if she has a delicious secret. 'People in Room 14. My God, Hannah!'

'They actually broke the bed this time?'

She leans close, but then we both see Owen, the pink-faced young sous-chef, buttoning his whites as he heads for the kitchens. We are never allowed to gossip about guests, not in public; we break apart, guiltily.

'See you later, Elena!' I chirp and she grins, and we get on with our days. Mine takes me down the corridor into reception. I say hello to Danielle – local, dyed blonde, harshly pretty, lots of make-up, thirty, smart, friendly, yet always that bit distant. She's possibly sleeping with Logan Mackinlay, the Mackster, the genius head chef. Or she did sleep with him, and they've stopped? Gossip about staff also circulates; I hear some of it.

Danielle is looking in the BOOK.

Ever since the day we reopened, the Stanhope has kept a grand, old-fashioned Guest Book. We did it deliberately, to give an echo of the Stanhope in its heyday. It was my idea.

We could have used tablets and e-signatures, like everyone else, but instead we had an old guest registry bound in tooled leather, and we bought some fine Visconti fountain pens to go with it. This told the arriving new guest: this hotel does things differently, and luxuriously. Sign your name here, please. We insist that *everyone* signs. This book is like the Stanhope's family bible. It never lies, and it contains all the truth.

Whenever I see the Book I get a tiny puff of pride. My idea.

Now I climb the big grand circular stairs, one of the glories of this historic building; late last year it was restored with blue-and-white-striped Regency-style wallpaper and hung with authentic paintings of coastal East Anglian scenes, red-sailed boats on the Stour, oystermen toiling at Mersea.

Every time I climb these stairs, I get another little lift: because I helped the design team source the wallpaper, wanting it to reflect the sky and air and water outside. The lovely paintings and sketches came from Oliver, who probably already owned them, hanging in one of his many houses.

Into the office. It's quite modern and open-plan, but still stylish.

Loz is already at work, absorbed by the screen at her desk. The assistant manager. Forty-three. Divorced. Funny. Dark-haired. Part Italian. Sardonic. Lapsed vaper, reverted smoker. Loz Devivo. When I came here – it seems so long ago, yet it was less than two years – I asked her how she got her faintly unusual name. 'Sweetheart,' she said, 'I was christened Lola Devivo. Imagine being called Lola Devivo? Everyone just assumes you do sex work. And *Lolly* Devivo makes me sound like I do sex work in tartan miniskirts. So, I went for Loz.'

Loz is silent now – she mouths an amiable, distracted hello, then returns to work.

Plonking myself on one of Oliver's thousand-pound office chairs, I turn on my screen. A big image of the salt-white Atacama Desert fills the space: my computer wallpaper. No water there at all. Not a drop. Literally the driest place on earth: Yungay, Chile. Clicking through, I go to the website I also set up and designed when I arrived here.

This was one of my main tasks, as brand manager, recruited and promoted from my position as PR girl in the Maldives. Build a brand. Make us a fancy website. Make us glamorous again. That's what Oliver told me, urgently, eagerly, his handsome face wide-eyed with passion.

And so, I did. And my first true task was to change the name of the place. For years the hotel had been known as the Stanhope Gardens Island Hotel. A name which, I decided, was both off-puttingly long, and a lie. There are no grandiose landscape gardens, just pretty little lawns and nooks: the island is far too small, and ninety-eight per cent of it, anyway, is ultra-protected, publicly owned, don't-pick-a-flower primordial ancient woodland, a site of special scientific interest, full of sacred old trees, rare birds and mammals. Red squirrels, dormice, hares, pine martens. We are super proud of our pine martens.

We are not so proud of our gardens, which are merely agreeable. So, I got rid of 'Gardens' and shortened the name to *the Stanhope*. And as soon as I did, I knew I'd aced it. THE STANHOPE. It captured the history and felt luxe without being pompous. When I told Oliver, his greyish-green eyes lit up. Yes!

Sitting back now, I page through the website. I am still proud of it. All those elaborate photo shoots! Took us months. Wine bottles artfully posed by the brasserie windows. Sunlight shot-slant through the rich ruby liquid. White-sailed yachts visible outside.

That single image took us two days to get exactly right, to give the sense of discreet, effortless luxury, but without any bling. After we went live – website, adverts, fam trips for journalists – bookings doubled in a month, then doubled again. Oliver bought us all champagne.

Click. Another shot. Outside. The river blue and benign. Oysters gleaming on the half shell on a sunlit table, with shallot mignonette on the side. A lovely young woman in a summer dress holds a parasol; I remember she was actually freezing. It was autumn and she kept swearing at the photographer to *Get a fecking move on, wanker.*

11

Another shot. The jetty. Freddy Nix the ferryman. This shot is to show you that the Stanhope is *extra* special: sequestered – in six years of hotel PR you get to learn that tourists love the word 'sequestered' – on its own unique island, with muntjac deer in the hazel-woods. The ultimate English bolthole.

Frowning now, I lean closer. There is a distinctive boat in that photo. Is it the little speedboat I saw in the dark this morning? Possibly. Hard to tell.

A prickle of unease, more than the usual, reaches my typing fingertips. Lifting my head from the screen, I start to ask Loz if she saw the boat or knows anyone who owns a fast black speedboat. But she's gone. I didn't hear her leave. I was too absorbed. Must be lunchtime.

My phone chimes. Message. Mr Moody Fiancé. Ben!

Han, babe, we've only gone n dunnit

I type back, smiling. My man speaks. The man I love. My gastropub chef with the sexy tattoos. Just by messaging, he tells me: life is not all bad. I have *him*, for a start.

Done what? Exploded the pub? I warned you
about pressure cookers

Haha, funny lady. No no we've got a full lunch service, first time ever, 30 covers, zero no-shows. Kev says we turned punters AWAY!!

My smile broadens. He is clearly and sincerely thrilled, and he should be: building a foodie pub is harder than most people can conceive, perhaps because it is so rarely witnessed.

12

Wow! Darling. I am SO proud of you! If only I was there, we could drown ourselves in Nyetimber. You deserve this. You worked so hard. You must celebrate 🥂

Pause. *Typing* . . .

Hannah, we will celebrate. Maybe a quick drink at the Stannie tomorrow? And you WILL get off that bloody island. I'll carry you off if I have 2!

Oooh. Manly. I like. Yes please tomorrow 👍

OK gotta go, mad here, but yay xx

He goes offline. I set the phone down, stretch, still half-smiling. *Ben* believes in me. Maybe he is right to believe in me? I do rather like the concept of him literally carrying me away over the waters. A young bride at a threshold.

Standing up, I cross the office to the windows, and I take this good energy and I tell myself to *enjoy* the grandiose view of the Blackwater. Be positive.

I look out. The little black speedboat has gone from the jetty. It came in the darkness, and now it has stolen away. Across the Blackwater. I guess that's not strange. We have some *very* rich guests who are used to doing exactly as they please.

3

The English fizz is finished; the bottle lies on the floor. We must have kicked it over in our passion. The glassy flutes are drained; one is toppled. My heart is still beating from the sex. In an agreeable way.

Ben is climbing out of bed, and into his clothes: rugby-player legs in dark jeans, muscled arms punching through white shirtsleeves. I'd like to lie back and admire, but I also want to see him off, on the ferry: because every moment of his company is precious. In my isolation.

'Hey, slow down. I want to come to the jetty.'

He looks my way, buttoning up the shirt. 'Babe, you don't have to.'

I meet his gaze. Meaningfully. 'I do. You don't know how much I miss you.'

His handsome face softens, into boyish kindness, making him look more my age, twenty-eight, than his, thirty-four. He leans close, kisses me – soft, tender, much softer than the kisses of half an hour ago. Then he surveys the room, the bottle, the glasses, the roiled bedsheets everywhere.

'Looks like a bomb went off.'

'Don't flatter yourself. A minor grenade.'

He laughs, happily, as now I race into my own clothes. He looks my ways and says, 'Come on then, woman. Hurry.'

Obediently, I dress, until I am coated and booted – though the dying day is mild. Arm in arm we walk down the corridor, through reception, then we clank down the shingle to the jetty; the bright red regular ferry is not far away – it breasts the modest waves of the Blackwater, bouncily, cheerfully. A boat in a kid's book. One that might talk to trains.

My head is resting on Ben's firm shoulder. I still feel post-coital, a little dreamy. Twilit. Ben is silent. I lift my eyes, look at him. 'You OK?'

He is staring, pensively, down the island, at the unused part of the hotel, the east wing, the empty rooms. Or maybe the darker woods that begin immediately after-wards. Or he is simply staring at nothing, just thinking, remembering. Ben has moments of random sadness. He lost his mother at an early age, as I did: it is one of the things that bonded us from the start.

'Ben?'

He snaps out of it. 'Ah, sorry, Han. Just pub stuff. Orders. VAT. All that.'

I squeeze his strong, cheffy hand.

'I am proud of you, what you've done. Everyone was so sceptical and look.'

'Thanks, sweetheart, but . . . long way to go yet.' He glances away. 'All right, the ferry's here. I must get back before Charlie attempts a roulade. Loads more bookings tonight!'

He grins, I smile, we wave, and off he goes. Leaping from the jetty down onto the ferry, which is otherwise largely empty. For a few moments I watch the boat as it pushes away and revolves, heading for the mainland, as I cannot.

My mood darkens instantly. I am *sincerely* proud of my fiancé. The man I love is doing great things. He's

15

been a chef in his pub for a while, but he only took over, entirely, a few weeks ago. So, this sudden success is wonderful.

But what if it does *too* well? What if it consumes him? Then he will have even less time to come here and see me.

And thus, my solitary confinement will intensify.

4

'Where are you, Han?'

'Ohh, have a guess.'

I can hear the buzz of a London restaurant, or a bar, beyond Kat's silence. It is 3 p.m. So, this is what, a late lunch, a daylong bender, mega-early drinks?

She drawls, 'OK. I'll have a guess . . .' The bar noise briefly ebbs, and I enviously imagine her taking her drink. Swizzling it. Popping an olive. Saying, 'I know! You're in Buenos Aires. That famous steakhouse, the one we visited, gap year, by the water. Cabaña Las Lilas! Remember? You've gone back there! Wow. Nice one. No, hold on, wait, you can't go back there; we did a runner. My idea wasn't it? Soz boz, apolibobs.'

I laugh as I stride along one of the narrow lanes that thread the Dawzy woods. Magpies crark in the oaks as twigs snap under my walking boots. It is thought that the island was named, many centuries ago, for them: the crows and magpies and jackdaws. There are so many birds here in the woods, as there are out there on the saltmarsh. Birds everywhere. Birds arguing in the boughs, or sieving the muds, or skimming the waves. Watching us. Watching me.

Is someone watching me?

I turn, alerted, peering through blackthorn: this eastern lane is lonely.

Nothing. Paranoia is another symptom of my syndrome. I must control it.

My sister says, 'Han?'

'That doesn't work.'

'What?'

'Adding soz boz to apolibobs.'

'Eeeesh. OK, OK. I promise to do better, Robinson-bobs Crusoe-dogs. Ooh, uh-huh? Another martini? Whyever not? Thank you. I think six should be about right. Yep.'

I have no idea who she is boozily chatting with. Probably another rich boyfriend. She has so many. She toys with them; they seem to enjoy it. I'm just glad she is also talking to me, in between drinks. I miss my sister fiercely: one of the worst aspects of being Robinson-bobs Crusoe-dogs is that I am physically distanced from her, the person who – along with Ben – is closest to me in my life, my world, my everything.

We were close even as little girls: born about a year apart, and with similar looks, practically twins. Except Kat has always been *that* much prettier and cleverer than me. It is as if I am the beta version, the prototype, and she is alpha, the finished thing.

Her cheekbones are decorously slanted; mine are unimpressive. Her button nose is perfectly retroussé; mine boasts a tiny, annoying bump. Her blonde hair is lush; mine looks OK if I make a lot of effort.

When we were kids, everyone said how pretty we were. When we grew up I remained just that: 'quite pretty', 'kinda pretty'. Meanwhile, my adored and indulged younger sister Katalina Langley, Kattydogs, KattyKat, Kat, the Tarot-reading, stargazing, wit-cracking, handbag-losing, super-funny, multilingual, microskirted, underwear-forgetting, ukulele-playing, ultra-dyspraxic, weed-smoking, French-ballad-singing,

18

rune-reading, rebel chick schoolyard star of St Osyth Comprehensive, Maldon, was – and is – *beautiful*.

That's what boys would say to me at teenage parties. They'd sidle up to me with a glass of beer in hand, as if they were about to chat me up, and then they'd sip their beer wistfully and gaze into the centre of the booming room where Kat, in her denim hotpants or tiny red 'ironic' cheerleader skirt was, inevitably, surrounded by a bunch of guys competing like puppies for her attention and those wistful boys with the beers would sigh, and lean closer, and say to me, 'You know, your sister is really *beautiful*.'

After that they'd stare moodily into their beers, and every so often the more polite of them would quickly blurt, 'Oh, sorry, I didn't mean to . . . you know . . . you're um you're um, you're really beautiful too . . .'

Sometimes I would kiss these lying boys; occasionally I'd even sleep with them: these crumbs swept from Kat's table, unnoticed.

I didn't mind. I don't mind. *I never mind.* Kat is Kat and I adore her, and she gives all the love right back. We do everything together. Best friends, sisters, soulmates, sometimes even more than that. It was Kat, aged about six, who playfully started adding 'bobs' and 'dogs' to words, or 'jogs' or 'pops' or 'gogs'. A kind of personal Pig Latin but even sillier. Mum and Dad picked up a bit of it, but in reality it was our private sisterly language, shared solely by the two of us, and sometimes it could make us laugh for hours at the best ones: the stupidest, most pointlessly elaborate.

Soz boz, apolibobs.

It's actually not bad.

'Kat?' More buzzing bar noises. 'Kat, speak to me. I'm marooned on a bloody island.'

'Sorry, Han. I was trying to show this barman how to make a dirty martini. But he got confused and used bitters. I think I'm done now. I want to go home to knit cardigans for dogs. Blind dogs. Blind dogs for the guides. What a brilliant idea for a charity. Or cats, dancing on their hind legs. A cat with a face like Jane Witham. Remember that? Haha. Are you OK?'

'Yeah, I'm OK.'

'You sure, babybobs?'

'Yes, it's not easy, but yes. I'm coping.'

'OK, OK. I promise I'll come visit as soon as P.' Another pause, enviable laughter, then she's back. 'How's Ben? How's Mr Moody Fiancé?'

'He's fine. Frantic. Pub doing really well.'

A tinge of self-pity has entered my voice. Loneliness emerging. I fight to suppress it, by walking faster. The wood is opening out onto yet another steep shingle beach. I am reminded, for the nineteenth time today, that I am stuck on an island. The enormous coastal Essex sky is pale blue, yet lively with a regatta of racing clouds chased by a warm, stiffening wind. Sporting weather.

The tide must be out: at the end of the shingle, I can see tracks of the waterbirds – avocets, oystercatchers? – in the beige-grey gloop of tidal mud. Their prints are so delicate. The same Japanese letters repeating in a long, sad, lovely curving loop.

Kat has gone completely quiet again. But I can't hear the frizzy bar noise any more. Where is she now?

'Sis?'

'Outside. Uber. Got Tarot sesh later. Then Deliveroo. Wank. Bed. I've drunk too much.'

'It's not even four o'clock!'

'I know. God, I know. Am I an alkybobs?'

'Possipops.'

We both chuckle, and then . . . I stop. The question replays. Why *does* Kat keep postponing her much-promised visit to Dawzy? I know she is *super-biz-dogs* in London, reading Tarot cards for money, having lunch with helpless adoring businessmen who buy all her exquisite lingerie, volunteering a day a week at the homeless shelter, doing the odd comedy burlesque show – she's turned her dyspraxia into an erotic art form: falling off lap dancing poles, accidentally losing her bra – nonetheless she's not exactly a hard-pressed heart surgeon, she has ample spare time, and can pick and choose the days she works, or the weeks she thinks fuck it, and goes travelling in Kerala *again*.

Yet she doesn't drive here, doesn't get on Freddy Nix's ferry. I am less than two hours from London. Yet, no sister for ages.

A thought pierces. A sad, terrible thought. I am sure I am right.

'Kat, tell me the real reason you don't come here?'

Silence. I hear a car door slam.

'Kat. Tell me.'

She sighs, hard, long. 'Han, darling . . . I . . . just . . .'

'Is it because of what happened, that night? It is, isn't it?'

A short, sharper silence. Then: 'Of course it is, Han! It *haunts* me. I have *nightmares*. I know it's much much worse for you but . . . But oh God, it was so awful. I mean, it was my fault. I started it. Skinny-dipping? Midnight? Brilliant idea, Kattykogs, just brill, oh Kat you fucking idiot. Why am I such an idiot? I'm so so sorry.'

'It wasn't your fault! Everyone was doing it; everyone was drunk.'

'No. You can't excuse me. Jesus.'

'Kat?'

'Oh, fucketty-fuck I'm crying now. I miss you so much, Han. I'm drunk and I'm sad and the driver is worried about me, keeps checking the mirror.' She laughs through the tears. 'I'd better go, before he climbs in the back to console me. Why do they always want to console me? Bye, darling. My delicate firebrand darling! Goodbye! I will come, I promise. I love you. I WILL.'

The call ends and I pocket the phone. Watching a grey-and-white seabird wheel across the salty Blackwater just in front of me. Graceful and free.

Guilt throbs, as I think of Kat's words. Because it *wasn't* really Kat's fault, not wholly, not that night. I should have done something. After all, I've always been the responsible one, the older sister, the one who finished her degree and got a proper career. And that night I was literally the Responsible One, a member of staff – and I didn't stop them.

Worse than that, I actually went in the water with them: eagerly, happily, enthusiastically. Something I've never properly admitted. Not even to the inquest, when I had to give evidence by video link to a courtroom in Colchester. I just told the court I was worried, so I followed.

It was a lie. I had to lie. I'm a liar.

5

Evening falls, noticeably earlier than the last time I checked. My room grows dark; I have yet to turn the lamps on, a pathetic act of resistance against the encroaching armies of autumn.

What will winter be like?

I try not to think about that. I stare at the window. Tonight, I will close the curtains, shroud my jailer. I must. Fuck exposure therapy. There is a limit.

So, I go the window. Aaaaaaaand . . . I do not close the curtains. I gaze out, and I yearn.

The autumn evening is sadly beautiful. A faint mist drifts gauzily across the Blackwater, down to Bradwell-on-Sea, as if it is the long, slender soul of the dying river, suspended above it.

High above, the first stars glint luminously through the estuarine mist, like diamond studs on blue velvet. Venus? Jupiter? Kat would know.

Squinting into the gloom, I see that Freddy Nix is once again loading his ferry at the jetty. Some have big suitcases: departing guests. Quite a few. Others hop down the steps onto the big red boat with little or no baggage: staff. Freddy gives every one of them a cheery grin. Freddy is quite the lad, nearly fifty. And he knows, and is warmly welcomed in, practically every pub on the estuary from Jaywick to Heybridge. He lives in

Goldhanger with a twenty-five-year-old girlfriend. His latest. Georgia Quigley. Works for Mersea Oysters. Delivers fish to the Mackster.

Roughly half the Stanhope's staff commute across the river daily on Freddy's boat. Most of the rest have rooms here, but go to the mainland at weekends, and for holidays. Top management come and go as they please.

Just one person stays here forever. Robinson-bobs Crusoe-dogs. Me. Stranded with the polecats and screech owls. Soon they will become my only real friends. And I will sit in the woods, muttering incantations. Communing with the yews.

Enough. I *cannot* spend another night in my room, listlessly reading novels chosen mainly for their length so as to use up time, or apathetically engaging on social media, roiling with envy for everyone who has a life.

I could call Ben in Maldon? But no: I can't. The fiancé will be knee-deep in *jus* and *moules*: running his three-man gastropub does not allow for leisurely video calls at 7 p.m.

Drink, then in the Spinnaker, the hotel's more casual bar. Staff can drink in the Mainsail – the brasserie – but it's really meant for guests and eating.

Smartening up my clothes – nice jumper, proper shoes – I exit.

The bar is at the centre of the hotel, near reception, the other side of the brasserie: it is a swish, bright, airy space with views of the little terrace at the back, where there are pentagonal wooden tables, overhung by patio heaters. Pictures of famous yachts hang on all the Spinnaker walls. Huge, aristocratic vessels from the 1920s. Some of these boats surely came here for the famous cocktails, back in the Stanhope's first incarnation as a pleasure palace.

Tonight, the Spinnaker is chattery, but not remotely rammed. That's fine. Don't want a party. I'll probably never want a party again. Choosing a place to drink, I glance out of the windows at the tables, swimming pool and the outer wall of darkened woods. The terrace is deserted, the patio heaters switched off. It is utterly empty.

Pulling out a stool at the bar, I flick a smile at the barman, Eddie.

'All right, Eddie?'

He smiles warmly. Nice guy Eddie. Aussie. Quite handsome. I believe he is sleeping with a maid. Everyone sleeps with everyone else. Big and isolated hotels are always like this. In the Maldives it was one of two things you could do: snorkelling (which was fabulous), or sex with another staff member (variable).

'Evenin'. Usual, Hannah?'

'Indeedy doody.'

I don't know where that came from. *Indeedy doody?* A creaky old phrase from Dad, probably. Eddie does not seem to notice the odd answer. He is at work. I watch. It is always interesting to watch someone expert doing a task they love. First, he pours a lavish shot of prize-winning Mistley gin, then he scoops a silver shovelful of chunky ice into a big bowl of glass. After that, he deftly lobs in preserved orange, juniper berries, cardamom and his special bespoke hit of chilli, then the juicy foam of Framlingham Tonic.

Eddie is serious about his drink making. I am serious about my drinking. It is my solitary escape, my own ferryboat to Goldhanger. I am the only one not sleeping with anyone else: not even my fiancé, because his visits really have dwindled.

Lifting the drink, I inhale the tingle of fizz, savouring the eager anticipation. Eddie makes fabulous G&Ts.

25

'Staying here long then?'

Ah, Christ. A talkative guest. Often, I like to chat with guests, but tonight is not one of those times. I just want to get quietly sozzled, alone, in a bar. Yet I cannot be rude.

Gluing a pro smile to my face, I turn to the guy on the next stool along. Fortyish, nice jacket, velvet loafers.

'Yes, been staying here . . . a while. You?'

He extends a hand. 'Ryan. Here with the wife, Melissa, wedding anniversary! Twelve years! Good God!' He laughs at his own words, as if being married itself is a joke. 'Just for one night, though. We've got a table at the Mainsail. Is it as good as they say?'

'Yes,' I say. 'It really is.'

It is my job to promote the hotel, but the restaurant requires no promoting. It is genuinely brilliant. When Oliver bought up the Stanhope, he knew he needed a great restaurant with a great chef. The hotel has a nice little gym, a sweet little spa, an elegant heated pool, but that's it. Unless you *love* sailing or birding or hiking on beaches or hearing legends about maidens being kidnapped by piratical smugglers – or dealing with Leon our imposing, impatient Swiss-German concierge with the extraordinarily nice wristwatches – there isn't *that* much reason to come here, especially off-season, when the pool is closed and the sailing frigid. So, Oliver is offering the best food and bev for thirty miles.

I pursue the point. Brightly. 'You've not heard of the chef? Logan Mackinlay. Scottish, headhunted from the Connaught in London. They say he'll get his first Michelin star next month. Not that he cares: he's his own man, a proper genius.'

Ryan beams with satisfaction. 'Sounds good. Not so much of a foodie myself, but the wife loves it. Just as

26

long as she's happy!' He shrugs, contentedly. 'Anyway, it was her choice, coming here – she works with the hotel management. We're getting a discount. Result!'

He grins as he sips from his flute of champagne. We chat aimlessly for a while, but mainly in a way that ensures I know that he's doing *really* well in real estate. As I knock back my own drink, I think about what he's saying. About his wife. Melissa. I have heard the name. Oliver has mentioned it. On the finance side, maybe a banker, in London? Not my field.

Ryan tilts back the last foamy drop of champagne, then looks at me with a conspiring eye. 'Did you hear what happened here in the summer?'

A pause. This is the one thing that stops me drinking in the Spinnaker every single night: fear of being asked this question. What do I reply? Oh yes, I was there; I made it all worse. Call the cops now.

'No. Some kind of party that . . . went wrong?'

Just a bit, Han.

Ryan shakes his head. 'I had a friend who was here that night. The party. He tells me it was *wild.*' Ryan is blushing faintly. 'The girls, you know. Ah. Naked girls. And some of the rumours!'

There are *rumours*? Beyond what I know? Rumours of *what*?

I desperately want to hear the rumours; I desperately do not. What if they involve me? Or Kat?

I am not going to hear them anyway. Ryan veers off, in the excited way people have, when they have good gossip to impart.

'What's crazier is *this*. Apparently, there's some woman here, trapped, because of the drowning thing. She's actually got a fear of water. Imagine that. She can't get off the bloody island.'

I open my mouth to speak, but I have no idea what to say.

Ryan doesn't mind. He continues, with gusto, 'Freak show, right? And there's more. Melissa says the some of the management are just *desperate* to get rid of this madwoman, get her away. *They want rid of her.* But of course, they can't, because she's stuck. She can't cross the water!'

He sits back, happily awaiting my reaction to this deliciously weird story. I am trying not to tremble, trying not to give anything away, trying not to obviously be that same madwoman.

'Ah!' Ryan gazes over my shoulder. 'Sweetheart. Hello.'

I turn, concealing my fierce anxiety – or so I hope.

A tall, blonde, attractive woman wearing a discreet pearl necklace has appeared at the bar. Ryan stands up and pecks her check. 'Darling, you were ages!'

The woman sighs, sits on a stool. 'The babysitter called. Louis was playing up. I had to sing him a song.'

Ryan chuckles, switches his attention: between the wife and me.

'So, Mel, I was just telling this guest your story, about the madwoman who's trapped here.'

My heart hurts. Out of the side of my eye I can see Melissa. She is staring at me intently. I know this gaze, have seen it several times: it means she knows me. She's seen pictures, social media, wherever. Or I've been pointed out by the same management who, apparently, loathe me.

She knows exactly who I am.

Ryan rambles on, 'Isn't it creepy, the woman who can't get off, yet everyone else can and she just wanders about—'

Melissa kicks Ryan's stool. The toe of her expensive

shoe makes a clanging sound against the metal leg. He turns, confused, as Melissa tilts her head, discreetly, but not that discreetly, in my direction. Silently saying: that's *her*, you stupid, blundering oaf.

Ryan's blush goes from pink to crimson.

Melissa speaks, coldly. 'Nearly eight, Ryan. Mustn't be late for dinner. They have Brancaster natives.'

Still blushing, Ryan rises and says a stuttery goodbye and briskly follows Melissa like a loyal hound.

I am left alone with my gin, my chilli, my juniper berries and my brooding thoughts.

Desperate to get rid of her.

6

Kat, Then

Kat Langley sashayed through the Goldhanger boatyard, carrying a large, deliciously soft leather bag over her arm, enjoying the sensation of the hot June sun on her bare arms. Enjoying the sensation of the male gaze on her long, suntanned legs. All around her, men were painting boats, unfurling sails, examining keels – and now half were pausing, open-mouthed, tools in hand, to watch the young woman swinging along the duck-board.

Let them look, she thought, *because they won't be looking forever.* She might still pass for twenty-one now, at the age of twenty-six, but one day she would cross that inevitable line, and the male gaze would not be so easily snagged.

That was the key to life, Kat had long ago decided. Live as if you were born this morning, and you will die this evening. Seize each day like it is food, and you are starving. Kat was especially determined to enjoy the big party tomorrow. The midsummer celebration of the

Stanhope, successfully brought to life, in part, by her clever, hard-working sister. *Well done, sis. You earned it. Here's to your island.*

But where was the ferry? Gazing between a couple of skiffs raised up on blocks Kat could see the silver glitter of the river, the Blackwater, and Dawzy Island – green and hazy in the distance. Yet the little jetty was empty. There would usually, surely, be guests here, waiting with suitcases, and maybe staff. Especially today, twenty-four hours before it all kicked off.

Maybe she'd got the time wrong? It was noon. Yet she was sure that was right. Noon.

Dropping her big bag, Kat crouched, opened, and rummaged for that precious slip of paper. Why hadn't she just written it into her phone?

The bag, as usual, was a ghastly mess, and totally chocka. She had successfully brought her second favourite ukulele, denim shorts, a Jaw harp, her much-thumbed Tarot deck – Rider–Waite – a fabulously diaphanous summer dress for tomorrow night, two pairs of shoes, flip-flops, swimmers, a big book by Ursula Le Guin, some favourite stones from Avebury, a pure white bird's feather she had just found, about an eighth of weed, one half-smoked blunt, two credit cards, one of them smeared with argan oil, spilled last night; but, yes, dammit, she'd forgotten the one thing she needed: the note containing the ferry times for the island.

'Fuck.'

She'd probably left it at Dad's place this morning. They'd reminisced about Mum: how Kat had inherited Mum's scattiness, her forgetfulness, but also her good looks and vibrancy.

Whenever she went to see Dad, in his frowzy sheltered

housing, he always did this: he always made sure, with hints, smiles, jokes, hugs and extra special curranty biscuits from his tin, that Kat understood she was his favourite, the indulged younger sister. And every time Dad did this, Kat felt even more awkward, wanting him to stop. *Don't tell me this, Dad. Enough – think of Hannah.*

Because it had been like this all their lives. If Kat dropped a glass when she was seven, which she did weekly, ah that was just her dyspraxia, to be forgiven, laughed away. *Oh, you silly little thing.* If Hannah did anything similar, which happened about once a year, she got a scolding.

Hannybobs, I'm sorry.

The latest visit had been particularly awkward. Because Dad had finally told her the real story about Dawzy and Mum. How Mum had loved the sacred island with its foxes and ravens and witchy old yews, and how she had loved it in other ways, bad ways, wrong ways, sad ways. Ways that made Dad cry even now.

Squinting in the sun, Kat wondered: was she going to tell Hannah? She would have to at some point. But not this weekend. It would be a downer, a mood-kill. Why spoil the party?

Live this life like you were born this morning and you will die this evening.

One more rummage in the bag produced nothing. The note was definitely lost.

Sighing, Kat fished out her phone and texted Hannah . . .

Hey sis sorry. I'm a big crapola. I forgot the ferry times, lost note where I wrote 'em

Typing . . .

Can't believe Kat Langley of all people has lost something? Unprecedented

Yeah yeah, Captain Sensibobs, but what should I do? Where is he? It? Ferryman. Frankie Fred, Thingy? I remember him from before. Thingy? Isn't it noon? It's noon. I'm here at noon. NOOOOOOOOOOOOOON

Pause. Typing . . .

Just checked. Sorry no ferry, not till 4. It's hourly TOMORROW for the party

Oh Pish. I'm stuck here till 4?! Doof. There's nothing to but look at buoys. Or get leered at by bosuns. What the fuck are bosuns?

Wait. Idea! Regular ferryman is Freddy Nix & he *always* drinks in that pub by the marina. The Discovery. See it? Grey hair, 50, lecherous seadog type. Go and bat your lashes and he might taxi you over. Presume ur wearing something absurdly revealing?

Yep! 😜

Haha. Can't fail

Am I rlly that prdictble? *sad face* N E WAY. Fangoo, sis, love you, see you ASAP xxx

U too xx

Phone in bag, Kat marched down to the pub. As soon as she pushed the door open, she saw him: Freddy Nix on his own with a nearly finished pint, nattering lazily with the barman.

Hannah, it turned out, was right. He didn't need much persuasion. Freddy took one look at her face. Then at her top. Then at her legs.

'Of course, darlin', have you over at Dawzy in a sec.'

Leading her out of the pub, he walked them to a quieter part of the marina.

'Here we go. Your own water taxi.'

Kat looked down: at a small, sleek black speedboat. An expensive little toy of a thing. Unexpectedly chic.

'Hop in, love. Sit at the front so I can steer.'

She obeyed. Freddy followed.

As they carefully puttered into open water, Kat realized, very quickly, that Freddy had positioned her so that she was sitting at the front of the boat, considerably higher than Freddy, enabling him to look right up her skirt. Which he was doing. Brazenly.

'Nice boat,' she said.

Freddy smiled, with the hint of a leer.

'Yep. Proper fast. But there's no hurry today is there? Got plenty of time. Enjoy the sun.'

Plenty more time to look thirstily up my skirt, Kat thought, but she said nothing. His masculine adoration, helpless and hungry, was quite poignant. And it *was* a pleasant crossing. The breeze freshened with the scent of the sea just beyond.

'So, you're Hannah's sister, right? Sure I've seen you before.'

'Yep.'

'Nice lady, Hannah. Done great things. Manager loves her. Nice fiancé as well – they're a great match.

34

He's a chef over in Maldon. But you must know all that.'

Kat nodded. Staring over the waters.

They small-talked for a while more. Seabirds circled noisily above. Leaning out, Kat trailed a lazy hand in the water. It was surprisingly cold, despite the hot sun.

Then she felt the boat drag, suddenly, to the left, downriver. Like a car being pushed by a strong gust of wind. She glanced at Freddy, offering a puzzled face.

He nodded, faintly grimacing. 'Yes, weird riptides here. Unpredictable. Because of the river hitting the North Sea. Near the islands. There's actually an old name for one of them. Fisherman use it. Or used to.'

Kat looked at Freddy, waiting for an explanation. Freddy was staring into the Blackwater, as if he could see something, or someone, down in the depths. Pensive. Then he raised his gaze, and pointed to another island, green and low.

'Near the Stumble, and Royden Island, that way, that's a dangerous riptide, but it doesn't last.' Freddy's frown deepened.

Kat asked, 'How dangerous?'

'Well, they used to call it the Drowning Hour. Often at midday or midnight, I heard. Course, it doesn't drown anyone these days – river's too cold to swim in, modern boats too good – but decades ago it took a few fishermen. No one really knows about it any more. Local folklore. Like the witches, and the virgins.' He chuckled, but the chuckle was uncertain, or unmeant. 'Anyway, yeah. The riptide. I only know about that, cos I learned it from Grandad. Fished cod. Most hobby sailors at Goldhanger haven't a clue.'

'The Drowning Hour,' Kat repeated. They were near

the Dawzy jetty. She could see the sun on the glorious bay windows of the hotel. 'It's a creepy name.'

Freddy smiled, shook his head. 'Sorry! Not trying to scare you, darlin! Don't normally mention it; just occurred to me, feeling that current.'

'Oh, I'm not scared,' Kat said, truthfully. 'Not scared at all.' And then she shifted her legs, partly to make herself more comfortable, but mainly to give Freddy one last tormenting glimpse of her golden thighs, so that she could watch him suffer.

7

Hannah, Now

'Hannah. You busy?'

I look up from my screen, in the silence of the big empty office. It's the boss. Oliver. Poised at the door. I saw him arrive this morning, striding through reception, confident, assertive, himself. In jeans and a pullover with the flick of silver in his dark hair; he somehow makes jeans looks well judged. Kat tells me that I obviously fancy him. She's likely right. But I successfully hide it, or so I hope. He's married. I am engaged. He's the boss. He's at least fifteen years older. He's been very kind.

My answer is stammered, nervous. 'Um, Oliver, no, not massively busy.'

Not massively? Not *remotely* busy. This morning has been one of the rare but *really* bad ones. The mornings when apathetic despair overtakes me; when I lack all motivation, and find it hard to send a single email, despite the endless hours in hand. I know it's wrong. There's plenty of work. I live in fear of losing my job – what the hell would I do then? Live in a mud hut in the lightless oakwoods? And Oliver has had every reason to fire me. My role at the fateful party, my reckless irresponsibility.

And now I know that someone in management is desperate to get rid of me. Who is it? Oliver? Leon? Alistair? Loz? Someone in the London office?

The phrase resounds. *Get rid.* The way the guest said it, so vehemently. *They want rid of her.* Like they don't just want to eject me from the Stanhope, or just kick me off the island, more like they want to disappear me: to bury me or drown me.

'Hannah?'

'Sorry, Oliver. Daydreaming, what can I do?'

'Something's up. Come to my office?' The tone is sharp, and headmasterly.

'Of course.'

Hastily I turn to my screen. It has various tabs open, all of which show beautiful pics of faraway, unreachable places. Deserts, glaciers, mountains. Rio, London, the mini supermarket in Heybridge.

Closing the screen, I follow Oliver down the corridor into his office, like an obedient and dutiful schoolgirl. He sits at his desk as I glance around. I've only been in here a couple of times. Like Oliver himself, the room is quietly yet assertively masculine. And rich. Leather the colour of old claret, hardwoods the colour of coal, ultra-abstract paintings. A luxuriously enormous bay window offers a grandiose view of the Blackwater. I turn away; I don't want to see it. *One of those days.*

'Here,' says Oliver, taking a seat at his desk. 'Look.' I follow him again, glancing at the framed photos next to his computer. Two young blonde kids smiling on perfect little ponies, somewhere exceptionally sunny. California? Oliver in a pristine waxed jacket with a broken shotgun over an arm – hunting pheasant, or grouse, perhaps. Oliver and his lovely, perfectly blonde wife, laughing, in skiing gear, on the purest white Alpine snow.

I wonder if he ever gets tired of perfection.

But then, I doubt it really is perfect. There must be some sadness in there. Because there is always sadness somewhere. Occasionally I've seen Oliver – caught him – gazing into space, alone, expressing a wistfulness, maybe even a fear or a loneliness. Definitely a vulnerability. It probably made me fancy him more.

'So,' Oliver says. 'This is it.'

I lean closer, as he clicks his computer keyboard. Opening one of our social media pages. It shows a photo I posted yesterday: a bevelled glass of scotch glinting in the Stanhope's library, a roaring out-of-focus fire behind it and a menu placed enticingly on a mahogany table. It is all a terrible cliché, but I know this stuff works. The menu is the Mackster's new autumn special: venison, grouse, wild mallard; Colchester oysters with wild boar sausages.

Oliver scrolls down. 'Check this.'

I read quickly. And I see. And I say, 'Shit.'

Right underneath the photo, the first, anonymous comment is: 'Yes, why not go stay by the Blackwater, in the No Hope Hotel, on Drowny Island. Be sure to have a nice swim!'

The next comment is a series of laughter emojis. The next thirty comments are in the same vein. Mockery, evil jokes: 'you know that place is cursed'; 'they used to kill witches there – have they started again?'; 'careful, they might put poison in the pinot noir'.

Oliver sits back, glances up at me. Frowning. Green-grey eyes quite cold. 'You didn't notice this?'

It is my job to notice this, to be on top of social media, every day. 'Sorry, Oliver, must have forgot. I was just about to—'

His sigh is short. Terse. He's kind but he's not *that* kind. He likes making money, and the Stanhope is his expensive private passion. He's pumped millions into it. Yet he is also a businessman. He wants millions out of it.

'Get on the case, Hannah. Disable comments: now. I've checked our other media, these . . .' he shrugs '. . . *tags* – Drowny Island, No Hope Hotel, haven't spread. It's just here. But if they go viral?'

'I'll do it right now. Sorry.'

Another short, possibly disapproving sigh. 'Please. And after that, try and think of some decoy.'

'Sorry?'

'A distraction, a fresh promotion, something unusual, vivid, not just a new menu with partridge and figs. Get some new publicity. *Good* publicity. Perhaps something big for Christmas.' He pauses, goes on, 'December can be a great month. And we need a great month.'

'I'll do my very best, I promise.'

He eyes me. His frown softens. 'I know it's hard for you, Hannah. I can't imagine what it must be like. *Stuck.* Every day. Must be relentless. But . . .' He shakes his head, and I see a tiredness. 'Business is already down. Might be coincidence, might not. But if it really dries up; we lose all our bookings? I'd have to . . . I don't know . . .' He swivels, looks out of the bosomy bay window. 'I don't want to lay people off. That's all. I don't want to send everyone home.'

He returns his gaze to me. He knows I can't go home. I have no home. I have a weird kind of jail. So, he's warning me. I might actually end up alone, in this jail.

In my mind I see *me*: pacing the shingle beach, in the darkness of December, and behind me a shuttered building, devoid of people. As the darkness gathers. Alone on a wooded island, my head snapping around at the slightest noise, alert to the smallest crackle of twigs. The noise of an animal. Or a human who shouldn't be there.

'OK, Oliver. I'm on it!'

His smile is silent. Sincere. 'You will get better, Hannah. Keep at the therapy.'

I make more promises, say goodbye. I return to the quietness of the office – Loz is at meetings in London – and I actually work hard, all day, checking recent bookings, counting new ones, assessing possible cancellations, thinking of possible promotions; I work so hard I am surprised when I look up and notice the windows are darkening with twilight. Blue turning to a gentle, rosy grey.

Kat loves this time of day. She has a special French phrase for it. *L'heure entre chien et loup*. The hours between the dog and the wolf. And I've always liked the phrase, without quite understanding why it works. Or maybe I just like the way Kat says it, in her hyper-exaggerated French. Making me laugh.

My shoulders are stiff from typing and scrolling. Enough. I yawn and stretch. Work has made me better, distracting me from my state. After switching off my computer, I amble over to the window. Not afraid of the river. Not. I am not. I must expose myself. I must not give in.

I gaze out, startled.

Standing on the river-beach is a hare. Caught in the moonlight. Perfectly still. And it is staring up at me.

I know little about hares, except that they are quite

41

rare, and more poetic than rabbits. And I also know they are meant to live in fields, so no one really understands why they live on densely wooded Dawzy, which has no fields.

Maybe they are simply trapped here, like me, caught by the waters, desperate to escape.

But why is it standing, so still, and gazing up at me? I have seen TV nature footage of hares on their hind legs like this – but that's when they're boxing, mating, in spring. This is very much autumn. And now I am slightly unnerved. By a beautiful yet immobile wild animal thirty yards away. I want this beautiful creature to go, stop being weird, leave me alone, go back into the woods, *go back to wherever you came from.*

Please.

Still, it will not move. It does not seem frightened. I open the window, with a creak. *Still* it won't move. The behaviour is inexplicable. It just stands there, erect, stiff, whiskers tremulous in the breeze, right in the middle of the narrow, steepening beach.

Then, abruptly, it runs. Scampers. Gone. Because someone is shouting at it. Leon. He obviously wanted *rid of it.*

And now Leon turns, and stares across the waters, intently, as if he is waiting for an important guest. Yet no one is coming, not tonight. I've seen the bookings.

8

As still as that hare, I wait. Surveying the hurrying waves, racing from Southey Creek to Tollesbury Fleet.

It is a dank, windy morning. Cold. Avocets are sifting the waters, close by. Unperturbed by my presence. To my left, there is a row of eroded wooden spars – the spine of a rotting boat. The spikes are armoured with blue mussel shells; they march in a dutiful straight line, into the waters, until they drown, and disappear.

A shiver. A memory. It gets colder. Pulling up the hood of my cheap, old anorak, I feel the first gentle pittle-pattle of chilly rain on the plastic. Like a small child being slightly annoying. Tappety tap tap. Impatient now, frustrated now, I gaze out, across the Blackwater, to the distant marina at St Lawrence, the dull white blocks of the dead Magnox power station. Where is the ferry?

I check my phone. There is no mobile signal on Dawzy, but Oliver has spent trillions on the best Wi-Fi to make up for it. He spent trillions on the best of everything, from the cedarwood in the sauna to the CCTV in the corners to the single-estate coffee in the mornings. The amazing Wi-Fi means you can call, via your app, from the loneliest spinney, or the ghostliest sand spit.

But I have no need to call. *There.* A familiar, friendly sight reassures me. Freddy Nix the Ferryman. His chunky red boat is abroad the burly waves, navigating between red buoys and white buoys, crossing from Goldhanger. Carrying my saviour. I hope.

The pathetic bout of rain has ceased. Unhooding myself, I hurry down to the jetty, as Freddy throws a rope, eyeing me.

'Hello, darlin'. Could ya?'

I take the offered rope and pull it. He hops out of the boat, strangles a mooring bollard, winks up at me.

'Thanks, love. You look nice, scrubbin' up well.'

'Freddy, I'm in a crappy anorak, and old jeans.'

'Ach. Rubbish. Give me a girl with a bit of tangle in her hair.'

As Freddy deals with the boat, I stretch to see. A couple of guests with suitcases. Some staff. Two newish Polish waitresses, who try not to look too hard at me. The Woman Who Is Stuck Here. I smile back. Firm. Defiant. Where is he?

There.

A man steps up onto the jetty. And smiles. 'Hannah Langley?'

Disappointment floods me, quite painfully. I don't know why – probably I have been watching too many American soaps with high production values – but I expect doctors, especially heroic doctors, and I so want this doctor to be heroic – to be *dashing*. Or interestingly rugged. Or *something*.

My new therapist is stoutly over sixty. Tweed jacket, mustard-hued waistcoat, jowls and spectacles. But he *is* meant to be good. A specialist in phobias. My last therapist – vague, well-meaning, motherly – handed me on to him just last week. I am a difficult case. And this is his speciality.

'Dr Kempe. Hello!'

The new doc eyes the white, almost-weeping sky.

Sceptical. 'Call me Robert. Not a nice day. Shall we go indoors?'

'Please.'

We walk briskly to the hotel. In reception I see Alistair, the manager, talking to Leon: murmuring, and nodding. He eyes me. Looks at the doctor. Alistair's thin grey face is scowling. Annoyed that he is being overheard, or interrupted; or annoyed, more likely, that I am wasting worktime on my stupid therapy. I know he would have me sacked tomorrow. We do not get on.

Yet he has resented me since day one. Pretty much as soon as he arrived in the spring. Or not long after. Kat tells me he fancies me and resents that weakness in himself. But Kat thinks everyone fancies everyone, probably because every man she meets fancies her. I've even caught the Mackster eyeing Kat up, *from the kitchen*, and he rarely allows anyone to distract him when he's actually *cooking*. The roasting crab shells get all the love.

Jowly Robert Kempe apparently does not notice this tight little exchange with Alistair. Which is somewhat dismaying in a supposedly expert psychotherapist.

We go to a corner of the otherwise-empty library, with its lovely, big wood-burning fire. I order coffees for us both. When they arrive, Robert takes out a note-book, and says, 'I don't want to get straight into therapy today. I just want to get to know you. Hear your story. Your life story, as it were.'

I am perplexed. 'Ursula didn't tell you? She said she would hand over all her notes!'

He soothes me with a faint smile. 'She did, she did. But, in my experience, and I do have a lot of experience—' he chuckles, self-deprecating '—there's nothing like hearing it from the patient. Indeed, it's essential.'

'Where should I start?'

'At the beginning. Childhood, parents, schooling, and so forth.'

It's a story I have got used to telling, these past months, to doctors, therapists, the stubbornly curious, so I know how to reel it off. Like a list of bullet points.

As the coffees grow cold, and are renewed, I tell him My Story. The early childhood in far north London. How we moved to Maldon when I was about seven. A place that I much preferred. A little house by the river, a view that perhaps gave me my first yearning to travel. *Where does that river go? Where might it take me?*

The doctor scribbles notes. Looks up. 'Parents? Siblings?'

'Mum was young, Welsh, vivacious. Hippy chick. Astrologer. She handed all that on to Kat. I got my work ethic from Dad I suppose. Didn't matter, we were super super close as kids, me and Kat. She was born thirteen months after me.'

The doctor nods.

I continue. 'We got even closer when Mum died, of cancer, very sudden. I was ten, Kat was nine or so.'

'I'm sorry. That's hard.'

'It was.' I blink away the hint of tears. *Mummy.*

'Your father?'

'He was always much older, if you know what I mean. Mum was probably out of his league, looking back, I mean; she was really pretty. He had us very late. He used to be a teacher. He's retired now, and quite frail, lives in sheltered housing, still in Maldon.'

'I see. I see.' Scribble, scribble.

I look at his thick notepad. 'How relevant is this?'

He hesitates, the pen poised. Answers, 'Losing a parent so young, at such a tender age, that's an obvious cue

46

for anxiety. But also, your father: an older parent can make children especially aware of illness and decline.' His gaze is firm. 'The combination is doubly unfortunate, and destabilizing. We are, however, running ahead of ourselves. Please continue.'

I tell him the rest, briskly, a bit bored now. I tell him about the year I took off university, just so I could do Kat's gap year with her: across Asia, Africa, South America. Working as we went to pay for the next airfare. I explain how this brilliant year gave me a lifelong love for islands, the more romantically obscure the better: Ko Tao, Chiloé, St Kilda, the Andamans.

I don't touch on the irony: that this love for islands led me back here, where I am trapped: on an island. Robert eyes me inscrutably, as I go on, 'Kat was different. She fell in love with India and Peru. Also LA.'

'And after university?'

I speedily recount. Ticking the boxes. A couple of rubbish jobs. A couple of rubbish boyfriends. Then the move into hotel PR.

Robert lifts a hand. 'Why PR?'

I shrug. 'I'm good at it. I remember people, conversations, opinions, desires. And I'm good at branding or selling a place; no idea why. And,' I add, softly, 'it allowed me to travel.'

'OK.'

I continue briskly. My first hotel PR job in London. The next, Malta. An island! Then the dream job, a big hotel in the Maldives. Awani Fushi. Coral reefs. Scorpion fish. Meeting Ben. Mad sexy chef. Falling in love. Engagement. Then the second dream job. The Stanhope. Another island. Big promotion. My old home, near my lonely dad, nearer my lovely sister. I finish the story with a bit of a flourish. 'It was basically a miracle. Just as I heard about this refurb, here, I also heard about a brilliant old pub, in Maldon, full of potential, needing a new chef. Ben got the gig. It was perfect. He came back to Britain first, a few months before me. And Dawzy is an island I knew vaguely as a little kid. We did a few family trips here, when it was the old hotel, nearly ruined. Pretty woods. We stopped coming here after Mum died though.'

I stop. I say no more. I am slightly lying here: or being evasive. I'm not telling Robert Kempe the *full* story about the Maldives. How Kat flew out to the Maldives, to see me, and to go scuba diving, drunk. How one day she went swimming naked, at night, in front of multiple guests. How Ben came out to check what was causing the fuss: my naked beautiful sister, like a mermaid, nude and giggling above the starlit corals. How Ben went basically mad with anger. *This could get both of us sacked!*

It did not. But he was right. It could have. Ever since then, theirs has been a prickly relationship. Kat finds Ben driven, and uptight. Too ambitious. Taking over his own gastropub. He finds her annoyingly messy. Always dropping things. Like her bikini bottoms.

These days, I barely talk to him about her. It makes it all easier.

And I don't tell Robert any of this either; because, of course, it paints my beloved sister in a bad light. It makes her look blameworthy, even a bit mad: a pattern of behaviour, repeated that fateful night a few months ago. A pattern that I should have foreseen, and should have stopped, because she was so capable of encouraging others to chase her shapely bare ass into the waves.

'That's it,' I say, a little tartly, and unfairly.

'That's good. Very helpful. Thank you.'

48

For a few minutes we sit and talk. He tells me about phobias. He talks about my phobia, and my related post-traumatic stress disorder.

'It is essentially, perhaps, a form of agoraphobia. Which was first diagnosed centuries ago. The French called it *la peur des espaces*, or *horreur du vide*. The Germans called it *Platzschwindel* – which means "square dizziness". I've always liked that.' He smiles. I do not. He goes on, 'As I say, you have a form of this, something we might call aquaphobia or thalassophobia, perhaps with a tinge of topophobia: fear of a certain place. Aquaphobia is notably common. Many people fear water, especially deep water. The difference here is that you have really quite a severe case, and, of course . . .' His next smile is sadly sympathetic. 'You are, most unfortunately, stuck on an island.'

I nod. Mute. When does the damn therapy start?

Robert picks up his coffee cup, cradling it like precious porcelain. 'Ursula tells me you've had pretty much the full set of reactions?'

'I have.'

I could list them. But he surely knows them all. As he said I've done the full set. Flashbacks. Anhedonia. Vomiting. Hallucinations. Nightmares. Paranoia. Numbness. *Derealization*. Choking. Tonic immobility. Clawed hands. Intense chest pain. Blurred vision. Fainting. Anger. Irritability. Dry mouth. Lump throat. Fear of madness. Diarrhoea. Nausea. Brain fog. And actual full-on paralysis.

'A couple of times I have wet myself. In public. That was fun.'

The doctor shakes his head in a melancholy way, puts down his cup.

'So,' I say, 'can you please cheer me up? This is quite depressing.'

49

My hopes hover, as he replies, 'Yes, I think I can. I have successfully dealt with cases like yours; they are far from insoluble. Indeed, I am pretty certain that a course of intense therapy, exposure, cognitive behaviour, and so on, would essentially cure you.'

More exposure therapy? Fantastic. I try to hide my scepticism, and my pessimism. This is a new doctor, a specialist – he might be better. He *has* to be better. I want to believe in him. I ask, 'How many sessions? To cure me?'

The doctor tilts a thoughtful head.

'More than ten. Maybe twenty. It is not an exact science.'

'And how often can you see me?'

'Once a fortnight. Possibly more.'

I gaze at my supposed saviour. 'But that's twenty weeks! Or forty weeks! Almost a year?'

'No, no, no. Please. That's pessimistic. I would hope to have you off here by next spring.' He leans forward, pats me reassuringly – and patronizingly – on the knee. 'It's just one winter. Just a single winter. That's all.'

9

My one day off. I am therefore in the Spinnaker at 9 a.m., enjoying a solitary pot of tea. The place is deserted. It is quite often deserted at this time of day – it is a bar – but today it feels especially quiet. The wooden tables outside are unused, despite the autumn sunshine. The heated pool has now been closed, capped with a roof of stretched plastic, and it will stay like that till spring.

And, if Dr Kempe is right, I will do the same. I will stay like this till spring. On the island. Static. Immobilized. A medieval peasant caught dancing on the sabbath, cruelly turned to silent stone.

The thought makes me faintly nauseous, and dizzy. So, I must avert my gaze. It is the only way to cope with my increasingly horrific predicament. I must not look ahead, because ahead, for me, there is only sadness and loneliness and maybe worse. It's the same principle as not looking down as you walk a tightrope.

Therefore, I focus on the now, this day, this tea, this moment.

And work? It's my off day, but all the days are similar, drifting one into the other, blurring. I often find myself actively forgetting what day it is and have to ask Loz or Leon or Freddy. I'd like to ask Ben, but he's so busy; I'd like to ask Kat but she's always partying and though she makes me laugh, hard, and I love her dearly, sometimes the contrast between our lives – her absolute freedom, my total imprisonment – is too painful.

When Kat calls – which she does, often, she's a good sister – I sometimes sit there, filled with guilt, and let the phone cheerily dance and vibrate, and I let the call go to voicemail. And later on I listen to her funny, extroverted messages – *Hey, how's the Hotel of Doom, Hannybobs. Talk to me. Why do you never answer?* – and sometimes I quietly cry.

Work!

Oliver wants me to concoct a new Christmas promotion, something to distract from these negative labels attaching to our social media. They are not that bad yet, not that numerous, not that viral, not that clever, but he's right, they are a potential menace: I know the danger. I've seen other hotels get ruined by a few months of bad internet publicity.

Work, Han.

What can I possibly use for this promotion? Something unusual and quirky about the island, or the hotel, something I haven't already showcased?

Maybe Ben *can* help. I pick up my phone and go to recent contacts. There he is. Moody Fiancé.

> B, are you busy? Need help! Damsel = distress

He replies immediately.

> **Never 2 busy for u, sexy. OK that's maybe a lie lol but pub is shut. How can I help? Xx**

Ah, thank you Ben. As I gaze down at his words, the xx's, the written kisses, I remember the first time we actually kissed. In the Maldives, on the beach by the yoga place. It was a cliché of a kiss, the warm surf around my bare ankles, his muscled arm around my waist, him pulling me towards him, my yielding mouth to his red lips. Kissing Ben, falling in love with Ben, felt as if I was ascending to the sunlit surface out of a deep ocean of loneliness. I didn't realize I was lonely until I met Ben. And then I was lonely no more.

And other kisses, too. The tender kiss when he proposed. The fierce kiss when I flew back from Malé and he showed me the gutted new pub. We kissed as if we were starvelings, hungry for each other. Then he made salad niçoise. With just-made bread. And then the eager kisses as we stripped each other.

Those were good kisses. I am marrying the right man. If I can just get off this island.

> Oliver wants me to have new ideas. Promote Stanhope. Dunno what to do! I've tried so many angles. Thoughts? 🫠

I wait; he responds:

> **Tricky. V tricky. Maybe asking wrong guy ha. I'm just a chef, babe, this is your gig. Hotel PR. And ur great at it! U will find something!**

> Ta. Racking brains but got 0. We've done so much publicity. There's a limit

This time he replies before I can finish.

> **I kno. How about the Strood! That's a mad thing. Unique to Dawzy. STROOD?**

As soon as he types this, and as soon as I read it. I get the tingle. Yes. Maybe.

Whoa yes could be. NOT BAD! Thank you, B. Thank you. 😌😍😍

Ur welcome. OK have to go, deliveries. See ya xxxxxx

Setting down the phone, I ponder. This really could be something. The name, alone, has that uncanny ring. And it is entirely unique.

The Strood.

The Strood is the old Roman causeway that used to connect Dawzy to the mainland. It was built, it is thought, so that Romans could come and harvest the island's famous oysters. Romans loved the oysters of Essex, especially the Blackwater, most especially Dawzy. They were packed into fast chariots that could, legend says, take them from Colchester to Rome in three days. I seriously doubt that it is true, but I know Pliny the Roman historian definitely said 'the only good thing to come out of Britain is oysters'.

He was, it is thought, expressly referring to the oysters of the Blackwater River and its environs. Mersea. Dawzy. Colchester. Maldon. You can still see the remains of Roman and Anglo-Saxon oyster beds around the island now, though the oyster harvesting has mysteriously shifted to the mainland coast. Perhaps the oysters escaped.

No one knows when the Strood finally drowned beneath the Blackwater. It was always, it is suspected, a tidal causeway, a long snaking road that disappeared under high tides, cutting off the island; and as the centuries passed, the mercurial tides and currents got higher, the sea levels rose, the Strood struggled, like a swimmer in trouble – I shove the image away, away, away – but then it was finally submerged. Probably around the tenth century. And Dawzy became a proper island.

And yet, the ancient road is not entirely dead. In especially, freakishly low tides, which accompany certain weather conditions, the right stormy north winds – usually in bad winters – the Strood reappears miraculously, for an hour or so. A revenant. A spectre of Rome. Like the ghost of a legionnaire. Freddy Nix told me, when I arrived, that it happened three years ago. Mid-December. For just one hour. Some locals came to marvel. A few even crossed, in the moonlight, just a forty-minute walk on a two-thousand-year-old road.

Generally, I try not to think about the Strood. Because it is all-too-tantalizing, as it is, of course, a possible route off the island for me. A road of Roman cobbles that I could walk. An open door in my jail. But no one can predict when the Strood might arise, once more, for that precious hour. The tides here are so moody, and weather is weather. Therefore, the capriciousness that is the Strood feels like another part of my punishment, a cruel addition to my imprisonment. Yes, there is a theoretical way out, but no, sorry, it probably won't happen.

But now I'm thinking about the Strood, thanks to Ben. And the temptation is overwhelming. Who's to say it won't just reappear on a brisk autumn day with bright sun and a fresh wind? And even if it doesn't – I know it won't – it might be a great new way to sell the hotel.

Zipping up my old anorak.

Let's do it, Hannybobs, let's go see the Strood.

10

The lane that leads to the Strood – or, rather, where the Strood used to be – is probably the longest on Dawzy, circling the southern shore. So, I grab one of the Stanhope bikes, which is tilted against a rowan tree, just beyond the pool, its stout steel frame glinting like silver bones. These bikes were my idea: to have a few dozen chunky-wheeled bikes, lying around and about, which guests can pick up and use, and then leave behind wherever.

No one is going to steal a bike, after all. For a start the thieves would be pretty conspicuous on Freddy's ferry, carting off a large, cumbersome bicycle painted all over with the words THE STANHOPE in our bespoke font.

Oliver immediately agreed. 'Bicycles! Yes. Do it!' He saw the logic. Make the island an Enid Blyton island, a place full of grown-up kids on a magic, freewheeling holiday. Make everyone feel about thirteen years old.

It has worked. The bikes are very popular. Maybe the bicycles worked too well, injecting a sense of youthfulness: everyone acted like a naughty teen *that* night.

Pedalling hard down the muddy lane, which is painted with fallen golden maple leaves, I overtake two middle-aged guests, quietly walking the woods, hand in hand.

'Hi! Sorry! Thank you!'

They smile and wave at me, uncertainly: I see them in my bicycle's mirror. Usually I walk, like the guests, around Dawzy, because I have so much time and walking takes up time. Now I am in a hurry, though I am not sure why. The chances of the Strood reappearing right this minute are approximately zero point zero zero. For the Strood to do her Here I Am Again stage magic, there has to be, as Freddy says, the freakish low tide – *no*, the big storm – *no*, and all of this probably in midwinter. It's October.

This is pointless. No, it isn't. What does Freddy know? He thinks I look sexy in this ten-year-old anorak, in muddy jeans and muddy trainers. He's likeable, often charming, but his libido makes him an idiot. He positively *drools* over Kat. He was there that night when she stripped and dipped: salivating. The naked Langley girl: the younger, beautiful one. But then he was just one of many men who gazed, longingly, at my sister, laughing, dancing, teasing the world – and stripping naked, with a wild cackle. Wilder than I've ever heard it, that night. Something strange in her voice.

What happened to her that night? She has never explained. She refuses to talk about it. Too much guilt, perhaps. Like me.

I've reached the ancient oyster beds. Built by the Romans, worked by the Vikings, abandoned by the Normans. Grids of low, ancient, dark wooden palings, like rotting old fangs, rise from the waters: draped in green and tawny seaweed.

I am, therefore, at the far south-west edge of the island. The Blackwater is especially deep here: deep and fast. Poised on my half-tilted bike, I look at the river where it is becoming the estuary, determined to immerse itself in the North Sea. It is one of those typical Dawzy moments when you cannot tell in which direction the tide is flowing: the waves, maddened, seem to rush, hither, thither, whatever, wherever. Almost angry. Certainly chaotic. Like my mind. Seeing things. Hearing things.

Just get rid of her.

Calm down.

Slowly, deliberately, I breathe the tangy air. Gulping it down like chicken soup for the paranoid. From this shore of Dawzy I can see the flat, saltmarsh greenery of Royden Island: the famous bird sanctuary where no one is allowed to go. I can hear all the happy birds over there: honking, hawking, queeling, zhoozhing, a constant yet invisible party, celebrating the lack of humans. Perhaps this is what the world will sound like, when we are all gone. I almost yearn for it. For the world to get rid of us. The humans. We've had our chance and we fucked it up. Give it back to the birds.

Standing high on the pedals, I race on, squirting autumn mud. The narrow path runs around the steep, grey beach, and then, finally, it rises – and I am at the furthermost western edge of Dawzy. From here, I can see the wharves of Heybridge, and then, the quaintly climbing houses and churches of Maldon, perched on their pretty toytown hill, medieval windows flashing in the slanted sun.

Maldon. Famous for salt and beer and battles. That's where my dad is now. All alone, and still missing Mum. I must call him. I must. I find it so hard. He makes it hard.

And there it is: the start of the Strood. Where the island ends, the ground sharply dips, but a camber of cobbles rises.

And then falls away.

Dropping the bicycle to the ground, I accept the obvious disappointment. I didn't really expect the Strood to have reappeared as if on call, this afternoon. Did I? Perhaps I did, somehow; perhaps I am that much in need of hope.

Let me go.

I cannot go, I cannot get over it, not today. The Strood isn't going to do my bidding.

Stepping to the edge of the waters – causing a drowsy flock of dunlin to lift and flee with superb, choreo-graphed, anti-predator panic from my scrunching boots. I stare down. I have a vague, dimly lit memory of doing this as a kid, coming here to look at the Strood with Mum and Dad and Kat. We must have been seven and eight. The memory is on the edge of dissolution, it is so distant.

And the Strood has not changed. It is still a tease. At this outermost edge of the island, the very moment it first shows itself on the Dawzy shore, it slips shyly into the cold grey waters. For the first hundred yards or so, I can follow her tantalizing route: the lane of careful Roman stones, curving underwater, is just visible in the depths. But a little further out, it dives too deep, concealed by darker water.

How low must the tide get for the Strood to be completely revealed and usable? Lifting my gaze, I look across to the other side. If I'd brought my binoculars I could probably see where the Strood is said to re-emerge on the opposite side of the river, somewhere around Mundon Wash, that watery network of Jutish ditches and Anglian dykes, rattling reeds and soft treacly muds so deep and oozy that they can swallow a pony, a place where tides run so fast they can outrun a man. Somewhere in that half-land, so I have read, the Strood hauls itself out of the water, and flops exhausted on the shore, like a survivor from a movie shipwreck.

Going back to the bike I sit down on a damp tree stump. And I realize I cannot use the Strood as a selling point. Come and see a famous road you can't see? No. It is a unique thing, Ben is right, but it's not much of a selling point. Not really.

So, what can I use?

Whipping the phone out, logging on to Oliver's superb Wi-Fi great signal even *here* – *how* does he do it? – I search. *History Dawzy Stanhope*. Much of it I know already: I learned it when I first arrived and did the rebranding. I know the Roman and Saxon stuff. I know there was a lonely Elizabethan lodge here: probably a hunting lodge for the deer. I know the grand Regency house, the lovely core of the Stanhope, was built for a famous Admiral Stanhope, who made his money from Jamaican sugar, and by marrying well. The marriage was not happy, partly because the admiral was notorious for bedding his female servants, and when he ran out of kitchen wenches, he brought new women in, perhaps by force. Women have been unhappy on Dawzy; maybe I am just another in a long line.

Bird noise distracts me. The frightened dunlins have returned. The birds sit on the waters, gossiping and chittering, as I scroll down. A cool wind is kicking up.

More pages.

In the Victorian era the building was greatly extended to make it much grander. Some muck-and-brass indus-trialist making a statement. Hence the enormous east and west wings, like cathedral naves. Already, by then, Dawzy was known for its dense woods and precious wildlife. The house finally became a hotel in the 1920s and was immediately fashionable, attracting post-war partying Londoners: a luxurious hideaway, a little English Eden, perfectly located for metropolitan getaways; sufficiently close but sufficiently discreet. A spot for adultery, pheasant-shooting, and champagne with room service. Glasses spilled on rugs, rumpled bedsheets on lazy afternoons.

Maybe I could use that? The hotel's faint, titillating notoriety? Throw a few Christmas parties with a Twenties theme. Flapper dresses. Yes, maybe.

Because there isn't much else. In the war the building became an orphanage. When it returned as a hotel, in the Fifties, its appeal had dwindled. No one spent a penny on the place; they ran it ragged. And so commenced its sad, slow decline, supported only by loyal locals, increasingly shunned by lavish Londoners. In the Sixties it enjoyed a brief new flicker of fame, when tabloids talked of ghosts and spells and witchfinders, who supposedly tossed poor old village crones in the Blackwater currents, to see if they floated. I guess they sank.

After this modest, belated notoriety, the hotel vanished from sight, once more. Idling along as a decent old Essex gaff, quite popular on Sundays for its carvery, known by locals for curious legends, doomed for bankruptcy nonetheless. That's the down-at-heel hotel I can vaguely remember from when I was a little girl. Autumnal walks in the woods. Dry Yorkshire puddings. Lumpy gravy. Me and Kat giggling at the table and Dad telling us off.

And then, almost two decades later, Oliver Ormonde came along with his squillions. Ba-da-boom.

The waves lap, louder. The dunlins ride the wash from a fishing boat, placidly floating up and down. My eyes grow tired.

Work.

Opening an app for notes, I start to type. *Perhaps a Halloweeny Christmas party? Use the legends. Ghosts and witches. Ravished virgins. Talk to—*

No. No no NO. I stop abruptly. What am I thinking? The island – the hotel – is already regaining a kind of notoriety. 'You know that place is cursed.' 'There's where they drowned the witches.' Do I seriously want to remind our visitors of *drowning?*

Exhaling with frustration, I erase the note from the app. Go back. Go back. First thought best thought.

Yes. Yes, yes and yes. The Twenties theme is my winning bet. Return the Stanhope to its glorious, roaring days, when it was new and sexy. A minxy little bolthole in the Blackwater. Liberated women in slinky dresses, dancing to scandalous jazz.

Tip tap. My fingers dance. This feels better. This is working. This idea might be it.

I am in the flow-zone, until I am not.

Bird noise: again. This time much louder. Deafening. All the birds in all the trees are letting out alarm calls. Thunderous applause of wings. What is it? What has frightened them?

There. Something in the water. What is it? The waves are choppy.

And now I see it. A little dog, drowning.

11

Where is it from? Why is it in the water? Frantic, I search the waves, the shores, the emptiness. The lane behind me. Nothing. No one to help. No sign of anyone. It is just me and the choppy river and a drowning dog.

The dog looks young, almost a puppy. Where is the owner? How did it get in the water? I guess it could have fallen in from someone's boat and they didn't notice. Or maybe some cruel bastard casually threw it in: an unwanted pet, getting too big.

I am paralyzed, watching the dog drown.

I cannot go in the water. I am too frightened. I cannot help this poor animal. Yet I cannot just watch a dog drown. Can I?

'Help!' I try to scream. 'Help! Someone! Please help!'

My feeble shout is feebly returned by the echoing trees of Dawzy woods, which gaze at me disdainfully. The whole empty world seems to be looking at me with contempt. *Just get in the water and save this animal, you stupid woman.* And that is, of course, what I would have done four months ago: dived in without a moment's hesitation. Naturally. That's what you do. I am a very good swimmer, like Kat. Dad and Mum both made sure of that.

But now? Now I am not a good swimmer. I cannot swim at all. Memories of that night roil in my mind as

I look on, helpless, at the drowning dog. Memories of bodies in moonlight, naked people, thrashing, laughing, flirting – then screaming. Dying. And in those snarling waves? I close my eyes, shudder.

Yet I must save the dog. But all I can see . . .

Blackness.

No.

Eyes open again, I edge closer to the water. But I can't. I am trembling with the panic, my throat filling up with that familiar choking. As if I am drowning in air. Heart going mad. Nausea. Stiffness. Blurred vision.

Not that blurred: I can see the little dog has now seen *me*. It barks at me – *save me, lift me* – as it goes under a big, curling black wave. It will die any moment. And I am rigid and helpless and hot urine is running down my leg. It's happening again. The shame is intense. A pathetic woman who cannot save a drowning dog about ten yards away, who cannot control her bladder. I might as well not exist.

Again, the dog goes under. Possibly for the last time.

I step forward.

Into the water. I am stepping into the water and the fear and horror tumble insides me. Cold cold cold water over my feet.

I hear screams. Human. That night. The terror.

Another step. More screams. HEEEEEEEELP.

I cannot do this. The dog is weakening; it is almost motionless. One more big wave and it will die. For sure. I have to do this. Another step: now I am waist deep. The dog yelps, seeing me near, and then it sinks again, paddling desperately and helplessly. Now I start vomiting. Another step. Puke is tumbling from my mouth, from absolute fear.

Here it comes, the last big killing wave. I am covered

in my own vomit, my bladder is voided; yet I reach out deep into the repulsive water, and I shudder, and I grab and I feel the dog, warm in my hands, somehow. Warmth in the cold. A body. Touch.

Save the dog.

I get a firmer grip. Lift the little mongrel from the Blackwater. This sodden, grey-brown, furry little soul.

Save it. Do it.

I can do this. Wrapping my arms around the dog, I stagger backwards, almost falling. A few more yards. The shore. The Strood. The woods. My jail. Let me get there. Please please please. One two three, help me help me. Yes.

Yes?

Soft mud, shingle, more vomit. The seabirds wheel above me, carolling their alarm. But I did it. Dropping to my knees, spitting out water, I open my arms and let the dog go. It shivers, shaking the water from its fur, creating a brief rainbow in the chilly, angled sun. I am wet with river, vomit, pee, and tears. Snot pours from my nose.

Still on my knees, I gasp the last of the fear away. I look up. I am panting, freezing, ridiculous. Alive.

The dog looks at me. Tilts a cute head. Seems stupidly, perfectly fine.

Then she licks me.

Hello.

12

'Hannah, darling, they won't let you keep it.'

I gaze at my fiancé. Ben looks tired. But chefs always look tired, especially chefs running a newly bustling gastropub.

'Why can't I?'

'Just think about it. All the problems. You have to work in the office, and she's locked in your room all day? That's cruel.'

'He. She's a he. Checked.'

'Hah. OK.'

He chuckles, and rubs his face with a scratched, reddened hand. Burned and plastered. He works too hard in that kitchen. His stubble, which I normally like, is getting too long; he also needs a haircut. His dark fringe falls over tired grey eyes.

It was his eyes and energy that first attracted me and, of course, the flex of his hard, tanned, muscled, and nicely tattooed biceps as he toiled in that hot kitchen in the Maldives, among the marbled wagyu and spheres of foie gras. Chefs doing cheffing can be so sexy. Ben is a sexy man.

'Also, that dog must surely belong to someone else.'

'I don't think so! He didn't have a collar, nothing to show ownership, no chip. I've been online, searching for notices of local pets gone missing. There's nothing.

I reckon he was chucked off a boat. How else did he end up in the Blackwater? A puppy that got too big, so they dumped him. It happens.'

'OK. OK.' He attempts a helpful smile. 'Look, Han. I know you're lonely, I know you'd love a dog. But what if he wanders about? What if he came in here?'

I gaze about at the oaken, historic, nautical grandeur of the library. Portraits of famous sailors and buccaneers gazing down at empty leather chairs. Where is everyone? Normally there would be a dozen people in here, with champagne, or kir, or prosecco, or G&Ts, or Aperol spritzers. Standing by the log fire; playing backgammon or cards.

Ben is right. A dog would look pretty conspicuous in here, even on a normal, busy night. Pets are not explicitly forbidden at the Stanhope, but they are certainly not encouraged. I've never known a staff member keep a pet.

Yet I am dead keen to keep this rescued hound. I nearly sent myself mad saving him. I conquered my phobia, if only for a few minutes. The experience was so horrific I am even more phobic than ever, which, in turn, makes the little dog, *my* little dog, ever more precious.

'But I *am* lonely, Ben.' I give him a fixed stare. 'A dog will help. And who else will take him?'

'Someone.'

'I've even given him a name!'

'You have?'

'Yes. Greedygut. That's what Mum's dog was called. And he is greedy!'

'Won't be cheap.'

The irritation prickles. Ben is trying to help, but I want more than doominess or negative advice. I want encouragement. Putting a hand on his arm, I say, 'Perhaps I wouldn't be so lonely if you came over more often? This is your first visit in, what, a week? More?'

Ben shakes his head; guzzles his foamy beer. 'You know my situation, Han. I run a business 24/7. We're just beginning to turn a profit.' He checks his watch. 'In fact, I need to get back soon.'

'You're not staying over?'

Apologetic eyes. 'No. Sorry.'

A painful pause.

'You haven't stayed over in weeks. Months.'

'The pub needs me every night.'

'It's not *that* busy. You stayed over before the summer. Is it because of you know what?'

He eyes me, warily. Suspicious. Fearful? I press the question. 'Is it some kind of PTSD, Ben? The scene of the tragedy? I understand if it is, but just tell me. Everyone is scarred by that.'

He looks relieved. 'No. No. Not that.'

'So, what then? Are you getting bored of me? Do you want to end it, with the mad lady stuck on the island?'

'Of *course* not! I love you! I'm just making a buck so we can one day have a life together. Wasn't that the plan?'

He sounds kind-of-convincing. But not entirely. Perhaps he is embarrassed. I often wonder if he does have his own shade of PTSD, but he's too macho to admit it. Ben is proud, manly, ambitious. He can barely talk to the Mackster because he is jealous of the more famous chef; maybe that same testosteroney pride means he can't reveal his vulnerability.

As I drain my white wine, a couple of guests stroll in. They remind me of the wedding anniversary couple. The woman who recognized me.

I can't let this opportunity go. I have to ask, even if it comes from nowhere. 'Ben, have you . . . heard any rumours? About management, and me?'

His frown is perplexed, sincere. Fair enough: it's an abrupt question.

'*Rumours?* What do you mean?'

'I know it sounds paranoid, but I met this guest who works with the Stanhope office. Her husband didn't know who I was, and he told me someone wanted rid of me. In the head office. Or here.'

'*Jesus.*' Ben shakes his head. 'Hannah, there's bound to be rumours; it was in the news. Frankly it's lucky the hotel is still going. My advice is stop digging up the past. It does you no good and you *will* scare off guests. And then someone really will want to get rid of you. And if you lose this job . . .' His voice is mildly raised. He swivels his empty glass. 'Please. Enough, darling. Perhaps we just need another drink. Can you order one?'

I recognize his tone. He really doesn't want to continue this conversation, and I don't have all night with him.

Glancing over his shoulder, I see Julia serving the other guests. One of the local-born waitresses: blonde, fun, young. Just ending her day shift, probably.

'Julia, can we get another Peroni?'

She turns, looks at me and Ben, appears startled. Gazing at Ben with an expression. Of what? Embarrassment. Awkwardness? As if she fancies him, or even, no, as if she's slept with him?

No. Julia is not like that. Nor is Ben. Ridiculous.

'We're all out of Peroni. Sorry, Hannah. Something else?'

Ben is oblivious. He turns and smiles warmly at Julia. 'No drama. I've probably had enough anyway. Ta.'

Julia vanishes. We sit there for a moment, silent.

'Ben, let's just go to my room. If you only have an hour left.'

'Sure.' A hint of a sexy smile.

It's a short walk to my room; as soon as I push open the door, Greedygut bounces up to greet me, licking my hand.

Ben laughs. 'I suppose he *is* kind of cute.'

'I told you!'

'Young, huh? Bit of spaniel in him? Springer maybe. Beagle as well? He'll be a great sniffer dog.'

Greedy barks, excitedly. Ben turns to me, with a questioning expression. I say, 'I know I know but it's OK – I've got a bone to distract him! The Mackster gave it to me.'

Reaching for a plastic bag on a high shelf, I throw Greedygut the hefty beef bone. He leaps on it with his usual relish. Gnawing with glee.

We both know what happens next, without needing to say it. Quickly, expertly, Ben strips me, as I unbutton his shirt, his jeans, then we topple on to the bed, and have sex. Forceful sex. He flips me over, pushes my face into the pillow and pulls my hair back: as if reining a horse. I let him do it all. I quite like this rough sex, him taking charge, me letting go; Ben has always been into this, but it's more intense this time. It's been more intense for a while.

Maybe he is venting his stress. Or maybe, just maybe, it is anger. At *me*. Locking him into an engagement with a madwoman trapped on an island, by her own stupidity. He can't just dump me: that would be cruel. But maybe he wants to be *rid of me*, as well.

When he's finished, he jumps off the bed and dresses – immediately. Faster than ever. Saying, 'That was nice.'

71

'It was certainly quick.'

'But you did come, right?'

I put my arms in my shirtsleeves, looking at him. Laconically.

I say, 'Soft, what light through yonder window breaks?'

He laughs. 'OK OK. Sorry for the lack of romance. Truly sorry. I can't always do ten hours of tantra.' He chuckles and leans and kisses me, briskly. 'Things *will* get better when the pub has settled down. I'll come over for a whole weekend. Winter will be quieter anyway, at least until Christmas.'

Winter.

Slipping on my own jumper, I remember what Dr Kempe said, tapping my knee like a reassuring uncle with an anxious young niece about to go to uni. *It's just one winter.*

I'm not sure I can do a whole winter.

An idea reappears, an old, bad idea, but one that won't quit. It has been needling me, from within, for months.

'Ben, if I get absolutely desperate, would you reconsider helping me? Doing that getaway thing?'

He shakes his head. 'Really? This again?'

'Yes.'

'You mean the pills.' He scowls, deeply disapproving.

He always scowls when I mention this: my crazy idea is that I take a whole load of sleeping pills, knock myself out, maybe drink a bottle of scotch if I have to, then Ben could – literally – carry me, unconscious, on to a boat so that I can escape Dawzy. At midnight. A mad midnight flit.

His sigh is almost a growl. 'We discussed this, Hannah. What did your last doctor say? It could be extremely

72

dangerous, messing with this phobia. I don't want to be responsible if it all goes wrong, mixing pills and booze.'

'But—'

He won't let me speak. 'And even if it works, which it surely won't, then you haven't cured yourself. You'll also lose your job, because you won't be able to come back.'

'But if I am absolutely desperate? Ben? Please?'

He gazes at me searchingly. Then he pecks me on the cheek. Impatient. 'Do the therapy; that's the only way off. And now I have to go – ferry will be here any minute.'

'I suppose . . .' I say, feeling suddenly, acutely sad. My loneliness has, if anything, been intensified by Ben's visit.

'Hey,' I say. 'I'm sorry if I was snappy. I do love you, you know.'

'And I still love you.'

We share a final kiss; a much better kiss. Thank the Lord. Then the door opens, and shuts, and my fiancé is gone. Greedygut gnaws at his bone. I sit on the rumpled bed, the darkening sky pressing silently at the window, and I think about the waitress – her startled, flushed expression. Looking at me and Ben.

Julia. She was here that night. The night of the Drownings. My unsettling curiosity grows – even though I know Ben is probably right, and I should let it go.

Rumours?

Scanning my phone, I realize I don't have her number; but she is on the hotel group chat: StanhopeStuff. Most of us are on it. It's a great way to organize shifts, tasks, events. And sometimes share gossip, without giving out personal numbers.

I find her avatar; it says she's online. And she'll be knocking off around now, her day shift done.

Hey, Julia
Sorry if this sounds a bit mad, but is there some bad vibe between you and Ben? Felt a little odd this evening, maybe just me!
Hxx

I don't have to wait long. She must be back in her room, as bored as the rest of us. The answer pings.

Haha no! Silly. I was just surprised to see him. Isn't his pub doing brilliant? He must be busy, am I right?
J x

I put down the phone. She is, indeed, right. Of course. And Ben is right: enough of this.

I gaze at Greedy. He has finished his bone and now he's giving me that cock-eyed glance, head tilted, puzzled yet expectant. As if I am surely about to do an exciting trick. Or he is about to pee all over the carpet.

He needs a walk. I need a walk.

Smuggling him out of the hotel, wondering how long I can keep him as invisible as possible, I guide us both onto the shingle, where the towns of the mainland twinkle, distantly, enticingly, across the moonlit river. It is a calm night with barely a whisper of river-wind. There's even a lingering hint of warmth in the salty air. The old hotel glows, richly, from its many windows. I can see prosperous people inside, going to dinner, climbing the Regency stairs, pulling velvet curtains shut.

Only one end of the hotel is dark and silent. The east wing. The long, old, nave-like wing, with its dark and arched windows. The great refurb has yet to reach this side of the Stanhope. It is like a corner of the nineteenth-century world barely touched by imperial civilization. Guests are only put here if we are absolutely desperate. Otherwise, no one goes there.

Greedy pads ahead, heading east into the deepening murk, probably looking for birds. He is weirdly obsessed by birds, simultaneously overjoyed that they exist, yet frantically bewildered by their ability to fly. Perhaps he was once a bird. Perhaps he is a shapeshifter, my witch's familiar, like in the book my mum had, the book I hated. The one with the hanging witch.

My dog is almost out of sight. I call into the softness of the night, and then I stop. Alarmed. More than alarmed.

There.

My heart thumps as if I am trying to swim in the Blackwater.

Through the gloom I see a pale face at a window in the east wing, where no one ever stays. Where no one ever goes. A pretty young woman, gazing sadly out.

And now, already, she is gone.

Running up the shingle, I approach the east wing. Which window was it? They are all the same. Repeating arches. I peer in through one window, then another, then another, but I see nothing, just vague shapes of furniture in the gloom. Nothing.

There is no one in the east wing. I imagined it. I must have.

Behind me, Greedy barks.

13

Kat, Then

There. A face. Sister.

Loudly, Kat called out, 'Han!'

Hannah was hurrying through reception in her typical work clothes: tidy skirt, ironed blue shirt. She turned and ran over and they hugged; and then stopped hugging, at exactly the same time.

'Sis . . .'

A mutual step backwards, more happy smiles. Kat considered her sister. They were still *almost* a mirror image, inside and out. The same blue eyes, blonde hair, same Langley smile. Then they both laughed, at exactly the same time.

It had always been like this, that telepathic link. As Hannah chattered away, Kat remembered, with a pang of sadness, how it had been like this the day Mum had died. They'd telepathically run to each other, crying, along the landing, in the old house in Maldon, the one with that view of the curlew-crying river. Two little girls dimly aware that Mummy was in hospital in a way that made grown-ups *whisper*; two little girls who knew, somehow, that something terrible had just happened.

They'd cried together for an hour, sitting beside one another at the top of the stairs with the dusty orange carpet and the peeling banister. Hugging, holding hands, knowing nothing except that Mum was gone.

Kat snapped out of her memories. This really was not the weekend to mention Mum too much, not with Hannah, not after what Dad had said. *Dawzy and Mum? Who could have guessed?*

Hannah was still talking.

'You look stressed,' Kat said. 'Slow down! Have a banana.'

Hannah chuckled. 'I wish I could. Been run off my feet all day, all week! Organizing this. Christ, Kat. It's like we're invading France, armed with Bollinger.'

Her wide gesture took in the adjoining corridors, brasserie, spiral stairs, everywhere thronged with people fetching, carrying, preparing.

Kat contemplated the scene: it felt like the day before a very big, marginally royal wedding party. A sense of anticipation filled the hotel, which had every door and window flung open to the glorious June sunshine. The day was hot already; tomorrow was meant to be even hotter.

A male voice called over. Authoritative, from high above.

'Hannah, could I grab you for a moment?'

Hannah swivelled, obedient, gazing up.

Aha, Kat, thought, *the boss*. The handsome older him. Oliver whatsit. Coming down the stairs towards them.

Oliver was wearing a pale linen suit and a blindingly white linen shirt unbuttoned by just the right amount so as to show a tanned chest, and dark chest hair: one more button undone would have been a bit too private-jet-to-Dubai. Perfectly judged.

Kat watched, curiously, at the way Hannah fluttered eyelashes at her boss. Oh yes. Oh, definitely yes.

Oliver came over, smiled at Kat and she said hi; then he looked back at Hannah.

'We've got some fantastically obscure problem with the caviar. Not enough oscietra, apparently.'

Hannah frowned. 'Er. OK.'

Kat watched on as Oliver St John Xavier Charlemagne Sexybobs laid a hand on Hannah's shoulder. 'Sorry. I *know* it's not your department, but you're just so *good* at this. Could you come and smooth things over? Don't want Chef to quit. Not today. Unideal.'

Hannah nodded and smiled and blinked rapidly. In fact, Hannah practically *curtseyed*. Then she turned to Kat. 'Sorry, sis, I've just got to, y'know. I mean, it's work—'

Kat beamed. 'It's fine! Go work!'

Hannah waved as she walked away. 'You've got a room, somewhere? Check Danielle, on reception, or Julia. Catch up with you later!'

'Cool. No drama.'

Hannah and Oliver disappeared. Kat could hear the familiar Scottish accent of Logan shouting loudly, probably at a piece of hake. Then all she could hear was the deafening rattle of glasses and cutlery as more workmen came piling through, pushing trolleys, ferrying white tablecloths. Others were lugging wooden chairs, lush bowls of flowers, setting up tables, indoors, outdoors, everywhere.

Kat took out her phone and messaged Julia.

Where are you? I'm here! Is now a good time? x

Almost immediately, a response. *Typing.*

Sure. I'm in the bar, now is good 😉

Kat knew exactly how to find the bar. Left, right, here: pictures of royal yachts, big jugs of Pimm's, that Australian who made the fancy cocktails. Plenty of people were drinking already; children were happily splashing in the little swimming pool through the open French windows.

Julia was in her waitressing kit. 'Kat!'

'Bro! There are rumours I've got an actual room?'

Julia smiled and kind of winked. She led Kat, wordlessly, out of the noisy bar, through a hallway, past a big, dominant portrait, then into a carpeted corner.

'You got a room in the west wing, tonight, near Hannah.'

'Great. Coolio. Uhm . . . And . . . Er . . . did you?'

Kat didn't want to say it loudly; she didn't want to say it at all. Just in case. But Julia nodded, hesitant, smiling.

'Yep. It's coming tomorrow.'

'Everything?'

'The whole lot – 2C-B, ket, and a couple of grams of coke. Everything.'

Kat clapped her hands. 'Yay.'

Julia turned, about to go, then paused. 'There's one more thing, Kat. We're really jammers. Chocka. So, tomorrow we might have to move you.'

Kat shrugged. 'God, I don't mind, I'll sleep by the Strood. Where ya putting me? How bad can it get?'

'The east wing.' Julia frowned. 'It's not the nicest part of the hotel. But . . .' she grinned '. . . you probably won't even notice, will you?'

Kat laughed. 'I hope not.'

14

Hannah, Now

On the steep shingle beach, I tickle Greedygut behind the ear. He pants, pink-tongued, happy and adoring. Practically bursting with loyalty. I've already learned he loves behind-the-ear tickling, and I have learned much more. The dog is an education. He teaches me how to calm down, and how to think of something other than my imprisonment, and the tragedy, and the awfulness of everything. He is one of the few things keeping me sane, by the mere fact that I have to look after him, feed him, walk him. Play. He teaches me that there is hope, maybe.

And he keeps me level-headed. This is the third day since I saw that face in the east wing, and I am now pretty convinced I saw nothing, and yet as I scrunch my way up the shingle, I look towards the east wing. At that endless Victorian brickwork, and the long row of black, empty, arched windows.

Greedy yaps, at just the right time, dragging me back to reality. And to a much more pressing question. How do I get to keep my beloved rescue dog? Alistair had been adamant. No pets allowed for staff. Loz refused to intervene as I pleaded my case. She literally ducked behind her computer screen as Alistair told me, with a definite relish, an obvious pleasure in the hurting, that Greedy had to go. He actually, said, 'There's a dogs' home in Chelmsford – they'll take him. Rescue dogs and all that.'

I nearly burst out crying, with outrage: *but I already rescued him!* Instead, I kept my mouth shut. Mustn't give him an excuse to sack me.

I am defeated.

Greedygut barks joyously at a heron perched on a hummock of grass. I tickle him again, resisting tears, saying, 'Shhhh, Greedy, shhhhh. Tis but a bird.' He stops barking and instead, and for no reason, does a little happy doggy dance on the shingle. Round and round and round. And this forces me to laugh, again, despite everything. The dog is a source of life, distraction, laughter. And I must let him be taken to some awful dogs' home?

As Greedygut runs up and down the narrow beach, I gaze out, away from the hotel.

It is a cold October afternoon, curdling into evening. Distant ships emerge out of the murk, then disappear, as if they can barely be bothered to exist.

Lights. On.

I turn. The hotel lights are going on as the darkness falls on us all. One light, in particular catches my attention. The biggest bay window on the first floor. Oliver's office. I saw his big white boat berthed earlier. He must be on Dawzy, and he must be in the office.

A hope.

Dare I?

In my favour is this: last night I sent Oliver my ideas for a big Christmas theme, to distract everyone from the bad publicity. A series of special Twenties dinners, dances, murder mystery parties. The idea came out of my furious research: I fortuitously stumbled over invites and menus that the Stanhope – in its earliest, fashionable incarnation as a hotel – sent out to those affluent, adulterous Londoners. My idea that is we copy these Gatsby-era invites, font for font, word for word, make it ironic but fun.

In the kitchen we'll take some of the fancy old-fashioned French dishes – *Caille double Perigourdine, Darne de Saumon a la Royale, Salade Mimosa* – and get Mackinlay to update them in his genius modern-Brit way. Chuck in some 1920s jazz with a modern beat, add lashings of swanky period cocktails: Brandy Alexandre, the Hanky-Panky – and, so I told Oliver, people will positively flock. They are bored. It's a cold, rainy autumn, heading for a frigid winter. They are desperate to dance. And in December they will dance the Charleston in the Stanhope.

That was my idea: and Oliver loved it. He emailed back within the hour. *Brilliant, let's do it!*

If I take my case to the ultimate boss, right now, I might get a hearing.

Stomping along the shingle, I return Greedygut to the room and give him a tennis shoe to chew on. Then I walk fast – before my bravery fails.

Approaching the door to the boss's office, I hesitate. Then I knock.

A dark, familiar voice. 'Yup.'

As soon as I enter, my stomach tumbles with disappointment. Alistair is also here. Standing by the windows, talking with Oliver, who has his feet up on his desk.

The boss gives me a grand, welcoming smile. 'Hey. Our genius PR girl! Sorry I shouldn't call you *girl*. Am I allowed to call you *genius*?'

I blush. 'Hannah is fine, but thanks.'

'I'll call you genius if I like. So, anyway . . .' Oliver takes his polished shoes off the desk. 'How can I help?'

He's clearly busy. I have little time. Dry-mouthed.

Alistair gazes at me. He's also smiling my way, but it is shrivelled, maybe gloating. I suspect he knows what I am about to say, and I suspect he knows I am going to be rebuffed and humiliated.

'It's about that dog I found. Rescued.' Oliver frowns. I go on, 'I know Alistair thinks it's a terrible idea, not allowed. I just thought, well, uhm, you know, uhm, maybe?'

The frown deepens; Oliver sighs. 'Alistair did mention this. I am afraid he's absolutely right.'

'I know. I know,' I rush on, heedless, 'but I am so bloody lonely, Oliver. Stuck here, on the island. That dog, somehow, he helps. A whole lot.'

I mustn't cry. I despise women who use their tears to manipulate men.

Oliver regards my evident distress. I allow one tear to fall. No one is perfect.

His hands are churched: fingertips lightly pressed together. 'Well. Well. I don't know.' A long, tormenting pause. He half nods, half shakes his head. A tight, precise sigh. 'You'd need a distant room with direct access to the woods, or the beach. Impossible otherwise. Can't have a dog going through the common areas.'

At the window, Alistair stiffens. 'Oliver—'

The boss raises a hand, silencing him. 'The east wing.'

Alistair protests again. 'No way.'

Oliver glances at Alistair with a hint of contempt.

'Calm down, Alistair. It's just a room.' His glare is chilly. 'A room no one is using. In a wing no one uses.' He glares pointedly at Alistair. 'And it has an external door.'

'But fuck. That wing.'

Alistair is swearing at Oliver? I've never heard Oliver and Alistair argue like this. Oliver stands up. He is bigger than Alistair. More powerful. Taller by a good few inches, six foot three to five foot seven.

'That's enough. Really. *Enough.*' He turns and gives me a brief smile, a smile that says *I am doing you a big favour, be grateful.* And he is, and I am. 'Hannah it's the last room down at the end, big windows, a door to the beach. It's not in the best condition.' He shrugs. 'But if you move there, you can keep your precious pup.'

'Thank you,' I say. 'Thank you thank you thank you.'

Making good my escape, I leave the office, but even as I close the door, I can still hear Alistair, almost shouting. He REALLY doesn't want me to stay in the east wing. Why? Can it have anything to do with what I saw? The face at the window? Surely not. If there was actually anyone there it was probably just a maid. They must maintain it sometimes. Although why at night?

I have no idea what's going on. And I do not care.

I can keep Greedygut. For the first time in many months, I feel something in my chest, or my heart. Somewhere in there, a warm, bubbly feeling. I think it is happiness. It is already gone.

15

My new room is very big and, as Oliver warned me, rather stale. It has old yellowy wallpaper, peeled in places, and there are cigarette burns in the 1970s fitted carpet that look like dark spots of acne. No honey-waxed parquet and hand-woven Isfahan rugs here. The bed is big, bumpy, brass.

The only signs of any refurb are the new painted ceiling, some new and modern lighting, and one pricey, elegant, wall-to-ceiling mirror. That's as far as they got before the restoration abruptly stopped, a few months before I arrived. The plan after that was, apparently, to complete the refurbishment of the east wing this autumn; but the events of That Night, and the confusion that came after, meant everything got shelved way into the future. Oliver says he'll get to it next year.

My new incomplete home is, also, as far from every-where else as it is possible to get inside this labyrinthine building. Mine is the very last room in the east wing, which is, of course, otherwise entirely deserted: devoid even of pale, anxious faces in windows. Unless mine counts.

I am right at the end of a long silent corridor. Beyond my room the woods, beaches and barking birds begin. I am at the edge of civilization.

Greedygut snoozes on the bed, next to me. Snoring,

in fact. Shutting my laptop, I ease myself off the mattress, put on running shoes and walk over to the heavy Victorian door, and push it open. Stare down the length of the shadowy corridor.

My gaze is rewarded with utter silence.

The corridor stretches away into nothing. Rows of doors are resolutely shut. Nothing stirs; no one else is here. No one comes. No one goes. No one cleans the unused rooms. No guests have noisy afternoon sex. No maids gossip and laugh and smoke, illicitly, by flung-open windows. Which means I surely did not see anyone, and it also means I'll have to clean the room myself. I don't mind. I get to keep Greedy. But I do wonder if something happened to me would anyone hear my cries and come running? I could probably scream continuously, and no one would ever hear.

Back into my room. It has those same arched, almost-ecclesiastical windows, kind of Victorian Gothic, and they inevitably look – if I am in the mood to look – onto the rushing, estuarine Blackwater. Next to these churchy windows is the reason I am here: a proper exit. An external door, opening directly onto the shingle. Maybe this room was used for deliveries a century ago, or it was occupied by someone who needed outdoor access.

On the mighty bed, Greedy has woken up. He looks bored. I am bored. My work is done. It is late afternoon. The sickly light will soon be dead.

I gaze at my listless dog.

'Walkydogs? Beachybobs?'

The transformation is instant. He's learned this patois super quick. Tail wagging, joyously, as if he has a powerful if primitive motor lodged in his butt, he leaps from the duvet, and runs to the door. Mewling with

86

suppressed desire. Wagging ever more furiously. I chuckle, grab a coat, and then some binoculars; I am using the binos to birdwatch, but I am also using them as exposure therapy.

Rob Kempe has instructed me carefully: the more I simply look at the water, the more I will tolerate it; the more I tolerate it, the closer I will get to that moment, that unforeseeable, beautiful moment, when I am locked up no longer. A day that seems to recede from me, every day I get nearer.

It's a chilly, dank afternoon. I scan the horizon. A V-shaped arrow of geese is flying, languidly across the grey sky, dipping and rising like a sine wave. A south wind carries the scents of farms from across the scurrying river. Silage? It smells like cider. It smells of rural England and country lanes.

Deeply, hungrily, I inhale. Oh God, how I'd love to be on a *farm*. Walk along a *field*. Stare across sweet green *meadows*. Everywhere on Dawzy is so enclosed: by the dense black woodlands, which only end at these clinking pebbled beaches, sometimes so steep they are essentially cliffs. And anything that isn't wood, or beach, on Dawzy, is the great hotel, or tiny walled gardens.

At least I do have the beach. As Greedygut pants eagerly ahead, I take out my binoculars to observe the geese. They are wheeling around now, manoeuvring in perfect formation. Showing off, maybe. Though no one watches, apart from me.

And Danielle, the receptionist.

She's just over there. A few yards away. Unaware of me. Wrapped in a furry hooded anorak, gazing across the waters, having a crafty cigarette.

Greedygut gallops back, barking at everything. Danielle turns, startled, sees the dog, sees me. Her frown softens.

'Hello,' I say.

She nods. 'Hiya.'

That's it. I don't quite know what to add. We've never really bonded, Danielle and I – not because of dislike, just too much work. We are busy colleagues. Or we were. She arrived a few months before me. She's got a new man on the mainland and disappears every weekend. If she ever had a fling with the Mackster it is over.

And now we are together, alone, on a beach, and it is just beginning to rain. Again. Danielle shakes her head, exhaling more smoke. 'This fucking island.' Another drag, another plume of grey-blue smoke. 'Fuck this fucking place.' She offers me a look. 'Sorry, Kat. I know it's way worse for you.'

'No, it's OK. Really. I get bored of people sympathizing all the time.'

She shrugs, takes a last puff, drops the cigarette, and slowly, forcefully grinds it out with the toe of her trainer, as if she wants to hurt the island.

I am curious. Greedygut is getting cold, and the rain is not abating. Why not?

'Do you want a cup of tea? I've got a kettle in my room.'

Danielle looks surprised by the offer, but not offended. 'Sure. Why not? Getting Nix at six. Thank fuck.'

16

Pushing the sturdy external door, I let us all in out of the rain. The door shuts behind us and the ceaseless birdcalls are muffled.

Danielle takes off her anorak and drops it on the bed, stares around, mouth slightly open. Her roots are showing.

'Never been in *this* one.'

'It's a bit tired, isn't it? But it's got this door, which is all I want, really.'

'Uh-huh. For your new dog, right?'

The kettle is on; it hums into life.

'Yes. Greedygut. Please, sit down, enjoy the peerless luxury. I even have a biscuit. Somewhere.'

She smiles, politely, and sits. Wearing less make-up than usual. Heading home, mask off. I can see her looking around my new home: at the mirror, the brass bed, the poxy carpet, a pile of books still waiting to be shelved.

'I'd ask for extra wages if they locked me in here.'

'Sorry?'

'Ah, nothing.' She grins sadly, showing teeth that are faintly stained with red wine. And now I see there is tannin on her lips. Drinking, in the afternoon. Her voice, now I pay attention, is discreetly but clearly slurred.

'Shouldn't say anything. Not you. Not you. Ta.'

She takes the tea. Asks for three sugars. I stir it in.

Her jumper is blue, homely; her jeans have a couple of rips. She is off duty in all senses.

'Are you all right, Danielle?'

Now she laughs, but it is dark. 'Soon as I get off this fucking island, I'll be fine.'

'What do you mean?'

Danielle drinks the hot tea, rather too quickly, says, 'Had enough. But it's a good job, right, so I have to stick around, don't I? Don't we all? Just have to stick around. And then they put you in here? You, of all people. The woman who can never get off the island. Fucking mental. Cruel.'

'I really don't understand, Danielle. What is it about this room?'

I am alarmed, again. I wait for an answer.

Greedygut whimpers in the corner. Probably hungry. I will feed him soon. Danielle looks at my dog.

'He came outta the water, like magic. I heard?'

'Sort of, yes.'

'You dived in, by the Strood. That's brave.'

'I couldn't let him *drown*.'

'Course not. But, the dog, the dog, that . . .' Her slurring is worsening. 'The dog means you gotta live here. In the east wing. FFssshh.'

She stares at me. Unblinking. She may be drunk but her focus is sharp. Her brown eyes look into mine and I realize she is scared.

'You never wondered why they never finished doing this wing up?'

'But they intend to, no? It was going to be this year, but after the . . . accident, it got delayed.'

'Nah. They won't ever. Not now. It will always be like *this*.' She looks at the mirror. 'You know some of the staff won't come down here?'

'Danielle, are you actually saying it is . . .' I can't say the word. It is too ludicrous.

She shrugs. 'Who knows? Imagine buying a great big hotel and only then you realize you've got this *atmosphere*. Too late.'

She stands up. Unsteadily.

'Freddy Nix at six. Ta for the tea. I'm sorry, gotta go. I'm sorry.'

She goes over and picks up her coat; slowly puts it on. Speaks. 'You know, a few weeks before you came, there was a maid.'

Greedygut whimpers, again. Dani says, 'Yeah. We had this new maid, from Hungary, Mira. Her English wasn't very good, but anyway they gave her a job one day – and she got it all wrong, got the numbers all wrong. She went to turn a room in this wing, the east not the west, and a few minutes later she came back crying, sobbing, like she'd seen something properly terrible, something horrific.'

'What do you mean?'

'She was superstitious, you know, Catholic, wore a cross as big as you like. Anyway, she left the Stannie the same fucking day. Wouldn't talk about it. Gone. So, what the fuck happened? Who knows? Management doesn't like us to talk about it, of course.' Danielle buttons her coat and turns to me. 'I'm sorry, I'm sorry, I've had a drink. I shouldn't have told you, but—' She reaches out, squeezes my shoulder, firmly, kindly, trying to help.

The human touch in the middle of all this isolation makes me want to cry, even as her words unnerve me.

'But *no one* tells you *anything*, Hannah, because of what you're going through. Everyone tiptoes around you, but it's not fair on you. So, I'm sorry but I'm not sorry, and I'd better go. If you want to get me sacked, please do, then I've got an excuse to get off this *fucking* island. Bye.'

She opens the door. The east wing inhales the cool air.

I stand here, looking out of the door, as my thoughts race away like a hare fleeing a dog. Have they put me all the way down here in the east wing for a reason? It could be a complex way of getting rid of me. But why?

I can feel a vague chest pain, while I breathe in the scents of the Blackwater. I know the pain well: tachycardia. Racing heartbeat. But this is not phobia. It is a new and deep unease.

17

Kat, Then

'Omfguhhhhhh . . . mmmmm.'

'You like it?'

Kat nodded, sighed exuberantly and took another forkful of the dish. Closing her eyes, she tilted her chin towards the ceiling of the Mainsail brasserie. Wondering if she looked absurd, not caring.

'Fucketty hell. *Delicioso*. What is that in there, the fruit, some kind of pear?'

Hannah smiled back. 'It's a local pear. Chef goes out to all the farms every week, never stops working.'

'He's still a genius, isn't he? The Mackster. Who knew that pear goes with smoked . . . whatever-the-fuck-it-is.'

'Eel.'

'Eel Really? Hah. Again!'

'Sorry?'

Kat set down her fork. 'I had eel, like, last Wednesday. Eel. With the new guy.'

'K.'

'He only *ever* takes me to these pricey seafood places.

He's got some obsession with tracking down these mad things. What are they? Ushuaia king crabs! That's it.'

Kat watched as her sister leaned closer, inquisitive, asking, 'But which new guy is this? A *new* new guy? Or the same new guy?'

'No, this is a *new new* guy. THE new new new new new new guy.'

'You mean new – for about a week.'

Kat pretended to be horrified. 'I'm not that bad! Am I? OK I am. Anyway, I'm keeping this one, if I can.'

They resumed eating. Kat noted, as she savoured the amazing eel and pear – and some kind of Japanese condiment? – that her older sister's blonde hair was neatly and very recently cut for the big day tomorrow.

Hannah spoke. 'So, let me guess.'

'What?'

'The new new guy. About forty-five? Banker? Lives in Chelsea?'

Kat chuckled. 'Close! Forty-seven. Lawyer. Knightsbridge.'

'God. I *was* close.'

'Madam?'

Kat turned and nodded eagerly at the waiter offering to pour more wine. As he topped up her generous glass, she stared around. The Mainsail was busy, with just the right amount of buzz: loud enough to energise, yet without making private conversation difficult. Whoever designed this space had clearly thought about the *acoustics*.

'Forty-seven is pretty old, even by your standards, Kat. Doesn't the age gap ever get to you?'

'Nah. I like it.'

'Daddybobs issuedogs?'

'Ha yes, OK, but also,' Kat darkened her voice, conspiring. 'Don't you ever notice it?'

'Sorry?

'Young Men Today. What are they about? Have you talked to a guy in his mid-twenties recently?'

'I guess, a bit, not so much . . . Why?'

Kat threw up her hands. 'Christ. Christ They're just so . . .' A pause, seeking the right word. '*Vapid*. They talk about computer games. They laugh at non-jokes. They're terrified of offending. It's *dull*. The older dudes aren't scared. They have higher sperm counts.'

'Er . . .'

'It's true. Ooops. Ugh!'

Kat looked down. Her knife was spinning to the floor. A waiter rushed over to replace it. Kat was very used to dropping things. *Dyspraxia*. It came in handy sometimes. Men sought to protect her as she fell over.

'Anyway, yes *and* IQs have fallen – I reckon you can actually see it in young men. They're like boys.'

'Not young women?'

'Maybe not so *much*. *We're* not so scared to offend. Well, I'm not anyway. Oh God, I'm *still* hungry. Shall we share a dessert?'

They shared a dessert. Kat laughed as she took her first mouthful: poached fruit in sloe-something. *Divine*. Logan Mackinlay's IQ had clearly not declined. She thought about Logan's rugby-playing shoulders, and that sexy Scottish accent. *Aye, Katalina Langley* . . . But no. She purged the thought as best she could. Be a good girl this time. Just for one weekend. She could do that? Couldn't she?

Hannah was reminiscing about Mum, and Kat joined in, even if it made her want to fess up and tell Han what Dad had said. But she couldn't. She *could* still chat about Mum, though. For a few minutes Mum could live again, here on Dawzy Island, where they used to come as a family.

'Remember that mad book she had? The one on the occult, the big encyclopaedia, with all her writing in it—'

Hannah laughed. 'God, yes. Of course, I remember it. The one with the witch picture. Hated it. Tooooo creepy.'

'Really, I *loved* it. It had everything. Spells and potions, and unguents. I'm still not sure what a fuckin' unguent is.'

'Didn't she always make that toothpaste during the full moon?'

'Oh my God, yes!' Kat laughed, overloud, making diners at another table frown. She didn't care. They chatted some more, about Mum, then Kat remembered. 'Oh my God. I forgot to *tell* you.'

Hannah looked back, alarmed, eyes wide. 'Jesus. Kat? What is it?'

There was a long pause, then Kat said, 'Cellulite.'

'What?'

'I've got fucking CELLULITE. Found it this morning. UGH!'

People were definitely glancing over. Kat beamed at them.

Hannah was laughing. 'You've only *just* got cellulite? I've had it literally since puberty.'

'You *have*? Well, I've joined the bloody gang.' She shook her head, theatrically mournful, enjoying the absurd drama. 'And it's all over my ass, man. I got in the shower and looked down and it's bubble-wrap city down there. Ants could use my bum as a skate park.'

Another snort of laughter from Hannah. This felt good. Kat liked making her sister happy.

Downing her wine, Hannah asked, 'How is your room?'

'S'gorgeous Han.'

'You're welcome, Kat. Least I could do.'

Kat shook her head, cheerily. 'Don't be daft! I'm getting it for *free*. I'm verrrrry lucky. Your boss is generous.'

'He is.'

'And quite, you know, attractive?'

Hannah's smile was measured. 'Stop!' A meaningful gaze. '*Seriously.*'

Kat got the message. *I see you, sister.* 'OK Han. OK.' Kat allowed herself a big yawn. 'You know, I'm wagama-ma'd. I'd better go sleep.'

'You have come all the way from London.'

'And drunk way too much. Need sleep. Everyone's been so kind, even that lechy dude, the sea dog, telling me about the hour thing, the danger. Seee you tomorrow. D'ya need me to—'

Hannah gave Kat a reassuring smile. *Everything is taken care of.*

Grateful, sated, Kat wove her way out of the brasserie: aiming for her room, *just down here*, trying her best not to fall over. She really was properly drunk. Somehow, she managed to card her door, fall into her room, fall out of her clothes, fall into bed.

Ping.

Blearily, she lifted her phone. A message from him? No. Not this weekend. Never again.

Kat turned the phone off and lay back on the pillow, staring up into the darkness. Tomorrow she would go looking for that special place, Mum's place, where it all changed.

18

Hannah, Now

Morning sun makes dazzle-patches on the Blackwater. Resolutely, I ignore it. Not one of my good mornings. I woke up sad, and kind of scared. Even Greedygut didn't cheer me up.

I do not believe in ghosts. I am not my witchy, Tarot-reading sister. I am not my zodiac-reading, horoscopical mother. I am practical Hannah, the one with the proper job, the girl with the sensible career. And yet what Danielle said has stayed with me.

So, I'm in the Mainsail brasserie, in an empty corner. Fuelling up on toast and caffeine, suffocating my fears with food, trying *not* to remember happier times. That dinner with Kat, the night before it all happened. Should I have seen the signals in her even then? What drove her to that wildness? She won't tell me even *now*. Yet I need to know.

I can hear the chatter of guests idling by the buffet table, choosing types of omelette, marvelling at the *jamón ibérico de bellota*: an entire leg of the finest acorn-fed, black-trottered Extremadura ham, horizontally skewered on a vicious cast-iron spike.

Guests are invited to carve themselves as much of this ultra-premium ham as they like at breakfast, even though it costs about ten thousand quid a slice. One of the ways Oliver lured the Mackster here, away from the flash and cash of London and the crucial restaurant reviewers, was with stuff like this: the absolute best ingredients. Just like the coffee I am drinking. From Ethiopian beans.

Pouring another, I check my phone. Ten minutes till work begins.

Should I call someone? Kat? Probably too early. She may be sleeping off a hangover, or canoodling with her newest. The new new new newest.

Bracing myself, I opt to call Dad, who rises at about 5 a.m. so that he can start his full day of doing nothing, as early as possible.

I select the number. His mobile rings and rings and rings, nagging away in that room in Maldon, then goes to voicemail. His husky, quavery voice tells me: 'Hello, you've reached Peter Langley. Please leave me a message after the beep.'

Beep.

Oh, Dad. Really?

I know he is lonely. Widowed and alone and bored in his sheltered housing. But I'm alone and bored and practically widowed on an island. We could console each other; we could compare notes on isolation, lockdown and tedium. And I love my dad. I miss him. It is such a shame he is so distant. So prickly and difficult. He's not like this with Kat. He's *never* like this with Kat. I don't mention her to him in case I sound jealous. Which I'm not. Even though I could be.

I try again. Thinking. *Just answer me. I'm here. For you. Be there for me? I miss you and love you.*

Beep.

I don't leave a message. I'm not sure what to say. So, I stare at the phone with its wallpaper pic of me and Kat as kids: running hand in hand on a riverside path, sprinting gleefully towards the camera. It is one of my favourite photos. I think Mum took it. We are about seven and eight; our faces express the kind of happiness you only get at that brilliant age between four and nine, when nothing has ever gone wrong, and all of life is amazing, when the existence of *anything* seems a miracle. Ladybirds, trains, windy days.

Wind. Air. Yes. I need some air before work. Grabbing my things, I thread my way through reception. Danielle is not here, for which I am glad.

On the way out, I pass Leon, the concierge.

Leon glares at me. He glares at a lot of people. But he says nothing: he knows he can't boss me around. I am PR. Nothing to do with him. Instead, he smooths his dark hair over his big head, pompously stands at the doorway like he is guarding a monarch.

Where does he get this attitude from? He's been here since the start, before me, and he is a puzzle. A Swiss German, in coastal Essex. There are lots of Swiss Germans in hotel management. Sometimes it feels as if they are all Swiss German, but Leon is just the concierge. Yet he seems rich. How much do they pay him? Maybe too much. Hence his arrogance.

On to the breezy, sunny, chilly beach, I see Logan, the chef, talking with Owen, the sous-chef, both in their whites, taking a breather from the kitchen, down by the lapping water. As I approach, Owen waves a goodbye, to both of us: kitchen business, I presume. But

Logan lingers. He offers me that modestly handsome face. Sturdy white teeth, blonde fringe, hint of Viking red in his stubble.

'Hey, Hannah. Have you found a teleporter yet? That could work.'

He likes to joke with me. I like to joke with him. He and Loz are maybe the only two people on Dawzy with whom I can have friendly, bantering conversations.

'No teleporters yet.'

'Shame!'

'At the moment my main hope is getting kidnapped by pirates. At least I'd get to see the Aldi in Heybridge.'

Logan gives a low chuckle. 'Aye, that could work.'

We gaze at each other amiably. Though I can also see stress in his eyes.

'How's the kitchen?'

His sigh is meaningful. He runs fingers through his hair. 'You've seen the bookings, Hannah – not great. Not terrible. But definitely down.'

'Cheer up. I've got some PR ideas, might work. Twenties theme. Gatsby parties, Sazerac cocktails, flapper dresses.'

He grins. 'Oliver told me; he really likes it.' A brief check of his watch. He needs to be elsewhere. He's waiting for my permission to go.

I hesitate. Can I really ask this next question? I'm not sure I can. It will make me seem disloyal.

'Hannah. Turbot doesn't order itself. Georgia's waiting in the kitchen.'

Georgia Quigley. West Mersea Seafood. Freddy's girl-friend. Somehow it is all linked, and sometimes it feels like a chain-link fence around me.

The only way to say this is to say it quickly. 'Logan, this might sound a bit odd. But have you ever heard,

101

like, stories, about the east wing? Weird things happening there?'

Logan Mackinlay looks at me and says nothing. And then he faintly blushes.

'Logan?'

He's thinking, delaying. So, there is *something*?

Then he says, 'Noooo. Nothing. Don't be daft! It just needs a damn good paint job. Anyway, I really do have to order up the horse barnacles. Got Spanish guests coming.'

'OK. OK. Sorry to bother you. I'm being silly, I guess.'

He eyes me hesitantly. Do I see a flash of sympathy? 'Logan, please don't tell anyone what I just said; everyone already thinks I'm crazy.'

Another pause. Until he says, softly, 'You know, I don't think you're crazy at all, Hannah.'

And then he puts on his blank face, once again, and walks away.

19

Dr Kempe sits in the old wooden armchair in my old Victorian room with the old slumland wallpaper and looks sympathetically at me. Frankly, I feel older than anything around us. I'm like an old crone from the seventeenth century, prone to toothless delusions. Surrounded by imps. The staring hare. The magical dog. The face in the window that was not there.

I am one of those witches they chucked in the river by Royden.

'So, Robert, am I going mad?'

'No.'

'What about the hare? The face at the window? Is it possible I'm seeing things?'

'Possible. But hallucinations are rare in phobias or anxiety disorders, and if they occur, they tend to be restricted.'

'In what way, restricted?'

'Mild auditory hallucinations, like tinnitus, maybe stray voices. Nothing more elaborate.'

'Well, I don't get *those*.'

Tea, mug, sip. Gentle smile. 'So, I think you should calm down. The mind is prone to creating human shapes and faces out of nothing – coats that become monsters at night. Cheese graters that smile. It is universal in childhood. But not a hallucination.'

I remember the dressing gown on the door that became the crooked-necked witch when I was a child. So that's true enough. The young Hannah is still inside me, maybe.

'And the hare?'

'You probably just saw a very friendly hare!' Robert's laugh is well-meant but jarring. He stops laughing, aware that I am unamused. 'I'm serious, Hannah. These are just animals. The island is full of them, is it not? And what was the other thing – the ghost story from your friend? It was a ghost story, and she was rather tipsy, you said?'

'She was drunk. Really quite drunk.'

'There you are then. Safely ignored.'

I nod, half-heartedly.

He affirms: 'All these fears and anxieties, they will go away. We can *make* them go away.'

'Does that include Alistair? Be quite nice if he went away.'

Robert smiles sardonically. 'The manager. The one you don't get on with?'

'Yes.'

'I believe I have met him: short, thin, peevish?'

'Bingo.'

The doctor nods, leans over and tickles a sleepy Greedygut behind the ear, just in the right spot. Greedygut does a kind of doggy purr, tail swishing, lazily.

'He's the one that didn't want you to keep the dog, correct?'

'Yep.'

'Well, you were absolutely right to stand your ground. Greedy here is an excellent innovation. Just from his need for walks, he'll keep you going outside, exposing you to the water daily. And keep you company, too, of course.' A thoughtful frown. 'Indeed, it's fascinating that you managed to dive into the water, to save him. It shows you *can* do it, in extremis.'

'But it was *so* extreme, Robert. I puked, wet myself, horrible. I never ever want to do it again; I nearly had a heart attack.'

'Yet you did it.' The doctor's smile is fatherly, encouraging. 'It gives us something to work on.'

He reaches into his mustard-coloured waistcoat, looks at a pocket watch like a character out of Dickens, maybe the fat older guy who rescued Oliver Twist. I am warming to Dr Robert Kempe. He calms me; he allays my fears. I feel better for seeing him. He will cure me. He *must*.

'I'd better be going soon. The ferry is at six, isn't it?'

'Uh-huh. Freddy Nix at six.'

The doctor is standing, reaching into his briefcase. He offers me a piece of paper. 'This is a list of the therapies we discussed today. Cognitive stuff. Next time we can go back to practicalities. I am sure I can get you paddling.'

Paddling in the Blackwater?

The concept alone makes my throat tighten.

Robert pushes the door open, and I follow him out into a blustering sunny afternoon. Salty winds, billowing clouds.

The doctor gazes at the wide horizon, 'The skies over Essex are the most beautiful in the world. You know who said that?'

'Yes. John Ruskin. And didn't he actually say Thanet?'

Robert smiles as we scrunch across the pebbles. 'Thanet is a few miles away. You do have *such* wonderful skies here – the combination of water, distant hills, the saltmarsh. So much space, under heaven.'

'It doesn't feel like heaven.' I sigh. 'Can I leave you to it? Got some work waiting.'

'Of course, of course.' He buttons his raincoat. 'I have just one more question. Slightly random.'

'Go on?'

'Have you ever thought of flying off the island? In a helicopter? It would be absurdly expensive, but if there was an absolute crisis, something medical.'

I gaze his way, unsurprised. Everyone who knows me eventually asks this question.

'We looked into it. There's no space. Helicopters need quite a big, flat area to land in. The beaches are far too steep, and everywhere else is densely wooded and protected. You'd have to chop down a thousand historic trees, kill a million pine martens, and then you'd go to jail.'

'Ah.' Robert nods. And frowns.

'And I'm too scared to cross the Blackwater in a boat, so a plane or a space rocket would probably be the same.'

'I see. I see. Well then, therapy it is.'

'Therapy it most definitely is. You are my saviour. I hope.'

He smiles, trying to be reassuring. But the smile is a little pained. The frown returns. 'You know, I'm going to look into accelerating your therapy. See if we can find more time. You really do need to get off Dawzy.' He glances left, towards the hotel, which stares disdainfully over us, towards England. 'It's really not good for you here. I get that.'

He reaches out a hand, touches mine, squeezes it, and then turns and trudges to the jetty. Nix at six. And I am left wondering whether he thinks the Stanhope is bad for me because it is sending me mad, or whether the Stanhope is bad for me because it is Bad.

20

Kat, Then

The day of the party. Morning sunlight streamed, thronged, dazzled through the lavish bay windows of her room; the Blackwater glinting hints of azure had maybe never been bluer.

Finishing the last of the apple from the breakfast buffet, Kat looked at her clothes hung in the wardrobe, or slung in the drawer. What to wear during the day? Summery and casual, for sure. And definitely a bikini beneath. Slipping-off clothes. She stepped into her bikini, then pulled a simple pink-and-skimpy summer dress over it. Buckled up gladiator sandals.

A knock. Gentle. Twice.

Kat opened the door.

Julia stood outside, smiling. 'So, do you want to go to your next room? This one is needed for . . .'

'People who actually pay.'

Julia chuckled. 'Yeah. You ready?'

'Gimme *twoooooo* minutes.'

Kat extravagantly swept everything from the bed into

her big bag: the books, Tarot cards, drawing pad, head-phones, natural sun oil, all her clothes.

'That's some pretty fast packing.'

'I'm used to making getaways.'

Julia grinned. 'Then let's do it.'

Julia led Kat her through the hotel, past reception, where she paused. 'Ah wait I forgot.'

'Sorry?'

'Got to sign you up – over here!'

Opening a large, lavish volume, Julia got Kat to sign in, practically using a quill pen. Kat marvelled. The Stanhope was always so *posh*.

Then they walked past the gym, the spa, the little glassy atrium that led to the north wing, then around the sauna into a long dingy corridor. Kat had never seen this bit of the hotel before.

Julia carded a door and ushered Kat inside. The room was small, unadorned, old-fashioned, and OK. Maybe a bit of mustiness, something not altogether pleasant. A bit of a chill? It didn't matter. Kat didn't intend to spend much time in here, not today. As Kat dropped her bag and exuberantly tested the bounciness of the bed – quite bouncy – Julia said in a whisper, 'Here. Two gees. Maybe have the ket and the rest later.'

Kat took the little slips. 'Thanks, Jules.' Reaching into her bag, she found her turquoise beaded purse and handed over cash.

Julia thanked her, rolled her eyes. 'Must go – chaos now.'

'Sure.'

As Julia vanished, Kat sat on the bed and stared at the little packet. Why not? A peppish start to the day. Carefully opening the wrap, she tapped out some white, crushed-diamond coke, drawing a crystal line down the cover of her big book about astrology. Then a rolled paper note. A sniff, a sigh.

As the coke buzz surged, Kat glanced out of the window. The sun, the blue, the beckoning day. She had to get out there. But she couldn't be bothered to walk all the way back through the hotel. Maybe there was a quicker exit?

Out of the door, she turned right, heading for the other end of the corridor. Logic dictated there must be another way out of this huge empty wing. She came to the very last room. The door was wide open. She stepped inside. Big brass bed, peeling wallpaper, surprisingly big mirror, and yes, on the other side of the room, high, rather churchy, Gothically arched windows and an external door, heading straight onto the shingle beach. Again, an atmosphere, not very nice.

But it was handy to have this way out so near to her new room. Kat pushed the external door and stepped into the gorgeous sunlight.

The cocaine was now singing in her brain.

Let Everything Begin.

21

Hannah, Now

Greedy is whimpering at the door. I can hear him in the dark of my room.

It's mid evening, 9 p.m. at least. I am trying to sleep, get an early night – and failing.

And yet the idea of going out there into the cold, damp, autumn night, of looking at the Blackwater, fills me with sickly unease.

But Greedy won't stop whimpering and I don't want him peeing all over my already-manky carpet.

I reach for the sidelight, making yellow brightness.

'OK, Greedy. OK. Couldn't you have done this two hours ago?'

The dog looks up at me, happily, panting an answer, as if to say, *Yes, I could but now is more exciting, isn't it?*

Ah, my dog. He is a life support system, a miracle from the water.

The night is cold. I throw on layers: thicker socks, big jumper, and a coat, a scarf, and now at last I can open the door. Greedygut scampers out into the darkness and the noise of the birds. The gulls call out, over there, invisibly, on the saltings. Another bird is wailing louder, nearer, unseeable in the murk. Is it an alarm call – or maybe it is mating? I do not know. Other birds flute and squeeeal, as they flee across the clouded moon.

Greedygut races off, to do his business. I inhale the cool scent of freshly exposed marsh, the rotting hanks of briny seaweed: calming myself. It was raining hard earlier this evening; now it has cleared.

The moon appears as a cloud recedes. It is bright, nearly full, like some lantern held aloft by a loyal servant, trying to help, to guide me away, but I cannot be guided, because I have nowhere to go.

'Greedy?'

Where is he? I scan the shoreline. Flints and shingles shine wetly, like polished iron in the generous moonlight. Left, right, the beach is empty. Then I hear his playful yap. He is happy. He wants to stay out here.

Perhaps I should let him: I have nothing else to do. Dr Robert Kempe wants me to 'expose myself' to the Blackwater, and it doesn't get much more exposed than this. Staring at the river for an hour, or more, through a chilly autumn night.

Sitting down on a tussock of dried seaweed, I wait and shiver in the cold and dark, gazing out. Simply doing this is possibly helping me, even curing me. And so, I wait some more. The hotel is silent and black behind me. Guests numbers are still gently falling. Only the west wing is being used at the moment, so much of the hotel is dark.

The urge to go back to bed is fierce. But I want to do this. I want to face the river for hour after hour, expose myself as I have never done before.

Ten thirty p.m. Nothing. The fear laps at my feet. I have been staring too long, maybe. I haven't been this near to the Blackwater for so many continuous minutes since then. I can feel the first tickling choke in my throat. I think of that maid, Mira, the Hungarian, and what Danielle said: *a few minutes later she came back crying, sobbing, like she'd seen something terrible, horrific . . .*

No. It was just a ghost story. I must not frighten myself with ghost stories: not when reality is grim enough.

Eleven p.m.

I can hear something. A distant door closing, distant chat.

Two men have emerged from the hotel. The moon, however, is wholly hidden behind a black cloud.

They are striding down to the jetty, a long way down the shingle, black silhouettes in big raincoats, even darker than the sky. What are they doing here so late?

Ah.

More movement. A low light coming across the water. It's that boat again. The chic, fast black speedboat. I am sure it is. The one that comes and goes at odd hours. I watch it puttering – no, purring, this is a pricey machine – over to the side of the jetty. It looks as if Freddy Nix is at the tiller. The other two men are getting ready to embark as they near the slimy wooden steps. I cannot recognize anyone from this distance.

Binoculars? Dammit. Back in my room. Do I have time? No.

The men are already walking along the jetty. Is one of them Alistair? Maybe. Do I recognize his walk?

From behind me, Greedy barks, far too loudly, running tongue-out to my side.

'No,' I whisper, fierce, in his fuzzy ear. 'No, Greedy, shhhhh.'

The two men have already turned our way, maybe hearing the bark – and, somehow, by the way they move, the dark tilt of shoulders, I feel a sense of being menaced. These men do not especially want to be seen. What if I am caught watching them?

They want rid of her.

'Greeedy. Shhhhh, please. SHHH.'

Obedient, he copies me, as we crouch down quiet and low. We are a long way away, just murky shadows, or nothing at all.

The two men are going. Down the steps, into the boat. The motor starts. It is too late.

No, it isn't. Just as the boat wheels out into the water, the moon reappears. One man is steering away: his face invisible.

The other man is looking to his right. I recognize him. Older. Late forties. Silver hair. Firm chin. Aquiline.

But where do I recognize him from?

Then I remember.

22

Back in my room. Greedy in his basket. Wrapped up warm. The river hidden by the curtains. Too much river. Too much Blackwater. For tonight.

My gaze is locked onto my phone. Trawl the net.

The man I saw is on TV. I am sure of it: I've seen him on a screen. A banker, lawyer, businessman, or an actor who plays that sort of role. Yes. Something like that.

Yet I cannot track him down. I'm dicing with every combination of words that might capture him. Silver hair, aquiline, alpha, mid-forties, banker, famous . . . My tired thoughts drag like boots clogged with mud. I am getting odd looks from Greedy, as if he senses my fears. My dog who thinks he's a bird, maybe he can see into my mind. What did the maid see down here, in the east wing?

It is 2 a.m., and sleep is falling on me like a huge, tumbling wall. It is too much. I have just enough wakefulness to slap my laptop shut and push it across the bed before I am sucked down into sleep, as if I am falling in the pony-drowning muds of the Mundon Wash and I think of men in fishing boats and the ghostly face at the window I . . . I . . .

No, stop

NOOOO
STOOOOOOOOOOPPPPP

I am dragged from sleep, by *a scream*. A terrified, human scream. Shrieking: *No, stop*. It is a woman's scream, abject, horrified, helpless. Or did I dream it? I did not dream it. Maybe I dreamed of myself, drowning in the Blackwater; maybe I did too much exposure. This is not true. I heard a woman shrieking: *No, stop,* in anguish. I heard it. Awful. It echoes in my head.

And it was here, in the hotel. Not next door, but not far away. In the east wing, I'm sure of it.

I glance at the curtains. Grey-blue light surrounds the black cloth. It is dawn.

And someone has just screamed in curdling fear and pain. Not far away from where I lie, half paralyzed.

23

Not paralyzed. I have to do something. I run out into the corridor but see nothing. Empty rooms, closed doors. A darkened row of rectangular denials, with the night-lights innocently glowing.

But I heard it – I know I did.

I walk down the corridor, waiting for another terrifying scream. But I hear nothing. The silence is heavy. Did I dream it?

I did not dream it. It came from around here. Outside Room 6, I wait, listening close to the locked door. So many locked doors. I cannot hear anything, except the muffled hush of the cold Blackwater River outside the hotel. It sounds like someone breathing.

The next door. More silence. Yet that scream?

I cannot wait. I reach for my phone. *Do it.*

Dial 999.

A female voice answers. Welsh accent. Warm. 'Hello. Emergency services. Which service do you require? Fire, police, ambulance?'

'Um. Um. God. Police.'

'Hold on, just putting you through.' A pause.

A new voice, another woman with an Essex accent. 'Go ahead, please this is Colchester Police. Where are you?'

'The Stanhope.'

Even as I say this, I get my first proper doubts. Like prickles of energy, but painful. What am I doing? Calling the police on my own hotel?

'Sorry, love, where?'

'The Stanhope. It's a hotel. On Dawzy Island. In the Blackwater? The River Blackwater down from Maldon.'

'Ah. Yes, yes, I know it.'

'Please, we need help.'

'Are you in immediate personal danger?'

'No. No no.'

'So, what is the purpose of your call? How can we assist?'

'Uh. God. I – I heard a scream. A girl, or a woman. Just as I was waking up. Somewhere in the hotel.'

The policewoman makes a puzzled sound, says, 'A scream? What kind of scream?'

'Like someone being hurt, I don't know, someone saying: *No, stop*. Like – like she was being badly hurt, or something awful, violent.'

'Have you witnessed anything?'

'No, I can't see anything. I didn't, I mean – it's dawn. It was just as I woke up.' I refuse my doubts, I think of the true and piercing pain in that scream. *No, stop*. 'But I definitely *heard* it, I am sure. Please send someone, please.'

'All right, love, stay calm – we'll send someone. It'll take a while to get to the island. Stay calm, OK? What's your name?'

'Hannah Langley.'

'Are you a guest at the hotel?'

'No, I work here. PR. I'm in Room 46, in the east wing. I'm right at the end – that's why it's hard for me to say exactly where it was, the scream, the girl, I mean.'

'All right, we're on the way. We've got your number.'

117

'It only works on Wi-Fi.'

'That's fine. We can reach you. Just go to your room and stay there.'

The call clicks off. I stare at the phone. I do my duty and go back to my room, and I stare at Greedy, sleeping peacefully. So, he didn't hear anything? The doubts return like an inevitable tide.

I walk to the window and pull back the curtains and *expose myself*. The autumn sun is up, doodling silver squiggles on the river, and the waterbirds are out there on the low tide, sifting through the soft grey mudflats. Everything appears normal. What have I done?

Yet that black boat in the night, those two men, one of them maybe Alistair. And the Hungarian maid who saw something, and the face in the window.

Again, I step out into the corridor and the silence now is reproachful, contemptuous of my over-reaction. It is all perfectly ordinary out here: the hotel is just waking up. I can hear the distant clink of the kitchens, phone alarms going off, that means maids waking up. I sense them yawning, showering, the smell of coffee, the first baked bread, the murmuring voices: good morning, good morning. All the people I know and like here: Logan, Eddie, Oliver, Loz, Elena.

I have called the police on *them*.

No one is screaming. Everything is normal.

This is a disaster.

Standing at the window, I take out my phone and call 999 again. The same woman puts me through to the same woman: Colchester Police.

'Hello, this is Hannah Langley. I called you earlier.'

'Yes, I remember. We're on the way; we've organized a boat. Just stay calm.'

'No, please don't come. Sorry.'

'What?'

'It was a mistake. I made a stupid, stupid mistake. I think I dreamed it. I have these bad dreams. I'm stuck on this island you see. I'm so sorry – please don't tell.'

'You don't want us to come now?'

'No, please, it will be terrible for the hotel, the guests. We can't have police here, not again.'

'Sorry?'

'We don't need bad publicity, please. I made a big mistake. I'm sorry for wasting your time.'

The woman hesitates, whether from irritation or concern I don't know. Her next words have a sharper tone. 'This is all being recorded, Miss Langley. Now, please tell me, I need to know you aren't being forced to say this, so just say yes or no to my next questions. Is there anyone with you?'

'No.'

'No one is forcing you to say this?'

'No.'

'Do you want us to come to the hotel or not? Yes or no?'

'No.'

'Very well, we'll call it off.' She goes away, comes back. 'And please, look after yourself. You sound . . . *distressed.*'

'I know. Again, I am sorry.'

The call ends. The phone is limp in my hand. I am skewered by doubt. Did I hear the scream or not? Maybe it was just guests having rough sex. Dawzy, after all, is known for its sensual pleasures. And its terrified women.

No, stop.

Maybe I heard myself scream. Because this is what I feel inside.

No, stop. Stop it all.

24

Morning, yawning, pretending to work in the office, Loz across the way.

Coffee, drink. Eyes, rub. Work, if I can. I've thrust the farce of the police call from my mind. I pray the Colchester police will file it away somewhere obscure, and it will be forgotten, especially my name.

I can't be sure I heard anything, though I think I did. It sounded pained, terrified. But I was half asleep.

I need to speak to Robert Kempe. Get me off this island.

And what about that man? The one I've seen on a screen?

I yawn extravagantly, attracting odd glances from Loz.

No, stop.

The pain in that voice, something sad, yet animal. Brutal.

'You OK, Han?'

'Sorry, Loz, yes I'm fine, just a bit tired. Greedygut kept waking me up.'

She smiles. 'Love dogs, but they can be a total pain. Like having a baby, someone once told me. That's why I never had either. Hah!'

She goes back to work. She's been immersed in her screen all morning, juggling rooms for guests. We're getting more bookings, for Logan's dinners, and we're getting the first interest in my Christmas parties, the Twenties themes. The hotel might actually be reviving. The irony is fine and sharp, like a shiny new blade.

No, stop.

'Loz, you better come.'

It's Leon, at the office door.

Loz looks up. Frowns.

'Oliver and Alistair are in London. So, you'd better deal with this.'

'With what?'

He grimaces. 'Police.'

'What?'

'Yah. Freddy just called me; he's bringing them over now.'

Loz mouth drops open. 'Police . . .'

I try to hide behind my computer screen. This cannot be a coincidence. The police did not ignore or forget my call after all. Perhaps they aren't allowed to? I reported a fearful scream, so it could be that they *have* to investigate.

I have ducked so low behind my laptop screen that I am practically crouching. A child hiding from angry parents. My only hope is that the police are discreet. Would they give out my name? If they think I am in danger perhaps they won't. I peep over my computer screen.

Leon is striding towards the big bay window. The blustery sky frames him as he gazes down, presumably at the jetty. His voice is tense, angry. 'They're already here. We'd better greet them.'

Loz glances my way, but not suspiciously, just in a what-the-hell way: eyes rolling. With an extroverted sigh, she swings her coat from the chair, sticks her arms in the sleeves, and follows Leon as he marches out of the door.

Rising, I creep to the bay window. I can see Leon and Loz on the grey shingle down there with two police officers, their caps under their arms, talking. Freddy Nix's boat is berthed at the jetty; he loiters in his cabin.

I try to lip-read, but from this far away I can't. They could be saying anything. *We believe a girl was recently murdered in the east wing; can we have a quick look? Or: One of your staff is insane and needs to be sectioned. She hallucinates screams.*

The autumn day is cold: everyone is coated and booted. Loz and Leon make gestures to the officers, clearly saying: *Come inside, come in, come and be warm. Have a coffee.*

I can imagine the first guests noticing this, ogling, wide-eyed, as they head for breakfast, turning and pointing as they see this little drama on their way to the brasserie. Why are there police here, on the island with the reputation? This is where they had the Drownings, isn't it? What is going on?

I must pretend to be normal. Slipping back to my desk, I try to work, sending out more invites, frantically distracting myself with emails and PR puffery: *Come to our Christmas dance, there will be Savoy cocktails. There will be langoustines and foie gras and faux gemstones and feathered headbands. There will be fancy period cocktails: Sazerac, Dubonnet, Bee's Knees.*

And . . .

Loz is back. That didn't take long. Ten minutes, tops.

I attempt my best calm, innocent face as she drops her coat over her chair. She sees me looking over. Her smile is unexpected, and somehow vague. 'A prank call. A bloody prank call – 999! Probably some bastard in a rival hotel, that posh new one in Burnham? Anyway. Jeez. Never a dull moment in the Stannie.' She chuckles darkly, shakes her head. 'Sorry, there probably are a few dull moments for you, Han.'

'It's OK.' I force a fake laugh of my own. 'So, there was no big problem?'

'No, they were just doing it out of courtesy. I don't think there are going to be show trials. Not this time, at least. Anyway, these bookings, your Christmas stuff, this definitely looks better.'

She is already back in her work. Her screen reflects bright on her face. She works hard, Loz. She likes it; she is good at it. I am relieved: amid the anxiety it looks as if I have got away with it.

Yet Loz's expression was unreadable. Her distant smile a little strange. Is she lying to me, or worried about something else?

I need answers. And there is one person, above all, I need to talk to. One person finally needs to give me those answers.

25

When I call Kat, she picks up immediately and says, before I can speak, 'I just aligned my spine with a tree.'

'What?'

'Dude it was amazebombs. Try it. I'm on Primrose Hill. Near that place we scattered some of Mum's ashes. Coz William Blake saw spirits there, didn't he? God, how many places did we scatter a bit of Mum? The whole world was her ashtray. In life as in death. Do you remember how in Maldon when she was tryin' to hide when she was having a cheeky blunt in the back-yard, she drank a glass of whisky to cover the smell? Like, that's better? Yeah, Mum, thank God you're a dipso, not a vile smoker of WEED—'

'KAT!'

She stops. I turn. Noise. I see a couple of maids taking a walk, looking at me, with pity. I am the woman everyone pities.

I walk on, down the wooded path, and out onto the steep shelf of pebbles. I can hear the river breeze through the blackthorns as I gaze down at the Strood. Today, it is teasing. The tide is out, and I could step onto the grey, well-set Roman cobbles and walk for at least ten yards. Only then does the Strood slip, like a startled stone mermaid, into the depths. Only then would I drown.

'Kat, I need to ask you some questions. Again. You know what they are.'

Her silence is somehow sullen.

'About that night, that whole weekend. It's time.'

The silence persists. The little river waves lap at the green toes of my wellies. A cormorant stands on a muddy rock, oiling itself, then staring at me, mildly affronted: as if I am some kind of voyeur. Greedygut stares at the bird, hypnotized, as ever.

My sister still says nothing.

'Please, Kat?'

'What would you have of me?'

'Everything. Tell me.'

She sighs. 'But. Han. You. Know. I. Can't.' Her voice is deeply strained. 'You know this. *We've been through this.*' I hear the chink of a lighter, the sharp inhalation of smoke. I picture her walking on Primrose Hill. I picture all of London laid out before her like a banquet in the late afternoon light, the autumn leaves in piles designed for kicking by couples in beautiful jumpers.

Out here in my different, lonelier world, the first of the pink lights go on in Maldon, across the Blackwater. So far away from the untouchable mainland. Escape from this enclosing nightmare.

'Please try, Kat. I know it's traumatic.'

She snaps back, 'Traumatic Yes, just a tiny fucking bit. I saw them. Dying. Screaming . . . Drowning. I can't go back to that. Trauma dogs. Traumadogs. Like your dog. Greedygut. Greedygut and Rutterkin. Like Mum's dogs. Such weird names.'

This is mad. I am pressing her too hard. 'OK, but still. Kat—'

'No, you don't get it!'

I stop myself. Her trauma is really real, is maybe

worse than mine. She has never been able to talk about that night. But maybe before then, the hours prior?

'OK, OK. Forget the night, I want to ask you about the weekend, the party. Why you were so wild, before . . . the bad stuff. Because I have new reasons, new reasons I need to *know*. Things are happening. Here.'

I can hear her puffing – either on a cig or weed – as she heads home to her lovely flat in Belsize Park. Where she is surrounded by agreeable pubs and restaurants. Maybe she'll spend the night with her rich new man friend in Hampstead.

Jealousy stings: her trauma may be as bad as mine, but she is FREE.

'Please. Can't you tell me *anything*?'

Morosely, she responds, 'Like what?'

I seize the moment. 'OK, I'm hearing there are rumours about that weekend. And everyone in the hotel, is behaving . . .' How do I phrase this? I think, and I try: 'Well. There are weird stories, scary stories, bloody ghost stories. Especially about the east wing. And the management want rid of me, like, *really* rid of me. I even thought I heard a scream this morning, a woman – in fear or pain, I don't know. I just don't know what's going on. And I wonder if it's connected to what happened that weekend.'

Again: I get the sisterly silence; but I can also hear the sound of cars, in her background. More envy. How I long to hear a car, see a noisy truck, encounter a traffic accident, worry about street crime, anything. Give me it all. Pollution, congestion, litter. I haven't seen litter in months.

Suddenly: 'You *should* be scared, Hannah.'

The answer hits me: physically. I actually step back, as if confronted by danger, right here. 'What do you mean?'

She inhales again. Definitely smoking. Stress smoking.

126

'I mean, Han, I haven't told you before coz you're *stuck* there on that awful place and I really really didn't want to make it worse for you. So, I bit my tongue. But, oh Christ.' She falls silent.

'Kat?'

A tense hesitation, then: 'You really think it was all an accident, that night?! Some people, some things, they are dangerous. On Dawzy, they are evil. So . . . So yes you should be scared. Just get off that island however you can, just do it. Please. It's not safe at all. Because of them. Those animals. Staring.'

Anxiety surges. 'Who? What?'

'I can't say. You just – you won't understand.'

'What, Kat?! What don't I understand? Tell me!'

'I'm so sorry, Han. I can't. I'm not allowed, I shouldn't even be saying this.'

And now she is crying. My sister is so stressed by all she is crying.

'Calm down. Explain. Please. This is way too frightening.'

'I'm sorry. Can't. Forgive me. Needadrink.'

And then I hear the nothing. The silence again. She's rung off.

I think about calling her again, but it feels helplessly pointless. She won't say any more, and what she has said is sufficient, in its own mad way.

Left alone, I gaze at the busy, grey waters. The Strood is slowly drowning as the tide rushes in. Kat has now made it all worse.

A flapping noise. The cormorant lifts its oily black wings and takes to the darkening sky as if it has also heard the terrible news – and needs to escape. Greedygut barks, as if he wants to follow.

The fear burns in my throat.

26

You called the police???

I reply to my fiancé, fingers slightly trembling. I've waited
two days to tell him all this: I didn't want him to think
I am getting even crazier. But I need to speak to someone,
and Kat won't talk and Dad won't even answer and
Ben is my friend *and* my lover. And he is reassuringly
level-headed, most of the time. When he's not raging at
rival chefs who get stars.

Standing in my smart work clothes in the silent,
screamless east wing, I type away, ready to go to work.
Ready to be normal. Terrified of shadows. *Typing.*

Coz it sounded so fkn real, Ben. The scream. Too
late now. 😑

Don't get it, Han. The cops came anyway?

Yes. Mad. Know. Loz says they tld her it was a
prank call but did they really? Dunno who 2 trust

**Jeez. Well u can trust me. We will get you off
that island. We have to!**

Is my fiancé suggesting what I think? I need to know:

Are you saying you'll try it? Knock me out, drugs?
If it gets rlly bad?

A pause. I picture him in his kitchen in his pub, his beloved *mise en place*. Knives ready to be sharpened. Ready for a day of the work he loves.

No. I don't think so, it's 2 dangerous but. Fk. I don't know. Maybe in the end if we have to. Keep calm for now, baby. Talk tonight? Work now xx

Sure. Love you. 😘

Ben has done what he can do, at his best. Calmed me. Firmed my resolve. I can do this. I can fake normality.

Corridor, reception, Regency stairs. Office.

Loz is already in here. An empty coffee cup on her desk.

I need to speak to her. Or my brain will go blackberrying again. Plucking dark fruits, in thorny brambles. I need to speak normally to someone in real life, not on a screen. I need to be human.

'All good, Loz?'

She looks up. 'Sorry?'

'Business? How we doing?'

She grins cheerily. 'Not bad, not bad. Your idea is working. Re-enacting the Jazz Age, special dances. Foxtrots. Tangos. Whisky. Oscar. People seem to like it.' She flexes her fingers, returns her attention to the screen. 'OK. OK. So, do we put the regulars in the suites? Some of these new guests are super rich.'

She's talking to herself again, which she often does. Loz

doesn't need my input, she's done this for years: ranking guests by importance, prestige, likelihood to return, social media profile, not *too* many Chinese or Russians – though you never admit this because it will go viral and destroy a hotel, as it did in the Maldives. All the Maldives hotels have racial quotas, but no one talks of it.

A pang. How I wish I was back there now on the Maldives. Long before the horror. My blue Eden, snorkelling with Ben. The fish surrounding you, like golden snowflakes floating in a deep blue outer space. Ben.

'What the hell?'

Loz is gazing at her screen from a distance, like she has developed an allergy to computers.

'What's up, Loz?'

She puts a hand to her mouth as if she is watching a brilliantly scary horror movie. Something has alarmed her. She's not listening to anything else, including me. I watch as Loz winces, squints, stares at the screen, winces again.

'Another one?'

Speed-reading now. Shaking her head. Another click. Another screen.

'Shit.'

Crossing the office, I put a hand on her shoulder. She turns, startled, at my hesitant touch.

'Loz, what is it? What's wrong?'

She exhales, heavily, gesturing at her computer. 'See for yourself.'

I lean closer and look.

'Shit.'

Cancellations. At least half a dozen of them. Even as I am reading the latest – curt, impersonal, via a hotel booking app – another email appears: '*Very sorry but we have to cancel. I'm sure you understand . . .*'

I look at Loz. 'But, why?'

'No bloody idea.' Pointing at the screen, she says accusingly, 'Two more. Just in. *God*. They are ALL cancelling.'

The two of us contemplate the screen, hypnotized. A traffic accident turned into hotel management. Loz snaps to her senses. 'Get Oliver. Alistair. They're need to see this.'

I find them in Oliver's office, happily discussing the dinners and dances.

Five minutes later: half the Stanhope's management is crowded around Loz's screen watching the same motorway pile-up of cancellations.

Oliver is pale, frowning, tensed; Alistair keeps glancing my way, sharply, as if he's already decided this is my fault. And perhaps it is.

'Some of these cancellations, some of these are regulars,' Oliver says, addressing the room. 'We know them. We have their details.' He turns, focuses. 'Alistair, Loz, call them up, find out what happened.'

Loz and Alistair disperse to corners, making their calls. I stand here, still mesmerized by the emails. The cancellations are *pouring in*. Like dreary rain through a broken roof.

Oliver contemplates the screen with a heavy frown. We all know what this means, potentially, financially, reputationally.

Loz returns. 'Got hold of Helen Bradyll. She says they got an email this morning. She's sending it through. She also said . . .' Loz shrugs '. . . she's sorry.'

Oliver laughs blackly. 'That's nice of her.'

The email pings onto Loz's screen. Oliver stoops, clicks, and we all read:

Dear Mrs Bradyll,

We understand that you intend to visit the Stanhope Hotel this weekend. You are surely away that it was the scene of a notorious accident, and the drowning of several guests, last summer. What you may not realize is that the stretch of water where these guests died is known locally for a terrible riptide: the so-called Drowning Hour. Allowing the guests to swim there was, therefore, criminally negligent. By visiting the hotel, you are visiting the scene of a murder; you may find your dancing is interrupted by detectives. See the police here, in this photo – they came a couple of days ago. If you wish to know more, visit www.thedrowninghour.com. *We suggest that you cancel; as you can see, we have your email address.*

The email is, of course, unsigned and anonymous. From an email address set up especially for this message. And attached to it is a photo, of the two policemen on the beach, the Colchester police that I called. Someone took a photo of that moment from inside the hotel. The police are talking to Leon, as Loz walks back up the beach to reception. Everyone in the photo is frowning.

It looks awful.

Oliver takes a deep breath, then clicks on the website link. It delivers a blank. The website is already down.

Loz interrupts, 'Helen told me there was something on the website, a bit out of some old book. About the Drowning Hour thing.'

Alistair barks at the screen, his voice falsetto, 'But it's all bollocks! Ridiculous!'

Oliver answers coldly, 'Hardly matters, Alistair. This

is a superb takedown. Of course, everyone will cancel. Who would come to a hotel after reading *that*? And seeing that photo?'

Alistair yaps, again, 'But I don't get it! Why do it this way? Like, clandestine? Why not just put it all online, like those stupid messages? Just make it all public.'

Oliver shrugs. 'Because they did not want to attract *too* much attention? And the police might take an interest in *them*. That damn photo. *And* if you want to damage us commercially this is just perfect. Quiet. Subtle. Deadly accurate. Targeted emails to known and valuable clients. From someone who remembers all our best customers.'

He goes silent. I sense that everyone in this room is trying not to look at me.

27

It is 2 a.m. Greedygut wheezes asthmatically in his sleep.

My eyes are dry as I stare at the blur of the ceiling. In the dark of my room, in the dark of the Stanhope, in the dark of Dawzy Island. With the kreeeeees of the night-birds winging over the Blackwater. I can't sleep. Of course I can't. My mind keeps replaying the week's turmoil on a grisly loop. From the weird black boat to the scream that wasn't there to the call to the police who I didn't want to come who came anyway. And now the new and real menace to my job, to the hotel.

Grim. I turn over another pillow. Help me, head, help me. I need sleep. I want oblivion, not reality. I wish my brain was a machine. Switch OFF. Computers are so lucky. They have Sleep Mode.

Maybe it is just too hot? I drag myself out of bed and lift and open the big window. There. Crawling back to bed, I feel the winds lift the old curtains, then caress my face towards unconsciousness.

And I lie here. And: no. I am still awake.

Finally, I give up, and I decide to apply myself to the present. And an idea.

That email that sabotaged us. What did it mention: *the Drowning Hour?* And Loz said that one cancelling guest, Helen Bradyll, had told her there was something about it on the website – which conveniently disappeared

– in a book? I haven't yet examined this, because of the whirling drama of the day; but now I have time. Plenty of time. An entire winter on an island.

Taking up my phone, I search: 'the Drowning Hour'.

Nothing.

Nothing?

Nothing. Or, certainly, nothing relevant. The phrase is used in some song lyrics by a couple of different bands, one lyrical indie, one death metal. Fitting. Otherwise, it is, as far as I can see, barely used at all. It is in some strange Celtic or Scots folk poetry—

> *. . . life deep down the drowning hour's a dour tower o' paler power how the hour randies sour candies I am gem jewel of moss when given freedom and room but . . .*

That isn't it. So, I take my search further, deeper, into the bowels of the internet, nearly at the bottom, then at the bottom. I cannot find it.

I do not understand. Was the entire thing a lie? A convincing hoax? I am on the last page with any relevant results but all it does is repeat the earlier hits. I have run out of options. Can there really be something that isn't on the internet? The internet is everything. It contains the world. This, apparently, is not of this world.

Phone set down, I muse.

Mrs Bradyll said a bit out of some old book.

I try one more time. The phrase along with the word 'book'.

And?

Yes. Here it is. I get a little giddy as I read, a rush of adrenalin. The phrase, it seems, can be found in the pages of this:

Mehalah, a Story of the Salt Marshes, by the Reverend Sabine Baring-Gould, published in London 1880

I can see why I could not immediately find it. Doesn't get much more obscure than an entirely forgotten novel from the late nineteenth century.

I read, as Greedygut stirs, with the birds calling outside.

The book apparently describes a tragic love affair, and it is set here – Maldon and Mersea, Dawzy and Virley – and touches on the history of smuggling: men ferrying brandy, tobacco, and fine Holland lace, in the deep of the night, up the Ray and the Pyefleet. Men who came in the dark, who hid from the moon, like the men the other night.

The search offers me a facsimile of the book, in its dense, old-fashioned, blurry, nearly Gothic black type.

It begins:

Between the mouths of the Blackwater and the Colne, on the east coast of Essex, lies an extensive marshy tract veined and freckled in every part with water. It is a wide waste of debatable ground, contested by sea and land . . .

Debatable land. That is too apt. It argues with me, the land. The Strood positively taunts me.

Skipping on.

A more desolate region can scarce be conceived, and yet it is also possessed of unusual beauty. In summer the thrift mantles the marshes with shot satin, passing through all gradations of tint from maiden's blush to lily white. Thereafter a purple glow steals over the waste, as the sea lavender

136

bursts into flower, and simultaneously every creek . . .

The prose is pretty; if a little starched. But I don't want to read for pleasure. I want to find this menacing phrase *the Drowning Hour*. Does this historic book website have its own search engine? Where is the little magnifying glass?

There. I click.

Seabirds shriek, outside, in horror at my discovery, as I type in 'the Drowning Hour'.

There is just one result, a few pages from the beginning, amid some more rolling description. But one result is all I need. And here it is.

Mrs Bradyll was right.

At noontides, or spring tides, at solstices and equinoxes, the sea asserts its especial sovereignty over this region, creating difficult and capricious currents that must be negotiated with care. Between the beautiful, wooded isle of Dawzy and the wild, desolate island of Royden, and near a shallowing called the Stumble, one current in particular has earned a fearsome reputation amongst the water people. When the time is right, this ripping tide has been known to devour men who do not swim well, or swallow skiffs that are captained badly. In the taverns of Maldon, over a jar of ale, smugglers and fishermen alike will afrighten the visitor with the old stories, claiming that even the sea-mews and the otters have learned to avoid the Drowning Hour, hard by the Stumble . . .

There is no more. There doesn't need to be. My insomniac brain, already fizzing with tiredness, now brims with acid, scary thoughts.

I have recalled one of the things Kat told me, when we had that dinner before the big summer party, when she raved about the Mackster's food. *Everyone's been so kind, even that lechy dude, the sea dog, telling me about the hour thing, the danger.*

It made no sense at the time. It was said so quickly, and she was pretty drunk.

But now the implication is clear. And I'm good at remembering conversations.

Kat knew about the Drowning Hour.

And she swam to it on purpose.

Why would she do that? She probably would not have feared the tide itself: she's a remarkably strong swimmer. Yet she would also have known that people would probably follow her into the water: they always did, the naked girl with the infectious laugh, getting everyone excited. Just like in the Maldives.

This is why she never wants to talk about it. It explains everything. Kat encouraged people into a dangerous tide. Lured them.

28

Kat, Then

The sun was hot. Almost Maldives hot. Kat stretched herself, eyes closed, luxuriating, lying back on the posh, sturdy, dark-wood Stanhope sunbed. Soothing sounds bathed her, just like the summer sun. The sound of young women splashing and laughing in the pool, the chirpy squeal of glasses being set down, the batting back and forth of agreeable questions and answers – more drinks, ladies? a cold flannel, sir? – it was all so amenable it made her wonder whether she should get that tattoo on her ankle after all.

The symbol Mummy loved. A hexafoil: the six-flowered lily. Warning the men: here is a witch. You hold this naked ankle; you hold a bare-assed witch. Good to give them some warning. Mum's island. Bad Mum.

'Madam?'

She opened one eye. A young waiter, perfectly smart yet casual – pressed linen, cream shorts, tanned and muscled calves – was hovering expertly. Not intrusive, but alert. A tray balanced on one deftly splayed hand, like a pentafoil, the five-fingered lily.

'Would you like anything to drink?'

Kat mused. Opened both eyes. She noticed the waiter glancing, just for a moment, admiring her bikini, and her body, but only for a slice of a second. Professional.

'What time is it?'

'I'm sorry?'

'I mean, is it past noon? Am I allowed a little . . .' She paused, deliberately. '*Stiffener?*'

A brief, manly chuckle. 'It is a party, madam. And this is the Stanhope. You are always allowed . . .' he also paused, deliberately '. . . a *stiffener.*'

They exchanged glances. There it was: that bright neurochemical flash of mutual desire. Addictive. Kat reminded herself: *behave*. At least for now.

'I know, I'll have a glass of something with bubbles. What do you recommend?'

'We have some excellent English fizz. Nyetimber. Very, very chilled.'

'Oooh, yes please. Thank you.'

The waiter vanished, as if he had dematerialized. Kat sat up, checking she was surrounded by everything she needed. iPhone. Shiseido aftersun cream. Home-made sun oil infused with herbs foraged under the newest moon. Half-read novel about Caribbean mermaids. AirPods. Check check check. All good. All good. The only thing lacking was a man to polish her sunglasses, which were slightly smeared with the coconut sun oil.

Kat recalled that they'd had one of those in the Maldives. A polite man who patrolled the enormous infinity pool, charged with the solitary task of cleaning guests' sunglasses. But then the Maldives also had underwater restaurants with reef sharks ogling your risotto, and steam rooms made entirely out of Himalayan salt, and overwater spas where lissom therapists administered four-handed Ayurvedic rubdowns, and poured ointments from cowrie shells onto your breasts, leaving you suspended between sleep and heaven.

No, Kat decided, the Stanhope wasn't quite the Maldives, but it was still first class, in an English way.

And Maldivianly hot and sunny right now.

Conversation drifted over from a nearby table, where two men were toying with an early lunch. Ceviche, it looked like. The older man was nearly fifty, clearly prosperous: subtly luxe watch, excellent choice of sandals. The other guy was in his twenties, very good-looking, pink cotton shirt, girlish.

Gay, Kat decided. *Gay couple.*

She tuned in to their conversation. Older Gay Guy was British; Younger Gay Guy was American.

'It's true. This place has a kind of spiritual *terroir.*' Older Guy hesitated.

Younger Guy interrupted, 'George, did you really just say *spiritual terroir?*'

They both laughed, quietly.

Older Guy went on, 'It is the case, though. The quality of light here, the infinite skies, the density of what must be primordial woodland, the endless noise of the birdlife. It is special, but what makes it unique, haunted, brilliantly strange, is the context.'

'Meaning?'

'It's particularly brilliant because it's juxtaposed with so much bleakness, even ruin. Think of that brooding power station, on the mainland.'

Younger Guy smiled. 'Uh-huh. You know this tuna is exquizz. I think these must be fennel tops.'

Older Guy sat back, glass of white wine in hand.

'I've often thought there's a sublimity to great unspoiled landscapes *right next to ruination, or mundanity*. Both are elevated. The Sonoran Desert lapping at the exurbs of Phoenix, both become amazing by the combination. The sordid little mining towns of the green Welsh valleys. You need *both*. The North Circular, right by Hampstead!'

'I part company at the North Circular.'

A wry laugh.

'Yes, maybe a reach. I think you're correct. Fennel tops! Superbly done.'

Kat turned away, considering their conversation. The haunted specialness of Dawzy. They were right. Dawzy was beautiful not just because it was beautiful but because it was surrounded by desolation, by muddy marsh, tacky holiday camps, desolate shores, wintry marinas, ruined things. Tinkling lanyards. Salty jetties. Stiffened flags. Dark Age churches, Elderly men with sticks and dark glasses and flat caps gazing at the grey waves as a brutal wind whistled through wires and chains meant for absent boats.

Weatherboarded houses. Red naval mines. Eroding pillboxes. The Saltmarsh Trail. Unoccupied benches chewed by saline gales. Furled and wintered masts, in the dead marinas: masts that rose at night into the frigid dark, like a forest of fleshless spines. Long bones pointing. And all of it surrounding precious Dawzy. With all its hares and merlins.

Kat was falling asleep. She was stopped by the arrival of the wine.

'Your glass of Nyetimber, madam?'

'Ahh, thank you.'

The waiter set down the flute. And a little saucer with some concoction of nuts and olives.

'Fabulous. Those look like the best nibbles *ever. Nibblissimo!*'

The waiter chuckled, then did his vanishing trick again. Kat sipped at the super-cold, delicious sparkling wine. She could see that four men were looking at her, in the way the waiter had. *That* way. The men, realizing they were being observed in return, sharply and politely averted the male gaze, and continued their walk into the sunlit woods.

One of the men, Kat recognized. The owner. Baron Maximilian Tollemache III, Duke of Derrr, Oliver Ormonde. The second was the manager, much shorter, gaunt, always pale. Alistair?

The third and fourth, she did not recognize. One was tall. Silver hair. The other – right next to him – was younger but had similar features, a son perhaps. His gaze was even more penetrating than Oliver's.

Katalina Langley happily popped a nut in her mouth and chewed. It was delicious.

29

Hannah, Now

November rain whips across the arched Gothic windows of the north hall, the hall we were going to be using for the Twenties-themed dances, which surely won't happen now.

The hall, this morning, is full of subdued people. Waiters talk, quietly, with waitresses; the Mackster chats morosely with Danielle. Are they swapping supernatural tales? Or discussing my sister, luring people into the dangerous water?

I force this thought from my head. I chat to no one, though almost everyone is here: all the staff assembled for a Special Team Meeting. I've been expecting this. Oliver has been closeted in his office for days, assessing things with Alistair, and Loz. Leon. Logan. Occasionally me. I do not know what their decision will be.

The rain is brittle and gusty. I gaze out, watching the ancient trees of Dawzy bend, yielding to something cruel. Leaves mercilessly stripped away, one by one. Autumn as a form of slow torture.

Taking out my phone, I text Kat again.

> We HAVE to talk about the weekend. ASAP. Did
> you KNOW about the Drowning Hour, Kat?

She never replies. Maybe she will never reply again.
The murmuring ceases.
I turn.
Oliver, Alistair, Loz. Like a trio of magistrates, entering
court. They climb onto the stage.
Oliver starts. 'OK, guys. I'll keep it brief; we all have
work to do.'
My heart flutters: mixed feelings. If we have *work to
do*, they're not shuttering the hotel.
'We have work to do because we are determined to
keep the hotel open through the winter.'
Relief spreads through the rest of the staff. It is
palpable: a relaxation of limbs, faces. Oliver's voice is
confident, calming: he is a natural leader. Six foot three.
'We've been looking at bookings, very carefully. And
they're not as bad as we feared. It's not great, but
it's not a disaster. We've had plenty of cancellations,
but also new enquiries – Logan is still popular! And
we're dropping our prices, just as we did after the
summer.'
He surveys our upturned faces. Letting the word, sink
in. *Summer*.
'Remember, people, we endured *that*. We made it
through the awful tragedy of the Drownings. Something
infinitely worse than this. We will, therefore, cope with
this as well, and next year will be a fresh start. This is
still a fine fine hotel, thanks mainly to you guys. We
may have to furlough a few people, close a few doors,
but we are not shuttering! So, please remember: have

145

faith, be your best. We can do this.' He lifts his gaze. 'Does anyone have any questions?'

Eddie raises a hand.

Oliver nods. 'Go ahead.'

'We all heard about this email. The book? The Drowning Hour thing? Well, some of us are wondering. Will there be, like, any more police stuff? New investigations, all over again?'

Oliver nods, thoughtful. 'Fair question. *Good* question. Ah . . .'

We wait for his answer. But he looks at Loz, then at Alistair, as if he does not know. Loz goes to speak, but Alistair interrupts.

'No, there won't be. The inquest made its findings; they are not minded to reopen it.'

More relief: Stanhope staff are half-smiling, not something I've seen a lot of recently. I'm just not sure if *I* am relieved. A significant part of me *wanted* police here, again: to find out the truth, to see why Kat is so scared.

And yet, there is now the other thought. Maybe I don't want the police here: if Kat is implicated in the deaths it might be better if it is all hidden away.

Oliver gestures to Alistair. *Go ahead.*

Alistair steps forward. 'All right, everyone, that's the good news. This, I'm afraid, is the bad.'

No more smiles. I see Logan staring with unconcealed distaste, at our manager. At least I'm not alone in that.

Alistair looks down at us. 'We went over what happened – that day, when the cancellations came in. Pretty clear that the takedown – the mass emailing – was highly organized and well targeted. The emailer, whoever it was, had access to our database. They knew the email addresses of all our customers; in fact, they knew *exactly* who'd booked.'

His gaze is level, shrewd, unblinking.

'We could've been hacked but it seems unlikely. We've checked – and double-checked. And of course, there was a photo, taken of the beach, from the hotel. Consequently, the person who did this was in the hotel at the time, and they *must* have access to our files. It is very probably a member of the Stanhope's staff. Which means . . .'

He pauses, for dramatic effect. I didn't know he had such theatricality in him.

'Which means – that the person who tried to destroy this business, your jobs, this hotel, is almost certainly standing in this room right now.'

I wait for him to add 'and we are going to find that person', but he doesn't. Because he doesn't need to. That is their next job. Our job. To sleuth down the villain. And get rid of them.

Oliver, Loz, and Alistair exit the hall and the rest of the staff silently follow, until it is just me, alone in this historic room with its early Victorian gables, resembling a nave.

The rain attacks the window, again. Like a crazy knife killer in the street. Slish slash.

THE MOON .

30

Given up trying to call Kat. Ben is helpful, but now obsessed with roast bone marrow. So, I'm trying to call my dad, again.

My father answers at last. His voice is croaky, yet shrill. Husky, but not in a good way. Oh, Dad.

'Peter Langley?'

Why does he always say this? He can see my name on the screen of the mobile. He knows who is ringing. That's why he is able to evade so many of my calls.

'Dad, I've not forgotten your name. I'm your daughter.'

I can hear the wheeze as he sits down. In that musty room. Plate of fig rolls. Mug of tea.

'I've not forgotten that either. That you're my daughter.'

'OK.'

'Not something I'm likely to forget.'

Already awkward. Why?

He mutters something about pouring another cup. 'Hold on, Hannah.'

Phone in hand, I stare despairingly out at the cold, sunlit Blackwater rolling its way to the sea, at the shingle and rocks, the seakale, sea-beet, and sea-campion. Everything here eventually becomes the sea. Maybe, if I am stuck here long enough, I will become the sea-Hannah.

Dad returns. 'What is it you wanted?'

I prickle. Do I need a reason to call my own father? When he knows I am marooned on Dawzy? I understand his attitude, in part: I get that he thinks I deserted him, that I was the one who went off travelling, and then working. Malta, then the Maldives. Unlike Kat, the smarter, lovelier, younger sister who, despite spending half her life drunk or high, stayed behind and keeps him company.

'I just wanted to chat, Dad. It gets lonely here. Anyway, how *are* you, Dad? Are you OK?'

He is so silent I can hear the tinkle of the teaspoon. Two sugars. Dunk the biscuit.

With a voice saying *this is an effort* he answers, 'I get along, Hannah. I'm all right.'

'That's good. Really good. Dad, you know I miss you. God. So much. You and Kat. As soon as I get off this island, I'm coming to have cake with you! Two cakes!'

He hmms, as if he is uncertain about it. Uncertain about what? Cake? He asks, 'How *is* the therapy going?'

'It's OK, actually, maybe. I've got this new guy, new psychotherapist, Robert Kempe. He thinks I need fifteen or twenty sessions, but then I should be largely cured. But that still means a winter, here, on the island, on my own.'

My Dad says, 'Oh.'

'Dad?'

'Well. That's a shame. Still . . .'

Still?

'Still, you've got a good job. It could be worse.'

Can he care so little? We used to be quite close. Never as close as he is with Kat; but he would sit with me on the old doggy sofa and read me stories in his kind but quiet, schoolmasterly way, when Mummy was teaching

Kat to ride a bike down the riverside on sunny Maldon days. We were also close *as a family*. Before it all went wrong.

'Thanks, Dad.'

He sniffs. Says nothing.

The silence is like an ache in the air. I open the window, to fill this void. The oystercatchers cut across the boundless Blackwater sky. Kleeeep. Kleeeep. Stalks of dried hogweed rattle in the wind, which is picking up as the November sun declines.

Greedygut is lying on my bed, one eye open, watching me.

Enough. Straight to it. Why not. I am stuck on an island in a river.

'Dad, why are you like this? Whenever you take my calls, which is hardly ever, we have these strained conversations. It's ridiculous. You're lonely. I'm lonely. I love you. You're my dad.'

'Yes,' he says tightly, as if he has selected a word that will displease me. 'I'm lonely.'

Oh, Dad.

'Then let's talk properly?'

Another painful silence.

'Not today. I'm not especially in the mood. Lose yourself in books, Hannah. You always loved books. Atlases, detective books. More than Katalina . . . even more than . . . Mummy.' His voice quavers. So much memory is compressed into his little throaty syllables. Mummy.

I reply, 'As soon as I get off the island, we will *all* have a party – me, Ben, you, Kat! Everyone.'

Total silence. Throbbing. Angry? He's had enough.

'I must go now. Goodbye.'

The call dies. That's my lot. Three minutes in three weeks. With my own father.

Opening the window further, I breathe the cool, salty air. Trying to calm myself.

The lowering sunlight is sparkling on the sprinting waves. The tide must be fast, right now.

I circle back to my memories. *When it all went wrong.* The afternoon he told me and Kat that Mummy was dead.

We'd already sensed it: two young sisters holding hands at the top of the stairs. But he still had to do it. Inform the children. Like making an official announcement.

Our Auntie Lottie had been looking after us. Keeping us fed in the kitchen, distracted by toast, even as Katalina sniffled, and I stared at blackness. Then Dad came home from the hospital, his face all pinched and sombre, and he said, 'Girls, can you come into the front room?'

So, Kat and I went in and sat on the sofa, covered with flamboyant throws knitted by Mum. Dad sat opposite, his skin under his hollow eyes as grey as dried ashes. Wearing his jumper with a hole by the collar. We always had moths in Maldon.

Then he sat forward, swallowing. Unable to say it. Mouth twisted, as if he was in physical pain.

Kat broke the terrible spell by yelling at him, 'Daddy. Tell us. TELL US. What's wrong with Mummy? Where is she? Is she coming back from hospital?'

We all knew the cancer was vicious, out of control. Devouring her daily. In weeks, she'd withered. There's only so much that adult whispers can hide. Kat and I had sensed it.

'She's dead,' Dad said bluntly. 'Mummy's dead. I'm sorry.'

When he said this, he seemed to visibly shrink, collapsing in on himself. Shoulders cringing. Starting to sob. I'd only ever seen Dad cry a few times, but this was different. He broke into pieces in his own hands, cradling his own head.

Kat ran out of the front room. I bit back my tears and went to Dad and patted him on his quaking shoulder and said, 'There, there,' but he didn't notice so I gave up and went slowly upstairs to Mum and Dad's bedroom and I found her favourite perfume, one of her home-made ones – witch hazel, sandalwood, geranium, almonds – and I opened the bottle and I poured it all over myself, wanting to smell of her, wanting to keep her alive. Mum. Don't go, Mummy.

The scent evaporated. Katalina found me hours later in the corner of Mum's bedroom clutching the perfume bottle. Tears dried; eyes vacant. She sat down next to me, and we said nothing until it was quite quite dark. And the river flowed endlessly past the house; and inside I felt all my childish happiness go with it.

31

Quiet. Far too quiet. It's a Sunday in November, so it will never be busy, but we have just twenty-four per cent occupancy. The hotel is so empty you can hear it. Lying on my bed, staring at the lights, I listen to the ominous nothingness out there in our bars and brasseries, spa and reception. The many empty rooms, doors wide open, other doors locked all the time; all of it getting emptier by the day.

The curtains are closed against the grey afternoon sky. Greedygut is out there, somewhere. I just let him roam now. It doesn't seem to matter when there are so few guests. No one has complained, and I've trained him not to go towards reception or the jetty, where he might easily be seen.

Instead, he gallops left, towards the eastern end of Dawzy, to the old wartime ramparts, where the island looks to High Collins and Mersea, the gasometers and fishing boats, and the endless wind farms in the further seas, their arms gyrating, signalling urgently, as if they are trying to warn us, but we are too far away to hear them.

My mood descends. If I lie here any more I will spiral down and down – and out. I know the way it goes. Brooding turns to anxiety, which turns to a fearful despair.

Up up up. Forcing myself into shoes, I head out of the room, pace down the silent hotel corridor, the always empty yet hag-ridden east wing. Ascending the mighty spiral staircase, I aim for the office. Maybe I will do some work, even on a Sunday.

I push the door.

It doesn't open.

Locked? It's never locked. One of the modest joys of this job is that you can come and go as you please, work in here late at night, wander the woods at dawn.

'They lock it.'

I turn. Elena, the maid, probably finishing her shift.

'They do? Since when?'

Elena shrugs, crooked smile, always friendly. 'Sundays, and evenings. Lots more locked rooms now.' She chuckles. 'Less to clean!'

She passes on, humming a tune, heading for her bed, maybe a video call with her boyfriend in Wroclaw. She is one of the few people not sleeping with anyone else in the hotel. I wonder how long she will stay in the Stanhope.

Once more I gaze resentfully at the locked door. Then I spin around and head downstairs into the brasserie. I ask Eddie for a coffee, and he listlessly serves me a macchiato. Delicious, of course. I sip it at a lonely table, for the brasserie is otherwise deserted. I avert my face from the celebrated view. The Blackwater doesn't need me to look. I sense, however, it is looking at me.

My phone waits patiently for me to decide what's next. I could call Ben; he should be off duty. I will call Ben. He and Kat are the only people I can rant at and let it all hang: except that Ben *never* wants to hear about Kat. That prickly dislike is still there.

'You.'

155

It's Alistair. I didn't know he was on Dawzy. He usually crosses the water at weekends, and escapes. As I cannot.

A scowl is twisting his narrow face as he approaches my table. His finger jabs, angry and hostile. 'What did you do, Hannah? And why the FUCK did you do it?'

I gaze at him blankly, trying not to be bullied. 'Sorry?'

'We've been through the list, exhaustively. We've checked everyone, taken us days. No one has any motive. None of the staff. Except you. And you had all the booking information. And *you* researched all the history when you first got here. The Drowning Hour.'

'I don't understand.'

He gets closer. 'You did it. No one else.'

I wonder if Alistair can see Eddie, lurking in the shadows of the bar, polishing a glass with a Stanhope tea towel. I wonder if he would act like this if he knew there were witnesses. Maybe he doesn't care any more: this is a new level of anger.

'Why would I do it, Alistair?'

My words are too meek; he spits his.

'Because you are fucking mad.' He chops the air. 'That's why. Doesn't need more explanation than that.'

'I'm not mad. I have a phobia.'

He sneers, and I detect weakness, but also something else. Real fury. And fear. He is scared as well. And perhaps he believes what he is saying.

'We've all seen you, Langley. Talking away. Wandering the island, muttering on your *phone*, jumping at fucking *ghosts*. It had to be someone mad because it's such a mad thing to do, so it's you – there aren't any other mad people in here, just you. Right? Course it was you. It was YOU.'

'It was not.'

'Who the fuck else then?'

'I don't know!'

'No one else makes sense. What possible motive would they have? Why destroy this business? But then we come to YOU.'

'Jesus. Just stop.'

He doesn't stop.

'You're stuck here; doesn't matter to you. You can't escape, and you hate it all because you're crazy. Because of what happened. And we can't say anything because we all have to feel sorry for you, because of your condition. You and your crazy whore of a sister. You did it.'

I stand up. Not meek now. 'Alistair, I am really, really sorry that you are about *four foot seven*. I am sorry that you would lose a fight with a *hen*. And I am sorry that this has impinged on your masculinity all your miserable life, but it really does not make me guilty of anything.'

He pauses just long enough for me to know that I hit my target, then he says, 'Wow. Go you.'

'Yeah, I'm going.'

'Go and pat your ludicrous dog.'

'I will, shorty.'

I walk away. I am bleeding inside somewhere but I am also defiant. I will not let them do this. I am Hannah Langley.

And I need to offload this. Safely away from the bar, I pick up my phone and text my fiancé, describing the scene.

He replies, just as quick.

Never liked him

He's effete, & a dick 🙈

157

But why did he do it?

F knows, maybe he actually believes it. They are
all freaking out about the bookings. We're way
down

What if they close, babe? What will you do?

Don't care. Have to get off. Need therapist to
fix me

U do need a bit of fixing

Thanks

**Sorry, i am trying 2 help! Got mad work as
always**

Need 2 be proactive. Work it all out. The boat, the
face, the silver-haired guy

Silver-haired guy?

Someone. Sure I told u? So much weirdness.
Ghost stories. NEway they come/go on this boat.
At night.

Don't go all tin foil hat, babe xxxx

But there IS something going ON. Underneath
it all

**OK. Just stay calm, don't go crazy, & I will come
visit soon. Promise**

Please. You know I'm in the east wing now. Right at the end. Lonely down here!

They put you all the way down there?

Yes. I wanted it

Bit bleak, Han?

I didn't even know you knew it. Anyway it's got a bed and a door to the beach. Come see me!!!!

I will. DEF. Gotta go in a sec. Neil bringing mussels

Going now. Love u

Ben?

Please come c me in my bleak little room in my spooky old wing

PLZ

32

The office is probably busier than the lobby, or the bar, or the brasserie. Or the entire island. The Mackster is in a corner with Alistair, and Eddie, talking through menus. We're having to reduce and rethink. Take items off, budget, make it all leaner and cheaper but without looking as if we are actually doing that. Fake it with a *new* autumn menu, more innovative vegetarian options (cheaper). More on-trend autumnal offal (cheaper). There won't be any *jamón ibérico de bellota* for the rest of the winter.

We are also doing the dreaded *furloughing*. Julia and another waitress, Kaitlyn, went today: sent off the island on half pay for a week or three. It is generous of Oliver; he could just lay them off. He wants to retain his team. Can he?

I look at the Mackster; he is the key. He is talking with Alistair by his rarely used desk with its special Stanhope laptop fixed to the desk with wires, as with all the computers – as if we're all about to steal stuff.

While they talk, Alistair and Logan lean apart as far as possible, like two divorcing royals who can't yet tell the press.

Logan clearly doesn't want to be here. He doesn't want to be with anyone in management. He probably dislikes his desk, which is why he does most of his paperwork in his precious kitchen, smearing passata on spreadsheets. He shouts even more at crustacea these days, I hear him as I pass the brasserie kitchens on the way up here. His frustration rises. Lobsters get claw-hammered. We have a beer sometimes, me and the Mackster, and his jokes get darker by the day.

Here and now, he sends a little eye-roll my way, and I do the same back.

And yet, why is he even in this hotel? The Mackster could go any time. He could be working in any number of fancy restaurants in London, in Soho, Shoreditch, Mayfair: ascending places with waiting lists, packed to the rafters with hedge fund millionaires and their polished Slavic wives, Michelin stars raining down on him like lava bombs at Krakatoa, as Kat once put it.

So why *does* he stay? It does not make sense. Professionalism? Apathy? Love?

Oliver is sitting with Loz and Leon. They are – they told me – wondering which parts of the hotel they can shutter without making it look as if the place is being butchered, without giving an impression of despair. Because, Oliver reassures us, despair would be unjustified. We've had bookings for Christmas, quite a few, so despair isn't drowning us – them – yet. But in the meantime, we must limit the damage, get through to Christmas, then build on that, and recover. New year, new chance. People will forget; rumours die down. One more disaster, however, and we're kaput.

Do I care? I certainly don't want to end up alone, and I do still have some lingering loyalty to the place. Even if I am now imprisoned, I once channelled all my passion into this hotel. And it remains lovely, even as the shadows deepen in the corners, and the woods grow quieter. Maybe it grows *lovelier*. This morning I saw a pheasant strut boldly past the covered pool, then stare into the bar, as if we are in the zoo and the creatures gawp at *us*, trapped inside.

I look across at Oliver. Could it actually be him? Behind whatever this is? An attempt to close the hotel? Cover up something that happened here, the stuff that still frightens Kat, the maids, me?

Peculiar if so. It's his business. And Oliver is kind. My room with the dog and the door. He gave me that. Made life with Greedygut feasible. He allowed Ben to come and go at all hours.

Oliver Seymour St John Ormonde.

Unlike others, he's never lusted after Kat, so I can't see any link there. And when he talks of the hotel potentially closing I *do* see despair in Oliver's handsome eyes.

That leaves Freddy. Alistair. Loz. Leon. The Mackster.

Freddy Nix? Beery. Garrulous. Lechy. Salty. A boatman with lots of mates in lots of pubs. Gossiping about the Drowning Hour, freaking out my sister. But he did not know she would do what she did, and he is always overfriendly to pretty young women.

Alistair. Loz. Leon.

Leon? Firm, distant, clearly frustrated. Oddly rich. Yes, maybe. Yet he was on the beach with the police when the photo was taken. So not him. Or he was working with someone else?

Alistair. Or Loz?

Something that has never occurred to me before. *Loz Devivo*. Funny, dry-humoured, chain-smoking, likeable, a proper friend – in the sense of person who will keenly hear honest confessions – now that Ben rarely visits. Yet I don't tell her everything, nor she me. I know so little about her. She does have access to all our databases. She could easily have done it. But she was *also* on the beach in the photo so she could not have taken the photo. And I do not begin to see her motive. But then, I don't know her motive for anything. Why is she even here, on an island, in the middle of the Blackwater?

Loz is looking at me.

'Need any help, Hannah?'

They are all looking at me. Leon, Alistair, Oliver, Logan, Loz, Eddie. Hell, maybe it is all of them. And maybe I am predictably paranoid, and prone to delusions. Symptom 17 on the lists. Topophobia. *La peur des espaces.* My *horreur de la mer.* I will be the girl who screamed, who wasn't there.

'Daydreaming.' I force a smile. 'I'm fine.'

They regard me. I regard them.

I put my head down and gaze into my own screen. Which is black. I have not been working. My face gazes back from the dull, unlit screen. Eyes wide. Full of thought.

The silver-haired guy. A sharpness prickles. A tingle of realization, like an inoculation in the scalp. I realize, now, where I saw him. It wasn't in a programme, movie, or TV drama. He appeared on my own screen. But it wasn't this one; it was my own personal laptop, in my room.

The idea takes hold.

I have seen that guy before on my own laptop. I just don't remember where. I must have seen a thousand faces on that screen, video calls, group calls; one of them was his and he was talking, confidently. That is all I remember. Who remembers every single face they've seen on a computer screen? I have that excellent memory, for names and conversations and human preferences, it's vital for hotel PR. But faces on screens? There are millions of them.

Maybe I can ask Kat. She might just answer *that* question, if nothing else. She, in turn, has a notably good memory for handsome men. And their phone numbers.

In my discreet corner of the office, I pick up the phone and dial Kat. It goes to voicemail. She is blanking me now. Maybe she senses my suspicions. Perhaps that sisterly telepathy works against us and drives us apart.

Kat. Kat. Kat. What makes you so scared of this island? What happened that sunny weekend?

33

Kat, Then

'Madam?'

Kat turned from her new lunchtime friends – Older British Guy, Younger American Guy, Actress with Bad Nose Job from Denmark, Giggling Art Student, Other Girl About Kat's Age – and turned to the waiter. It was him again. The one with the shorts. Smiling. Holding out a menu.

'Mm, yes please.'

Kat took the printed card and scanned.

Red gurnard, burnt Dengie chicory, and a warm green salsa

North Sea brill, foraged Blackwater sea-purslane, capers, and fresh home mayo

A salad of shoreline Dawzy herbs, Tollesbury potatoes, cold roast Middle White

This is clever, Kat thought, as she read on through. Very clever. The great Logan M was not just using as many ingredients as possible from the region, he was using ingredients from the Blackwater – in fact, using food sourced just a few yards from their lunch table; probably foraged this same hot, sunny morning.

'The Suffolk ceviche is impossibly good.'

Older Gay Guy was smiling her way as he offered this advice. Kat bounced a smile back. He had invited her to join their table, just for a drink. But a drink in the cooling shade, under the parasol, had turned into two drinks, then the others had joined, and now they were a proper lunch party. Slurping. Gossiping. Ordering. Happy. Anticipating. Party. Music. Kisses. Pleasure. Perfect sunny weather.

'Fennel tops,' said his younger American lover. 'Genius!'

'I'll have the Cromer crab, please.'

The waiter typed on his tablet. 'Guys?'

Older Guy and Younger Guy smiled, shook heads. 'No, it's OK, we've already eaten.'

'But we'd looooooove another glass of this *white*. What is it again?'

The waiter answered, crisp, professional, without hesitation, 'Rebula. From Goriska.'

'Huh?'

'Slovenia.'

'Ah!' Younger Guy nodded, face bright, 'Slovenia! Who knew?'

'I did.' Older Guy chuckled. 'It's the same as Ribolla. Same grape I mean. Across the border, in Italy. Top-notch food wines.'

The waiter went around the table, taking lunch orders. Kat made a mental note of all the names. Older Guy:

George. Young American: Joshua. Pronounced, languidly, Jaaaaaaashuuaaaa, like a swish Korean software company. Giggling Art Student: Phoebe. Other Girl: Alice. Actress with Bad Nose Job from Denmark was called *Signe* but Kat was already menaced by the notion she would forget *Signe* and actually say the words 'Actress with Bad Nose Job' across the lunch table, because it really was mesmerizing, the nose job: almost perfect, but very definitely not – too sharp. You could open wedding invites with that nose, which was a shame, as otherwise Signe was beautiful.

Everyone was discussing the menu, asking about the chef.

'Logan Mackinlay,' Kat said to the table. 'Lovely Scottish guy.'

Jaaaaaashuaaaaa looked surprised.

'You know all the chefs around here?'

She felt a faint flush rising. Quelled it. No need to be too honest.

'My sister does the PR here; that's why I got an invite. I come a lot. It's brilliantly eerie in the winter. I overheard you guys talking about it? The haunted quality. Totally right. I reckon the beach is dreaming, ha. I like to say *I am looking over the Blackwater to Goldhanger*. Where else can you say that? Ah, yeah, wine!'

The waiter poured for them all. Kat kicked hers back in two gulps. Asked for more. More was poured. The food arrived. She wanted more cocaine. Would he text? She rather hoped not. No temptation. Not tonight. Just have fun. But what kind of fun? Ket and 2C-B and coke kind of fun, and dancing? Maybe she could swim? No, she couldn't.

What did that seedy Freddy guy say? The Drowning

Hour. She couldn't swim. Too dangerous. Despite the glorious heat, and this lavish sun.

The conversation came alive with the food and bounced around the table. They talked in turns, quickly and easily. They talked of London, monarchy, Denmark, bacon with fish, meat with fish, ghost sharks, ghosts, superstition, astrology. Joshua, who seemed quite interested in Kat's denim shorts, despite being gay, raised an eyebrow, and asked, 'You really believe in astrology?'

Kat snorkelled more wine. Laughed. 'Astrology works and makes sense because it is a work of high art. A portrait of the universe and the heavens as they are *at this moment* – when everything relates to everyone else, intrinsically, the way all the figures in a great Renaissance painting are interpreting and altering the others, like Raphael's "School of Athens" daubed across the sky.'

The lunch table regarded her. Kat liked doing this. Surprising people. Sometimes she'd grab her ukulele and just launch into a song, klezmer, Albanian folk songs beloved by Byron, tunes by Simon and Garfunkel; at other times she'd speak Flemish to Belgians, or Portuguese to Brazilians, or Latin to old-school academics, which all jarred with the hotpants and blonde hair and made people pause, hesitant, changing opinions.

Kat went on. 'I also love astrology because it means we look at the stars, right? We don't look at the stars enough. We've lost them. The constant interaction with Jupiter and Polaris. Schoolkids walking home would once have known them as friends, accompanying them home to warmth and Mummy. Humanity is in a constant state of grief for the darkened heavens we have lost. The curve of a woman's waist to hip has the swing of Venus around the sun. And death has perfect night vision. Ah, God, I've had too much wine, right?'

168

George laughed; Bad Nose Job frowned faintly, perhaps displeased. Kat sensed she was dominating, in a potentially bad way, and she did need the loo, and she really needed some more cocaine in order to sober up.

Gotta pace yourself, Kats.

Smiling, apologizing, she excused herself and left them to contemplate her oratory. She threaded her way through the narrow gardens around the hotel, every space busy with tables and sunbeds and wicker chairs, with people tippling, laughing, chinking glasses, snoozing under sun hats, kissing, flirting outrageously, already. Hedonistic.

She went in through that little door at the end. Cool interior, out of the sun. Arched windows, awful carpet, big mirror. In there, Kat pressed on to her own room. Something brighter beckoned. Something in here: in her cute little turquoise beaded bag from Tangiers.

The miniature crystals in a wrap of white paper. The alkaline taste at the back of her throat. The silvery sharpness in her mind. Tilt. Head. Yes. *Death has perfect night vision.* Where did that come from? And yet it was true. Kat sniffed again. Yes.

The tingling high was so powerful that she had to sit down on the floor. Whoa.

For a few moments she remained there. The old carpet looked as if it hadn't been hoovered for months, possibly ever. The wine and coke were swirling in her head. And in her chest. Thumpety thump.

Kat knew what to do. She'd been here before. Stretching out, she lay flat on the floor, head back, letting her heart slow. Letting it all go.

Looking left, she could see there was a slip of folded paper lodged discreetly between the bedframe and the mattress: you'd only see it if you were lying on the floor, like this. Which had probably never happened since the Romans built the Strood.

Lifting an arm, she plucked the paper, and opened it, her face directed at the ceiling. And at the note. Which consisted of just two words, written in frail, girlish letters.

Help me

34

Hannah, Now

Out there, east of Dawzy, is Foulness. And Brightlingsea, And Churchend. And Wakering. Further north the names get even more English. Ancient and primeval.

Snape. Uffield. Falkenham. Sweffling. Yoxford.

Sweffling.

That's what is happening to me: a mixture of stifling and muffling. I have been *sweffled* on Dawzy. But I will not let it happen, I will escape.

Breathing deep I put a wellington boot closer to the lapping Blackwater, here at the far east end of the island, away from mocking eyes. Only Greedygut watches me, curiously, sitting like an Egyptian statue of a dog: perfectly still. There are few birds to distract him, not on this cold grey afternoon. I am in a thick coat, scarf, and jumper. Binoculars hang from my neck; I pretended to myself I was just going to do a little wildlife spotting, maybe see a Dawzy hare. Or a cat dancing on its hind legs. Yet I was lying to myself. I am here to do The Exposure.

'I'm going to do it, Greedy. Gonna paddle.'

He nods, slightly, as if he understands. Then a seagull whips past, and he looks up, yaps, and yaps again. Then more birds, merganser? Or plover, definitely plover. Greedy yips in his envy. Birds!

I place my right wellington boot about three inches in the water. A cold dread steals over me, a childish shiver of fear. Not delicious, like in a horror film, just pure running fear. Proper fright. The crooked-necked witch hanging from the door of my bedroom.

And yet, I do *not* feel a need to immediately remove my foot from the river. The reflex reaction is waning. Perhaps. I feel sick and uneasy, and my heart races – of course – but I do not feel scalded, nor that instant need to retract.

Another foot? I might actually put two boots into the Blackwater. Breathing ever deeper, I lift my left boot and – closing my eyes – I stamp it down, hard, onto the pebbles, splashing the Blackwater, making Greedy bark twice, excited, applauding.

I have both feet in the Blackwater. But my eyes are closed. I need to open them, or it will feel like cheating.

I open my eyes. I am standing in about three inches of water on a dreary autumn afternoon, and it feels like a day of immortal triumph.

'Greedy, watch this; I am going up to my ankles!'

I'm not sure I am going up to my ankles. My heart begins to pain me, the prickles of adrenalin are beginning to sting, the nausea locks up in my throat, and I start to see the dancing images, the Drownings, the helpless faces going under this same river, this Blackwater, this place of death, and then the bodies being ferried so efficiently to the busy North Sea, so the Chinese container ships out of Felixstowe can chop-chop-chop—

I am spiralling. Going down into the darkness.

That means I need to do this fast. Gripping my hands into fists I take a big step, fifteen inches further into the river, then a big downwards stomp. And a big splash. Done it. DONE IT. Now the second boot. My chest strains with the pain of my trapped heart but I do it. Splash. Two feet. Six inches deep. I am actually paddling.

'GREEDYGUT! *I did it*!'

My dog appears to smile. He is probably leering at a rabbit beyond me. He turns his head cutely, anyway. I know I turn him into a human, but I do not care. Sometimes I half expect him to talk back to me. *Well done, Hannah, that's probably enough for today. Look how fast I can wag my tail. Can we go for a walk where there are more birds?*

Greedy is right: that is enough for today. I have made it up to my ankles, six inches deep in the bloody Blackwater. That's more than I have managed since the Drownings. I will text Dr Kempe when I get back to my room and the warmth.

I am exultant. I *will* get off this nightmare of an island. The cure is *working*.

For that reason, I don't want to go back just yet. I want to enjoy the moment. The strained light of the day is fading, a rising fog embroiders the sense of autumn twilight. The grey is turning to a soulful, misty darkness. Stepping out of the water – carefully, slowly – as if I am wary of the landmines in my head, I step up the shingles and sit on some salty grass. Ben.

I did it! I paddled in the Blackwater. I think it's working!!!

Immediately, he comes back.

173

That's brilliant, babe. Do you want to celebrate?

Of course. 🥂 But how?

Got evening off. Charlie wants 2 have a go running kitchen. Could get water taxi, just for a bit? Cld be there in 30 minutes!

Please! 😊

Slipping the phone in a pocket, I am filled with some-thing like gladness, however fleeting. Even in the depths of this nightmare, there can be hope. I have paddled in the Blackwater and now my fiancé is coming to see me. Maybe we will have sex. I will touch another human. And another human will touch me.

And I will one day escape.

Lifting my binoculars, I look across the fogbound estuary. The dusk is thick and hazy. Through the mist I can just about see the dull white cubes of the dead nuclear power station. Some small fishing boats returning from the sea.

Lazily, contentedly, I tickle Greedygut behind the ear and he growls in his most amiable way. The moon is rising, clouded, foggy, but still impressive. Enough to gently illuminate the misted riverscape.

Another boat. Out there. Don't recognize it. Maybe it is Ben's water taxi? What is it doing? It doesn't seem to be heading for the jetty – or it is doing so in a slow roundabout way? Focusing my binoculars, I can just make out two hazy dark figures, plus the pilot.

One does look like Ben. Tall, male. His thick, black down jacket. The other is slighter, female; maybe she has her head on his shoulder. It is so hard to tell. They

174

are faraway; the thickening fog intervenes. From the body language, however, it is plain to see this is an intimate couple. She definitely rests her head on his shoulder, as the boat passes up the cold misty Blackwater, under the uncertain moon.

'Ben!'

I shout, even though I cannot be heard. They are too far away. I am panicked. I don't want to see this. No.

'Ben!'

The woman lifts her face, as if she can hear me, though she surely can't. She is pale, maybe sad. As pale as the woman I thought I saw in the east wing. And suddenly I am sure this is the same woman. I am *sure* of it. I don't know how I know, but I know. And now the woman on the boat on the Blackwater turns to face me, and I tighten the focus of my binoculars, with trembling hands, until at last it sharpens just enough, so that I can recognize her.

It is Kat.

35

The boat passes out of view, veiled by the riverine fog. For moments, hours, minutes – I don't know – I sit here. Paralyzed with sadness. Betrayal? Kat has been coming here. Has she been seeing Ben? I do not understand; I just feel anguish. Or maybe I misinterpreted. Yet I saw what I saw. They are either lovers, or much more friendly than I ever imagined.

And yet: why come here? She clearly really hates the island. Or she is lying to hide her real feelings, her true behaviour.

This cannot stand.

Ben said he was coming to Dawzy. It's here on my phone. Whatever he is doing with Kat it is written here on my phone.

Be there in 30 minutes!

Nearly thirty minutes have elapsed. Picking myself up, I run down the misty shingle, all the way down the shore, towards the hotel, and the jetty. Greedy barks as he follows, as if this is a game. The air is cold in my mouth; the tears are cold in my eyes. The fog is thickening still.

There. A boat is berthed. It looks like the Maldon water taxi. I can just make out its shape in the murk.

And I see a misted silhouette, someone walking up the shingle, alone, in the chilly and drizzly twilight, towards the welcoming yellow light of the hotel.

It is Kat. In a long black coat, elegant laced-up leather boots. She is here: brazenly. I guess she does not know I saw her with Ben.

I approach, yet she does not seem to hear my wellies, crunching on the pebbles.

'Kat.'

I am just ten yards away.

She doesn't turn.

'Kat, I saw you. On the boat. I saw.'

She is staring straight ahead at the hotel, her eyes fixed on something – or someone – I cannot see. Someone inside. She is expecting to be greeted. By whom?

'Kat, talk to me. Why are you here? What the hell? Kat?'

At last, she turns, but she doesn't really focus on me. She looks stoned. Zonked. She looks the way she looks when she's had way too much weed. And booze. Beautiful but blank, maybe beyond blank. Lost in her own world. Staring at the Pleiades, wondering about Aquarius.

'Kat, are you OK?'

Her eyes are glazed with vagueness. She looks beyond me, through me, around me, anywhere but at me. It seems she does not even sense me. She must be drugged up. And she wears a puzzled frown, as if she can hear a voice but can't tell where it's coming from.

'Kat! Stop it!'

Another voice. 'What are you doing?'

It's Ben. He's pacing up the shingle, presumably from the jetty.

I turn on him. Angrily. 'Why the fuck should I stop?

177

This is my sister. You brought her here?' I turn back to her. 'Kat, you were on the boat. I saw you together. What's going on?'

She says nothing. Then she nods, slowly. Now I see an incredible sadness in her expression, the same sadness I saw in the face of the woman looking out of the window in the east wing. That *was* her; she's been secretly coming and going.

'Hannah, for fuck's sake stop!'

I pivot back to Ben, my stupid fiancé. 'Why? I need to know. Why Kat is here. Why she came with you. I saw you both on the boat.'

He shakes his head, and I see something new in his face. *Horror.* Is he horrified that I have guessed?

'Hannah, you did not see Kat and me on the boat.'

'I did!'

'You didn't.'

'There's no point in lying. I saw you.'

'No, God, please – you really didn't.' He steps forward: anguish in his eyes; he lifts a placating, softening hand, and says, 'Hannah, you're not talking to Kat, because you can't.'

'Sorry?'

'You are not talking to her, because it is impossible. Because she is dead. Because your sister drowned. In the summer.'

I turn to look at Kat.

But there is no Kat. She is gone.

And I know, at once, that Ben is right.

36

Ben puts an arm around me. His touch is, however, unbearable. I so wanted a human embrace; now I want anything but. The sadness in me needs to be alone. To nurse itself, like a kindling fire. I don't know where it will end. What might burn down. Maybe everything.

'Please go, Ben.'

'What?'

The cold river wind lifts the hair from his handsome face. He wants to help; he really does. Yet I cannot be in the company of anyone, not now that Kat is dead.

'Please get the water taxi back to Maldon. I need to think.'

He makes a protesting noise, but he sees the conviction in my face. My numb face. There are no tears. Not yet. They will surely come. In armies.

'OK, I'll go,' he says. 'But I'm coming back. You mustn't be alone. You need people with you. People who love you.'

My fiancé gives me one more fierce hug and then he walks back down the beach. I follow him slowly, in silence, as Greedy trots beside me. Probably puzzled by his human talking to empty space, conversing with ghosts.

I watch as Ben climbs into the water taxi, talks to the pilot, explaining. I watch as they putter out into the

Blackwater fog. I approach the end of the jetty and watch until the boat is swallowed by the fog.

When I look down, I can see the Blackwater pass under the weather-beaten planks of the jetty. The old, old river that carries everything with it, all my hopes, such as they were. It is like the time we found out that Mummy was dead.

The tears are close, now.

At the very end of the jetty, I squint downwards. There is something down there in the dark water. Something pale. Maybe a skate. Or a large fish?

The possibility strikes me: a body part. Human flesh. My sister.

This is insane. It cannot be.

The white shape is surfacing. Surely it is a skate, I think. I look hard. It is not a skate. It is a human face.

It is Kat. It is her dead face, surfacing in the water like a Japanese Kabuki mask emerging from a blacked-out stage. Kat's face breaks the water, quite dead, and immobile, floating like a dead animal.

I gaze down in horror. I cannot look away.

And then Kat's face breaks into a sudden screaming shape, noiseless, but wide, her mouth open, eyes staring at me. As if she is screaming: NO, STOP, HELP! A scream of agony. But no noise comes out.

I cover my eyes with my arm, and I turn, and I run. I run as fast as I can up the crunching shingle.

37

Kat, Then

Help me

Kat sat up. Brought the note close, held it at a distance.

Help me

The paper was lined, roughly ripped from something like a school exercise book. Nothing else was written on the front or back. Kat turned it around, turned it over, looked for any other clues: a smudge, a tear, a spot of blood, a coffee stain.

Nothing.

The lined white paper was not faded by light; so, it might be quite new. But if it had been stuck between the mattress and bedframe, then no light would have struck it, to fade it, and it could have been there many years, like a kind of fossil.

Help me

The words came in and out of focus as the initial tide of the coke receded in Kat's mind. Help who? Help against what?

Another look.

The handwriting was blue, an ordinary biro. The style was simple, rounded, probably feminine, hard to say. Perhaps young? Yes, but not a child. Older than that.

Kat set the note down for a moment. Thinking. Why was it stuck here, in this unused room, in this unused wing?

Help me

Now Kat could actually *hear* it, in her head. A pleading female voice. Echoing softly, too softly, down the long corridor outside. Echoing in the empty rooms, echoing down the years, fading, unheard. A cry for help unattended, a last gasp: suffocated. Maybe no one else had ever opened this note before Kat. It was like an unexploded bomb, or maybe one of those cats they put in walls, mummified, to ward off witches. Kat was probably the first to read it since the words were written and hidden here, months ago. Or twenty years ago? Back when Mum came to the island.

No. That association was ridiculous. Kat decided: Not Going There.

It was a sunny weekend, a party on a beautiful island which, it turned out, her mother loved much more than Kat had ever realized. This was just a silly note concealed in a bedroom. Probably a childish game or a prank. Hide-and-seek. Kids trying to scare each other, back in the days when the Stanhope was the Stanhope Gardens Island Hotel and you could get a room here for pennies, and overcooked roast beef for a little more.

Folding the note, hiding the words

Help me

stifling the scream that came barrelling down the decades

Help me

Kat carefully slipped the note back into its hiding place. Then she stood up, smoothed herself down, checked herself in a mirror, breezed out of the door and headed back out into the blazing sun, which sparkled on the Blackwater, the riverscape minting all its millions of coins, of shimmering golden light.

38

Hannah, Now

My chin rests on my knees. My arms embrace my shins. My breathing is shallow, because if I breathe deeply it seems to let the pain in, as if I am inhaling hurt, and then I might start crying again.

The room is dark, the curtains half open, showing a silver fingernail clipping of moon. The tiny white rumours of seabirds flee across it.

Kleeeep.

It could be 9 p.m. It could be 2 a.m. I have cried so long that I have lost my sense of space–time. My room has been as big as a cathedral, then sometimes it collapses, the walls closing in, the floor rising up: as if it is trying to crush me against the light fixtures, my chest tightening, agonizing, fighting for breath because the sobbing tears took all my breath.

Katalina.

I know I knew; I knew I know.

She's dead.

I know you're dead, Kattykogs. I've always known.

I couldn't know; knowing was too hard. So I let you grow, in my head. I let you live. You came alive again, Kat, because the pain of accepting was too much, and denial the only painkiller; I couldn't lose you after Mummy, not you too, my sister, my near-twin, my soulmate, the little girl running hand in hand with me down the towpath in Maldon, down past the oyster houses, down to the Strood when we were tiny, down the seafront at Mersea to the wooden walls of the Company Shed: those sunny, breezy day trips when the gulls cracked and the sailing boats tinkled and we queued at the window and Mum bought us all spicy lobster soup in big grown-up polystyrene cups and we went back to the seafront to eat the food on benches, watching the yachts, giggling and happy, faces smeared with thick yellow butter and rich orange soup, eagerly spooning the soup down our mouths with all that lovely crème fraîche and dunking fat salty chips in the gloop and then we climbed back in to the car with Dad saying, *Don't get soup on the seats.*

And then when we got home, off we'd go again, bolting out of the car, irrepressibly happy, taking Greedygut for a run, away into the park, always hand in hand. Your smaller hand seemed to fit mine, as if we were meant to be touching: always.

Kat.

You are gone. You will never talk to me now. Will you?

The silence of the room is terminal, and solid. Surrounding me.

That's another reason I couldn't let you go, Kat. *The silence.* I couldn't bear the silence, not on top of my imprisonment. You were always the noisy one, the music in my life, the spontaneous ukulele playing, the boozy sing-songs, the cackling laughter – *Ohhhh, Hanny* – the

185

sound of another knife clattering to the floor, my stifled laughter at your salty jokes, the sound of you falling over and laughing, the drunken tearful calls that somehow ended with us laughing. *All* those times we laughed, argued, laughed, wondered, stayed up late at night age eight and nine to watch a star you said was special and moved and then we ended up singing our own made-up song to a star; two little girls at a big window staring up at the moon and the stars and crooning their own sweeeeet song. All those noises, all the marvellous noise and clatter and music of you, it was the heartbeat that gave the rhythm to my life and now this is gone?

The silence is all that is left. And a brief, sharp knock at my door.

My room is dark. The doorframe is a fragile rectangle of light: the corridor outside.

I manage to speak, my face painful from the sobbing. 'Who is it?'

'Me.'

Ben.

'I got a lift over from Freddy. Please, darling, let me in. You really do need to be with someone.'

His kindness makes me want to cry, again. I am done with crying for today. I know I will cry again tomorrow. And the days after that. Probably forever. Whatever. But my tired eyes are dry, for now.

'Come in. The door isn't locked.'

The fragile light expands.

He turns on a switch; light floods the room. My tall stubbled lover in his jeans and black down jacket, is gazing down at his pathetic, barefoot fiancée in her soft pyjamas, scrunched in the corner of the room, on the floor, embracing her knees as if they are children she must protect.

'Han. Jeez. How long have you been like this?'

He sits down on the floor beside me, puts a hand on my shoulder but I shrug it away – even though I yearn for his touch.

Not taking offence, he leans, unzips his rucksack, lifts out some documents. I do not want to look. Sidelong, I look. They are newspapers.

'I remembered I had these. I kept them, when, you know, we were still hopeful. Waiting for news.'

He puts a couple on the floor, the *Essex Chronicle*, the *Daily Telegraph*, carefully opened and folded so that the relevant headlines are easy to read.

Do I want to read them? No, but I can't resist.

Three Still Missing in Drowning Tragedy

The bodies of two partygoers, identified as Jamie Caule and Cicely Trezien, were yesterday recovered from the Blackwater near Goldhanger Marina. Three others – Katalina Langley, Najwa Haddad and Toby Wyne – remain missing, with fears growing . . .

The other is from two weeks later. July.

Search Abandoned in Blackwater Drownings

It was announced yesterday that the search for the three partygoers, still missing from the drownings at the Stanhope Hotel, Dawzy Island, has been called off. Speaking at the RNLI station in Southend-on-Sea, a spokesperson for Essex police said that the strong tides, cold currents and heavy shipping sadly meant that survival was now seen as impossible . . .

That silence again. Apart from Ben breathing.

'I'm sorry,' he says. I say nothing; he goes on, 'I did wonder . . . About you, what you were thinking, you know. Your dad said something. And I heard you were seen talking on the phone, with . . . with . . . you know.'

'My dead sister.'

He nods uncomfortably.

I take a profound breath. I need to talk. I really need to talk.

I open my mouth, and nothing happens, as if it has stopped working. My brain, my tongue, everything. Frozen.

Ben's face is concerned, sympathetic. *Please try.*

So, I try again. I open my mouth, and a kind of mumble is all I can manage.

His hand grips mine, harder, as if he can give me the courage, inject it into me.

Somehow, I start talking. Coherently. 'You lost someone, Ben. You lost your mum. You know how bad that is.'

He says, very quietly, 'I do.'

'So maybe you get it? My mum *and* my sister? Imagine. *Imagine.*' I force myself to go on. 'I couldn't cope, because it brought it all back, all the sadness of Mum, and also because I *saw* it. I mean, I saw Kat going under; I saw her go under. I was there, until I got knocked out, by the dinghy, the rescue boat. I saw her, screaming, being swept downstream, in the Drowning Hour. The darkness, her screams. It was too much.'

His hand feels hot.

I continue, fierce now. 'I woke up on Dawzy and already I had it. The fear. I was all over the place, breaking apart, and then one day, maybe that same week – she came back to me, on my phone. I mean, her number is still in there. All her messages, her life, our emails, stories, jokes, her face, everything – in photos, videos, voicemails, everything – it is like she *is* alive sometimes, and sometimes those first days I would call her number just to hear her voice, you know, her singing words, that joyful, funny voice, *please leave a messidge-uh*. And I would leave a message, and then one day *she called back* and I *knew* it wasn't her I *knew* I was imagining it but I had to believe. I wanted so much to believe because it made all the terrible pain go away. The grief, it was physical, a stabbing, a broken bone in my bloody heart, always hurting, so much hurt. The pain of the grief was *physical*; so, I took the call. From my dead sister. And that's when it started. And it was easy to believe. Because Kat is – because she was – always so *alive*, such a vivid presence. She was always that bit more alive than me. It was *impossible* for her to be dead, so I let her come alive again, in my phone, in my head, in my heart. Was that so bad? It made things bearable. It made *this* bearable. This awful jail. The island. Everything. Kat in my phone was a place I could escape to. That's how it started.'

I remove my hand from his and look at him.

'And now it's over. Now you've ended it. Now she's gone again. But this time forever.'

He shakes his head. I see a faint tremor of tears in his eyes. He rarely cries.

With a vivid wail my own tears erupt again, in sobs that could break a rib: gulping and fierce. I am rocking back and forth, epileptic with sadness, out of control.

I sense Ben as he leans close and opens his arms, and now I yield. I sink into his loving arms, and I press my weeping face to his chest, and I cry so hard that my throat burns.

39

I am pushing you, Kat, on a swing in the park in Maldon, overlooking the Blackwater, our favourite park with the fountains and the lido and the bandstand. Greedy the First runs around us: yapping happily.

You are about seven years old, so I must be eight or nine. The summer sun is strong and thistledown floats, and you laugh at all the golden sparkles in the air.

'More, Hannybobs, more, MORE! Push it harder!'

You always like the risk. The danger. I always love the sound of your laughter. It makes me laugh: a duet. Obediently, I push you harder, swinging you firmly into the clear blue sky. Greedy yaps even louder, responding to your excitement. I don't know where Mum and Dad have gone. But it doesn't matter. We are here, together and alive, in the green of Promenade Park, with the view of the river and Royden Island, with prams and picnics and an ice cream stand, where dogs bicker and people jog, and someone gives a pink balloon to an astonished little girl.

'More, Hanny, more more more more more—'

I do another big push to make you gurgle with happiness, but I push too hard, and something isn't right. I push so hard you seem to detach. Go away. Go too far. You do not swing back to me. Instead, your swing just goes up, and up, and up, and up, and away, and I stand there in Promenade Park and I watch as you soar.

I shield my eyes from the sun, with a trembling hand. You have gone from my sight, and now the blue sky gets blacker. It is dark now, and I am watching a pinpoint of light, wondering if it is you. It looks like that moving star we once sang a song about, standing by the window, two little girls, two sisters holding hands, and now there is not even a little moving star.

I gaze around. The darkened park is shut and deserted. Everyone has gone home. A chilly wind rips off the Blackwater, pushes litter down the paths. Fish and chip papers rolling like tumbleweed.

'Mummy?'

I am scared now. How am I in a park in the night on my own?

'Daddy?'

No one answers. I start running down the path to the gate that leads home and then I think I see you again: running away from me like a mist, a frail shiver of light, down the road, and I run up to the padlocked gates and scream, 'Katty! Kattydogs! Come back! Don't go! Help me!' And then I feel someone big and tall is running up behind me and I . . .

Wake up. With a pelting heart. Gasping. Alone. In my room. Greedygut sleeps in his basket. The hotel is silent and brooding. What day is it? Saturday? When did I see Ben? Three days ago?

I gaze at the ceiling, drained of life. My loneliness is intense, hardened like a diamond.

Robert Kempe comes tomorrow. He might help. He has to help.

Reaching for my bedside glass, I gulp the tepid water, and some of it spills down my chin. Drink more, and more. Willing my heart to slow.

I get these dreams every night now. Sad, yearning

dreams. Not quite nightmares, something else, dreams of absence and departure.

I am obviously grieving. It hurts much more than I expected. And I do not know why. Why is absence so much harder, so much heavier than presence? Why does loss hurt so much *more*? I have *lost* you, Katalina. You have gone into the darkness, and sometimes I am unable to breathe, as if I am buried, like a fossil. Or as if I have a fossil inside me instead of a heart.

I remember once when you talked about Mum, and you said something very strange and very striking. You said, 'Grief is the trace fossil of love – like the delicate fossil of a fern, a flower, even a handprint. The ephemeral thing is gone; what is left is harder, colder, enduring.' And I didn't really understand, yet I remembered it word for word, and now I realize why: because it is so true. The loss of you is the stone carving in my soul that will endure forever, even as the life you had was so brilliantly brief.

There is a sudden noise.

Rain is dashing against the windows, as if an illicit Romeo is standing outside, a young lover urgently flinging pebbles. After pushing back the duvet, I cross the floor and open the curtains. Romeo is not out there. Dawn is out there, a pale, cold, creamy mist athwart the estuary.

A crow squawks as it pecks at a fish bone.

Setting myself on autopilot, I go about my duties. I shower, dress, munch a listless breakfast. Then I go to work in the empty Saturday office, and I skip my lunch, and I work some more, and I come back from work. Then sit down alone in my room as the evening folds around me, with Greedy running down the beach outside.

I try to read. The pages turn; the words blur.
My phone pings. A message from Ben.

You OK?

He's being a good fiancé, taking time off from the
business to make sure I haven't done myself in from
loneliness and anguish.

I'm OK. Kinda. Doc Kempe comes tomorrow

That's good, Han. He will help

I pause, fingers poised, type:

It is quite tough tho, nothing 2 do, no one 2 talk
to. They're sending staff away. Just sit here, in this
room. I try not 2 brood but this F room

**I hear you, darl. God knows why they put u in
the east wing of all places. Mad**

You know why. The door 🫠

There's a pause. It is Saturday evening. He's probably
got several pots on the go, stock over here, bisque over
there, orders coming in, service, service.

What is it about the east wing, Ben?

The text is read, but it goes unanswered. I wait. And
I wait. Letting it hang in his mind. He is probably just
checking his fondant potatoes before sending them out?
Finally:

Just feels bit morbid. People who slept there.
Have 2 go doll. MayB later. Mad busy here ££££
Be strong. U can do this xxxx

And he's gone.

I am alone. In my room. In the east wing. With Ben's words in my mind.

People who slept there.

Or sleep?

No, ridiculous. I must not go down that road. I must be logical. He must mean some of the drowned people were put here? In the east wing. During the party.

I was vaguely aware that the east wing was used but for months I've either been in denial, avoiding all these thoughts, or convincing myself that my sister lives. She does not live. She's dead and she haunts me. That was her face I saw in the window, and her scream I heard echoing down the corridor. And it was all in my head.

But was Kat given a room in the east wing when Julia ran out of space? Unpaying guests were certainly shunted around. I could ask Julia but, of course, Julia is furloughed. One by one, doors are locked, people are silenced, sent away off the island.

A bark – Greedy is at the door.

I let him in, and he pants happily, full of fresh river air, the scent of hares.

A mix of beagle and springer? He'll be a great sniffer dog.

The dog was given to me, by the river, like a miracle. Perhaps he was given to me for a purpose.

'Hey, Greedy. Wait.'

He gapes a lolling tongue, happy to wait.

Out of the wardrobe I pull out the bag I never open, the bag I've long been telling myself I must give to Kat when she next visits Dawzy. But now I have accepted that she will not be returning to get all her clothes and possessions from that weekend. The make-up, ukulele, sunnies, Tarot deck.

As I set the bag on the bed it spills out and her perfume, the sun oil, the coconut and vanilla and scent of the summer, assails me. The emotions surge, a stormy, brutal tide, but I have to steady myself. Hold back the swell of grief, be firm and strong *for her*. I have to know what happened to her. That weekend.

'Here, Greedy.' I lean down and give him the shirt to sniff.

He sniffs, then looks puzzled as I almost smother him in the shirt.

'There, Greedy. That's Kat. That's my sister. Smell her?'

He cocks an eye at his mad new owner.

Does he understand?

Once more I smother his muzzle in perfumed shirt. It smells *strongly* of Kat, and tears prickle in my eyes.

'Come on, Greedy. Sniff!'

The instinct must be in him. Half beagle, half springer. Ben knows his dogs. Greedy barks. Yes!

Leading him out into the corridor, I give him a push. I don't care if anyone sees me. No one will see me. No one comes to the east wing, except me.

'Go, Greedy! Go! Find her. Find Kat!'

He canters down the corridor, then puts his nose to the careworn carpet. He turns, big ears flopping, doggy frown. He paces back, sniffs, looks at me, sniffs. He's found something. No, he hasn't. Yes, he has. His nose is practically buried in the carpet. Then he stands to attention. Pointing.

Directly at a door.

The door is, of course, locked. And it is Saturday evening. The drawers in reception will be locked until Monday morning.

Greedy barks, softly, pushing his wet nose at the door. Room 10.

40

Robert Kempe climbs, with a deep exhalation, off his Stanhope bike, and tilts it up against an ash tree. I climb off my own and do the same. The November sun hangs heavy in the pearly sky and the light glistens on the Blackwater, which is in a subdued mood.

It was my idea to use the bikes, to get away from the silence and spiders in the east wing. And all its many, many empty rooms. And carefully locked doors.

Room 10.

Robert says, 'That was enjoyable, if a little painful. I can't remember the last time I was on a bicycle! Probably twenty years.'

I say nothing, as is commonly the case these recent days. Only Greedygut makes me speak. *Here. Greedy. FETCH.*

Robert watches me as I watch the waters of the Stumble.

'So,' he says, in a throat-clearing way. 'This is it. This is . . . the place?'

'Yes. Where Kat ran in.'

I zip my raincoat tighter under my chin; the sun offers no warmth at all.

Robert turns and confronts the waters. The Blackwater is eerily quiet today. The brooding, superior quality of silence you find on terrible battlefields. He breaks the silence.

'How do you feel about it now? Looking at it, I mean.'

I shrug. 'I can do it. I *can* look at it, but that's all I can do. My fear of it is probably greater. I did some paddling the other day but now it feels I'm right back to the worst.'

His smile is gentle, and sad. 'Since your acceptance of Kat's death?'

'Yes.'

The wind tousles Dr Kempe's curly grey hair, making him look boyish, just for a moment.

'Do you mind if we talk about it?'

'No, no of course it's fine, Robert. This is the only way you can help me.'

'Well, then. I have one obvious question. How often did Kat materialize corporeally?'

I must look puzzled: he lifts an apologetic hand.

'Sorry, Hannah. I'll put it another way. What I mean is, when you, ah, imagined Kat as being alive, how often did you see her in the flesh, imagine she was actually present, in a room, say, or on the beach?'

'Barely ever. I saw her face, weeks ago, then heard her scream.'

He nods. Accepting.

I go on, 'The only time I really saw her was the moment Ben told me she was dead. Back up the beach. And I saw her face in the river. That's it. Otherwise, it was always on the phone.'

'OK. That's possibly a good sign. It means the delusions are not too severe.'

'They feel bloody severe! She was extremely real on my phone.'

'Sure. But a lot of people hear sounds of the dead when they are grieving. Recent widows hear a key in a door, a footstep in the hall—'

'Yeah – but I had entire *conversations*, Robert. Video calls. Long, long chats with a dead person. She's been haunting me for months.'

He tries to speak; I won't let him.

'And I'm finding it hard to deal with that. Because of what it means. Because it means that when Danielle told me there were ghosts in my room, in that wing, she was *right*, wasn't she? There *are* ghosts, but I *invented* them; I created the ghost. And my texts were like a *séance*.'

He shakes his head.

'Hannah, I'm not going to deny this is a setback. It does make your condition more problematic. But I am still convinced a good course of therapy will see you off the island.'

I put my hands on my hips. Trying not to look too desperate. 'By spring?'

'By spring. Yes.'

I take this in. Then I say, 'Please God make it happen. I *have* to escape.'

'We will. In the meantime, remember to keep healthy. Remember—'

'Do lots of exercise.' I go closer to the water, examining its sighing, tiny waves. 'I know, I know. I hear it from everyone. Fresh air. Exercise. Five pieces of fruit. I know all that. I am doing all that.' My voice is imploring; I hear my own neediness. 'I know all of this, but it doesn't help all that much. Because I am trapped in a place that *haunts* me, and it's not getting better. It is getting *darker*. Darker and *scarier*.' My despair rises. Remembering that face, screaming, in the water.

I rush on, dispelling thoughts. 'And – Robert – what if Kat comes back to haunt me again, properly, *materially*, and I know she's a ghost, but she's still there?

What do I do then?' I am close to tears, but I fight them. 'It would help if they found her *body*. Then we could have a funeral. A grave. Ashes. But they haven't, so we can't. Because she's not found; she's *missing*. Her body is out there, somewhere, floating past some fucking barge. My funny, beautiful sister.'

He squints at me, looking unsure.

I don't want *unsure*. 'Help me, Robert.'

We both fall quiet.

He is surveying Royden Island: its low, windswept trees fluttering with their last golden leaves in the chilly sun. The place of the birds. Then he says, 'Your sister liked Tarot, didn't she?'

I look at him, wondering where this is going. 'Yes. She did.'

The memory is a pang. The colourful, vivid Rider–Waite deck, still in that bag in my room. The Tower Struck by Lightning. The Devil with his lovers in chains. I picture Katalina laying the Knight of Wands in her flat in London and exhaling weed smoke and triumphantly saying, *Aha! I knew it!*

'She used Tarot all the time.'

'And with reason!' Robert says, attempting a genial smile. 'Why? Because Tarot actually works. It reveals our subconscious fears and desires through our interpretation of the cards. The Tarot deck can therefore, in a sense, predict the future, because we often act on those same subconscious wishes.'

I regard his smile, trying to interpret my own doctor. 'Go on.'

'You say these conversations with . . .' he hesitates '. . . with your sister, were quite elaborate.'

'Yup.'

'Recall that your mind created them, entirely. In that

sense, they are akin to dreams – they are messages from the subconscious.'

'OK.'

He tilts his head. 'This might be something that can help you to clear a way through the phobia. Try and remember what she said, in your conversations, because it was your own subconscious speaking to you. Trying to help, trying to message you. And if you can put it all together, you will heal all the quicker.'

I allow myself a brief smile. I think I get it. Try to understand Kat's messages from deep in my own mind, the same way she would read the Tarot cards. I like this idea, even if it frightens me.

Not safe, Hanny, not safe.

But everything frightens me. 'Thank you, Robert. I'll try.'

'Good.' He checks his watch. 'Anyway, I must . . .'

'Nix at six?'

'Yes.'

We walk to our bicycles. He climbs on; I climb on. In tandem formation we pedal down the narrow, beach-side path, the dark trees to our left. The birds are still oddly but profoundly silent. As if they are patiently waiting for the next scene.

And I know what that scene is. I have to investigate Room 10. And then I have to go inside.

41

The office is quieter than ever. Loz taps her teeth with a pencil as she scans data. A bright November sun dazzles outside the fine bay windows. Not a cloud this Monday morning. Huge Essex skies. Pure and blue. Like the weekend when Kat drowned, that same perfect sky. Tormenting me now, as it enticed her then. *Come swimming.*

Unless she was enticed by someone, or something, else.

Or she enticed them. And it went wrong?

I turn away from the windows, focus on my screen. And click.

Click click click click. What?

You need a password to access these files.

Someone has put all the prior guests records for June, the weekend of the Drownings, into a secure vault. I am sure they were open before.

I try an old password.

Incorrect password. Please log in again.

Why have they done this? Now? Months after the tragedy? Perhaps because it would have looked too suspicious, especially during or around the inquest. And yet, management has a reason to shove this data in a vault. Somebody on the staff has accessed them and tried to ruin the hotel by sending poisonous emails to known and confirmed guests.

The possibility of the hotel closing, entirely, and me being jailed here, alone, rips me apart a little more. Then it stops. I *won't* be the trapped madwoman. I have accepted my sister's death even though it makes me rage with sadness. I have also accepted that her death is deeply puzzling, haunting, *suspect*.

Something happened to her, and if I can work out what it was, I will heal *all the quicker*. Robert Kempe told me.

I try another old password.

Incorrect password. Please log in again.

I curse quietly. This won't work. I look up from my desk. Loz is engrossed in her task, whatever it is. Her hair is neatly bunned; she still makes an effort. I've noticed that many of the remaining staff – those not furloughed – looking scruffier: ties loosened, wearing yesterday's shirt. No one instructs them.

I could ask Loz for the password, but she might not have it, or she might not give it to me, and whatever the answer, my question will notify Alistair and Oliver and Loz that I am investigating the Drownings.

Down the spiral staircase I go, past the paintings of the red-sailed oyster boats on the Stour, and into reception. Someone is actually checking in? I hover on the third step, watching.

The new guest is a pleasant-faced man in his fifties with a discreetly expensive jacket, probably a foodie pursuing the Mackster's autumn chitterlings.

'My wife will be coming later, on the six o'clock boat.'

'That's absolutely fine. Enjoy your dinner!'

Danielle gives the man her best receptionist smile. It disappears as soon as he is gone, replaced by an apathetic frown. Then she sees me, and the frown softens to distant sympathy, but no more. We haven't spoken about what she said that afternoon in my room. She is probably embarrassed; she was so drunk. I don't want to add to her discomfort. She did me a large favour, even if what she said scared me.

Room 10.

'Hey, Dani.'

'Han. All right?'

'Yes. I was just wondering, could I see the guest book?'

'The Book?'

I have a lie ready to go. Like a loaf, which has risen. 'Yes. I like to look at it, because I get more of a *sense* of the guests when I see their handwriting. And I want to know what kind of people are *still* checking in so we can attract more of them.'

It's not the best lie but it seems to work. She shrugs, holds up her packet of cigarettes. 'No worries. It's here, do your worst. Maybe you could man the boat? Gasping.'

'Of course.'

She chucks on a coat, then pushes the sunlit, glassy door out to the Blackwater breeze. Cigarette shoved straight in her mouth, hands cupping a lighter, she walks out of view.

I approach the Book. The Bible of Reception. The Gold-Tooled Truth.

As I open the heavy leather covers, and riffle the big pages, it occurs to me that I have never looked in here, for the entries made during the weekend of the Drownings. I suppose I never wanted to, for fear of the memories. It was part of my denial.

I have to conquer that fear now.

A slight tickle in my throat. A vague, hesitant tremor in my hands. The thick, authoritative pages flutter and pass, and here: June 23rd. The weekend of the

Drownings. It is all here. No one has ripped out the pages. That would, perhaps, be too obvious. Or they just forgot that it's all in here. Or they are hiding something *else* online.

Infinite possibilities: the Book is definitive.

Yet there are so many names. Because it was a *party*. We were fully booked. And yes, it looks like they even put a few guests in the *east wing*, despite the shabbiness down there. And the *atmosphere*.

My finger slowly traces down the list of names, one by one, a roster of pain. How many went in the water?

Cicely Trezien

Toby Wyne

Both missing, both dead.

West wing. Near me. They were supposedly sleeping near me that night, yet they never came back to their rooms. They went under in the Stumble and their bodies were swept down the Blackwater, and probably got chewed up by shipping off Seawick; no one even noticing the flesh and blood in the moonlit sea.

Gone. Like Kat.

The tickle in my throat intensifies. I can't find my drowned sister. This is odd. What about the other names? Can I find silver-haired man? He could be any of these guests: there are many dozens of them, from all over – a lot of posh London addresses, or Paris, Brussels, Edinburgh, Dubai, plus a few Americans – New York, LA – some locals too, Goldhanger, Maldon, Mersea. There is money in Essex.

Voices? It sounds like Oliver and Alistair, down a corridor, near the Mainsail. I can't hide away. If they come into reception I will just have to brazen it out, with one manager who loathes me, and another – the boss – who is increasingly wearied by my troublesome presence and annoyed by my failings at work but is kind enough to hide it. Mostly.

Their voices get nearer. I am panicking. This will just look so odd, me in reception, poring over the hotel bible like some spy.

The voices dwindle. They've turned away.

I have to do this quick. Where is Kat? Her check-in was chaotic. I remember her running to me in the sunlight in this same airy reception, her swishy little skirt, long, tanned legs, sun oil. Hannybobs, laughter, sister, love.

Julia fixed her room; I was too busy. It was all so happy and frenetic and fun, and then fatal. Perhaps Julia came back, and they did it later?

Turning the page. Gulping sadness. Part of me doesn't want to find her, doesn't want the piercing experience of seeing Kat's handwriting, another last few molecules of her attaching to the page. I will cry. No, I will not.

I have found her. It is very hard not to cry. Her handwriting is so distinctive, almost a doodle in every letter. Extrovert, pretty, like her.

Katalina Langley, 47 Belsize Park Gardens, London NW3 7JL!!!

Why the exclamation marks? Kat often does this. Did this. Random punctuation, livening up the dullest things. Here, then, is an atom of her personality. I am really doing very well in not crying.

Now I must see what Julia wrote. It will be the first important secret I have unearthed, all by myself.

June 23rd, west wing, Room 39

June 24th, east wing, Room 10

206

Not unexpected, but still, it shakes me. Kat was meant to be sleeping there the second night, in a room not far from my new home, though she never put a head on a pillow. Who knew this, apart from Julia?

'Heya.'

Danielle is back. The big reception door is half open. I can smell the Blackwater.

'Nearly finished, having a second,' she says, pointing at a cigarette in her hand. 'Do you mind? One more min.'

'No, that's fine.'

Dani steps outside, taking a final gulp of nicotine. I have one last minute. Slamming the Book shut, I stoop down and pull out a drawer, rapidly spinning through little paper pockets. Keycards. All of them. North wing. West wing. Suites.

East wing.

The paper pocket is clearly inscribed.

I pluck out the keycard.

Room 10.

42

Don't have to hide anything this time. It looks as if I am just heading down to my own room. To feed or water Greedy. To let him out of the door to do his thing for an hour or two. He is increasingly autonomous. He loves the woods and spinneys. He is so much freer than me.

Room 10.

It's just like any of the other rooms, a blue door, not painted in ages, hints of peeling. Locked for as long as I can remember. Possibly the last time it was opened was when my sister opened it.

Or maybe not – I remember Julia bringing her my things, wordlessly, at the outset of my grief and shock – she must have quietly collected them from here, a day or two after Kat drowned.

Perhaps I can track down Julia, find her actual number, somehow; call her, ask her about all this. But again, if I do that, it might get back to Alistair. For now, it is better I do this all alone. Investigating the death of Katalina Langley, of Belsize Park Gardens. *London NW3 7JL!*

Ah, Kat, are you in here? What if I find nothing inside? That might be worse.

The locked door stares at me, defiant.

And I have *palpitations*. It's happening again, the

tachycardia. Like acid reflux, a burning in the lower throat, my heart going too fast.

I will not yield. Instead, I accept the pain – lean into it – and I take the keycard out of my back pocket, and I press the card against the circular sensor.

Bzzz. Green light. Enter. The door unlatches, with a click.

Even so, I pause. Momentarily, I close my eyes, think away the fear; then I step into the room my sister was given the night she died, maybe the room with her face at the window; maybe the room where Kat screamed, making me call the police to investigate a ghost. I open my eyes.

It is just a room.

I am not sure what I expected. Perhaps I feared and hoped to find Kat – materially realized – sitting on the bed knitting a symbolic vagina out of Peruvian wool, and smoking some very good weed? Turning to smile at me in that stoned, heavy-lidded way, saying, 'Heyyyyyy'. Maybe I merely wanted a sense of her person. Her perfume. An echo of her ukulele.

Yet there is nothing. There is less than nothing. The room feels voided. There's a hint of bleach. Someone has been in here and cleaned it, thoroughly, maybe more than once, which is unusual for the east wing. Of all the rooms in the east wing, the one that has been seriously cleaned is the one my sister was meant to sleep in, the night she died.

I walk around, seeking clues I do not understand, to a mystery that lies out of sight.

Empty wardrobes, big churchy windows, drab paint. I lift curtains to the relentless cold sunshine and drop them again. I open wardrobe doors and see they contain nothing, not even dust.

That leaves the bed. Kneeling down, I look under it. Nothing. No dust balls. No colourful knickers. No dead sister.

There is nothing left to investigate. Or nothing that a human could find. But a dog? Why not? It worked before.

Stepping out, I run to my own room. Greedy rouses, in his basket, tail up and happy, ready for his walk, but he will have to wait a few minutes. He has a professional task first. I step to the wardrobe and pull out the bag, take out the shirt. *Again.* 'Here, Greedy.'

Into Room 10. I give him the shirt. *Find Kat, find her.* But he doesn't need much encouragement. He knows his job now. He seems to enjoy it.

For a few seconds he noses around the edge of the room. Then he lifts his smart doggy head and runs to the bed. Barks. *Yap.*

The bed. The mattress.

So, Kat lay on this bed during the day? Before she went swimming?

Greedy's barking is loud. He wants me to look deeper. I pull off the bedsheet in one big tug. It gets caught on a corner, then pings away. Underneath: a mattress cover. Clean and white. And Greedy is still whimpering, intent on the mattress.

The mattress cover has been washed, or it is new. Sweating a little, now, I pull away the stretchy corners of the mattress cover, and immediately Greedygut leaps up onto the bed. He sniffs all over the mattress. Then howls, triumphant, and looks at me.

He is getting a scent here. I cannot see anything except a mattress. But a dog can discern molecules. He is smelling my sister's perfume, surely. She lay on this bed. At some point in the day. It makes sense.

But what good does it do me, to know this?

Greedy barks, urgently, tail swishing.

Perhaps there is something underneath? Yes. I see it in my frightened mind. A vivid red bloodstain, on the underside, so they turned it over.

I tug at the mattress. It is very heavy. I have just enough strength to lift it, at an angle, to look at the underside.

There is no patch of crimson blood.

Wait. Wait. A pause, a heart flutter, there *is* something. A piece of card. It was hidden between the mattress and the bedframe – and, as I drop the heavy mattress, expelling air, the card flutters away, falling to the floor.

Looks like a Tarot card.

Squatting down, I pick it up, and turn it over. The card is the Moon.

I don't know much about Tarot, even though Kat tried to teach me. But she did a few readings for me. She was good. *She intuited my subconscious fears and desires*. Because we were practically telepathic.

Sadness looms, and I ignore it. Instead, I examine the card. I know it is important.

Number XVIII. The Major Arcana. The Moon.

It shows a strange dog, and another sort-of-dog, on a lonely beach, howling at a moon that looks oddly like the sun. They appear to be on an island, or a promontory. A crayfish lurks beneath them, also gazing at the moon.

I have one more job. Tousling my dog – *well done boy, good boy, good boy* – I escort him back to my room and open the door to let him onto the beach.

Kat's bag sits on the bed, containing her precious, heavily used Tarot pack. Opening the box, I go through all the many cards carefully, one by one, arranging them in suits.

Her deck is missing one card.

Number XVIII. The Major Arcana. The Moon.

The card I found in Room 10 is Kat's card. She must have selected it, extracted it, and then placed it under her mattress. Presumably, for someone to find.

Perhaps she wanted that someone to be me?

43

I look at the Tarot card as Greedy yelps outside.

'Yes, Greedy, in a minute. Walkyjogs!'

The card is indefinably eerie. The two doglike creatures. Or maybe a fox and a wolf. A crayfish. Little
flecks of gold from a moon that looks like the sun.
There are two pillars in the landscape, which could be
an island. Like Dawzy?

A sandy yellow path leads between the pillars and
disappears into blue mountains, or fierce blue waves,
like the path through the Dawzy woods to the bucking
blue waves of the Stumble, and the Drowning Hour.

Did Kat see this card, and follow that path? I need
to know more about the meaning of the card. Opening
my phone, I search. There are hundreds of websites
that offer to educate me. I pluck sentences from
many—

*A lane weaves between two stone towers. Beyond these
towers, shadowy mountains seem to melt into churning
water. The eyes of the moon are shut, ignoring the
scene beneath. The moon symbolises mysteries, wilder-
ness, the deep unknown, illusion—*

If the **Moon card** *appears in your reading, it can indi-
cate fear, anxieties, confusion, and deceit—*

If you are in a relationship, the Moon can mean decep-
*tion or lies being unveiled – **unfaithfulness**.*

There is delusion here. There is divinity here. When you
choose to sink into the moon's still waters, your wisdom
will embrace you—

Words associated with the Moon: Danger, Deception,
Femininity, False Friends, Menstruation, Confusion,
Sexuality, Infidelity

Infidelity

Shutting down the phone, I slip on a coat, and step outside into the chilly daylight. I pick up a stick.

'Greedy? Fetch!'

My loyal hound bounces down the shingles. The wind is hard enough now to make my eyes water.

Infidelity.

I am thinking of Ben, in my blue Eden, back in the Maldives: the way he stared at Kat swimming naked in the corals. The way he kept staring at her. Kept staring. Kept staring.

At the time, I thought it was anger. Then they had that strangely fraught relationship, ever after.

And more: Ben has always had that particular aversion to the east wing, like so many others, but as if he knows it well. Personally. As if maybe he has been here? To Room 10. And more: the way Julia reacted to him in the bar, weeks ago, a sense of blushing shame, something to do with sex, and she was at the Stanhope the night of the Drownings.

And still more: Robert Kempe told me that the ghost of my sister is a Tarot card of the subconscious mind, telling me things.

I saw that ghost, on a boat, standing close to Ben. Like a lover.

44

Kat, Then

The narrow path led directly north across the island through the dense, dappled woodlands. The sounds of the sunlit afternoon – the weekenders drinking mojitos and Pimm's around the Stanhope's swimming pool – dwindled into the background, overtaken by ardent birdsong, and the summer breeze tinkling the leaves.

Everything was as her father had described, sadly, hesitantly, but with a kind of relief, back in Maldon. The oak trees, the low, red-painted wooden fence – fencing nothing obvious – and then woodland: brambles, hazels, rowans.

And then, yes, this was it. Kat stepped into a circular glade surrounded by bushes, florid with wild scarlet roses. In the middle of the vivid green grass, just as Dad had promised, was a bronze sculpture on a marble pillar. Victorian and erotic, it was a sensuous depiction of a maiden, near-naked, bronze hair flowing, face tilted to the left with her lips apart: a woman willingly seduced by someone out of sight.

Kat placed a hand on the bronze. It was warm to the touch as if it was heated from within, as if blood flowed in the bronze flesh.

At the edge of the glade, there was a wooden bench: white, humble, pretty, inviting, probably antique.

She recalled her father's words, in between chocolate biscuits and sips of tea, just yesterday:

We often went there, me and your mother, and sat in those woods. We loved that particular clearing. We had picnics on the bench. So, it felt especially cruel that she should meet him there.

Her mother fell in love not long before she died. Betraying Kat's dad. There was no glossing over it.

As the sun blazed and the birds trilled, Kat sat down on the bench and examined her reaction to this. Her mother definitely did something wrong, but it was also understandable. Dad was always that much older, stuffier, slower; Mum was so young, pretty, vivacious, full of passions and projects. Dad was never going to be enough. Maybe Mum was always likely to wander, eventually. She had tried to hide it from Hannah and Kat, not telling them she was slipping off to Dawzy. On the days she told them she was meeting friends, she was really meeting *him*. The lover. Kissing him here, by the sculpture, deep in the woods, in the beautiful glade. Sacred Dawzy.

She heard her father's voice, again.

That's one reason I reacted the way I did when Kat got a job there. Unfair of me, of course. Hannah knew nothing, but I couldn't help myself – it was too much to bear. Of all places, the Stanhope Hotel? It churned up all the memories of that terrible time. And then she died, and it was so painful, so very painful . . . More tea, darling?

The wooden bench, like the bronze, was warm in the generous sun. Unstrapping her sandals and kicking them off, Kat lay down on the bench. The sun tingled her skin. She had an urge to take off everything else as well. Shorts and half-buttoned shirt. Why not? No one would come here. And yet, maybe they would. Kat did not want to get her sister nearly sacked from *another* hotel. She decided to keep her shirt and shorts on, even as she wondered if her mother had done exactly *this* – lain down naked on these slats – as he blocked the sun above her. A man diving in for a kiss, as if plunging into coralline water.

Or maybe they made love on the soft green grass? The glade had an atmosphere: it was a cage of golden memory. You could easily imagine two lovers entwined on the grass beside the bronze of a nude.

Closing her eyes, letting the sun dapple her eyelids, Katalina could also *hear* it, the cry of desire, guilt, and pleasure floating down the many years. Betrayal, yet love. Sorry not sorry. Mum, still young, still beautiful, had fallen in love with the wrong man. It happened, it happens, it will always happen.

Help me.

Kat felt a memory stirring: it was a memory of the Maldives. That huge storm that raged all night above the atolls. A storm like a monster stomping up and down the horizon, swathed in dark mist, hurling jagged electric spears. Kat recalled how she'd struggled to wake, to watch the spectacle, but failed; instead, troubled by magnificent dreams, she slept on, even as she sensed the lightning play on her eyelids, forming pink and flashing silver veins, pulsing, pulsing.

And then, she sensed *him*. In the warm shadows.

'You're *her*, aren't you?'

Kat snapped to alertness. Eyes wide: feeling suddenly endangered. A man, in the dark.

And now he stepped out of the shadow. Into the clearing.

45

Hannah, Now

The card sits on my bare table in the evening lamplight; I scrutinize it for the eighteenth time, hoping that this time it will make more sense. My sister chose this one card from her Tarot deck and hid it carefully in her room, so that one day it might be found. To tell the future: literally. Because I am in the future, and she is now telling *me*.

But telling me what? Am I right about Ben?

Another look. The curious moon gazes down, with a melancholy frown, at the dogs, or doglike monsters, howling on the beach. The moon sheds golden tears, as if she weeps for what must happen. The sandy, yellow path leads uncertainly across the island to the blue mountains, which become waves, ready to engulf.

Deception. Confusion. Sexuality. Betrayal. Infidelity.

Why did my sister follow that path? And why does the stylized crayfish gaze up, out of the water?

Pushing the card away with a sigh, I rise. I need to interrogate people, not a Tarot card. I need to ask Julia.

I have different questions now. But she has been furloughed and I have no number. She's logged out of the hotel group chat. Everyone is logging out. No one returns.

Leaving Greedygut to his twitching dreams of pine martens I head out, and down the east wing corridor. As always, I walk that bit quicker past Room 10, as if it might entice me in. As if Kat might be in there, eyes blank, white, open and dead, but still staring, wanting me to join her. Then lifting her arm and trying to put her ice-cold hand in mine. Kat.

Luck. Just past reception I see Loz, probably heading for a supper in the brasserie.

'Loz.'

She turns, looking harassed. Like everyone else. The hotel is down to ten per cent occupancy. Barely functioning at all. Days from being closed?

'Loz, you don't have a telephone number for Julia Daubney, do you? The waitress—'

Her harassed frown persists. 'Jules, sure, somewhere, but why?'

'Just want to ask her about that weekend when my sister died.'

I've given up pretending. They surely know I am *investigating*.

'Ah, God. OK. OK. You don't need a number; you can ask her yourself. In person. She rotated back in yesterday.' Loz gazes around at the emptiness and silence. 'Probably for the last time.'

'That's great, so—'

'Likely in her room. Staff corridor, 23B.'

Up the silent spiral stairs, past the silent office, down the silent corridor, 23B. Knock.

'Come in.'

Julia is lying on her bed, in jeans and tee, shoes off, reading a gossip magazine. She looks at me, startled, her face shadowed with anxiety.

Straight to it. Enough evasions. 'Julia, I want you to tell me everything.'

'Sorry?'

'Everything that happened that weekend my sister drowned. When they *all* drowned. Because I've already worked most of it out, but I need you to confirm it. I *know* you know something. I saw the way you looked at Ben, back in the bar, that day he came over. You said you were surprised he was here, because his pub is busy. But it wasn't that, was it? Tell me. *Everything*.'

Her lip quivers. There is fear there.

She bites a trembling lip. What does she know?

'Tell me. PLEASE. This is my sister and she died!'

She surrenders, her eyes wide and pleading. 'I didn't mean to do it. Han, please, I just . . . It was – was all fun, a party, she wanted some – you know, the coke – and ket. I never, y'know, meant any harm.'

I hide my shock. Julia sold drugs to my sister. Ket. And coke. Explains some of Kat's wildness?

Maybe. But there is more. I know it.

Julia is burbling.

'Please don't tell anyone, Han? I'm so sorry, so so so fucking sorry. The guilt has been awful, honest. I never told anyone; I avoided the inquest – they never called me. Oh God, Han—'

She is crying now. And I feel a tinge of sympathy for her. My charismatic sister asking a young waitress for drugs. Katalina was hard to resist, with her charm, enthusiasm, beauty.

'I don't care about the drugs, Jules.'

Julia eyes me, nervily.

'I want you to tell me about Ben and my sister.'

Now she looks properly shocked. Her voice reduces to a hoarse whisper. 'No, Hannah. You don't want to know.'

'Yes, I *do*. I saw the way you looked at him when he was here a few weeks ago – you know *something*. You put her in that room, down there. Tell me, Julia, or I will go to the police about the drugs. If they ever find her body, they will detect the drugs in her system. You will go to jail. TELL ME.'

Julia shakes her head, tears liberally streaming. 'I can't. You lost her. I never told you because you lost her, your lovely sister. It's too *cruel*.'

'Not knowing is crueller. And I basically know already. He slept with her, didn't he? My fiancé slept with my sister in that room.'

Julia takes an enormous breath and pinches the tears from her eyes with thumb and forefinger. Shakes her head.

I enforce things. 'I *will* tell the cops about the drugs. Don't bet I won't.'

'Wait.'

'Tell me. What you saw, what you know. Right now. I am trapped on this island and surrounded by liars; I want the truth.'

Julia stares at the floor. A careworn, fading carpet, a bit like the carpets in the east wing. Then she lifts her pink-rimmed, tearful eyes, and says in a quiet quavering voice, 'It's much worse than that.'

'I'm sorry? How can it be worse?'

She manages a murmur. 'It was rape.' Then louder. 'Ben raped your sister.'

46

The only sound is muffled birdsong, outside in the frigid night. Silvery shapes in the dark, randomly wheeling round Dawzy, skimming the drowning waves.

Julia's statement is so unexpected that my questions have dried up. *Rape.* My soul shrivels at the idea. Rejects it. Why would he rape Kat if they were having an affair? Maybe one night he just took it too far . . . ? Or I have got it all wrong, and they weren't having an affair, and he just pushed his way into her room, and raped her? Would that have led her to hurl herself into the waters? To follow the path across the island to the big blue waves? Watched by the howling dogs, and the eerie crayfish?

Somehow, I find a quieter voice, buried under the anger. 'How do you know? Did you see it?'

Julia shakes her head. 'No, I went to her room, and I saw her, with – with Ben. I was gonna give her 2C-B or ket, but the door was, like, ajar, and I looked in: she was sitting very close to him and I saw him touch her face, the way you do, before a kiss—'

'Did she resist?'

'Oh yeah, pushed his hand away. Quite angry. I left them to it, went back to work.'

The blood begins to boil. I never understood that phrase before. *Blood boiling.* Turns out it is kind of

226

true. My blood *simmers* with fury. Veins and nerves sizzling with information.

Then I say, 'But that's not rape, Jules. It could be anything.'

'Later,' Julia says, choking the words out, 'I tried again later, but before I could, like, even knock on the door, Katalina came out. She looked all wild, dishevelled, tearful, y'know? I asked her what's wrong, I'm not sure she heard me, or realized who I was.' Julia sighs tearfully, tightly. 'But she said, "*He just raped me. He raped me.*" And then she ran down the corridor, and I never saw her again.'

I absorb all this. Then, I say, less aggressively, because I am also quite tearful, wounded by the truth, 'You said none of this at the inquest?'

'They never called me, Han! Thank God. I was terrified the drugs thing would come out.'

'Why didn't you tell me?'

She lifts her tear-streaked face. Eyes wide. Sincere. 'I couldn't tell you. You were lost in grief, Hannah. And, Jesus, I felt so sorry for you. You were trapped by your phobia. You looked suicidal sometimes. We all knew you were . . . seeing things, talking to Kat. Was there ever a right time to tell you this? What if it tipped you over the edge?'

What she says makes sense. I was in no fit state to deal with this *as well*. Losing my fiancé, isolating me further. *My darling sister raped?* Can it be true?

'Thank you, Julia,' I say at length. 'Really. Thank you. It's horrible. But it's better to know.'

'What are you going to do, Han?'

'I don't know. Get off this nightmare of an island?'

Julia bleats again, 'Oh God. I'm so so sorry, really, so sorry, for everything, I—'

I ignore her lamentations. Pushing open the door,

I weave back to my own silent room at the end of the haunted wing, now made even more poisonous by the appalling idea that my supposedly loving fiancé, the moody but handsome man who was soon meant to be my husband, maybe raped my sister about thirty yards away from my room. On the night she drowned.

Anger dances with sadness. Sitting on my bed, I barely notice as my phone rings. I let it ring through without picking it up. I reckon it is Ben. I cannot bear to talk to him, maybe ever again.

The phone rings again, needling, persistent. Loud and shrill, stirring Greedy from his dreams.

'For Christ's sake, you bastard, go away—'

I go the phone on my table to switch it off, but then I see who is calling me.

Kat.

I stare at the phone.

Can I?

The phone sits in my hand. Greedy looks at me as if I am a stranger. Cautious, timorous. Perplexed.

Ping!

I stare at the phone, with renewed horror.

Kat has left voicemail.

This is impossible. She is dead. But technically, she is only missing. No, she is dead. Of course she is dead. She drowned, along with her phone, in the Blackwater.

Yet someone using her number has just left me voice-mail?

Picking up the phone, I clench my teeth, and I erase the voicemail without listening to it. I must not let the ghost back into my life. I must keep the delusions at bay.

And then I sit here, wishing I hadn't done what I just did.

What if she had said *I'm still alive?*

47

It's that hare again. Standing, on its hind legs, completely immobile. Looking at me in the autumn twilight, which smells faintly and sweetly of woodsmoke. Essex farmers are burning brambles and underbrush. Mersea fishermen are clearing the decks for winter.

I hear the faint muffled thump of shotguns, men slaughtering pheasants in some woodland, like the sound of a bad battle in an endless war, and very far away. But getting closer.

The hare?

I step forward. Nothing.

Twenty yards away the hare, erect, stiff, keeps on staring at me, nose faintly twitching. Lifting my binoculars, I get a better view of the perfect, polished, amber-and-ebony roundels of its gem-like eyes, gazing right back.

'Shoo shoo shoo, go on. Please go.'

A loud barking. I turn. And I see Greedygut, galloping up the beach, tongue lolling from his hungry mouth as he hurtles eagerly towards me.

When I turn back, the beach is empty. The hare has vanished. Scampered, presumably, into the oakwoods a few feet to my left.

I march on. I am waiting for Freddy Nix to bring Ben over from Goldhanger. He should be here very soon, in half an hour or so. I've said nothing to him about the rape story, nothing about Kat. I just said, *Meet me in reception as soon as you get here. I've had a breakthrough; you have to see it.*

Because I have to look in his eyes when I confront him with the story of what he did to Kat. A video call does not drill down into the soul. And that's where I want to go. That's where the story leads: deep into the core of Ben. A man allegedly capable of raping the sister of the woman he supposedly loves.

'Come on, Greedy.'

Greedygut watches me skim stones; I watch him retrieve sticks. My walk is aimless, time-killing, fretting about my upcoming confrontation with Ben.

Something else.

Freddy Nix is already here, under a mackerel blue-black sky as the last of the light begins to flee upriver. His ferry is rope-tied, waiting in the misty, late November chill. He sometimes comes a few minutes later, or early, depending on how much he has left to do, or how much he wants the following job. And even as I think this I get a *ping* from my phone.

I'm already here. Reception. Nix was early

Hold on . . . I'll come straight away

But I don't move. I stay as immobile as a magical hare. Because someone is trying to get *onto* Freddy's ferry. It is the Mackster. And this is strange, because Logan Mackinlay never leaves the island at this time of day, an hour before the first early diner. He is always in the kitchen, yelling angrily, at himself, or the lack of yellow mustard seeds.

Logan has a bunch of bags and suitcases next to him. He is quitting the hotel?

Yet Freddy, it seems, is not keen to let him on. Lifting my binos and adjusting the focus, I can see there is definitely a confrontation. The Mackster is jabbing a finger, furiously, at Freddy, who is also clearly furious.

I watch, as Logan grabs Freddy by the throat, almost pushing him off the jetty. For a few stomach-tumbling moments, I think the Mackster is going to brutally push him into the Blackwater. Maybe I should run over. Intervene. Freddy is shouting, but he's weaker. And now the older man yields, cowers, raises his hands. He lets Logan Mackinlay on to the boat with all his bags and cases.

If the Mackster is quitting, this probably spells the final closure of the Stanhope.

I watch, pensive, as Freddy un-nooses the rope from the bollard, then kicks free of the jetty, and the boat churns out into the quiet river, the smoke of the evening like a grey-bluish gauze hanging over the waters.

Ping.

I'm still waiting

It's time to tell him. Surprise him, as I wanted.

I've changed my mind. Meet me somewhere else.

Pause.

Where?

Room 10. East wing. You know where it is, right? 😉

48

As soon as Ben walks through the door I know I am right. He looks at me too long and too hard. I am quite deliberately sitting in the only chair, so he will have to sit on the bed. That same bed.

My fiancé is clean-shaven. The stubble has gone. Trying to look innocent. I can hear duplicity in his voice.

'It's anarchy back there.'

I eye him. 'Sorry?'

'Hotel. Crazy. Think Logan has finally quit. Saw him with cases? Big arguments. Shouting.'

'Uh-huh. Uh-huh.'

He sees my lack of interest. He sighs then gestures at the open wine bottle on the floor by my side.

'Bit early?'

'Just felt like it. You want some?'

'Why not?'

I offer him a half-full glass, hoping our hands will not touch. I will never let Ben touch me again. Those strong, muscled male hands – shucking Pacific rocks, scissoring shoulders of pork, the hands I once so desired, to unzip, unbutton, *undo* – make me nauseous now. I see them gripping my sister, pinning her down, fingers closing around her slender white throat.

Our fingers do not touch. As he sits down on the bed, casting his coat to the side, I see little his wince. Ben allows himself to gaze around at last, eyes flickering, nervous, on edge; he must guess that I know something.

'Why this room, Hannah? Why not yours?'

Straight to it? Interesting.

'Oh, I fancied a change. Bored of my room. There's so many empty rooms now.'

He sips at the red wine, slowly; perhaps he is buying time to work out a story.

'Why don't you get a room in a different wing?'

He's almost taunting me. Daring me to say it.

'Why?'

He says nothing. He hasn't worked out a story.

'Have you been in this room before, Ben?'

He blinks rapidly, shakes his head. 'I thought you'd brought me here to tell me some news, some breakthrough?'

'Oh, I've made a breakthrough. Definitely a breakthrough.'

His chuckle is anxious.

My words are cold. 'Have you been in this room before, Ben?'

He drinks his wine and I do the same. Letting him wait. Wait some more.

Then: 'You have been in here before though, haven't you, Ben? That night last summer. The night she died.'

'What?'

Almost a squeak. Rodent-like.

'You bastard.'

He blushes. He tries to cover it by drinking more wine, but I can see a little tremor in his hand.

'Look, Han—'

'Look what? Look where? Look at the bed?' Anger rises. 'I spoke to Julia. The waitress. The one who saw you in here, touching Kat, caressing her, that night, her pushing you away.' Surging, now. 'I know what you did, you fucking bastard. I know what you did to my sister. I know that you raped her. Is that why she went in the water? Is that why she did what she did? You *raped* her, right? My own *sister. You fucking bastard.*'

The wine glass in my hand feels pleasantly heavy. Half rising, I hurl it at him. I don't care if it blinds him: but he ducks and the glass hits the wall behind, exploding in shards, wine splattering like a severed artery hosing red everywhere.

The violence is cathartic. The echoing silence that follows is broken only by one solitary seabird. Singing ardently. And then it, too, dwindles away, and it is just me and my fiancé.

Ex-fiancé.

Ben's shoulders are slumped, his eyes downcast. He reminds me, unexpectedly, of my father: when he told us about Mum dying in hospital. Something broken inside a man, busted forever.

Now he looks my way. 'For fuck's sake.' His voice is croaky. 'Han, I didn't rape her!'

'Julia says you did.'

His eyes seek mine hungrily, and I am surprised to find something real in there. Imploring, but sincere.

'Look, this is nonsense, Hannah. No!' A touch of anger now.

'Well, this is persuasive.'

'Really, Han. Believe me. I would never do . . . *that.*'

I say nothing now. It is all on him.

'Hannah.'

Nothing.

He puts his face into his cradling hands, inhales, exhales, rubs his eyes. Then he lifts his head and looks my way, and I see the tiredness, deep in the bones. Hard work shifts of sixteen or eighteen hours, and now this. A madwoman. But I am not mad.

When he speaks, his face is full of tension. 'It wasn't rape. I'd never do that.' A dry pause. 'But, yes, we did have sex that night.'

I say nothing. I scream inside, but I stay mute.

'She was so upset about . . . something. Maybe *things*. She hated this room. I tried to comfort her, maybe that's what Julia saw? And then . . .' He breathes deep, controlling his emotions. 'Then yes, we had sex. And it—' He glances to the side, unable to meet my gaze. 'It wasn't the first time.'

The silence folds us into its embrace. I breathe deep, sensing the pain in my chest like a blade. The worst of it is that I maybe, possibly, probably, believe him. I know Ben; I've loved him for years. He can be a selfish bastard, ambitious, driven, moody. Yet not a rapist. I just don't see it in him. And I can see Kat, in her wildness, her sexual abandon, sleeping with Ben. She loves sexy men. Ben is sincerely sexy.

And I am frightened by this sincerity, because if he is telling the truth, this is so much worse. If and when I believe Ben, I am back to my original, hateful suspicion. They had an actual *affair*. I was *betrayed*, by *both of them*, and most of all by my beloved sister. My other soul.

Fuck Ben. He can disappear from my life – he *will* disappear from my life – but Katalina? She betrayed me, for weeks, months, years?

And she is dead.

At last, I manage to speak. 'OK then. Let's say you're being honest.' I glare, determined. 'This affair. When did it start?'

He winces. 'Do we really have to—'

'Yes. Oh yes. Yes, we do. Because I'm trapped on an island in some haunted hotel – and I've just discovered my fiancé was fucking my sister the night she drowned. So, yeah I THINK we REALLY HAVE TO.'

He sits back, chastised.

Good.

Slowly, he confesses. 'The first time was in the Maldives. Just once. Then, then—' An intake of breath. 'I don't know, I wanted it more than her. It was me. Blame me. I chased her. She had so many men after her. She felt massively guilty about you. We had sex maybe once or twice afterwards, and then also that night, so that's three or four times, that's all, and it was my fault. I chased her.' He looks at me as if he knows we will never meet again because, even if I believe him, I will never forgive him. 'It wasn't rape. It *was* sex. She was so moody, tearful. Something was wrong, something had happened. She hated this room; she was sad about something, something to do with your mother and a man living here, way back when. She was drunk, she said she had some coke, we came back here, and then . . .' A pathetic shrug. 'It was all wrong. I'm sorry. I'm sorry. I'm really sorry. What can I say? I hope one day you can forgive me.'

'Don't say fucking *sorry.*'

He averts his face as if I have punched him. He sighs. And slowly reaches for his down jacket.

'Why did you do it, Ben?'

'What?'

He is getting ready to go. He's retreating. Like a coward. We will never meet again, I hope.

Once more with feeling. 'Why did you fuck my sister? My own sister. I'm your fiancé! The least I deserve is the truth.'

The jacket is zipped up. The seconds wait; the silence

is painful. He grimaces. And then he speaks, softly, clearly. Truthfully. 'She was so beautiful.'

The words fall into the space between us. I look past him, at the wild claret stain on the wall. There it is, once again. Your sister is so *beautiful*. The words I've heard all my life. I always accepted that it was the price of having her as a sister.

Oh, Kat.

My ex-fiancé says, 'I'll go. I can get the water taxi.'

I shrug. My thoughts are all about Kat. Why did she claim rape if it never happened? How could she betray me?

'Yes,' I say, 'I think you better go.' I stand up, hands on hips. 'And, you know, *Ben*, don't ever speak to me again. Don't call, don't visit, nothing. I never want to think of you again. I want to forget about you forever.'

This properly hurts him. I see it in his grey-blue eyes, a real deep sadness, maybe he did love me, and still loves me, despite everything. It doesn't matter now. Kat was just so *beautiful*.

His voice is almost a bleat. 'Please, one day, try and forgive me, Hannah. Please?'

My face is cold. Silent.

He exhales and walks to the door. For a second, he looks over his shoulder at me, as if there is some final thing he can say, even now, words that can rescue this catastrophe. There is nothing. I am unblinking. I won't relent and he can see it. And I can see it, in him. The sagging shoulders again. The defeated man: like my dad. I see maybe a hint of wetness in his eyes, then he opens the door, and leaves.

Alone, I listen to the faint wash of the Blackwater outside. I feel as if I am going deep into its turbulent waters, into the Drowning Hour.

I reach for my phone and seek out her name, her profile picture. I press 'call'.

It goes to voicemail.

'Hey, you, sorrreeee, not here, must be doing something vitally important. Leave a message-uh.'

The tone pings out. I hold the phone close to my ear for a few seconds, my eyes shut, my breathing tight, and then I say it.

'Kat, it's Han. Please call me?'

49

Kat, Then

It was him. The young guy. The one she had seen staring at her, before lunch, as she sunbathed by the Stanhope pool, who had paused with Oliver and Alistair, and the silver-haired man. Handsome, blonde, cheekbones, surely related to Silver-Haired Man?

His shirt was the blue of birds' eggs you find as a child. Kat couldn't see his eyes behind his chrome-and-black sunglasses.

'I wondered if you'd come here,' he said, looking her up and down, quite blatant. Making Kat feel, abruptly, quite self-conscious about her semi-nudity, lying down on a bench, shirt unbuttoned, no bra.

Swinging her legs around, Kat sat up, buttoning her clothes. And said, 'What does that mean?'

The man smiled. A blank smile: made even more meaningless by the sunglasses, hiding the eyes. 'You must know the history; you're her daughter. The younger one. Katalina Langley.'

Kat buckled her sandals. The glade didn't appear so

charming now. The bronze statue was suddenly senti-
mental and kitsch.

The blonde young man was still giving her that vacant
smile. Sharp, white, slightly animalistic teeth.

Kat shrugged, defiant, refusing to be menaced. 'I don't
understand.'

His smile faded, slowly. 'I can see you're her daughter.
It's obvious – I saw photos. You can't see anything in
me? I suppose not.'

Kat frowned. The sun was angled directly in her eyes.

Now the young man moved between her and the
light, so that he was a silhouette, the bright afternoon
sun right behind him, making a black shadow over Kat's
face.

Lifting a shielding hand to her eyes, Kat squinted.
'Well, OK. I saw you around the pool with that other
guy. Tall guy, with silver hair. *Distinguished*.'

The black shadow nodded. 'Yeah. My uncle. I look
even more like his brother.'

'You do?

'Your mother would recognize me. If she wasn't, you
know, *dead*.'

Kat stared. 'Oh my God, you're his son?'

Framed by the sun, his face was entirely dark.

'Elliot Kreeft. Nice to meet you. My uncle is Matthew.'

Kat dropped her visoring hand and shifted left to get
a better view. Now that the young man was no longer
in shadow, he looked less menacing. There was something vulnerable about him. Or something unbalanced.
No, that was harsh. Vulnerable, nervous, sad, yes. Sad.

Kat said, 'You know, I only found out yesterday. About
my mum and your dad. All of it, how they came here.'

Elliot sat down on the bench a metre away from her,
unnerving Kat again. His profile was sharp as he stared

across the clearing, the sun turning his finely cut blonde hair quite white – ghostly, silvery, like his uncle.

'You know all this was ours. We owned it.'

'Noooooo. You did?'

'That's how they met. You really don't know much, do you?'

Kat shook her head, needled.

Elliot's smile was cold. 'Your mother and father came here, and then Bryony met Andrew and everything changed, for everyone – for you, for me, everyone.' Elliot shook his head, took off his sunglasses. Turned to Kat and his eyes were coolish grey, very striking with the blonde hair. 'So, you didn't know we owned the Stanhope back then?'

'No. Dad kept it all quiet, maybe out of shame, I don't know. And, y'know, my mum died, soon after, from the cancer. He just wanted to forget I guess.'

Elliot regarded her silently, as the birds sang in chorus, as the warm summer breeze tousled the wild roses. Then he said, quietly, 'Yes, of course, the cancer.'

Kat shook her head. 'I don't like talking about it now. Terrible, too young, my poor mum.'

'And her poor daughters. Naturally. And she died so fast, I understand?'

Elliot put on his sunglasses once more. Eyes concealed. Gazing away from her, across the clearing, intently, as if he could see Kat's mum and his dad, kissing passionately, by the statue.

'You know your mother destroyed my family. Broke my mum, their marriage, left me very lonely, and then Dad of course. But still . . .' He paused. 'There's always the *cancer*. Isn't there? You think she died of *cancer*. So that's OK.'

Silence again. It felt deeply awkward now. Kat had

241

an urge to flee, to get away from this quietly spoken, disconcertingly beautiful young man. The whole encounter was so strange, and discomforting, as if she was casually sitting with a polite, well-dressed, yet disdainful ghost.

'God. I didn't know about any of that. I'm sorry—'

'Oh, don't be sorry, Katalina. My mother just drank. And my father gave up. We handed the hotel over to some managers, moved away, and it happened.' A sigh. Then: 'But the family ran out of cash and then we got such a big offer for the place. Remarkable really. Oliver and his friends paid so much, despite it all. For this peculiar old hotel. On the island of smugglers.' Elliot shrugged. 'Perhaps they didn't know the legends. The witches. The raped virgins. The *adulteries*. Do you like your room?'

'Uhm . . .'

'Perhaps your mother slept in one of them, with my father. I've often wondered which one. Maybe several. Fucking their way through the hotel, with my mother crying in *her* room. So many rooms. And now everything has changed – and yet it is the same, really, isn't it? The smuggling and the witches. The birds always there. Even at night. Everyone watching. And now I really need a drink. Perhaps I'll see you later, at the party.'

He rose and turned; wordless now. Kat watched him as he stepped out of the dazzling sun into the shadows, disappearing. She realized she was trembling.

50

Hannah, Now

'Here, Greedy.'

I feed him a treat as we sit together on a concrete block on the shingle in front of the Stanhope. The sun is bright on the choppy Blackwater, like the chaotic glitter of a badly chipped mirror. A keening wind keeps everything cold. Almost winter now.

'You want another?'

Eagerly, Greedy takes the little cheese-and-chicken treat from my hand, then he licks my palm, then he licks my face. Affection, maybe. It is not unwelcome. No one else can give me affection, not now Ben has gone.

Leaving me with all those troubling and puzzling words.

Something to do with your mother, and a man here, way back when . . .

In the first tidal rush of emotions, this had not made much impression but now it strikes deep, a throbbing chord of disquiet. Kat must have discovered something about Mum on Dawzy.

Searching my childhood memories returns nothing. A big fat zero. We came here with Mum and Dad a few times as little girls. We ate roast pork with soggy crackling. We played hide-and-seek; maybe had a picnic? We also went to look at the Strood. I dimly recall Dad telling us the romantic but spooky story: of the Roman road that disappeared, yet sometimes materializes.

The mystery blocks me. The wind prickles me. A crayfish.

Greedy stands, the cold breeze riffling his lush brown beagle-pelt. Sniffing. Seeing things I cannot.

'What is it, Greedy?'

His muscles twitch, his eyes stare, at the river, as if he can smell something in the rushing waves commuting down to the North Sea, streaming over the Anglo-Saxon oyster beds and their spars of rotting wood.

I have Greedy on the lead because we are near the hotel.

'Here, Greedy, off you go, run-go-search!'

Unlooping the metal hook, I release my dog. Eagerly, he bounds down the stoop of pebbles to the riverbank, then pivots and trots along the waterside, following a scented trail. It does not matter if he is seen by one of the seven guests who inexplicably remain because they too will soon depart, and then we must surely close. Logan Mackinlay has gone for good. Loz confirmed this to me, pale-faced, two days ago, the last time I went into the office. She did it with a tiny sigh, which was more than enough.

I haven't been back to the office since. No one has checked to remonstrate or see if I am perhaps dead.

'C'mon, Greedy. Home.'

We go home. I feed him. He sleeps.

Then I drift to the brasserie, where I have coffee and soup and sandwiches and see no one apart from the whispering or eccentric. Not Alistair, not Oliver, just Eddie, the odd waitress, a couple of maids. I don't know who has already left. I sense the staff dwindling, more furloughs, no bookings, no one checking in, no one checking out. I haven't seen Danielle in days either. It is as if they are all dematerializing, like Kat on the swing sailing into the sky, as if the hotel itself is disappearing into fog.

I want to call Kat. Speak to her. Let her explain everything.

Yet this is mad. I cannot call Kat; I must not dial her again. Though I am eager to hear what she says. She is only missing.

No. She is dead. Finishing my ham sandwich in the lonely big room, I focus instead on what Kat has already said, in our imagined conversations. I have enough material already. She is the Tarot pack in my head, and I have a good memory for conversations. And I remember how she used some odd phrases that jarred then, and jar now.

A cat with a face like Jane Witham. That was one. And another. *Delicate firebrand darling.*

And another: *Greedygut and Rutterkin.* And more.

Rutterkin?

Taking out my phone, I search, and very swiftly, I find these same phrases. And a coldness overtakes me.

These phrases *all* relate to witchcraft from the sixteenth or seventeenth century. Most of them phrases used by witches: in trials. And as for 'Greedygut' and 'Rutterkin' – they are the names of witches' familiars. The shape-shifting imps – demons – that accompanied the witches.

I never knew that my mother gave our dog the name of a witch's familiar: which means I have done the same.

But why does the ghost of my sister want to tell me, in her hinting way, anything about witches? I sense she is trying to tell me something about Mum. My witchy, moon-loving, Tarot-reading mum.

51

I call my father, again.

Phone, cold hands, tidal salt on the breeze, 07993 . . .

'Hello, you've reached Peter Langley. Please leave me a message after the beep.'

He's ignoring me, again.

Beep.

I'll have to do it by message, then.

'Dad this is at least the tenth time I've called you. Please pick up. *Please.* I'm really on my own now. Ben and I have split up. It was horrible. I learned . . . stuff. He said things. Oh God, Dad, please, if you won't speak to me, please listen to this. I know I must have seemed mad, talking about Kat, like she was alive. I'm so sorry. I know that now, but I know that's why you were ignoring me—'

Beep.

I have run out of time. Everything is running out, even as everything repeats. The world is on a loop. The same view, the same island, the same hotel, the same empty rooms. Where Kat left the Moon on a card with two howling dogs and a crayfish, meaning *betrayal, infidelity, deception.*

Phone, cold hands, tidal salt on the breeze, 07993 . . .

'Hello, you've reached Peter Langley. Please leave me a message after the beep.'

Beep.

'But, Dad, I get it. I know she must be dead. So, I'm not like that any more. And I understand why talking to me must have been too hard. I get that you must blame me, for not stopping her running into the water—' I choke a little on these words. 'But I really need you, Dad. I think if I can work out what happened to her, why she did it . . . If I can solve all this, then it might—'

Beep.

Phone, even colder hands, the sun receding behind thin, oyster-grey clouds, 07993 . . .

'If I do that, if I solve all these stupid sad mysteries, I reckon I will be OK. It's like I am blocked by the puzzle, but if I unblock that, I can heal quicker. My therapist said so. I dunno. But, Dad, at least that's what I *believe* and believing is all I *need*. My phobia is irrational; I can conquer it, with rationality. But for that I need help, your help, because—'

Beep.

Beep beep beep.

One more go.

'Because, Dad, Ben said something, before we split up. He said that Katalina had found out about Mum and a man, here, on the island. What does that mean? What happened to Mum? I want to talk about Mum. And the dog. And that was why we stopped coming to Dawzy, when we were kids? Please tell me, Dad. I'm your daughter. The last one left. And I'm scared and trapped. And I love you. You're my dad.'

Beep.

Beep beep kleeeee.

Dropping the phone into my pocket, I watch Greedy, who is still nosing the frigid riverbank. Excited by the scent of something wild, and animal.

Surely, if my father listens to those messages he will respond?

Surely.

Voices, just behind me: two young women standing outside the hotel, having a smoke or just taking the air, and talking. It sounds like Lara and Nancy, waitress and maid. I peer behind. It is indeed them. They can't see me, because a row of bushes helpfully screens me.

Their words are urgent, yet forlorn. Lara asks, 'What will you do?'

'Probably leave this week. You?'

'Same. As soon as possible. This fucking place freaks me out, all the rooms with no one in them, so isolating now. It feels like we're trapped.'

'It is what it is. But, yeah, I don't like it,' Nancy agrees.

They go quiet. Vaping, I think. I know Nancy vapes.

'Christ it's cold. Shall we go back inside?' Lara says.

'OK.'

They walk away and their voices are replaced by trilling birdcalls. Dunlin, and knot? I will surely know them all by the end of winter.

There is a *ping*. I have a message. My chilly fingers pick my own pocket, and I look down at the phone screen.

Look at the card

The message is from . . .
Kat

THE MOON .

52

The message has already gone. Is it because it was never there? Kat is in my mind, not on this phone, not out there alive; she is missing but dead.

Use her the way Kat used to use Tarot cards, a way of divining the subconscious.

'Greedy, get in. Here.'

I shunt at the door and Greedy and I step inside. The warmth is embracing, but it comes with the particular, insistent silence of the east wing, which feels fiercer than ever now.

A silence like a shrill siren, announcing Kat's death. It is all too much. Turning back, I open the door again, and leave it ajar: ushering in the cries of birdlife and the wash of the tide. I need the sense and breeze and smell, the careening gulls, the charging waves, a little white tug on the estuary, bobbing, desperately, in the chop.

Look at the card.

It lies on my table. Waiting for me to decipher its impossible symbols.

Pick up the Moon. Look at THE MOON.

The angry dog-things howling at the Moon's yellow tears, the yellow stylized crayfish below. The winding path across the island to the dangerous waves of the Stumble, the path taken by Kat.

I go back to my internet research.

The card portrays a night-time scene, where two great pillars loom. A dog and a wolf howl at the sky, while a crayfish creeps from the water. The moon is "dripping the tears of dew" in huge drops. Behind this disquieting image, is the unknown mystery, which even the Moon cannot reveal. . .

More. Deeper.

The Rider–Waite Moon closely resembles the Tarot de Marseilles, and both Moon cards are very different to older Italian cards, with their astronomers and Moon maidens. However, an uncut sheet of cards (the Cary sheet) from Milan in the early 1500s shows a very similar design to Rider–Waite; lacking only the dogs. So, it is highly likely that this eerie night-time scene, absent of human figures, dates back to the very earliest days of the Tarot . . .

So, it is one of the oldest Tarot cards, the most ancient of designs. Katalina would have known the importance and lineage of this particular card. Her knowledge was serious, just like Mum's.

Just like Mum. Also reading about Tarot. Absorbed.

Is that what Kat is trying to tell me? The card refers to Mum, not Kat? Or something they shared?

But I am not Kat. I do not understand Tarot. I cannot see patterns in the stars. I have never sat down in a very short miniskirt in the garden of a Hampstead pub with a fat glass of cold Sancerre and said, apropos of nothing: *You know, Han, all life is a life of crime, and we all get caught.*

I don't know anything. I don't even which one of me and Kat is really the ghost. I can't work out who has left who. I don't know who is pushing the swing, and who is left behind in Promenade Park as the lonely night falls, and the chip wrappers tumble. And I can't remember the very last time we were together, the actual moment we parted.

Emotions blur in my eyes. I step to the door, inhaling the smoke-tinged ozone of the estuary.

Framed in my own doorway, gazing at the twin white boxes of the dead power station, beside the old Saxon church, far across the churning waters, I dial Kat's number, just to hear her voice.

But this time she answers.

53

'Kat?'

'Sistahbobs!'

It really is her. My dead sister. I know it isn't her. It is the illusion of her, the ghost in the phone.

The river breeze is frigid. A crow hops jauntily along the pebbles.

'Kat, where are you?'

'Down here, look for me—'

'I can't. No.'

'Oh, you can or we can oh—'

'Kat, tell me about the card.'

'Card card card. Why not look for me!'

'You know I can't.'

'Why not, darling, whyever? I miss you. Sorry for everything, Hannyjogs, remember all that.'

She sounds as if she is crying. Why is she crying?

She isn't crying. This is just her voice in my head. And now she is rambling.

'Hey, Han, I had this weird thought. What if . . . what if God is, like really autistic, you know? An idiot savant?'

'Sorry?

'I mean. Imagine He can only do one thing. He can only create, and He does that brilliantly, but then He fucks up? That would explain it all. Wouldn't it? No?'

Her voice sways in volume, as if she is nearer, then further away.

'Kat. Stop this. Tell me about Mum.'

'Ah I wish, but I can't.'

'Please. What did you learn on Dawzy, that weekend? You discovered something.'

'Nothing. Nothing at all. There is *nothing*.'

'Kat?'

The ghost of my sister in my phone in my head is humming an indistinct song. Then she falls into silence. The hopping crow flies away, escaping into the low-hanging, rain-sodden clouds and now Kat stops singing and says, in a hoarse whisper, 'I love your dog. Greedygut. Love him like Rutterkin.'

There it is again. What is she saying? The witch's familiar. Where did she get these words?

'Explain.'

'No, I won't. You already know.'

'I do?'

'Yes. You already know, you just need to think. Nothing is about me, nothing is me, I'm not here, anyway.'

I should turn the phone off, but I can't do that. Robert Kempe, my saviour, has told me to interact with this *thing*. It *is* my own subconscious, talking to me, giving me a glimpse of my hidden fears, memories, wishes; trying to help, like the Tarot, like the Moon card.

The phone is silent. Has my sister disappeared? Her ghost vanished?

'Katalina?'

More silence. My phone is cold in my frigid hand. Then I hear, on the phone, Kat's laughter.

'You already know. Just think the fuck out of it. Don't

255

be a scaredy-cat. You read the detective books, you can do this. Oh, baby, do this.'

'Wait, slow down—'

'Keep seeing these freaking cats, dancing on their hind legs. Remember that? You do. You DO. THINK. WHERE do they COME FROM?'

I am wrestling with an echo that shouts. It is too much.

I hold the phone away from me, as I march down the shingle, down to the green-slimed shore of the Blackwater. A ray lies there, on the glistening rocks and broken shells. It must have died and been washed up recently, for it has not been pecked by the gulls. It is perfect. Gleaming. It is lying on its back, staring at me, a triangular, demonic, pink-white face, with zigzaggy teeth. Its tail curves away, sharply tapering, and spiky. Like the tail of a demon.

'Tell me about Ben, Kat. What happened? Why? He says it wasn't rape and I believe him. Did you betray me?'

Silence.

'Tell me everything, Kat. Tell me about the card. And tell me about Ben. Everything!'

The breathing becomes laboured, hysterical. And then she speaks.

'What will you have me do for you? Say, yes, I am sorry? No, I am sorry?'

'I want you to explain.'

She is not listening. She mumbles gibberish. 'Tout tout tout tout. Tout tout and roundabout. And then they could fly!'

I want to throw the fucking phone in the river.

'Kat, help me.'

She goes silent again. Then she says, more clearly,

'You really need to explore this island. Daddy liked it; then he didn't.'

'I will.'

'And look at that card again. The Moon! Amazing what you can see if you really look. And work out the weird words. You can do it!'

I have to know. I have to get her answer. 'Tell me about Ben!'

The river washes past. The seabirds pursue it, forlornly, pointlessly.

Kat is sighing, heavily, and at last she says, 'You know I always liked tattoos. I always wanted more *tattoos*. Maybe I wanted *his*.'

And then the call dies.

Is this a final admission that it wasn't rape? I think so. It surely came from my own subconscious knowledge of my sister, but it is here now. So, there it is.

But then another thought chills me colder than the Blackwater wind.

Perhaps this voice is not in my head. Kat's voice. Perhaps the conversation I just heard *is* what a real ghost would sound like? How would I know? *I've never spoken to a ghost before.* Just ones I made up.

I am standing on a beach by a wintry river, and I am wondering if I have spoken to a ghost.

54

Here it comes.

Oliver shuffles onto the stage of the north hall where he quite recently announced the determined decision to keep the Stanhope open and pauses awkwardly – which is unlike him. I know this time his conclusion is going to be different: he's already sent melancholic emails about renewed problems, about the price of furlough and Christmas cancellations.

'Anyway, guys, I shan't waste your time. You surely know what this all means.'

Oh yes, we surely do. I counted four guests today, on my screen, when I went into the office. I was the only person there.

I am almost the only person *here*. Silent Oliver is alone on the stag: there's no triumvirate, no Loz and Alistair. And standing in the hall, gazing up, is a score of people, not forty or fifty. No Leon, no Logan Mackinlay.

Oliver sighs and continues, 'It is difficult to put this into words. It is a very sad moment for me personally, but I know it is sad for all of us, for everyone who has worked so hard. However, in the light of all these problems, especially Logan, the time has come for us to shutter the hotel, at least for the winter, although we may open for a few days at Christmas.'

The hall is quiet, but not mutinous. We've all been expecting this. If anything, people look relieved. *Just get me off this freaky island.*

Oliver looks from face to face. 'We'll try to keep as many staff on furlough as possible, but it won't be financially feasible to do this forever – and we'll be sending out emails, letting you know if we have to let you go. Naturally, you may wish to quit anyway and look for other employment, as I have to admit the possibility that the hotel may not ever reopen.' He sounds choked. 'Not under this management, anyhow.' He also looks diminished. 'Because we want to keep the old place ticking over, a skeleton staff will stay on. Danielle has agreed. And Owen. And Elena. Maybe Loz during the week. Freddy Nix will still operate, come and go, though much less frequently, and Alistair and I will visit, to check on things as much as we can.' He glances my way. 'There will also be a few workers for the next days, closing it all down. And that leaves, of course, ah, Hannah—'

He doesn't know how to say it. The madwoman stuck here, who now walks down beaches where thornback rays lie dead: she won't be going anywhere.

Oliver fumbles some words, drops them, looks panicked.

I raise my voice, to help him out.

'Don't worry, Oliver, I'll still be here.' I lower my gaze and survey the diminished staff. 'If anyone wants to find me, over the next, ooh, sixty years, I'll be walking round and round and round the island, with my dog, then round and round and round again. Occasionally I might have a coffee in the Mainsail.'

This earns a polite chuckle. Oliver looks relieved. He smiles at me, sincerely, sympathetically. 'Thank you,

Hannah. I know it must be hard for you, but I think your timeframe might be a touch pessimistic. Your therapist will have you off here in a few weeks, I am absolutely sure.' He turns back to everyone and claps his hands as if he is winding up a pep talk. 'There it is, guys; I sincerely wish this was better news. It is what it is. However, we are not giving up, entirely. I have no intention of selling. Over the winter Alistair, the team in London and I will seek out a new chef, raise some new capital, and I very much hope we will be back. This is too good a hotel to go silent perpetually. And you know how much I, personally, *care*. How much I have put into this. And I know how much *you* have put into this. I will not see that effort wasted. This is, I fervently hope, just a pause. An interregnum.'

He walks to the edge of the stage, ready to go, then hesitates, remembering something.

'Finally, for all those leaving, please liaise with Loz who will get you a place on Freddy's boat. He will be doing several sailings to get everyone off the island. Thank you.'

Everyone except me. And the skeleton staff.

The others begin to disperse; this time I get ahead of them. I don't want to linger in that hall. Pacing the corridors, down through the east wing. I key open the door, let Greedy out to run wherever he likes. Then I sit, alone, on the bed. Brooding. Staring into space as if it will reveal its mysteries, even though it won't. Wondering at the mighty silence all around me, hearing the deep-time echoes of a once busy place, now deserted.

Ideas germinate in the quiet like flowers that grow in the dark. I try to thrust them from my mind, but it is hard.

Down to four, then. Owen, Danielle, Elena, me.

55

'Cats dancing on their hind legs?'

'Yes.'

I blush. It sounds crazier now than it did then. But Robert Kempe doesn't seem fazed, or even particularly surprised. Instead, he frowns in deep thought and sits forward: chin poised on two thumbs, gazing down as if he can read the solution to all my puzzles in the tired beige threadbare carpet of Room 10.

'It sounds like something from, I don't know, a fairy tale. Enchanted animals.'

I nod. 'Yes. They also come from witchcraft, witch trials, these images. And phrases. I researched.'

'And what else did she say?'

'Just lots of nonsense, half confessions, rambling.' I sigh heavily. 'It was not a fun experience.'

He gazes at me. His old eyes clear and unblinking; concerned.

I am sitting on the bed. The bed where Ben sat, the bed where Ben had sex with Kat, the bed where Katalina lay under him. I've brought Robert here, after our session of therapy by the river, to see if he will react to the *atmosphere*. He has not, in any way.

He has another question for me. 'If she speaks again, like this, maybe take notes, so you can recall them, examine them? As I say, your mind is fashioning these words. Treat them as dream symbols. For instance: what does a cat on its hind legs mean? What can it symbolize?'

'That the cat is half human?'

'Perhaps. Or something else. Delve into your subconscious!'

I want to say: *I'd rather not delve too much, thanks all the same, because maybe this is not what you think; maybe this is not my subconscious chatting away; maybe I really was talking to an actual ghost.*

I cannot confess this to my therapist: it is too clearly mad. I don't want Robert to think I am mad, and then abandon me as beyond hope. And, anyway, I have had an insight. A new route in the laboratory rat-maze of my mind has opened up.

'Actually, I do remember something. I had a period when I saw witches hanging – I recall that vividly. And other stuff too. Most of it came from a book my mum had. Kat loved it.'

Robert leans forward, eagerly. 'Then it is definitely something!'

'And Kat was into fairy tales. And horoscopes, crystals, palm reading, wicca, everything. Got it from Mum's book, as well. Maybe some of these phrases are in there, too?'

Robert nods. 'There must surely be something in this, some message from your subconscious mind, from childhood memories still inside you.'

'Yes,' I say haltingly. 'That could be it.' I feel a hint of resentment. 'Or maybe Kat just *wants* to scare me?'

He meets my gaze steadily. 'The imaginary Kat in your mind wants to frighten you?'

'Yes.' I try not to blush. 'Why not?'

He shakes his head. 'I doubt that, Hannah. Nightmares

aren't generally meant to scare, or, at least, not simply that. They are quite often meant to warn.'

We lapse into quietness. He gazes around the room, at the yellow walls, the modern lights, the bed on which I sit.

'It was there that you found the Tarot card?' He gestures to the mattress.

'Yep.'

'Can I see it again? The card?'

I keep it with me at all times now, the Moon in my pocket, the card of *betrayal, deception, infidelity*. I take it out of the breast pocket of my denim jacket and hand it over.

Robert studies it. 'And it is definitely hers?'

'It's missing from her pack, so yes. She must have left it here that night. Deliberately.'

He squints at the moon, the two howling almost-dogs, the catatonic yet staring crayfish. 'It *is* highly suggestive.' He sighs, giving it back to me. 'I wish I knew precisely what it denotes but will give it some thought. I promise.'

Frustration rises. This dialogue gets me nowhere. But maybe I am asking too much of Robert; he is a therapist who specializes in phobias, not a doctor of the soul, not an exorcist. If Kat really is here, in my brain, or in the hotel, I will have to get rid of her myself.

'So, Robert, you really think I should keep talking to . . . this . . .' *Don't say ghost don't say ghost don't say ghost.* 'To this *thing*? My imaginary sister?'

'Yes, I do.'

'But it's unnerving. I worry I'm losing my mind when I listen to her.'

'I'm sure. But remember you are not that unusual. For a start you are grieving, as we have discussed, but you are also severely isolated. The *sensed presence*, as it is sometimes known, is quite common in people who are stressed and alone – solitary mountaineers, Arctic explorers, round-the-world sailors – they often report apparitions, and crucially, the apparitions are often perceived as helpful in moments of great trouble.'

'Mine is a dead sister who speaks of cats dancing like humans.'

The smile persists. 'Hannah. It's really *not* that insane. Have you heard of Joshua Slocum?'

'No.'

'First person to circumnavigate the globe singlehand-edly, in 1895. He wrote a book about it, and he tells the story of how, one day, as he was stricken in his bunk with food poisoning, the pilot of Christopher Columbus's ship the *Pinta* appeared on the deck. Slocum claims, in the book, the pilot talked with him and advised him on the perils of white cheese, and then steered the boat through some heavy weather. Saving Slocum's life.' He nods at his own story. Emphatic. Trying to encourage me. 'The sensed presence clearly helped there.'

'So, I should let Kat steer my boat through this storm?'

'In a manner of speaking, yes.'

I am trying to believe but the idea deeply discomforts me. That rambling or rhapsodizing creature in my phone, or my head, or out there, or in this room . . . When she's like that I don't really want to let her near me.

And yet, Robert is the doctor, my saviour. Today he got me to paddle *eight* inches into the Blackwater. This is progress. Four weeks ago, I could not do that, unless I was saving a drowning animal.

I'll have you off the island by spring. Maybe he will.

A horn blows loudly. Freddy Nix's ferry.

Robert stands up and we go to my room, where he fondly pats my sleeping dog, and then we head out of the

264

external door into the wintry, saline dusk, where black-and-purple clouds glare down at the grey water. The Blackwater breeze is tangy with diesel and greenweed.

Wordlessly, we walk to the jetty. A line of people wrapped in coats and scarves against the winter twilight wait to board Freddy's boat: maids and waiters with multiple bags, suitcases, holdalls. Like a scene of wartime evacuation. The hotel staff are leaving. I notice that Julia is among them. She turns as we trudge towards the boat and waves. *Goodbye.*

I wave back, braving a smile, watching her hoist her bags and board the boat. Sent away for winter. I feel no animosity towards Julia. Yes, she gave my sister drugs – but it was my sister's choice to buy drugs. And Julia has told me all she knows, even though it makes no sense. Why did my sister say she was raped? I cannot suss it out. I do not believe Ben raped her. My sister has basically admitted her lies, in my head, even as a ghost, because I am told to listen to this ghost.

Why, then, would Kat lie to Julia?

Perhaps it *was* simply her shame at betraying me. Easier to lie.

'I'm afraid I've got some unfortunate news; I have hesitated to tell you.'

I turn, alarmed, to Robert, who is twisting his coat collar against the chill, getting ready to go. The gulls wheel in the twilight, beyond him.

He sighs awkwardly. Almost as if he is lying. But just uncomfortable. Guilty.

'My brother is ill, in London. I may have to go and help. For a few weeks at least. Over Christmas.'

Panic surges. 'So, you can't see me till January?'

'Possibly not. I am sorry. It's not definite yet, but I thought I should warn you.'

'But I'm going to be stuck here on the island with only three other people!'

My whine is childish, but I am childishly frightened. My situation worsens.

I see the pain on Robert's face. I blurt, 'Oh God, Robert, sorry, sorry. You have to go. It's your brother! Sorry.'

'We can stay in touch by phone. You can call any time you like. Hopefully all will be fine in a few weeks.'

'Dr Kempe?'

It's Freddy, rope in hand, ready to go.

I watch as Robert walks down the jetty and climbs down onto the boat. Freddy kicks the boat free and steers her away. I observe as the bolshie little ferryboat tootles across the wide, dark river, heading for Goldhanger – for roads and buildings, pubs and life, civilization and freedom. I watch until the boat has dwindled into the encroaching murk and all I can see is the chilled smoking grey of the estuary and the darkening sky and the distant orange smear of some Essex town staining the night sky, and all I can think is that phrase Robert used.

The *sensed presence*.

She is back there. In the dying hotel. Waiting for me.

56

Kat, Then

Kat sat on her bed, freshly showered, in Room 10, with the bitter-yet-minty taste of ket in her mouth. She never liked this taste, but it was worth it. She wanted to wipe out the memory of the young man in the glade, the son of Mum's lover.

And the party was upon them. A hot summer afternoon had dipped into that hour or two of siestas and showers and now a warm and diverting summer evening beckoned. Glasses tinkled on trolleys in the corridors. Sweet, hedonistic noises drifted into her room through the open windows.

Kat went to the window. Blue river and blue sky. The midsummer sun making a long, epic departure. A glamorous swansong. Paving the river with a golden road.

Singing. Laughter. Women carrying flutes of champagne walked barefoot along the pebbles, twirling strappy shoes on fingers, talking in the arms of boyfriends, husbands, lovers. Their chatter mixed with the distant music, and the air carried the scent of barbecues.

It was going to be a good party: if Kat could forget all this troubling *stuff*. Mummy betraying Dad and breaking up that young man's family. That quiet, beautiful, possibly disturbed young man. How could Mum do that to him, however inadvertently? And his peculiar emphasis on the word *cancer*, as if Mum had deserved it.

No. *Mum did not deserve it.* She fell in love. Love is a flower that grows anywhere it will. It must be accepted.

Mustn't it?

Maybe there was something else, something darker. The young man also suggested it wasn't even *cancer*.

Kat stood up, dropped the towel, and stepped into her summer dress, hooking the slender cotton over her shoulders.

She allowed herself one more look at the note, extracted from its hiding place and placed on the only chair.

Help me

Could that be Mum's writing, from all those years ago? This sad echo of a cry along the corridors. It did not make sense. Mum had been here having an affair. Regrettable, maybe: but her own choice. She had not been a prisoner. Unless she'd felt imprisoned by her own feelings. But that in itself was no reason to leave a note trapped between mattress and bed, for someone to find weeks, months, decades hence. And the coincidence was impossible.

She had to call Dad. Now. Kat reached for her phone.

'Peter Langley?'

'Dad, it's me.'

'Shouldn't you be at that big party? With Hannah?'

'I am. But, Dad, I want to know something.'

Dad said, in a reluctant tone, 'What is it then?'

She dived in. 'What *really* happened to Mum, and that man, on Dawzy?'

Silence.

'Dad?'

The silence persisted. The question was clearly shocking.

Through the window, the sun was descending, imperiously. The floating music grew louder. She yearned to get out there, go and have fun. But it was impossible until she knew it. She had to press on.

'Dad was it really cancer that killed Mum?'

Another pause, but shorter; he was still there. 'Kat.' His voice was choking. 'God no, Kat. Let's not talk about this.'

'I just want to know. What really happened? I'm in this bloody creepy room at the hotel, and—'

'You mustn't, you *must not*. I shouldn't have said anything. Just get off that island. I should have told you before, just leave that wretched place.'

'Dad?'

'*No.*'

Was Dad crying? And now the line had died.

Kat stared at the note on the table. Working it out.

Perhaps this was all *planned*. Perhaps her visit to Dawzy, this weekend, was meant to happen, from the beginning of the universe. Going to that little glade with the nude. Meeting Elliot Kreeft, who finally told her the truth. Sitting here being freaked out by a place and a note. Meaning this was *all fated*. Everything was and is *clockwork*. The stars and the cards: they *decide*.

And Kat surely wasn't meant to stay in the room alone. That was certain.

Go go go.

269

Opening the door, she stepped out.

A couple were just down the corridor. Two young women: kissing passionately. The taller woman was dark-haired; the shorter, barefoot blonde woman was on tiptoes, streaming her fingers through her partner's auburn hair.

For a passing moment, Kat felt embarrassed, forced to step around them in the corridor. But as she nervously walked past, she realized that they were completely oblivious to her. As if she wasn't there at all.

57

Hannah, Now

I watch as Danielle sips at her coffee in the vaulted emptiness of the Mainsail. Chairs sit upturned on tables; across the room an overalled workman is throwing dust covers over everything, turning the furniture into robed ghosts. The whole hotel will be shrouded, a dead thing ready for burial.

I can hear other workmen down the corridor, hammering nails, boarding up the most expressive and beautiful of the Regency windows.

The Stanhope will be ritually defaced as well.

Danielle chews her croissant listlessly. We've only made small talk in the forty-eight hours that have elapsed since the Announcement. It's time to ask her.

'Why *did* you stay?'

'Hmm?'

'For the whole winter? I'm just curious, Dani – you don't have to tell me. But we're going to be spending a lot of time together.'

She takes another hit of coffee. It is from a machine.

Eddie has gone, taking his perfect, single-estate Ethiopian bean, silky-smooth flat whites with him. All the other kitchen staff have departed, as well. How will we eat? How will this work? I will have to get food deliveries. Owen will surely be doing the manly stuff. Plumbing and roof-climbing.

Danielle swallows more croissant. 'Broke up with Andy. Last week. Perfect fucking timing.'

'Ah God, I'm sorry.'

She chucks me a weak smile. 'S'OK. Thanks. But yeah.' We fall silent.

All around us the workers are still doing their noisy, terminal business: slamming nails into beautiful wood, shuttering the lovely bay windows, mutilating a place I have loved, in my own way. As my mother must have loved it. And Katalina?

For a second, I get – yet again – the *sensed presence* of Kat. Perhaps she is just behind the switched off Gaggia. Perhaps she is waiting by the water oven in the kitchen. Perhaps she is under one of those new dust covers, waiting to rise up like a spectre in a bedsheet and say *Woooooooooo*.

More likely she is in my head, but that is scarier. She will have chosen the worst place to squat. There are areas in my own mind I never want to visit but might be forced to explore.

Danielle interrupts my thoughts. 'Also, I really need a job, and Alistair and Oliver offered me good money to stay.'

'They did?'

'Yeah, generous. Really quite generous. Made me wonder why, but I have a theory.'

I lean forward, intrigued. Out there, another nail goes into the coffin lid: *bang*.

'It's because no one else would stay. Really, no one. They're all spooked. Spending a winter on the *creepy* island with the Drowning Hour? No, sorry. Everyone was desperate to get away, so they had to keep upping the cash.'

I consider this. I do not like it.

Dani adds, 'You know they offered Logan a shitload, to stay, weeks back?'

'Well, I kind of guessed *that*.'

'Sure, he was the key to the hotel, but the thing is – he hasn't even got a new job. He just, like, *fled*.'

I gaze at Danielle, puzzled. My assumption was that the Mackster had escaped to some superior and glamorous new employment in London. Instead, he was so scared or furious he ran away? And in a manner that angered Freddy Nix? Why did he stay in the first place, then? The mysteries accumulate, tumbling on top of each other like compacting falls of snow that will turn to ice, leaving me in the middle, an eccentric creature lodged in the permafrost, preserved forever. Perhaps tourists will come from Maldon in January, when everyone is desperate for entertainment, to point at the Woman Who Got Stuck on the Island.

You can hear a scream in the east wing.

My coffee cup rattles as I set it down. Danielle stares at my tremoring hand. I try to calm my nerves. She asks, 'How about you? Are you OK? I mean, it's not so *bad* for me; I can get Freddy Nix.'

'Whereas I just walk round and round. And round.'

'Yeah. Fuck. How're you coping?'

'It is what it is.' I sigh hard and long. 'Jesus. I am SO bored of hearing myself say that.' I pick up the coffee cup: not trembling now. 'We are here with fairly shit coffee till spring. *That's* what it is.'

Danielle chuckles, laconically.

I say, 'What are you meant to do here? I mean, what are they paying you *for*? There won't be anyone checking in.'

Danielle nods. 'Yeah. Hah. I wondered the same, but there is still admin and the like and I will do all that. Sort bills, find some late payers to chase. I think they also just want a few people on the island through the winter to watch over it, y'know, to deter any unwanted *visitors*.'

She looks at me meaningfully as if she is about to say *the risen dead*, but she doesn't. Instead she says, 'And you? What're *you* gonna do?'

Sit in my room and talk to my dead sister on the phone.

'Not totally sure. They've got me on half pay, which is decent of Oliver. I won't exactly be spending much. And I guess I'll do a bit of PR: Oliver is talking about rebranding the whole hotel next spring all over again. He's desperate to cling on to it.'

'He is, isn't he? Desperate.' She finishes her coffee with a quizzical frown. 'Anyway, gotta go; have to sort some bills so we don't get cut off.'

She rises, takes her cup to the nearest sink, and rinses it. We will be doing all these things for ourselves from now on.

I ponder her words as she leaves. *So we don't get cut off.* This hadn't occurred to me but of course it is possible. And even if we aren't amputated completely, Oliver won't want to run electricity everywhere, at vast expense. Many parts of the hotel will darken.

Everything will darken, through the winter.

After rinsing my own coffee cup, I set about the day of doing almost nothing. I take Greedy for a walk in

274

the damp, misty woods. I stand at my unshuttered window and observe the rain come and go, wondering if I am brave enough to try and paddle a bit deeper, once again. Ten inches. *Twelve?* Exposure therapy means ever more exposure. But I am not brave enough today, so the Blackwater flows past, serene and unbothered, as if she is already forgetting about the anguished, disfigured hotel on the little green island.

As the light weakens, the workmen finish their boarding, shuttering, shrouding. I stand at my door like some fishwife waiting for her husband to return safely and I regard the men in the gloom, as they whistle and swear and jump on the boat. I watch as the boat putters out into the calm waters, reflecting the ragged clouds, charcoal and scarlet, gaudy with a wintry sunset over the creeks.

Then Greedy and I retreat to my room, just us two, a lonely little light in the shuttered hotel, a light right at the end of the east wing, in a huge building where four people sleep, scattered, isolated, each of them alone, like me.

I am frightening myself; I am frightened. We are so few.

Greedygut sleeps in his furry blue basket, ears twitching, probably dreaming of flight, yearning to grow wings and join the oystercatchers. So he can fly off the island, and maybe carry me with him.

I watch TV on my tablet: a drama series set in a fantastically exotic location – a city. Mesmerized I ogle the cars and people: women freely stepping into shops, a scene in a busy pub. A couple kissing in a wet street with traffic nearly makes me cry. I have not touched a human in ages. Will I ever kiss again?

The drama ends. I could watch more, but I don't

want to binge. I like this series, but I will need lots of TV to last me through the winter.

I can't think about the winter. Don't Look Ahead, as you Don't Look Down.

Turning off my tablet, I lie back, staring up, listening to the sounds of the now-deserted island, sleeping in its blackness. The deadened whoop of an owl in the Dawzy woods. Then the scathing cough of a pheasant, startled, rattly, out there in the bitter darkness.

I need that dark, cold air. Slippers on, I walk to the window, throw open the curtains, slide open the glazing, and breathe. My window is throwing a square of light onto the shingle. I see the silhouette of myself on the rocks. A lone human, looking out at herself. Listening to the wash of the absent river, eyeing the drifts of cold fog.

I think of what Kat said. *You must explore the island.*

Why not? It can't get much scarier. And I need something to do; I need to feel proactive. Taking control.

After throwing my coat on, swapping slippers for boots, I snatch up a headtorch. I grab the lead, then chuck it away: what does it matter? I just have to get out. And explore.

'Come on, Greedygut. Let's go.'

He leaps into life. I don't care where we go; I just follow the logical glow of my torch, a cone of light in the chilly Dawzy fog, the shreds of cold haze that writhe between the black trees.

The hotel is deader than I have ever known, in a state beyond silence. The gulls cry, invisible, in the dark.

Greedy runs into the black-eyed, fog-scarfed woods, as if he knows where he is going. He doesn't. I do. My torch shines on the damp, frigid little path, running north beside a fence. I rarely take this path.

I take it this time.
I don't know why.
Yes, I do.

58

Torchlight turns the mist into cold silver smoke, which slinks away between tree trunks as I walk towards it. Greedygut is behind me, hanging back, wary, or uninterested. Wary.

I know this path well; I know every path on Dawzy well. If I was walking here in sunny daylight there would be big old oak trees swaying in a soughing breeze, and a low, red-painted fence, then the woodland growing denser till you reach a clearing. In June it blooms with wild roses.

There is no colour now. It is all black and grey: sombre dark trees, tendrils of mist between trunks and branches. Vapour like ghostly ivy.

Greedy yaps in the dark.

'Hey, Greedy, what's wrong?'

He runs, pauses, and looks at me, head cocked, as if to say: why this path? Why this cold, dark route, right into the woods? In the middle of the night?

I look at him, with an expression, telling him: *I am just doing what I must.*

'C'mon it won't take long!'

He obeys with a sulky new walk. Together, we edge into the dimly moonlit woods, which are alive with night noises. Nocturnal things, best left alone. An animal stirring and rustling away, bushes shivering. Perhaps a badger? Then, just ahead, the low, alarmed call of an owl further down the narrowing path. My torch catches the heavy and lumbering beat of its wings as it flees at my approach. White. Snowy. Gone.

Blackness.

And now, yes, here comes the clearing, the wild rose bushes, though I can barely see them in the glow of my torchlight.

The floor of grass is dewy. A million teardrops twinkle as my headtorch beams down, then across until it alights on the bronze sculpture on a marble pillar. I remember *this*: a sculpture of a maiden, near naked, alluring, her bronze hair falling free, her pretty face tilted to the left, a woman willingly seduced by someone out of sight, someone up there, over there, approaching.

In the silvery torchlight the lonely bronze looks odd, not bronze at all: more like aluminium, or steel, or even polished bone. Solid moonlight. As I step closer, another owl hoots her hunting sadness. I examine the statue. The cold is turning dew into ice on the metal. A chunk of the pedestal has broken away, and a strange plant grows around the wounds, like a mouth surrounded by hair. Like human hair.

A frigid wind blows up, making the last leaves on the wintry trees tremor in alarm, waiting to be ripped away. And I know I have been here before.

Of course, I have been here before. I've been every-where on Dawzy before.

But I came here as a child, with Mum and Dad, on one of our last visits, maybe our last visit. We played hide-and-seek in this stand of woodlands.

Greedy runs into the foggy darkness, for no apparent reason; he is a grey shape dwindling as I stand by the cold metal maiden.

Was I nine? Or ten?

I have to work to retrieve the memory: it runs away like an untrained dog.

What happened here? Something to do with Dad. I found this little clearing and I hid behind the bench – the shape of a bench I can just make out over there.

It was a bright warm day, June or July. And I laughed with delicious fear as I hid, counting the seconds, hearing Dad stamp on the crackly twigs of the path, calling out with his gentle, cheering voice, 'I'm coming! I can see you, Hannah!'

Mum and Kat were somewhere else on another part of the island maybe; this was just a fun thing between Dad and me. Sometimes I liked having Dad to myself, because Kat soaked up so much of his love.

The glade stares back at me. I look up, like the dogs on the card, illuminating the black lacy branches with my cone of light. There are three birds up there: cormorants, perhaps. They are so big. They are too big. They look down at my disturbing light then flap away.

And back then?

A few moments later Dad emerged into the lovely glade with the roses and the statue, and he looked around. I was peering through the slats of the bench, and I could see his face: his expression was not cheerful any more, it was dismayed. Even angry? He didn't pretend to search for me; he just looked at the bronze, examined it briefly, scowled, then marched around the bench, saw me and said, 'Come on. Found you.'

No fun. That game of hide-and-seek was no fun because this place – this little corner of Dawzy, the statue on the marble – had put him in a mood. I didn't know why then, don't know why now.

Yet, as I look back, that whole day out was awkward.

Mum and Dad bickering on the boat over, and we stopped coming here after that. Something happened that day. The incident in this clearing was part of that.

It's a tiny fragment. But maybe it is enough.

The cold is intense, and a delicately cruel winter rain is pattering the grass, the bench, the black shadowy trees. Scents of pine, brine and decay.

I go back to the statue. There is a tiny plaque.

In memory of Jocasta Kreeft
Edward Kreeft

It's a name that resonates from my childhood. Like a particular scent evoking a whole period of life, a summer by a river, this name *Kreeft* unlocks a cluster of recollections. *Kreeft*. I can remember Mum saying that name, to a friend maybe, or whispered to someone as an aside – something wrong, something shameful? An unusual name, memorable. Dutch? Yes, probably. The double E in Kreeft. There are lots of old Dutch families on this coast.

The black birds are back. They ignore me. I watch, as the icy wind rips cruelly at a cloud, which roils and disintegrates, exposing the moon. Naked. White. There.

Greedy has disappeared.

59

Kat, Then

Kat pushed her way through the crowd. The Spinnaker was full of noise and music: full of people dancing, drinking, laughing, chattering, toasting, eating, touching, touching, touching. Every glass door was flung open to the terrace and the turquoise pool. People in linens and cottons: arms slung around bare shoulders, hands grazing an ankle, an ankle with a golden chain, red mouths smiling, meeting, kissing.

The sultry evening was flavoured with barbecue smoke, just enough smokiness to give the air a savour. Logan Mackinlay watched over the barbecue in his whites, as his sous-chefs served up grilled lobster in steaming heaps. A queue of hungry people laughed in the twilight.

Kat tried to remember her lines. This was all meant to be. She had no choice now. She was always meant to be in Room 10, in the hotel where Mum met her lover. She was just following her mother, again.

For a long hazy while, Kat wandered vacantly, among

the happy crowds, smiling, saying hi, accepting a drink, knocking it back, wondering how much could she drink, chatting with people she barely recognized, asking how much had she done. It didn't matter, it was always meant to be. Like Mum. Why did Mum die? Kat was beginning to understand. She would draw a card to explain, but she was sure what it would say.

'Hey.'

Ben. Mister Moody Fiancé, at the bar, talking with Eddie, who was exuberantly fixing up salty margaritas, perfectly rimed on the rim. Looking right at her.

Of course, he's here, of course he is; this is how it's meant to happen. This is where it all goes wrong.

Ben smiled broadly. Handsome as always, dammit. Black stubble, dark jeans, and a loose but pristine white shirt, unbuttoned. She could remember the sexy, discreet tattoos, under that near-perfect shirt. She had kissed those tattoos more than a few times. Was she going to kiss them again?

Slender white fingers and curling black chest hair.

Or not?

Kat rebelled at the idea. She loved her sister more than anyone. She was sad, scared, confused, drunk, and terrified of going there again, to that place of guilt and self-hatred. Yes, his smile was dashing, but that was all it was, a handsome smile. He wasn't especially clever, or funny. It was pure sex. But it was that, it really was. Sex. Absolute sex. Maybe that was how it was with Mum and her man.

'You OK, Kat?' Ben asked.

'Yeah, I'm fine.'

'You just look a bit shocked. Seen a ghost or something?'

'Seen about seven hundred. Oh yes. Oh yes.'

He chuckled. 'Eddie is making premier league margaritas. Wanna try?'

'Sure.' She took a rare empty stool beside him. 'I warn you I'm quite out of it.'

The stool was close enough to smell his bodywash. He was spruced. The white linen shirtsleeves elegantly rolled up, showing a copper-and-leather bracelet and his tan. Masculine. The arms muscled and hard from all that work chopping bones and cleavering meat. Pink bloody lamb legs carved with a flourish. She'd watched him work at the Maldives, sweating in the humidity, sexy stains on his whites, thick fingers vigorously salting down sirloins. That was when she'd first been tempted.

'You seen my sister?'

Ben eyed her. A brief, knowing smile. 'She's out there somewhere.' He gestured at the mill of people in the evening sun, dancing, laughing, by the pool. Live music drifted, Ibiza-ish, with a swishing, lazy beat. Kat watched the crowd, picking out faces. There.

Younger American Gay Guy was leaning against a door, arm around a very young blonde girl in a minuscule dress, his hand firmly placed on her hip, and she did not seem to mind. So, it was Younger American Bi Guy after all.

Kat thought about the feeling of a hand on her hip and temptation burned. She knocked back her margarita, tasting the crystally salt, crunchy, like quartz. She looked straight at Ben. 'Want some coke?'

Ben grinned, like a hound. 'You always have the best chat-up lines. What's a man to do?!'

Well, you could say no. You could refuse me. Please say: No, I don't want this guilt again.

'Where is it, Kat?'

'My room, pervydogs, my room. Shall we give it a shot?'

He was off his stool in a second, following her down the corridor of shame. It was inevitable. This was always meant to happen. No one gets to choose, not in real life.

They pushed their way into her room, and as soon as the door shut, he went to kiss her, pulling her around, pulling her mouth to his mouth, red lips and sharp white teeth, and this time she said, 'No.'

He looked bemused. 'What? I thought—'

'Just. Wait. Let's have some coke. First. God, the fucking guilt will kill me.'

They had coke. They talked, as the coke buzzed through. She talked about that afternoon, the strange young man. Mummy. Betrayal. Sadness. Ghosts. Statues. Dad on the phone. Ben looked at her as if she was a crazy woman. And maybe he was right. They did more coke. Sniffed it, licked it. He licked her wrist, and laughed. She let him kiss her.

Then she angrily pushed him away. 'No. We mustn't. Never again.'

He was persistent; she was drunk.

She slurred, 'I shouldn't have brought you here.'

'But you did.'

He's right. I did. Because I have no choice.

'It's my sister's hotel! What if someone sees? What if they tell her? I'd kill myself.'

She glanced at the door: it was ajar, anyone could have seen them already. She got up and closed the door and this time when she went back to the bed, he knew exactly what to do: he just grabbed her, took the decision out of her hands. Hard, powerful, hands, peeling off her clothes so quickly, as if he was ripping the fur off a hare.

He ate her. Face between her trembling thighs, forcing his head nearer, tasting. Then he was lifting her up onto the bed, fucking her. In the middle of the bed, from behind, as she reached for the pillows, grasping the sheets with white-knuckled hands. Then on the edge of the bed. Hard.

She said, '*Harder*.'

'You always like it so rough. Jesus.'

'You do too.'

'I don't—'

'Harder!'

He fucked her harder, then turned her over, face to face, and kissed her, hard. She bit his shoulder, clawed his arm. She felt him grip her throat, and then the grip loosened as he came, his whole body shaking, and she watched him, satisfied, sated, and then she came too, again, unexpected, for a third time, fierce, low, urgent. Her face trembled and she could not speak.

This is why, she thought, I've done this again. It's because the sex is so good. But it is only sex.

He flopped away and lay back, the sweat aglow on his chest. 'Fucking hell.'

Enough, she thought.

'Please go. Right now. I am never doing this again.'

'You always say that.'

'I mean it this time. I'm a fucking terrible person.'

He obeyed. Ben always obeyed her, everywhere but in bed, though in a sense he obeyed her there as well.

But we all obey, in a way, in the end. We have no choice. It's all in the cards and the stars.

Kat watched him as he scooped on his jeans, buttoned his shirt, and briskly left. He offered no words of regret or attachment. This pleased her in its bleakness. This was as it should be.

Covered in his sweat, Kat lay back, alone. And now, suddenly, tearful.

The guilt that hit her was so brutal it made her gasp. Like a stab.

She sat up, cried. She was betraying her sister, as Mum had betrayed Dad. Here, on Dawzy.

'Oh God, Hannah, I'm sorry, I'm so sorry, I'm sorry.'

The sob was brief, but intense, and then it faded. A bit like an orgasm, but an orgasm of sadness.

Katalina stared at the ceiling – the paint, the lights, the cracks, this strange old wing in this beautiful old hotel.

Noise filtered through the open window, getting louder. The music was picking up, even as the sun drowned in the Blackwater. Everything was fiercer. Giddier. Guiltier.

Kat rose from the bed, dragging a bedsheet as a toga, and went to the window. The evening music was brilliant with laughter and chatter in the sultry twilight. Kat shivered as the river breeze kicked up. She blinked back her sadness and turned, picked up the note on the little table.

Help me.

Who was it for? Did it even matter? The thing was written; the end was obvious. Angrily, tearfully, Kat got dressed, strapped her shoes. Did another line of coke for courage.

The dusk was darkening now, but welcoming. A warm, scented, smoky breeze came through the window. Enticing everyone to come out, come out.

Before she could *come out*, she was surprised by a knock on the door. She pulled. The door opened.

'Hello.'

Of course.

Of course, it would be *him*.

60

Hannah, Now

I twist around in the turning darkness of the clearing, as the moon shines down on the mist. That noise. But there is no one.

Is there?

Greedygut barks, out there, among the gathered trees. His yelp sounds lonely, maybe frightened. It is cold and damp, and my dog wants to go home: to the comparative safety of our sad little room at the end of the corridor.

My dog is right.

'This way, Greedy!'

He returns, lustily galloping into the cone of light.

'Let's go—'

He races ahead. He knows the way. He's running fast, as if he saw something out there, out there in the trees, and he knows we need to escape.

'Slow down!'

He doesn't slow down. He speeds *up*. He goes so fast, I fear I will lose him again. He could go anywhere, could magically disappear like he magically appeared. He could actually turn into the bird he wants to be, or thinks he is, and fly away, into the sky, like Kat on the swing in my dream.

I must not lose my dog. As long as I have to keep him alive, I will keep myself alive. The idea of not having him deepens my fear, intolerably.

I start running.

It is dangerous, running down a narrow woodland path in the dark. One exposed knuckle of root could send me spinning into the brambles, tearing flesh, spraining an ankle, but I need to find Greedy. The fog is thickening once more, like a sauce that curdles, out of nothing, out of water – something Ben would do, or Logan.

What is that? Who is that?

No one. There is no one out here. I did not see a face. There was no white face briefly looming between the trees. I have not seen anything.

I cannot see my dog.

'Hey! Greedygut!'

Greedy has vanished. Again. The torchlight shows shadowy trees, the fence, a distant hint of the hotel, lightless, brooding, in the murk and the dark. No faces staring at me.

No dog.

I run. Desperate.

'Greedy! Greedy!'

The cold air stings in my throat as I reach the emptied, leaf-littered swimming pool. The blue plastic covering is grey in the night. No Greedy here, either.

'GREEEDYYYYYYY!'

I resist the urge to panic. I have already panicked. I am sprinting around the hotel, running through the last of the woods onto the shingle, rocks shining in my torchlight like cobbles of tin.

'Oh my God, Greedy!'

There he sits, panting, happily. As if nothing is wrong. My dog!

Greedy. He is here, sitting loyally by the external door to my room, as if he is guarding it against the moon and the fog.

Sinking to my knees, feeling the damp through my jeans, I hug him, tugging back tears. 'Greedy, don't do that. Don't do that ever again. Don't run away in the night.'

He growls, but quietly. A friendly, loyal growl. I hug him again and then I sit back, looking at him. I shiver. Here I am on an island with the moon and the dog. It is very nearly the card. Have I worked it out?

No. But I *can* work it out. I know it, and by working it out I will stay sane. Yes.

The door opens. Greedy bounds in, happy to be home. The door is shut. Greedy goes straight to his basket, tired.

I can't sleep with the new information in my head buzzing, in there, trapped by locked glazing. Search the net, with Oliver's brilliant Wi-Fi.

Kreeft.

It takes mere seconds. It's an unusual name.

I gaze down at my little screen, eyes open, dry, unblinking.

Matthew Kreeft.

He's a senior lawyer. In Essex. Mersea. Same old family that once owned the Stanhope? Hence the bronze? Surely.

I search for his image. Silver-haired, distinguished, good-looking.

It's definitely him. Silver-Haired Guy. And now I can remember where I saw him on a screen. It was brief, but it was him. Yet it was not any movie, or TV show. It was a screen I had to watch, remotely, because I am trapped on Dawzy.

He was at the inquest in the court in Colchester into the Drownings. He was a lawyer at the inquest. A QC. Serious and important in black and white. A well-known lawyer? A highly useful man to have as a friend. Or partner. Especially at an inquest where you might want things quietly shelved.

And his older brother, Andrew, I now discover, was the actual owner of the Stanhope, because, yes, the Kreefts owned it for many generations. Andrew lived here for a while. Then the Kreefts moved away, though they retained ownership. Long years later the run-down hotel was finally sold, via some anonymous company, to Oliver.

Andrew Kreeft?

I have a growing sense of who he is, and his role. Although Andrew Kreeft is not so easy to research. Because he is dead. He died in a car crash, many years ago. About two months after my mother died.

The coincidence is too much.

I gaze at the image of this man, Andrew Kreeft, on my screen. There are a couple of these photos: news reports on the death. Alcohol implicated. Yet a veil drawn. But definite hints of suicide. Driving into a wall.

This man Andrew is handsome. Like Silver-Haired Guy. But with a kinder face, not so severe.

The picture is forming, like the Strood emerging from the Blackwater. In a winter storm.

What did Ben say? That Kat told him there was a link between Mum *and a man living on the island.*

Dad got angry with me when he just saw the name *Kreeft* on a statue.

Mum died so quickly, then this man Andrew drives himself, drunkenly, into a wall?

And the card Kat drew – the Moon of the Major Arcana – which means *infidelity*.

They were lovers. Mum and this man. I am sure of it.

Putting the phone down, I let the sadness wash over me, like water.

A lover. Mum took a lover. Then she died. Then he died. So soon afterwards. And then Kat died.

A message pings on my mobile. It is from Kat.

You're running out of time, Han

Look at the Card. Work out the Words

THE MOON.

61

The message disappears. Of course, it does.

I pick up the card from my bedside table. It is 5 a.m. I have not slept all night. I do not want to sleep. *Running out of time.*

I recall something Kat once said years ago, when we were teens, and I asked her about Tarot and she said, *If you cannot work it out, just stare at the card for a long as you can. Leave it, then return, hour after hour. If you allow it room, something will emerge.*

The last of the night-hours pass.

Two dogs
A crayfish
A beach
A winding path

Kat runs down that path under the moon and she jumps in the mountainous waters and she drowns.

I get all that; I see nothing more.
You are running out of time.
Why? What is going to happen to me?
I lie back. I can sense sleep tugging, like a bullying wind hauling on a tree. I am felled.

*

When I wake it is noon, rain chit-chatting on the window. I leave my walked and watered dog with his toy and his beefy stick and force myself to go into the deserted Mainsail. Tables and chairs all shrouded. No Danielle. No Elena. No one.

The portraits of the yachts and clippers regard me: the lonely woman. The heating is still on here. How much does this cost Oliver? He will surely cut it back very soon. Cold will rule.

But lunch first. Stepping into the big restaurant kitchen – like a steel tomb system with sinks for graves – I seek my own cupboard. Bread in hand, I open the enormous catering fridge, snatch some cheese and ham and make myself a sandwich.

I eat alone among dozens of empty tables and chairs covered by white dust sheets, like cars snowed under drifts.

Something creaks. A door opening?

I tense.

The door swings gently, to and fro. No one comes; no one goes.

'Danielle?'

She does not answer, because she is not here. The door swings to a halt.

'Owen?'

No.

The uneasiness tightens. I have a ghost in my room, on my phone, and in my head. Please not another one *here:* in the Mainsail. It was always one of my favourite places in the hotel. Before the Drownings. The grand Regency room, with the amazing view over the river, the happy sound of guests and waiters eating and serving, and the Mackster roundly insulting a gurnard.

That's what I used to say to Logan, to tease him: *You don't cook, Logan, you shout at gurnards!!*

Now, nothing. Most of the view is boarded up. The bar is locked and shuttered. Nobody orders Orford smoked eel. All is silent disquiet, and me, eating my sad cheese sandwich, staring at two dogs on a Tarot card, as if it will tell me the future of the world.

Going back to my room, I lie back on the bed. I am tired; I barely slept.

And start awake. Dusty eyes. Thirsty. Confused.

It's 9 p.m.

Greedy is lying on the bed beside me, eyes bright, waiting.

'OK, OK.'

Boots, coat, door, dog, beach, night, moon.

I reach the edge of the woods. Wherever you go on Dawzy, you are always either in the woods, or at the edge of them.

A tree creaks in the cold night wind. Loud and repetitive. As if a corpse is hanging there in the dark, swinging like a crooked-necked witch. Like the one in the picture that used to keep me awake, staring in dread at the dressing gown in the dark of my childhood bedroom.

The witch I read in *that book*.

Katalina. What did she tell me, in her ghostly way? *You can do a card. And work out the words.*

All the weird words. Like: my *delicate firebrand darling?*

Kat loved that book. Mum's book, with all the weird words of the witches, and then the words added by Mum. The grand old *Encyclopaedia of the Occult*. The same book Kat talked about the last time we ate together, the night before she drowned. I can see her now, in my head; hear her words, talking of the book: 'Really, I *loved* it. It had everything. Spells and potions, and unguents. I'm still not sure what a fuckin' unguent is.'

That book also had Tarot in it. I am sure.

With cold hands, in the cold salt air of the isle, I take out my phone. Text Dad.

> I need help, Dad. I need to look at Mum's book, the big encyclopaedia about witches and magic, the one she wrote in

I wait for a minute. Two. He does not reply.

> Please, Dad. Please help me. I might be in danger here. The hotel is empty now and I am scared, and this might be a way off, if I can work out what . . .

Pause. I can't finish this sentence; I can't write *what happened to Kat*. It will upset him, my poor dad.

I change it:

> If I can work out what happened to us all, and what is happening to me, it will help me get over this mental block, even help me get off the island

> Please?

Still no reply. I see that both of the messages are *Read*. But he does not respond. Greedy barks at me and my phone, as if he is displeased. Perhaps he is. Or maybe he is barking at a new scent in the night air, not the salt meadows or the cordgrass, not mudflats or fishing boat diesel, something else, something new, something resonant: smoke.

I turn. It's coming from the hotel. The east wing.

62

It's a fire. I can see the dance of flames on the window. It looks as if it's coming from Room 10.

Fear prickles. Room 10?

Has Kat started this fire?

This is absurd. *But what if she did?* She is dead. *But what if she did?*

Running up the shingle, chased by Greedy, I slam through my room, open the internal door. I can hear it now, the fire; see smoke pouring from under the open door, dark, oily, blinking out the scarlet nightlights.

The main lights switch on. The corridor is filling with smoke.

The roaring noise gets louder, like something weird, beastly, inhuman. Belching. And I tremble, here, at end of the corridor, where the hotel turns into brambles and puddles and boaking frogs. I watch the shadows cavort; I cannot move. Fear breeds fear.

The roaring noise is demonic. What is happening in Room 10? It is lurid. It is horrible. And maybe it is Kat and I have to get her out.

I run down the corridor, all the way to Room 10, and I turn, and see.

Owen is in the room, silhouetted by flames. A chair is on fire. Is there someone in the chair? Kat?

No. He has a large fire extinguisher, and he sweeps

the black nozzle across the blaze, nose buried in his sleeve to keep out the acrid smoke. The foam engulfs the fire, the flames retreat, they die – and I can see it really is just a chair, an old chair, empty, made with cheap yellow stuffing. That's why it burns so easily. Why was there no fire alarm?

Because this is the east wing. They never properly refurbished it. *We'll get to it next year.*

The fire is out.

Owen drops the extinguisher. It lands, loud and hard, on the floor. Owen is in T-shirt and joggers. He swivels to me and says, in a shocked voice, 'Jesus, Hannah. Sorry.'

I gaze at his bare arm. 'You're burned.'

Slow, dumb, he stares down at his livid red wrist, perplexed, as if he doesn't own an arm. Shock, probably.

'Fuck.'

'Wait, I'll go get stuff.'

I dash up the corridor to the cupboard by the sauna. With the first aid kits. Then I go to the silent kitchen – the tomb system of grey steel sinks – to get the cling-film.

I race back down the wing, not looking behind me, not looking at anything. No faces. Nothing. Not Kat. She's not here.

Owen is still standing where he was, gazing at the charred corpse of the chair, taking in puffs of dry foam and charcoal ashes. I spy a liquor bottle – tequila? – upturned, on the floor. The room stinks of tequila now that the smoke is dispersing.

Like a parent with a confused kid, I guide Owen into the bathroom, over to the sink. I can smell the tequila, vivid and fruity on his breath, as I hold his wrist. Which is already close to blistering, under the cold running water.

300

His brown eyes meet mine. I sense guilt. Maybe lots of it.

'We have to do this for twenty minutes. OK?'

He grunts. Then says, 'OK. OK. God, everything *hurts*. That extinguisher was *heavy*.' He winces as the water washes the burn. It is quite a nasty injury.

We are silent for a while, watching the flowing water, then I ask, 'What on earth are you doing down here, in this room? I thought you were in the north wing.'

Another wince of pain; a sigh of admission. 'I was up there but . . .' He is blushing. 'I got a bit freaked out. I mean, you know, spooked. I'm the only one sleeping up there! Elena and Dani are in the west wing. I woke up and I was like, just so lonely. I know. Embarrassing, innit? I decided to move.'

'So why didn't you go and sleep in the west wing. There's dozens of rooms.'

He shakes his head, flinching, inhaling the pain. 'They're all locked; the drawer with the cards was locked. So, I came down here and Room 10 was the only one that was open, and I knew you were down there, right at the end. I'm like a kid who wanted to be near Mum.' He blushes, again.

What he says makes sense. I have the keys to Room 10. That's why it was open. I look his way.

'And the fire? How did that happen?'

He offers me a guilty glance. I say, 'I saw the tequila on the floor.'

'Uh, yeah. Yes. Ouch. *Fuck.*'

'C'mon, soldier. Nearly done, two more minutes.'

He nods, grateful. And confesses, 'I got hammered, I was trying to deal with that loneliness, this empty hotel. All the noises, the bloody birds. Crying at night. Anyway, I guess I fell asleep in the chair. Then the bottle must

301

have spilled, soaking the carpet, skirting board – you know all the dodgy wiring down here.'

I nod.

We'll get to it next year.

We both look down at his bright scarlet burn.

'That will blister badly. You'll have to see a proper doctor tomorrow, maybe even go to A&E.'

He doesn't seem upset by this idea; I suspect he feels a sense of relief. *Getting off the island.* I wonder if he will ever come back. And even as I think that I strongly doubt he will. We will be down to three women, slowly being reduced: till I am the only one left?

'OK, we're done.'

Now I steer Owen out of the bathroom. He is wobbly, whether from shock, fright, or the drink I don't know. Probably all three. He sits down on the bed, and I sit next to him. He looks at his arm, frowning.

'Clingfilm?'

'It's better than a bandage. It's cleaner, sterile. Doesn't stick.'

He gazes on, marvelling, as I wrap the clingfilm around the arm.

'I look like forcemeat.'

He does: the arm is mincemeat – pink and raw. Carefully, I wrap another layer, encasing him in shiny plastic. I sit back in the now-silent room, surveying the damage of the fire, the white foam and grey ash, the blackened chair, the spilled tequila, and, yes, a sordid little evidence trail of burned carpet: from the seared skirting board. It was the wiring.

Owen follows my gaze and looks mortified, again.

'Maybe Logan came back and lit it himself.'

'Sorry?'

'This is one way to do it. I mean, do what he wanted.

Burn the bastard place down.' Owen's dark brown eyes glance around.

I stare at our sous-chef. 'Owen, what do you know about Logan? What are you saying?'

The blush is back. He is frightened, as well as embarrassed.

'Please. Tell me?'

He shakes his head. He looks truly boyish; he is only twenty-two. Then he says, 'It's nothing. Logan is a great chef, bit of a madman with venison, but a great guy. I mean – I guess he just got bored and wanted to leave, but he was . . .' An unconvincing shrug. 'Stuck. Y'know. They had him trapped in a contract. He was frustrated. That's all.'

'That's it. Just a contract problem?'

Owen grimaces from the pain. His better hand is clutching the injured arm. I will have to let this go. For now.

I meet his eyes with mine. 'When you go tomorrow, you're not coming back, are you?'

He doesn't reply.

'OK, Owen. OK. That's enough – for now. Go to sleep.' I press the point. 'Sleep in a bed! Somewhere else. Go back to the north wing, don't be lonely. And no more drinking, either.'

'Yes, Mum.'

I leave him yawningly grabbing his things and heading for reception – and then I pad down the darkened corridor and climb into my own bed and switch the lamp off, urging myself to sleep.

Yet the minutes drag past like wounded things. The room is hushed. The darkness heavy. The hotel decays in its ashes. I turn over, reversing the pillow, feeling the cool.

'Hannybobs.'

My blood is glacial cold. Meltwater.

She is here. My dead sister. My living sister. She's right behind me. She is lying in the bed. I can sense the heaviness of another body, weighing down the other side of the mattress.

'Hannah, you can't even give me a hug?'

I crush my eyes tight. Not going to give in, not going to turn around.

'I'm lonely, Hannah. Lonely and cold. You know I saw a pig dressed as a woman just now, just here. Right now. Total mad crap. What's happening to me?'

Not going to turn around. Sleep is coming. She will leave me alone.

'And there was this, like, stone, scarred with claw marks. Devildogs. Katty dogs. Hanny dogs.'

My eyes are screwed tight shut.

'Oh well, I'll go then. Pffyou. Tss.'

Let her go. Let her go. Focus on what Owen said. I hear the bed creak. I sense a body moving in the darkness, a creaking door, silence. She has departed.

Devildogs, devildogs.

What does she mean?

Kattydogs.

Hannydogs.

Two dogs on a beach. On a Tarot card.

And that big book in Dad's house, with all of Mum's scribbles, and Kat's own childish additions. And a big section on Tarot.

What would the Moon card mean to Kat? She could have, would have, taken her direction from that book. The book is maybe everything, now.

63

Owen and I stand on the beach, looking across the Blackwater to Goldhanger. We can see Freddy Nix's ferry, fighting the angry river. I do not mention Owen's multiple suitcases. He is obviously quitting for good.

Three of us left. The witches of Dawzy. Or three little maids. All going mad.

'How's the burn?'

He gazes down at his clingfilmed arm. Lurid and red. It looks painful.

'Hurts quite a bit. I'm going straight to A&E in Maldon.'

'Good.'

His eyes fix on me. 'You know, ah, I'm really sorry to leave you in the lurch, Hannah.'

His face – surrounded by a grey corona of fake-fur anorak hood – looks cherubic, even angelic. Too good and innocent to stay on Dawzy.

'Don't worry, we'll manage. Plenty of seaweed to eat.'

He laughs, but it is feeble. 'Try and get off, Hannah. There must be a way.'

'Hey, I'm not exactly keen to *stay*.'

The boat is nearer. Fire-alarm red against the grey water and sky. I can just see Freddy Nix in his cabin, languidly steering his little vessel to Dawzy. Slicing the grey-blue chop of an Essex estuary, swayed by North

Sea tides. The Drowning Hour cometh. Now is my only moment.

'I want you to tell me about Logan. What you failed to say. Last night?'

He flinches, and stammers, 'It – it was nothing. Contracts.'

'Owen, I'm stuck here. And this is bollocks. Tell me. Why did he hate this hotel so much, yet never left, till right at the end?'

His eyes glitter, with guilt or sympathy. I press the point. 'I have to know. I might end up entirely alone, for a whole winter.'

A timid breeze snags at Owen's longish dark hair, drawing it out from under his hood. He pushes it out of his eyes.

'Owen. You heard all the gossip. You guys in the kitchen, when you all stay up, drinking. I know how hotels work.'

Owen looks away from me. He looks east, down the bitter shore, all the way to the far-distant wind farms, gyrating in the cold North Sea: semaphoring danger our way, but urgently despairing at their failure.

I have one more button to push.

'If you don't tell me, I will have to tell management how the fire started. I really don't want to do that. We've always got on, you and me, but . . . This is my life. My sister's death.'

He sighs. 'OK. I genuinely have no idea why Logan stayed. The contract thing is what he told me, but I agree it sounds a bit feeble. It doesn't add up, right? But I really don't know what it was.' Eyes lifted, he looks at me, urging me to believe him. He pauses, thinking, adds, 'However . . . there is something.'

'Yes?'

'I was in the kitchen once, when Georgia was talking to Logan. Ages ago. He and Georgia were close. And Georgia said something strange.'

'What?'

'It was just before the police came, that time. Days before.'

I glance left. The red rescue boat is near. An ambulance to take Owen away. He must finish this story before Freddy Nix snatches him forever.

Owen looks like a schoolboy being dragged to class, but at last he says, 'OK, that day, I was in the back of the kitchens and Georgia was delivering fish and I overheard her tell Logan about the Drowning Hour. And she said she got it from Freddy. Freddy Nix knew. Only very old fishing families like his know about it, that old Blackwater folklore, you know? They keep it quiet; it's not good for boat trips and seal spotters, weekend sailors. But every few years – or so Georgia said – Freddy would tell someone to spook them out occasionally. As a salty joke. That's all.' Owen sighs. 'And that's it, Hannah. That's all I know! That's my gossip. You've got the lot.'

The logic slots into place, like oiled machinery. I muse, aloud, 'But if Logan knew about the Drowning Hour, that means – he could have sent the emails. To close the hotel, so he would be free. Released. Of course!'

Owen winces and clutches his injured arm. 'Dunno. But yes. It's possible.'

The ferry is berthed at the jetty. I look over Owen's shoulder. Freddy flops his mooring rope over the bollard. He glances our way but offers no wave, no friendly hello or laconic remark. He eyes me coldly, with a big dash of anger. Or contempt. I wonder if all of them have the same attitude towards me: Loz, Leon, Alistair,

Oliver, the rest. The madwoman who fucked up the hotel.

Owen picks up his first suitcase with his one good arm, slings it over a shoulder. Walks down the jetty and throws it in the boat. Freddy is leaning against his cabin, well out of earshot, surveying the chilly Essex waters. Bored. No one to joke with. He looks like a man with much better things to do than picking up a solitary passenger exiting a defunct hotel. With almost no one inside it.

I feel the desperation within me. Gestating.

Owen comes back for smaller bags. I pick one up, help, and say, urgently, 'Owen, when you reach Maldon, I need you to do me a favour.'

He frowns. 'Jesus, what now?'

'Please. It's not a big thing.'

A sigh. 'OK.'

I say it quickly: to get it over with. 'I need you to break into a house.'

'You fucking what?'

'Please.'

'Whose house, for fuck's sake?'

'My dad's.'

'No. I won't do it.'

'Then I *will* tell Oliver and Alistair about the fire.'

His frown deepens. 'Jesus. Who knew you could be such a ruthless bitch?'

'I am developing necessary skills.'

Despite it all, he chuckles, sadly, in the cold knifing breeze. 'All right. A favour. Then that's it.'

64

Seagulls are mobbing a pigeon on the grey beach, where withered brown seaweed tumbles dryly, rattling down the shingle. I watch through the window, the phone hot to my ear, listening to Owen.

'OK, I'm here. Sheltered housing. Saffron Court, just down from the roundabout.'

Owen tuts, down the phone, over there in Maldon.

'This is a pretty big bloody favour, Hannah.'

'I know, thank you.'

'If we're gonna do this, let's do it. Which is his door?'

'It's 68B. Blue. Potted evergreens outside.'

'I see it.' I hear him pacing the Maldon pavement in the wintry cold, puffing icy breath, scarfed against the December wind straight off the Blackwater. Now he pauses. 'Tell me again, Hannah, why can't I just go up, knock on the door, and ask for it?'

'Because he doesn't want anything to do with me. Because I upset him by believing Kat was alive. I distressed him, made it worse. And part of him blames me, I think, for her death. I should have stopped her, as the older sister.'

Owen comes back, 'So if he knows it's anything to do with you, he'll just slam the door?'

'Ninety-nine per cent certain. No, *a hundred per cent.* The book is so linked to Kat and my mum. Only I would want it.'

'OK. And how can I be sure he won't be in?'

I answer. Time is draining. 'Because he is a creature of habit. It's Thursday afternoon, four o'clock; he *always* goes to the quiz, in the community centre. He drives there in his green Toyota. Three until six. I've never known him miss it.'

'Mmm. OK.'

'Are you there? And there's no green Toyota?'

'Yes. I'm right outside, and there's no car, but who knows. I'm gonna check the windows, make sure.'

I can hear the crunch of his shoes on the gravel drive.

A silence.

'Owen?'

He whispers. 'Wait, someone is passing, Jeez I look so bad.'

I wait. And wait. I look at the seagulls toying with the pigeon. They've pecked it so hard a wing looks broken. They seem to have learned to do this, the Dawzy seagulls. Clever, cruel birds, that have learned to gang up on smaller birds, sharing the bloody meat as they kill.

'OK, she's gone. Some old girl with her shopping. Where's the spare key?'

'Under the third potted shrub, the red one. He always keeps it there.'

I hear the little scrape of pottery on tarmac.

'Found it.'

'Hurry up, get inside—'

'Not hanging about! I'm in.'

'Good.'

'The book?'

'It's called *The Purnell Encyclopaedia of Magic and the Occult*. It's big, and has blue covers, stars and moons – it will be on one of the bookshelves.'

I hear him move and stop.

'Wait, there's someone outside—'

'Owen?'

'Is it your dad?'

The waters of Essex rush by as I hang on the phone. I can hear Owen breathing, and breathing, then sighing. 'Just a delivery. That was freaky. What if he actually finds me here?'

'He definitely won't. If you're quick.'

'All right, I'm doing the shelves.'

I can hear him pacing around the living room. He says, 'No. I can't find it. Han, it's not here.'

'Shit. It must be. *Jesus.* Try the bedroom?'

'Really?'

'It has to be there! No way he'd throw it out. There's a few shelves in the bedroom as well.'

A creak of a hinge. Owen's in Dad's bedroom. I can picture the hanging blue dressing gown, imagine the scratched tumbler of water. A lonely old room. Old men should not live alone. I wish my dad had found someone else.

'OK, I think I've found it. Big. Blue. Yup.'

'Brilliant! Thank you! Now, quick, I just want you to take a few photos, and send them. That's all I need.'

'Uh-huh. Which?'

'Take a photo of the front page.'

'All right.'

An anxious little pause. My phone chimes. The title page of the book appears. It is what I expected:

The Purnell Encyclopaedia of Magic
and the Occult
London, 1974

And underneath it there are two large handwritten signatures. The first is *Bryony Langley*. My mother's flowing, extrovert hand, confident, a bit theatrical. Beneath it, smaller, more laboured, is my sister. It says *Katalina Langley (age 7!)*

I steel myself. I know this will be hard. I have a memory of what is in this book. But I need the proof.

'Hurry up, Hannah. This is creeping me out. It's worse than the Stanhope at night.'

'Sorry. Now . . . can you please go to the section about witches?'

'What section?' I hear pages riffling in his hands. He says curtly, 'There's are several. Spells. Potions. I'll give this two more minutes then I'm out.'

'That one. *Spells*, I think?'

'Here.'

A photo pings through the ether. I stare at my screen. The photographed page is useless, just a list of 'magical' plants. Mandrake. Hellebore. Larkspur. Monkshood. I can see several handwritten notes from my mum. One, ludicrously, says 'Tesco?' as if she thought she could buy Deadly Nightshade in the supermarket.

'Hannah?'

'OK, that doesn't work. Please go to the section about witch trials, the confessions—'

'Here.'

Another *chime*. I look. There's that vivid drawing, or woodcut, of a hanged witch, with the date AD 1664 in block Gothic letters. Her neck is obscenely crooked. This is the image that haunted me as a girl.

Underneath the horrible woodcut is text. One phrase is underlined in a firm hand. Maybe by Kat, or my mum. It is a spell used by witches at the Black Mass but extorted in confessions during a witch trial. I would have read this as a girl, when I browsed this book. I might have seen the underlining, because I *know* I saw the broken-necked witch above. The spells says:

Tout tout tout and thoundabout, and then they could fly

Scanning the rest of the text, more phrases leap up.

Delicate firebrand darling

And:

What would you have of me

And:

Cats dancing on their hind legs. One with a face like Jane Witham

My heart quickens, but not painfully: this time it speeds with a terrible excitement. I have unlocked something. All along my sister, my dead sister, really has been telling me this book is crucial, and that maybe all the answers I need are in here. The ultimate solution. Why the drowning happened, and how. I have worked out the words. They were pointing me here.

I have one more task. The most ominous.

'This is the last request, Owen. Can you go to the Tarot section? I remember it's near the end, there is a list of the major arcana and what they mean—'

'The major what?'

'The most important cards. It doesn't matter; I just need a photo of that page.'

A hesitation. He snaps, 'Wait.'

'What?'

Louder, 'Jesus, this really *is* your dad. I can hear his car!'

'No! Please. Wait. This is it. Just one more photo! Blame me if you have to!'

'He's at the door!'

'Owen – this is so important – you can run out the back door, but this photo—'

I hear fumbling, the phone being pocketed. I hear a door; I hear my dad, in the background. Shouting? I hear Owen: 'I'm sorry!'

Then my father's bewildered, quailing voice. 'What are you doing?'

'Mr Langley, I'm so sorry, your daughter, Hannah, she told me about the key. She wanted photos—'

'She did *what*?'

I hear Owen running. I think. A pounding sound. Trainers on tarmac. Fleeing my father's home. A reedy voice follows, my poor dad, still railing. 'I'll call the police!' The voice dwindles, Owen is still escaping. I hear him panting, heavily, sprinting along the cold Maldon pavement under the wintry streetlight, kerb stones glittering.

He comes on the line. 'Thanks a million for that, Hannah. What if he calls the coppers?!'

'He won't. I'm sure. God, I'm sorry. He hates fuss; he won't call them, but that last photo, I desperately need it. Did you?'

'Fucksake. Really? I just got busted burgling your dad. Oh, he never comes back before six. It's ten past fucking five!'

The line breaks. He's gone. I stand here, trying not to think what my dad is thinking. What damage I have done to our already fractured relationship. I may have alienated him forever, and for nothing.

Owen will not send me that last photo. I didn't get the crucial evidence.

And even as I think this, my phone chimes. Like a rebuke.

Owen did it. He has sent the final photo.

Steadying myself, gathering myself, suppressing the dread, I look down.

The page from the book is exactly as I remember it. All the major arcana cards listed, with brief explanations as to their meaning in divination. The Fool, the Magician, the Devil: each one with some florid notes by my mother, and a couple – childlike – by my sister.

And here is the Moon. Number 18. Near the bottom of the page.

The Moon.

Upright: Deception, Difficulty, Fear, Hiding, Infidelity, Duplicity, Insecurity, Mental Confusion

It goes on. And one word throbs with pain because it has been firmly circled three times, surely by my mother. And no doubt read, as a circled word, a hundred times over, by my sister. As a child, as a teenager, she would have absorbed this word. Associating it closely with this card. My heart hurts as I read it.

Suicide

65

I stand at my window, watching grey clouds slide over the vast and darkening sky. My face stares back at me, a woman alone in the glowing lamplight, wondering who else is here. I know who is here. She is here; she isn't going away now.

And I have to summon her. We need to talk, my sister and I. But I don't want to see her reflection, lying on my bed as she coils twists of golden hair around a finger, or tells me some filthy gossip with an eager, scandalized grin. I don't want that; I just want to *talk*. I have a question to ask her.

Stepping around Greedy, who twitches and wheezes in his sleep, I switch the lamps off. The room is now fully dark. The menacing reflections in the window have gone. All I can see through the window is what is *out there*: the last ragged orange lights of the winter sunset. The rushing river black beneath, sending its army of waves towards the North Sea.

'Kat?'

Waterbirds wheel. Kleeeeeeeee.

'Kat? Are you there? I know you're there.'

My sister does not respond. When I really want her, she refuses. Where has she gone? Perhaps she has left, crossed the water as I cannot.

'Kat I'm not angry, or anything. I need you.'

The waterbirds veer away into the blackness. All I can hear now is the wind on the bare shingle, across the confusion of waves, outside my room, in the cold Essex night. I know a major low tide is coming. I read the tides daily. But I try not to pin too much hope to it. The Strood?

And then Greedy emits a little, sleepy growl. As if he senses something, even in his sleep.

And then I hear a voice.

'Heyyyy. Hannah.'

The tingle of fear trickles down my neck and spine, like a leak of ice water, making me shiver. I really probably surely shouldn't be doing this. It is like kids playing with Ouija boards in a drama, stirring up demons and spectres. But what choice do I have?

I speak. 'Kat?'

'Hell-o! It's so bloody cold. Fuck ya doing?'

She's here. Sprawled on the bed, I imagine. I won't turn around, even though I yearn to see her bright, sardonic smile one more time. Resolutely, I stare out at the black clouds, funeral-veiling a big white moon.

'Tell me about the card, Kat.'

'What about the Moon? You still can't work it out?'

'No.'

''Tis only a dog. Couple of dogs.'

'Kat, please. Two dogs. What does that mean?'

'Sometimes I see cats, sometimes dogs. Look up at them Han. Look up. Up. UP.'

Her words fragment as if the ghost is breaking up, as if I am at the edge of a signal and she's a radio station fizzing into static.

'Tell me about the card! So, I should look up at the Moon itself?'

She's quiet, now. The birds are back in the sky, the

tiny white waterbirds in the big black Essex heavens. Coming, and going.

Kat speaks. 'Sweet sisterbobs, where are you?! Take away the cold.'

'I'll try. I will. But I have a question.'

'No.'

I have to say it. I have to.

'Did you decide that Mum killed herself, Kat?'

I sense her frowning, lying on the bed looking up at me, with my back to her, as I look out at the pebbly beach in the opulent moonlight. I believe I can smell her hippy-witchy home-made scent, just like Mum's.

But she is silent. I say, urgently, 'It's not true, Kat. Dad wouldn't have lied about it all this time. He couldn't have kept it quiet. It really was cancer.'

Kleeeeeee.

Wait. Hear her breathing.

When she speaks, the room is colder. Her voice is fast and clear, burbling water.

'But the *timing*, Hannydogs. Right after the doomed affair? Here? On fucking Dawzy? And Dad was very strange about her illness, not letting us her see her. What was that about?'

'No. I don't believe it. She died of cancer.'

'Yes OK. OK. Maybe I was wrong. All wrong. Anyway. The Moon, you see it. You hate me now?'

Her voice is pleading. Needy. Crying? If I turn around, I could go over and hug her. Comfort her. I resist, and say, 'It doesn't matter what I feel, Kat. Only thing that matters is what was in your mind. That night. And I reckon I understand, what it was, what happened to you. At least in part.'

The seabirds call in the dark as if they are calling to lost children.

318

A single tear rolls down my face. 'Because I've worked it out, Kat. I think *you* killed yourself. The suicide was *you*. I think it was all too much. You betrayed me, you were high, you jumped to some conclusion about Mum, you felt so guilty about Ben, then you drew the card, the Moon, that terrible card; the suicide card.' Another tear falls. 'You always listened to the cards! And you knew about the Drowning Hour. You knew where it was, so you swam towards danger, you swam towards death. You didn't want anyone else to follow, but they did, and it was too late.' Third tear, slowly tracing down my cheek, salty and warm. 'That's what happened isn't it? You killed yourself, Kat. It was suicide. Wasn't it?'

Greedy has stopped wheezing. I have stopped breathing. A seabird, a gull, flies so close to the window it makes me jump, its glaring eye, its savage beak, suddenly visible in the moonlight.

Kat says, very quietly, 'Yes. It was. You're right.'

Enough. I turn around: I have to see.

She's not on the bed.

It is dark but there is enough grey light to see that she is not here. Yet the door swings open, as if in a breeze. But there is no breeze.

319

66

Dani: Hey. Don't be a stranger, this bloody place is strange enough as it is. Come and join us. Plz. Mainsail. Wine!

I usher Greedy into the room and the warmth and text back.

Me: Sure, just settling the dog! Been for a walk. Gimme 2

I can do this; I can fake normality. My dead sister has, this same evening, told me that she killed herself, and I am not sure if I actually spoke to a spirit, a *sensed presence*; and I even wonder if it matters. Now I am going to sit at a table and sip wine like a normal person. I can be that person. My tears have long since dried, even if a hollow sadness remains.

Reaching for the dog box in the cupboard, I pull out a big chewy toy and toss it to Greedy.

'Here, boy.'

He eagerly seizes it, starts gnawing. Contented noises. He'll be happy for hours: allowing me to open the door, exit down the dark corridor, pace past the gloomy mess that is Room 10 – ash, damp, burned carpet – past the fleeting scent of peppermint, cedar, and birch that is the unused sauna, and into the Mainsail. Dust sheets and emptiness.

Near-emptiness.

Elena and Dani are, indeed, here, sitting at the only table not shrouded. A drained wine bottle stands on the table, next to another, newly opened bottle. There are three glasses, two full, and one for me.

As I approach, Dani offers me a weak but friendly smile. I pull out a chair and force a smile in return. I must try to hide the sadness. Don't want to frighten the last of us away.

Sitting down, I pour my glass, but I can already sense the terrible mood. This is not a cheering girls' night out, if such a thing were even possible in a shuttered hotel reduced to three occupants: on an island in a river on a rattly winter's night.

Elena looks pale, her dark hair drawn into a severe bun. Dani appears tense. I speak. 'So, I think Owen has actually gone for good.'

Elena nods, wordless. Sips at her wine.

Dani says, 'Yeah, he called me. Explained.'

Now I stiffen with new anxiety. Did he tell them about my dad and the house and the book? I do not see it in Dani's face. I simply see her frustration, and I see several big glasses of red. Slurring her words.

'Mental. The fire thing. *Mental.* What happened?'

'It was surely the wiring.'

Dani knocks back more wine. 'That's what Owen said. Makes sense. Jesus Christ, the east wing! Why did they never fix the wiring? Total shambles. You could move into any other room, Han, you don't have to stay down there with . . .'

Is she about to say a scary word? I am way beyond scaring. I talk to my dead sister, and she tells me things. I already *know* there are *ghosts.*

She says, 'With all that mess. It's not good for you.'

I see her logic, and I resist it. I am *used* to my room now. Greedy loves it. And it is, still, the only bedroom with an external door.

'That's kind, but I'll be fine where I am.'

'But wait.' She eyes me. 'There's more.'

'Meaning?

'I spoke to Alistair. He says they're cutting most of the power, to keep it safe because of the wiring, and to save money. The hotel will go dark, pretty much.'

A new flicker of fear. Growing quickly. I ask, 'When? *Where?*'

'Your wing, of course. And the offices. Spinnaker maybe not. The kitchen yes. Alistair said we can use the little kitchen here. The rest, I dunno.'

'When?'

'Very soon. They can probably do it remotely, just press a button in London?' Her smile is dark, but sympathetic. 'You're gonna *have* to move to the west wing, Hannah. Unless you want to live with no leccy, and, like, icicles in your shower.'

I sit back. Maybe it is better if I move. But I need that external door. I don't want to feel even more trapped.

Elena speaks up. 'I'm going as well.'

I glance at Dani; she looks surprised. She turns and asks, 'Elena? Why?'

Elena's reply is quiet. 'I have a family issue. I'm sorry, I have to go.'

I watch as she frowns and gazes off to the side. It is a tell. Elena is clearly lying. She just wants to get off this desperate place. I can see a new flicker of dismay on Dani's face. Which feeds my own anguish. How long before Dani flees too? She won't want to be alone on here, with the madwoman. If I am going to ask any

322

questions, I need to do it now, before they abandon me. 'Dani, do you think it is possible Logan sent the emails in November? To all the guests?'

Dani screws up her mouth, maybe considering what to say. Finally, she says, 'Yeah.'

'Really?'

'Uh-huh. Occurred to me once or twice. He was so fucking desperate to leave; they were so desperate to cling on to him, keep the kitchen popular. Maybe he tried to fuck it up so that it closed anyway, then he'd be able to go? They had some hold on him so he couldn't simply quit.'

'But what hold did they have on him?'

Dani shakes her head. 'Not a clue, hon. This whole place, there's so much weirdness.'

'I will find out. I'll ask Logan. I've tried texting already, but he doesn't answer.'

Dani chuckles, grimly. 'He still won't answer, never does.' She sighs. 'God, I need *nicotine*.' She rises, plucking a packet of cigarettes from her jacket pocket. 'Better go outside, I guess. Don't want to *burn the place down*. What a disaster that would be!'

She heads towards reception, for a cigarette under the stars. Now it is just me and Elena.

And Elena is looking at me.

She blushes. Then she reaches across the table, squeezes my hands tightly. Her eyes seek mine.

'Good luck.'

67

I watch at the door of reception, out of the cold, slanting, near-horizontal rain, as Freddy's red boat disappears into the enveloping murk, taking Elena with it.

It is raining so hard that the sky has joined the air and the river, melding everything into one sheeting wetness. My prison wall made real. You cannot see Goldhanger over the Blackwater.

Dawzy Island now has a population of precisely two. We are far outnumbered by the polecats. And the weather is meant to worsen.

Closing the door, I retreat, following my morbid moods around the mazy depths of the Stanhope. How much of the hotel will go dark? I will have to move, but I'm not doing it until I am forced. For now, I will assess what is left. Like here: the silent library, where everything has a tangible layer of dust, since it's not been cleaned in a week, or more.

A coffee mug sits on a mantel in the far corner. Left by the last guest, perhaps. No one comes to fetch it. There is no one to fetch it.

What do you do when there is nothing to do except to proceed from one moment to the next? Listen, I reckon. Listen to the musical silence of the Stanhope, the silent kitchens, silent bedrooms, silent bar and brasserie, silent corridor, silent sauna, silent office. I can *hear* it.

Bobs. Jobs. Lobs. Gobs. I committed suibobs.

Her voice in my head comes and goes. I can't control it. So, I flop myself into a chair, the same chair I used, so long before the Great Silence, when I once took tea with Robert Kempe.

Unpocketing my phone, I contemplate Robert's number. What has happened to him? He's turned into Logan, Loz, Ben. He promised he would help me, but he doesn't. My calls go to voicemail. My texts disappear into the ether. Maybe his poor brother is dying, or maybe he is another person with a reason not to talk to me. No one wants to talk to me.

Who else?

The rain crackles its answer at the nearest window. Another window creaks behind me as if it is being opened, as if someone is trying to get in.

No one is trying to get in.

I rise and I lock the nearest window. Shutting out the coastal Essex weather. Then I look at the next window. And I lock that, as well, though I am not sure why. There are so many ways into the Stanhope if you wanted to get in. But I still feel a need to keep everything out.

Slowly and methodically, I go around the library, doing the same to the other windows, screwing their locks tighter, tighter. So, Kat can't get out?

Back in the chair, I scroll through my phone. I *have* to phone someone. I have no one to phone. My mind frazzles in panic like the wiring in the east wing, which will soon be powerless. I am not powerless. I must have someone to phone.

My fiancé is exiled – I told him I would never talk to him again and I won't.

My dad? He was barely speaking to me before, now he surely won't speak to me, not after Owen broke into his house. I sent a message saying, *Sorry, Dad.* He hasn't even read it. And I cannot really blame him.

The list of my non-friends goes on. Owen won't speak to me. Loz has gone coldly silent. As has the rest of the management: Oliver, Alistair. Leon.

Help.

There is no one else in my tiny family. Dad's parents are dead; Mum was estranged from hers, so I never kept numbers. The only one I can find is Auntie Lottie, Dad's sister, but she lives in Australia; what could she say at 5 a.m. in Sydney to a niece she barely knows, stuck on an island in a river on the other side of the world?

I am becoming an island. I am my own island now. There is no way off me.

I stand. Greedy surely needs a walk. So, I must go to him: down the corridor, past the empty rooms and past Room 10, where the wiring is so bad it caused a fire. Why did they never fix the basic wiring when they *did* do the lights? Why do it in that order?

And what is this?

Someone has stuffed an envelope under my door. It must be Dani; there is no one else. I pick it up. Inside, there is a note, written in scrappy, hurried handwriting.

> Sorry. Can't hack this place any more. Got watertaxi.
> I'm sure you're right about Logan. If anyone can help it's the Mackster, he knew a LOT.
> Stay safe
> Dani

My heart thuds. I half-expected Dani to do this, but the reality is bitter.

The inevitable end I saw coming all those weeks ago has arrived. I am entirely alone; on an island I can't escape.

68

Alone. This is it.

There's a familiar taste in my mouth. Alkaline, yet metallic. It is the taste I get when I step too far into the Blackwater: the taste of exposure. Of rubber boots seven inches deep in the estuary. The taste of severe panic.

Alone?

I push open the door. Greedy yaps; I try to calm myself.

'Let's go, lad, walkytime.'

Greedy bounds out onto the shingle. The rain has abated but the wind is cold and buffeting, slicing down from the North Sea. Perhaps this is the forerunner, the scouting gusts of the promised storm.

Bad weather, in midwinter. Low tide? The hope is pathetic, but it fights for life. I try not to give it too much room in case I am disappointed. Storms, winter, north winds: all this equals the Strood?

No, it would be too much luck. The moment I am finally isolated on the island, a solitary queen of this cold, sad, wooded little Eden, that is the moment the seas part with biblical timing, and allow me to escape?

Greedy runs down the beach, chasing a black-backed gull. The gull lifts away, easily, contemptuously. It is enormous. With a beak that could take out a dog's eye if it wanted.

'Greedy, this way—'

He tilts his head, disappointed, but he obeys. We march on through the cruel wind.

I take out my phone.

> Logan, I'm stuck on the island, completely isolated.
> The only one left here. I need the truth. Why did
> you leave so quickly?

The message says Delivered. Then the message says Read. He does not reply.

> Please, Logan! I'm completely cut off! Help me.
> What do you know? How did they keep you here?

The message says: Undelivered.

He's disappeared. Everyone disappears.

Greedy and I trudge on together. I can sense the hotel watching me, even though there is no one in it. I am the only person on the island, the only person in this world. I wonder if, out there, in the other world, the outer world, anyone remembers me. Does anyone think of me? I am becoming a dim memory, already being forgotten. I will never get off this place.

Yes, I will.

I have to fight. Take the fight to *them*.

Steering Greedy back to my room, I leave him in his basket – and step into the corridor. The closed mouths of all the rooms in the east wing remain mute, except one charred and blackened space: Room 10.

The lights in the corridor are still burning bright. But for how long?

Not long. They are going to turn everything off. I do not have time.

Jogging down the corridor, I run into reception. Portraits of sailors, oystermen on the Stour, memories of guests – they all mingle into the oppressive nothingness. The quiet. The loneliness. The decaying light of a winter afternoon fills the Stanhope, but it will not last long either.

Up up up. That's what Kat said. Go up up up. Circling the Regency stairs, I make the first floor and run towards the main office. I want to know everything.

Twisting the handle, I press – and nothing. Locked. Who locked it? Loz? Elena? Dani?

It doesn't matter. Stepping back, I kick at the door. Furiously. Twice. Three times. It does not even quiver. This place is so solidly built. I wonder if I could break in even if I had a sledgehammer.

'Fuck you!' I shout at the walls, at the door, at the first-floor corridor. 'Fuck you all!'

The silence after my shouting is somehow worse. Emphasizing my solitude. And now evening is coming, and the lights are going.

Anxiety builds again. That steely taste on my tongue. The idea of being alone on this island, in this hotel, without electricity, is too frightening. A species of poison.

I must work out the card. The clues are here. My dead sister says so.

Racing down the stairs, I trot into the shadowy and vacant Spinnaker, and look at the shapes of dust sheets. The evening is enclosing, deeper, darkly. With a knot of fear in my stomach, I flick the switch – and they work. The lights flood the bar. It does not help much.

I shift, again. Reception. I look in the gym. Mirrors greet me, and weights, and dead machines, all doing nothing. It is just me.

Moving, running, I put my head in the sauna. The

old scent of cedar, the memories of bodies. Then I hear a noise in the corridor. Behind. The east wing. I turn. Nothing. There is *nothing*.

The Mainsail is empty. Reception is empty. Darkness falls on the hotel and I switch on every light I can, while I still can. All down the corridors. In and out of rooms, paintings of evil raping admirals looking down at me, this silly woman, as she runs into the library.

A creak.

Someone one is trying to get in, to get into the light, away from the dark. Someone—

No. It's just the wind.

An open window.

And now the anxiety hardens into something else. I locked all the windows in here, hours back. And yet, one of those long velvet curtains: it billows, like the bosomy sail of a boat.

A window is open. Someone got in.

69

My phone, my very last lifeline to other people, sits on the bar top in the Spinnaker, next to my mug of tea. Greedy sleeps besides me, nervily. I am slowly piecing together a logical explanation for the window.

I must have missed one. Yes, that's it. That must be it. There is no other solution. None, that is, which I will tolerate.

The wind whips the leaf litter onto the covered swimming pool. I watch the external lights of the terrace diminish into the wintry darkness. I can't afford to lose this remaining light: it is far too precious.

I sip at my cooling tea, marooned in my anxieties, as I look down at the Tarot card on the bar top.

I've searched the hotel for clues and all I find is locked doors. So, this card is the only way through, the only clue in my possession.

I contemplate it for a thousandth time.

Kat and I are on the island, Kattydogs and Hannydogs, staring up at the moon, or it might be the sun. The path stretches across the island to the Stumble. I still don't understand what the crayfish refers to, and I cannot work out the towers. Perhaps they are irrelevant. Two wings of the hotel?

A movement.

Greedy stirs. He sniffles, cocks his head, gazing around

as if he is looking at a bird, bewildered yet excited. In a way that says he doesn't understand. What has he sensed?

The door behind me squeals. The door is opening.

Greedy is alert, growling: low but steady. The prickles of unease run from my mind to my fingertips. I cannot bear to tun around and look. But this time I must.

It is Kat, coming into the bar.

I swallow dryness. Swallow again.

Where has she come from?

She doesn't acknowledge me. She is in her favourite coat, a long, lavish red winter coat that she found in a charity shop. She is so good at finding amazing clothes in charity shops, throwing them together, looking fabulous. I always envy her this.

Kat acts as if I am not here. She saunters across the empty bar and sits down at a metal table. She's carrying one of her embroidered bags from Morocco. Or India. Setting the bag down, she looks inside. What is she looking for? Her big headphones? A book?

It's a book. A novel, with a florid, acid-trip cover.

I watch, mesmerized, as she reads. What is she thinking? I have to speak to her. Maybe she has something to say to me. Drawing all my courage, I try, 'Kat?'

She ignores. Does she even know I am here? Am I here? How do I know that I am not the ghost? She might be the real one.

'Kat? Please?'

Now she turns her beautiful face – and frowns in confusion. Looking at something over my shoulder. Then she shrugs and returns to her book.

She is locking me out. It is almost impossible to disturb Kat when she's deep in a book. We are both such avid readers.

Quietly, she turns the pages, transfixed. Then she turns, frowns again, looks around, as if she has heard a voice. Perhaps she has, perhaps there is someone *else* that *I* can't see.

Then she looks right at me: on my barstool, by the empty counter, where Eddie used to mix his dirty martinis. Her frown deepens, as if she did not expect to see me here.

She opens her mouth, and tries to speak, but no sound emerges. She opens her lips and closes them. Dumb. Mute. Saying nothing. Her frown deepens into distress. As if she is surprised and frightened by this: her own inability to talk.

Yet now, finally, she talks. 'It's so *quiet*, Han. Where is everyone?'

The shock of her speaking is, somehow, worse than the muteness. She is smiling. The smile is dreamy, distracted.

I struggle to reply. 'They've . . . all gone. It's just me.'

'Whoa, bro. Really? All alone?'

'Yes.'

'That's creepaloid. Aren't you a bit spooked?'

I am not sure how to answer this. How do I talk to the dead, if I am not sure they are dead?

'Sometimes. Yes. Yes. I'm scared of what it will be like, at night.'

'Can imagine.'

She puts down the book, gazes around, eyes wide, as if she doesn't quite recognize where she is.

I ask, 'So where have you been, Kat?'

She pouts. 'Meh. Loafing about. What about you?'

'Me?'

'Where have you been, Hannydogs?'

'Nowhere, I mean, just, just, just, just . . . wandering.'

Greedy growls at Kat. I lean down and ruffle his fur, shushing him. He must not scare her away.

'You're looking at the card, aren't you, Han?'

'Yes. I'm trying to work it out.'

'Good. Good. Want some help?'

She pushes her chair back as if she is going to come over, sit next to me, look at the card. A greater horror suffuses me. She might touch me. Right now, that seems appalling.

'No. It's fine. You don't have to.'

'Sure?'

'I can do it by myself. I have to do it by myself, don't I?'

Her blue eyes survey me. Eyes like mine, but more beautiful, sharp, sad. Something in them broken. The girl who killed herself.

'Yes, you probably do.'

My mouth is so *dry*. Hard to speak.

She looks at me; she frowns sadly. She is the sad face in the window. Now she says, 'I'm sorry about Ben.'

Tears prickle behind my eyes. Kat's face is also twisting into some deep emotion. She always gets so emotional so quickly – laughter to sadness in seconds, and back again.

Kat is nearly crying, and I am properly tearing up, as well. The living and the dead.

'I'm sorry, Han. I don't know why I did it. Fuckola. You're my best friend. Why did I do it? *Why?* Can you forgive me?'

I want to weep. I cannot allow this. I say, slowly, 'Of course I forgive you. You're my sister.'

She rubs her tears with the heel of her hand. 'Ach. Look at me. Stupid *me!* Fucking idiot! Derrrr.' She stops crying now, nearly as abruptly as she started; instead, she turns, gazes inquisitively at the door. 'Someone's coming!'

'No . . . They're not. I'm all alone.'

'Really? Both of us?'

She turns back, looking at me. 'You really need to work out the card.'

'I know.'

'Because I'm going into the woods.'

My heart stings. I want to reach out. I don't want her to go. I really don't want her ghost to go. Maybe she isn't a ghost any more. Maybe she is here, and alive. Talking to me. In that long red velvet coat that makes me jealous.

'Kat?'

My sister shakes her head. Then she stands, shoves the book in her bag, and walks to the glass door that leads onto the terrace. It is dark and windy out there, the storm still coming.

Kat pushes the door and the scent of the evening rushes in. I watch as she walks beyond, past the pool: her red coat turning grey, and greyer, until she is swallowed by the chilly deeps of the Dawzy woods.

For a few minutes I keep staring out. Greedy copies my gaze.

Then I see that the glimmering terrace lights, which illuminate the cover of the swimming pool with their frail silver glow, have gone out. Walking over to the wall, I throw the switch to turn them on again.

They stay dark. The bulbs have gone, or – much more likely – the power has finally been cut.

I was warned. Dani said they would maybe keep the lights on inside the Spinnaker – but that the rest of the hotel would go dark.

I look around. Sensing the danger. Sensing it coming,

over the water. In which case, I can at least defend myself. And there are knives kept behind the bar, big fat folding knives Eddie would use for slicing limes and lemons.

I cross the room, reach and take one of the knives, and put it in my back pocket.

And now, I brace, as Greedy waits alongside me, softly growling. How much of the hotel has been shut down?

I open the door that leads to reception – and I get my answer like a slap. Outside the Spinnaker, I can't see two yards in front of my face. The only light comes through the glass doors: faint, filtered starlight from the wide, black Essex heavens. Just enough to make out the ghostly reception desk.

And the air in the darkened hotel is suddenly cold. And getting colder. They've turned the heating off as well. Just as the breeze picks up outside, tapping the glazing with rain. Winter storm coming.

I am on my own in an empty and almost lightless hotel.

I hear a noise. Could be anywhere, a footfall, upstairs? I look up, at the useless dead lights. Is there someone up there?

Greedy yaps.

There.

Yes.

That noise, *again*. It must be human! Or maybe a trapped bird, that got in through the window. Or a fox. Or a hare. Or something in a corridor, staring at me, in the solid dark, just a glint of its eyes visible.

Again, I feel the fierce urge, to fight back, resist, defend, I have to do *something*. But there is nothing I can do. I am flailing. I have lost, I am done. The riddle is too difficult. I cannot work out the card. I stand here, trembling, frightened, and I look up at the ceiling, the useless lights, and I want to howl, like a dog, at the moon.

Like a dog, at the moon.

Kattydogs and Hannydogs.

There is no light in this place, but it burns in my mind. I see it. I get it. Abruptly, I understand what the Tarot card is saying. Look up, up, UP.

Up.

The lights, Hannydogs, *look at the lights*.

We are two girls, on the same island, looking at the exact same lights.

THE MOON .

70

The card shows two dogs looking up: Kattydogs and Hannydogs.

We are looking up at the lights, in the hotel. Not the moon, not the sun, not the sky.

The lights in the east wing.

The rains slaps, again, on the glass door of the Spinnaker, like an order. I must go to my room and see if I am right.

But the darkness is so intense, and in the corridor of the east wing the darkness is much much worse. Denser. Forlornly I try the lights, just in case, flicking the switch. Nothing. The power is gone here, as well.

Greedy runs ahead of me and is quickly lost in the yawning blackness. This is a kind of dark I have not experienced before. There are no windows; this corridor is wholly sealed from the outside. A throbbing weight presses on my open eyes, as if I am blindfolded.

Walking in this blackness feels too dangerous. I might walk right into someone. There is no one, of course. But what if someone is down there? I would never see her; I would walk straight into her cold, wet arms.

So, I drop to my knees, the rough comfort of the carpet under my hands. I am crawling down the corridor, until I sense something close to me, breathing, heavily.

It is masculine, or even animal. Not Greedy.

Very close. I sense hot breath. In the solid dark. Panting.

'Kat?'

An answer out of the dark. 'No.'

I can't tell where it's coming from. Behind me? Close? Or just above. But I have to ignore it. Or Kat. That's if it is Kat. Perhaps it is *not* her. Maybe it is one of the other people who drowned. They might have come back as well. The boy. Toby. The girl, sliced up by the container ships, her head gashed open, grey sludgy brain showing, blood on her fingers. Reaching for me in the darkness, reaching for help in the Blackwater, hard by the Stumble.

Hurry up, Han.

Standing up, I run down the rest of the corridor. I don't care. Got to move, got to do this. Hurry.

My room. My keycard. Will it still work? Without electricity?

A click. It is just magnetic code. It works. The door swings open, in here there is some meagre light from the Gothic windows, which are a portrait of the Blackwater, a triptych of the shingle and the seabirds under the stars.

Bed, bag, where? Have I lost it?

No.

Headtorch.

I put it on my head and switch the light. The beam is not great, the batteries are old, but the light is enough to reveal the rest of my room. And then a shape, moving. It is Greedy happily trotting into the room. He cocks a doggy eye my way. Oh God, thank God, I still have Greedy. My only friend.

Sinking to my knees, I hug his doggy neck.

'Hey, Greedy, we're gonna get off this island. I promise. We will. I've worked it out.'

He licks me, puzzled. Maybe telling me to get on with it.

He's right. *Tick tock*. Someone will be coming, if they are not in here already. They've isolated me *perfectly*.

Going to the bed, I hurriedly pile pillows and cushions up to make a kind of platform. The beam of my headtorch makes zany shadows on the walls.

The platform of pillows and cushions is unstable. I can't reach high enough. This is a Victorian room: high-ceilinged. Desperate, I spin the torchlight around. *Suitcases.* Jumping off the bed, I lug the cases up onto the mattress. Make a firmer, taller platform.

Is it enough?

The little hi-tech spotlight is tantalizingly close. It floats above me, in the grey. I reach up, straining. I can just touch the silver casing of the fixture. But I don't know how to get at it.

Spring it out: with that blade.

Taking Eddie's knife from my back pocket, I click it open, and try again. The beam of my headtorch is weakening, the light is dying with the time. But if I jemmy the blade under the chrome, it must pop out, because there must be a way of replacing it. No bulb lasts forever. No matter how tech. And this is hi-tech. Why would you install such fancy lighting in a barely used wing of a hotel if, at the same time, you couldn't be bothered to fix faulty wiring? Or even add a lick of paint.

Leaving this wing unrefurbished: it was almost as if someone wanted to divert attention from the east wing, make everyone forget it. Because you were using the wing for something else. Because boats were always coming and going, you wouldn't notice a few at night, bringing people down here. They had to have a hotel, to disguise what they were doing *here*.

343

The casing resists me. I lever the knife blade, harder. Quickly. There. The casing yields; it moves. This is it. I swivel the blade deeper, cutting the ceiling. And there.

Pop.

The light casing is prised out. It dangles in mid-air, right in front of me. It looks strange, an exotic fruit of electrics. With the knife I slice the wires above so that I have the whole contraption in my hand. Jumping off my tower of pillows, I sit down on the bed and twist the light fitting in my hand. Examining it. Because here it is. The Moon from the Moon card. This is it.

The fixture is a trinity. Next to the bulb there is a tiny microphone, and a miniature camera. They gleam in the torchlight: expensive, precision tech.

For filming people, in these rooms. For filming men. With women. I am sure.

71

My hands are shivering. The miniature camera trembles in the torchlight, like a piece of jewellery, but more precious.

So, they were making films, in here, in the east wing. I bet I would find cameras like this in every room, in this wing. Filming people having sex. Films they could use for blackmail, for power, for leverage.

My mind springs to the finish.

It fits with the history of Dawzy, of course. The island of pirates and kidnaps, of witches and smugglers. The island where the wicked admiral quietly had his way, raping maidens. A place where you could do awful things, almost in plain sight.

And then again, in the Twenties, the rich and scandalous parties. This was a place for adultery, so near to civilization, to London, yet so deliciously and helpfully remote. Still the same. Dawzy is *still the same*. You could so easily bring girls here, quietly, in quiet boats, maybe traffic them. It is the perfect place. Disguised as a hotel. You'd need powerful lawyers as friends if anything went wrong, like an unwanted drowning. Like Matthew Kreeft. And you really wouldn't want a novice Hungarian maid coming down here, by mistake, to see something going on. You'd get her off the island straight away.

I tremble, in the cold, staring at this truth, the little

gizmos in my hand. The cascade of the solution feels like a slot machine, paying out. *Chukka chukka chukka.* It all adds up. They surely lured or swayed or enticed important people here, maybe offered them the women, or had them seduced in the bar. And then they filmed them: having sex, illegal or perverse or whatever. With that kind of compromising evidence, you can do so much, make so much money, pay your staff absurd salaries, like Leon, with his crazy wristwatches. Leon.

And I am sure that Kat discovered this, and I am sure she worked it out: she left a card to tell the future.

And maybe the card was, at the same time, a suicide note. In typical Kat style.

The logic hardens, like ice forming, yet speeded up.

I can get over it.

Standing, I put the light fitting in the pocket of my down jacket It might be evidence, which I need. But it is not enough, not yet. What can I do with it? Call the police and say, *I found a tiny camera; they were filming people?* The police will laugh at me, and scoff. I am the madwoman who prank-called them because of a ghostly scream. And that's if the police aren't implicated, as well. If they've got a senior lawyer, why not senior police?

I need more. I need help. I need to persuade Logan to help me. Bluff him?

Crossing to the blackened window, taking out my phone, I text him.

> Logan. I know the answer now. I know what they did to you. They filmed you. They filmed everyone. It was sex, wasn't it? I know. That's how they kept you here. And they needed you here because they needed a successful hotel for cover

The text is delivered. It is not read. But maybe he sees it anyway.

I wait. Greedy growls in his sleep. The tiny birds wheel across the cloudy sky, as the rain falls on the river. A dirty night, getting dirtier. The Blackwater chops with white wavelets.

> LOGAN. I am going to the police. Telling them everything. But I want more evidence. You need to help me. I will tell!

The text is also delivered, and unread. Maybe he has blocked me entirely, and won't see my messages, as he doesn't take my calls. I know what they did here, but it doesn't get me out of danger, and darkness. It doesn't get me off the island. I am still stuck. Even though I have worked it out.

I need more proof. And I still need to know exactly what happened to Kat. Right at the end.

72

Kat, Then

Elliot Kreeft. This is the beautiful blonde young man, standing in the doorway, stepping through the door, without being asked. The son of Mum's lover.

He looked the same as he had earlier on, in the clearing with the statue. The same cream suit and pale blue shirt, the same golden hair – somehow silvery in the evening light from the window. Nothing out of place; maybe he always looked like this.

Elliot looked around the room. Assessing. He looked at the bed still obviously disturbed: by sex, by Kat and Ben, bedsheets slipping to the floor, pillow still punched where Ben had forced her face into the cotton.

Elliot looked pensive.

Kat had to say something. 'What do you want?'

'Not much. This is just a visitation.' He regarded the bedroom once more, then he crossed to the window, his back to her, staring out at the Blackwater and the fading colours of the sunset. 'It is a lovely evening, isn't it? So long, they are so long. You know?'

'I guess.'

'These midsummer twilights on the Blackwater. I always loved them as a boy, loved them and watched them, but then we had to leave. And sometimes you think they will never end, and the darkness will never come. But it always does.'

He turned to face her, the purple twilight behind him: finally becoming night. She watched his mouth, his eyes, as he talked.

'Over Royden, over the Stumble, over the woods. I used to look for the Strood, knowing the old road was there, under the waters. Drowned in the river.'

For the first time, Kat felt a sense of physical menace. Yet she could not understand why. He wasn't saying anything threatening or doing anything obviously scary. Maybe it was guilt. She had drunk too much, done too many drugs. And the guilt over Ben was profound, and the sadness about Mum. She felt barely attached to sanity.

She lifted a hand, protesting. 'OK please, I don't know why you're here. I don't know what you want from me.'

'Nothing, Katalina. Just wanted to see you, in the flesh.'

'What does that even mean?'

Kat could hear the shrillness, even panic, in her own words, as she spoke. 'Look, I'm really, truly sorry about your dad and, y'know, what my mum did, but Mum died as well – it's not like we didn't suffer.'

'You spoke to your father.'

Kat did not understand this. She did not understand much, any more. She could hear the party, but muffled, far away. The strain of music, the white noise of laughter, everything turning incoherent. She shook her head. 'How do you know?'

'Come on, Katalina. Think.'

'What?'

'You could always say it was rape. I mean, it could almost have been rape, at the beginning.'

Her disquiet was growing, fast. Elliot was reaching into his pocket, bringing out a phone. He gazed down at the screen, absorbed, for a moment, then looked up. He lifted the phone, to show her.

She leaned over, squinted at the screen, and recoiled.

It was a movie, high-resolution, excellent sound. Kat stared through her tears at the images, listening to herself, listening to Ben.

'*Harder.*'

'You always like it so rough. Jesus.'

'You do too.'

'I don't—'

'Harder!'

Kat shuddered and looked away. Whatever happened, her sister must *never* see this. It was horrible. Kat glanced at it once more, then averted her face. Watching it was like some out-of-body experience when, close to death, you float above yourself, staring down at your body in the hospital bed.

Ben on top of her, her white fingers raking his dark hair. The desperate sighs.

They must have filmed *everything*. All of it. Her sucking him. Him eating her. Everything. It all looked so crude, so brutal, so terrible, on a screen.

Elliot smiled, as if puzzled. 'You don't want to see more?'

She shook her head. 'No.'

'Interesting.'

He put the phone back in his pocket. Gave her that strange smile again.

'They capture everything. All the girls. With extraordinary fidelity.'

Kat looked him in his eyes, expecting to see triumph, but she saw nothing. Maybe he could be persuaded.

'Please don't show that to my sister. I beg you. It will just break her heart. She's my best friend. Please. I'm sorry about the past. Your family, but please.'

He shrugged. 'As I say, you might possibly claim it was rape, unless you can think of something else? To distract attention?' He gestured, airily, towards the window. 'She will see it otherwise. Or you could vanish, steal away in the night, perhaps, run away from trouble like your mother. Do that and no one will know; no one will see anything.'

She did not know what to say. She watched as he walked past her, to the door, where he hesitated.

Then he was gone.

For a long while Kat stared at the open door.

The sky had entirely darkened. The music played. Kat sat by the window and rubbed some cocaine on her gums. Let it lick down her throat, trying to blur it all out. Just pretend it didn't happen, the video didn't exist.

It was impossible. She watched the moon come out. Sensed the Drowning Hour approaching.

She blinked back the intensity of her sadness, leaned over the little table and picked up the note.

Help me

Was it Mum? Surely not. Did it even matter? Carefully, angrily, Kat ripped the note into a dozen pieces and hurled them out of the open window, watching the confetti blow along the dusk-lit shingle.

Then she took her Tarot pack from her bag, opened

the box, took out the deck. Slowly, thoroughly, she shuffled the pack. Then she closed her eyes, and thought, with intensity, of Hannah, Mum, Dad, the Kreefts.

Eyes wide, she selected the top card, and turned it over.

The Moon, inverted.

Mum's card. Now Kat and Hannah's card.

The Moon, and the dogs. The crayfish and the path. Across the island to the Stumble.

Slipping off the bed, she lifted up the mattress. Positioned the card. Where the note had been stowed. It seemed right. The card was Kat's very own note, left for others to find. One day.

After that she dressed quickly, strapped on her shoes. The night was dark now, but welcoming. A warm, smoky breeze wafted through the window, tinged with the scent of burnt wood and meat. Enticing everyone.

73

Hannah, Now

How much time has passed, with me lying here, in my coat, in the freezing dark? Maybe ten minutes, maybe thirty. The wind moans outside, chasing the river to the sea. Maybe it *is* time to call the police. Tell them: I am mad, and I see ghosts, and I have found a tiny camera, please help.

I still can't call the police. They would still laugh at me. Or tell Oliver, or Alistair.

My phone chirrups.

I've got a message. Hope dazzles me.

Logan?

No. It is from a number I do not recognize. But it is ominous, whoever has sent it. Cold panic prickles. Pins and needles.

Don't call me or text me. It's dangerous. They monitor everything, messages, everything. The system is hacked. Intranet. They know everything. I shouldn't be doing this, but maybe this app will be OK. You are in danger

I type back, bewildered.

Who is this?

Anonymous phone. Shouting at gurnards

It is Logan. Our in-joke. Realization stings, and it brings deeper panic. Of course. The hotel Wi-Fi. All the hi-tech everything. The tablets for waiters, the smart-home lighting, the remote-controlled everything, the whole Stanhope intranet: it is all linked, and we *all* depend on the Wi-Fi. They might have been reading every message, or listening to every call, accessing every email, all the time I've been here.

Another message.

> **Search. Might still be there. Stored. Where I worked. I didn't take it with me. It was so evil. Wanted nothing to do with it**

I reply:

Look for WHAT?

Logan is *typing*. I lie here, on the bed, in the dark, in the sulphurous cold. Stiff with tension. Hurry up, Logan. Please. Save me.

Logan is not *typing*. He has vanished. I stare at my phone, bewildered. The app is disconnected. I check the top of the screen. No Wi-Fi.

The signal is down.

I wait, hoping. It could be a glitch. Or it could be part of the whole plan, shutting down the power – and now this as well.

I wait some more but the Wi-Fi is still dead. Heart fluttering, sitting up, I search in my settings, with cold, clumsy fingers. Toggling Wi-Fi on and off.

There is no network. No Stanhope5.

It's done. They've turned the Wi-Fi off, remotely. Alistair, or Loz, or Leon, or Oliver. Whoever. It might be coincidence, or maybe they've read my messages about police and cameras. Either way my only link with the outside world is broken. Without the Wi-Fi, I cannot talk to anyone. I cannot call or text. I can't ask for help from the mainland, from the outside world. They warned me, quite blatantly, they would do this. And they have an excuse: the wiring.

Health and safety, we have to cut the power.

But I am not entirely defeated. I am isolated but I can fight. Because now I have something on them. I have Logan's words. *Might still be there. Stored. Where I worked.*

Breathing the cold air deeply, twice, I turn on the headtorch. I must go and look in the kitchens, where Logan worked.

I didn't take it with me. It was so evil

74

Out Out Out Out Out Out Out Out Tout Tout
Out.

I step to the door, looking back for a moment. No. Let Greedy sleep. I may need him active later. I surely will.

The door opens to a silent, icy, darkened corridor. My headtorch is beginning to flicker. It has minutes left. I do not have batteries. Everything narrows down to this point. A singularity.

I gaze along the corridor. The many locked doors. A row of refusals. No one will say.

Evil.

Could they have filmed something worse than just sex? What might I find? Did they make a film of her murder? Is she still here?

Her body was never found.

I shudder, from frost, and alarm, but I have to do this quickly, before they get here. I am certain most of the higher management is involved in this. How can they not be? It is such a big thing. And they – all of them – must surely be coming. The rain is pattering the window; the storm is close. They will have to cross soon.

My breath is silver vapour as I walk, caught in the feeble torchlight. I am making ghosts: exhaling them.

Kat says, 'I am not here.'

But she is here, in the dark. I can just see her face. White, then gone, retreating, retreating. Her voice mumbles into quiet. A moan. Like sex.

I run on, not much time left. Thinking. Running. Past the cedar of the sauna, around reception, past the big register with my dead sister's name in it, into the deeper shadows of the Mainsail, with the boarded-up windows and the shrouded tables.

I slow as I approach the hotel kitchens. Both flaps of the big door are open onto a void of black. I do not remember opening these doors so that they stay open. You have to push hard. I would remember that, wouldn't I?

Who opened the doors?

There is an evil thing in the kitchens. Perhaps I am about to go in a room where I will open a big freezer door and I will find Kat in pieces in clear plastic bags, her body dismembered, the crime recorded on camera. In here, in the freezers. Her severed head, with ice on her pink-white lips, frost on her eyelashes. All chopped up, like pieces of a cow, frozen for later, chalky white bones in stiff pink meat.

It might be something like this. Logan did say evil. And he is not haunted like me. He is sane. He's a chef. He makes bearnaise sauce. If he said *evil*, he did not mean *ghosts* or *witches*; he possibly means *murder*.

Perhaps she survived the Drowning Hour, but they found her, and they killed her. Which means it wasn't suicide at all. It was murder. Is that it? The Moon is murder?

The big open door waits. I drag myself towards it, and step inside the echoey kitchens.

The silence is extraordinary. Oppressive. Worse than

the total dark. I look around, startled as well as scared, and realize why it is such a strange silence: all the machines have been switched off, the machines that are *never* switched off. The freezers and fridges, the micro-wave clocks. The food will be rotting now, as the fridges defrost; water and juices will ooze in the dark.

My frozen sister will be melting.

I have to look in the freezers. Have to do it. This is the most obviously evil thing you would find in a kitchen. Frozen bodies. Sliced-off faces frozen into eternal screams.

The freezers wait. Big steel things. Big steel tombs. Glinting grey and silver in the torchlight. The horror is a poisonous taste in my mouth. I swallow it away and pull open the freezer door.

It is empty.

They emptied them? They emptied the freezers. Or, at least, this one.

There are two more. The next is also empty. Cleaned out. Deep shelves of nothing. Water drips onto the floor as it begins to defrost.

The last freezer. I throw it open. This one is not empty. I force myself to rummage in the shelves, throwing my torchlight into the chilly gloom. There is frozen fish here, some vegetables. Peas. No severed human heads. A bag marked 'curry leaves'. Logan's writing, just visible in my dying torchlight.

There is something evil in there.

There is nothing evil in here; the evil must be else-where. Frustrated and fearful, I slam the door. I look left and right, and my torchlight alights on grey shapes: hobs, sinks, grills, sous-vide things I don't understand. Copper pans. Blenders. Colanders. Gloomy in the dark.

A noise does not make me turn. There are *no* noises.

There is nothing here. It is just a kitchen in a dead, frigid hotel; eerie and silent and devoid of light, but still: just a hotel kitchen. I am angry now, angry with Logan. He said to come here, where he worked, where I will find the truth. And there is nothing here, just a freezer containing no body parts.

So where is this evil?

Moving between the dancing shadows, I pull out drawers of rattling cutlery. Nothing. I yank open the watery caskets of the fridges. Nothing. I look under unused tables. Nothing. Nothing.

'Fucksake. Enough!'

My pulse rate is crazy fast.

My shouts trail away. The hotel does not respond. The dark, silent kitchen is simply waiting for me to fuck up. Maybe the evil thing in the kitchen is me. Maybe I have been sent to find *me*.

And then.

Corner of my eyes, I see it.

Her.

A grey, shaded figure walks briefly, quickly, past the kitchen door. The figure was stooping, looked frightened. Is it Kat? Or is there someone else here? I run out into the Mainsail and look left, and I see something moving out there, beyond the dust sheets and the shrouded tables, but she or it is gone.

It was not Kat; it wasn't someone else. Madness surrounds me. I have a few hours left, maybe a few minutes. I have to work out what Logan meant.

Where I worked.

Stored.

75

Perhaps I am not looking for hard evidence, perhaps I am looking for data. Movies. Files.

I leave the Mainsail and run into the icy reception. Look up. The main office. Where Logan has his desk, which he rarely used. And his company laptop, chained to the desk. So rarely opened. Would not have bothered anyone. Might have been overlooked.

Stored. You can store *data* as well as things.

Urgency sings. And my headtorch blacks out. The batteries are dead. And now I am surrounded by a greater darkness. But there is just enough light from the stormy night sky through the unboarded windows. Running up the spiral steps, nearly tripping in the gloom, I reach the landing and can just make out the main office door.

I turn the knob. It is still locked. Of course. But this time I have an idea.

I remember when Owen got burned, when he dropped the fire extinguisher. *That thing was heavy.*

There is a similar, large fire extinguisher in this corridor like the one in the east wing. I grope along in the darkness.

Found it. Extinguisher. And yes: very heavy. But that's what I want.

Dragging the big metal canister down the corridor, I

grip and lift it. I can do this. I think. I swing the cold steel around, crazy, round and round, like an athlete; and I let go and the canister hurls against the door and in an instant the hinges splinter, the wooden panels implode.

The door is cracked open. Kicking away the fangs of the planks, busted by the blow, I step over the threshold.

The office is so cold and so dark.

Loz is sitting there, at her desk. She turns and smiles at me. Then she disappears.

Ignoring this, I hasten across, and strike my shins against a table, didn't see it in the dark. Pain throbs.

Here. Logan's desk, his old Stanhope laptop, chained to the desk. The old one he barely used because he barely came here because he hated everything about this place. For so long he was trapped, like me. They kept him here, the great chef, so crucial to a relaunched hotel, or so crucial to making it *look* as if this was an ambitious and renewed hotel, quite near to London yet perfectly isolated. Suitable for other purposes.

A failed hotel with no guests would attract attention: if boats kept coming and going. Especially boats with girls, with human bait. They needed a *successful* hotel. And then the Drowning Hour fucked it up.

Reaching blindly for the chair in the near-complete dark, I yank it around, sit down, open the laptop . . . and then I pause, in realization.

There is no power. The laptop may not work. The battery may well have drained down. It is chained so I cannot move it, plug it into the sockets in the Spinnaker. Whatever battery is left is all I have.

I open the laptop and it springs to life, glowing with coloured light. The corner of the screen tells me the battery has nine per cent of power left. I must be quick.

I enter, I go straight in: no password needed. Logan *really* did not care.

Logan's wallpaper shines: a photo of grilled sardines and lemon wedges on a plate, somewhere sunny, foreign. The battery is down to eight per cent already. I have maybe twenty minutes. Or less. Before they come. They are coming, I know it. My bet is they will have seen those messages from Logan. Or they will see me working on this computer. They are monitoring everything, always.

Here. Documents. I click.

No.

I click on more files, and folders.

No.

Seven per cent power.

I search the Wi-Fi settings.

There's a network I have never seen before. Part of the secure intranet, exclusive to the island. I don't know how this works, but it obviously works. The network is called Strood99. They named it after a road that no one can walk, except on very rare occasions. Poetic. I am praying that they gave Logan access; he was the head chef, after all. The network is stored on his computer. Downloaded, integral.

But will the intranet be working, and can I access it?

Still seven per cent.

Soon they will be here to silence me. So easy in the cold and the dark that surrounds me. The rain is gravelly on the big bay windows that stare out at the river and the saltings.

I click on the network: Strood99.

A screen appears. Name and password required. Either I am lucky, or I am not.

I type Logan's name. It autocompletes.

I hover over the password.

It autocompletes.

Another screen opens. A series of folders. One is called Eastwing. The laptop is down to six per cent. I click on 'Eastwing', and a further screen appears. I feel as if I am walking through a series of ghostly doors, which magically dematerialize as I approach.

Name and password required.

I type Logan Macki – and it autocompletes. I go to the password – it autocompletes.

The last door is open. A document called 'videos'. I click on the folder.

Access Denied. Network Shut. See Admin.

Anger boils. So, it is turned off, or encrypted, or whatever. It was never going to be that easy. They have beaten me at the end.

'Fuck!'

I want to hurl the dying laptop across the darkened office.

But.

But I remember what Logan said. Stored.

Logan said *stored*. The laptop is down to five per cent. This is the last minute or two. Stored can also mean cached or saved in Logan's history.

I go to the search engine. I click on history. The last day he was here before he fled. November 18.

My mouth hangs open. In shock. Yet not shocked.

It is here. They are here. All the people. All the ghosts.

His laptop has accidentally *stored* a series of images. I can already see bodies. Naked.

I recognize one face immediately. My hand hesitates, trembling, fearful, but I click on it.

The image expands and fills the screen.

There she is. My sister. She is naked, on a bed, staring up, mouth open in pleasure, eyes shut with pleasure, as a naked, muscled man licks between her legs. My fiancé.

I can hear a strange sound in the office. Then I work out what it is.

My sister is sobbing in the dark.

76

Speedily, I sift through the images: naked girls, naked men, girls tied up, girls being whipped. The Mackster must have looked for quite a while: in shame, or horror, or lechery, or whatever. Working out if he could risk it: quitting. *See what we have on you, Logan.*

The images are high quality, but they definitely look like screenshots. Clearly there are videos, originally, the source of these shots. And a lot of videos. This must have gone on for many months, maybe years. Here is one girl screaming, her wrists handcuffed to a big iron bed, a shadowy figure next to her. Is she being raped? I see lashes. Bruises.

It looks as if she is being raped, and she's not the only one. Lots of frightened girls. I see their terrified faces on big pillows gazing up at the camera in the lights, evidently unaware they are being filmed. Here is Silver-Haired Guy. He's on his back with a girl riding him, and the girl is far too young, maybe fourteen or fifteen.

Here is another face I recognize, from TV, a man, a politician. Really important people. So, they definitely enticed *powerful* men here – with young female flesh – then they filmed them, then maybe they blackmailed them. Police, lawyers, politicians, businessmen, therapists even? – giving the Stanhope power over so many.

Everyone. A place the police would not investigate because they filmed the police with underage girls, too.

Evil.

The laptop is down to four per cent. I stare at the screen. I have worked it all out and I feel dead. My sister. Suibobs. So much pain. Screams down corridors. Sex and whips and underage girls.

And then the Drownings stopped them. Too much attention. But they wanted to start again. Maybe people came over to enjoy the videos: so, management would convince them it could start again. Matthew Kreeft. On that boat. Yet they had someone in their way, a problem: me. A woman stuck on the island, who might see too much. Who might start investigating the death of her sister? As I am doing. As I have done.

Suicide.

Get rid of her.

As the hotel shuttered maybe they saw the benefit of closure. A real chance to get rid of me, that annoying problem woman with the phobia. Isolate me, then do it.

I look down at one last image. The laptop is about to blink out.

The image shows Leon, with a very young girl. She is naked and, on her knees, sucking him; he stares up in bliss, face captured crisply by the camera. His big fat Rolex glitters on his arm.

This is hard evidence. I have seconds left to do this. Leaning down, I yank open the drawers of Logan's desk. They are full of pens and notebooks and detritus and spoons and recipe books and a data stick with a colourful picture of the Stanhope in the sun.

Yes.

I plug the stick into the laptop and swiftly copy the

photos over to the stick. The laptop is down to two per cent but it doesn't matter. I've done it. Here, in the dark and the cold, I have the truth and the evidence in the pocket of my jeans.

Now what?

The laptop sparks out. All the light has gone. I rise, still feeling empty, and dulled, and sad, despite the vague thrill of discovery, and I walk across the silent, shadow-filled office to the big Regency window and gaze out at the Blackwater.

This is it.

I have to try. I have entirely solved the problem; I have cracked the riddle. I know what happened to my sister, and now I must see if my phobia is dissolved. As my stupid therapist promised.

Out and down, I run through the darkness to the reception door, press it to the blowing wind, stinging with rain. The storm is still promised, but it is not here yet. It is still possible to cross from Goldhanger. Surely, they must be on their way. They know I am onto them. Oliver and Alistair and Leon can't risk allowing me another week of life; I might have found something. I *have* found something. I have found *everything*.

Running down to the shore, crunching old crab shells, sniffing the tangy air, I gaze at the marching waves, in the dimness. The water is well out; it is a very low tide. The lights of Goldhanger are distant twinkles, moistened and tiny orange jewels. Taking the deepest breath, I step into the water.

It feels OK, and then at once it feels terrible. My head is vivid with images, as if I have been poisoned in my soul. I see Kat, drawing the suicide card, leaving it under the mattress then running out, running to the water. This water. Black water. The Blackwater.

I gasp at the horror, jumping out of the water, onto the wet pebbles. I cannot do this. The Blackwater is evil. There is puke in my mouth; here it comes. I am retching into the river, clots of food, acid tongue.

It is impossible. My heart is pained. Agonies of thumping. My phobia is worse than ever. I still can't get off the island. Not on a boat. Not swimming.

There?

I hear it.

Now. I hear the puttering of an engine, in the dark; I know this sound. There is a boat coming down the river, getting closer, through the blustering drizzle. The boat is approaching the jetty. There are four figures on it. Oliver, Leon, Alistair? And a fourth. Freddy? Piloting? They seem to be carrying broken sticks.

I stare harder. Not broken sticks. Shotguns.

I have about a minute before they tie up the boat and jump onto the planks of the jetty and come for me. I can guess what they want to do. They want to threaten me with the guns. Make me run into the river, in fear of them, and then they can watch me drown, and then they can say it was suicide.

No messy shootings, no strangulation in the Mainsail. If I drown, then there are no witnesses but them. It is quite brilliant. For them. Isolate her, scare her, kill her, and make it look like suicide. She was unbalanced. She said she was seeing ghosts.

Sad, mad copy of her sister.

Then reopen the hotel and start over, in the spring, with some new girls. A new PR girl.

I must stop them. I can stop them. They must not be allowed to do this again, which means I have to survive.

I am sprinting up the chiming shingle into reception. They can probably see me from the jetty. But I don't care. Heedless, I run down the darkened corridor, stumbling in the dark, falling into my room. The dog looks up, through the gloom, as I stumble inside.

'Greedy. We gotta go!'

Greedy stands, shakes himself. Grabbing his collar, I lead him to the external door. No choice now. They will be here in seconds. I just have to hide on the island, in the woods maybe, somewhere. But where? And what can I do then?

Greedy runs out, yapping. I follow, onto pebbles, hissing at him, 'Shush! Shussssh! Please.'

Did they hear? I can see their dark shadows moving up the beach, carrying heavy torches, which send out powerful beams, catching the rain in sparkles. The shotguns are lofted and ready. They look as if they are going hunting at night for rabbits. Except that they're hunting me.

'This way, Greedy!'

We run into the darkened woods. Just like Kat last summer.

77

Kat, Then

Kat ran down the wooded lane, listening to the fading music of the party. She was leaving it all behind, the people kissing and fucking, the drinking and singing. Tears stung her eyes. Why did she say that stupid thing to Julia? Rape. It wasn't rape. She'd made it all worse, given herself even less choice. The shame was too much, the movie too ugly, the sadness too intense. Dad, Mum, the Kreefts, everything.

She had no choice at all.

There were people behind her. She didn't care. She didn't want to see anyone, ever again. She wanted to travel to the furthest place of all, further than India, further than Isfahan. She'd always wanted to go to the faraway place, and here it was all along: the most exotic place of all, coming to her.

The path opened out onto the beautiful river. The full moon in a clear, sweet sky was shining down on the grandeur of the Blackwater. The air was filled with birdsong; they called even at night, these beautiful birds, on the island. It would be the last thing she heard, that and the waters of the Drowning Hour.

Kat stripped off her dress, and slipped off her strappy sandals, leaving them on the beach. Then she ran straight down the damp pebbles to the shore. She knew it would be cold, even on a warm midsummer night, but that didn't matter – she wasn't going to swim for long. She would stop swimming by the Stumble, and let the river do its job.

She gasped at the cold, the chill of the waves on her ankles, thighs, stomach. The cold was good: it washed everything away. Cleaning and remaking. Kat sucked in her breath as the water made it to her heart. The memories stung as they returned, a slap of icy water on her face. Breasting the waves. Remembering. Dizzy with cold, maybe already drowning.

Kat was a little girl again, in Promenade Park, running with Hannybobs in the sun in Maldon. Running to get a 99 from the ice cream van, laughing, licking it off their faces. Sisters.

The water was cold cold cold, so cold. She gasped as she swam towards the Stumble, fighting the current already. She could hear voices, shouting, panicked. Had people followed her? She didn't want that. She didn't want anyone else to drown. Kat needed to drown. Hannah would never know what she had done. Unless she found the card and worked it out. Let the card decide. For itself. It had already decided once.

Suibobs.

The water glopped into her mouth. It was terrifyingly cold out here. She could feel the famous riptide now, tugging at her legs, pulling her in, and down. It was fierce. They did not lie.

The Drowning Hour.

It was dragging her away, down to the sea, down to the depths. Memories, memories, blurring. She could see her mum kissing the man, Dad smiling sadly by a bicycle, a flower, Marrakech, a man in dusty Rajasthan, the taste of sea urchin, that jewel, walking into her flat in Belsize Park, a scent, ylang-ylang, embroidered cloth. The water, the water in her mouth. Too cold. The tide was intense.

Let it go. Let it all go. An end to crying. Never cry again. It would always be sunny in Promenade Park and time is an illusion. We never die; we just think we do. We come and go like waterbirds in the dark, moving in and out of existence, cycling like tides, like this dark river forever carrying itself towards extinction. Mum, Dad, going, going, sad. Still here. We are always here.

She saw people in the water, then the water pulled her under. Dreamy colours now. Floating in the water, bare legs kicking feebly. Magenta, blood, dark bronze, coralline, cold pink. Skin. A cold pink sun underwater, moonlight.

Bird. Avocet.

Kat went under again, swallowing water, inhaling sadness. The end of a path. Just a thing.

Hannn

Mum

See me, see me.

Deep, black.

A

78

Hannah, Now

Run, hide, where?

Oliver, Alistair, Leon will be searching the hotel, my room, the Spinnaker. They will soon realize that I must have fled out here, into the cold and the gales.

Greedy runs ahead of me. If he runs too far, I will lose him.

'Slow, Greedy, slow down!'

He turns, eyes bright in the darkness. It is cold and wet and dank, and I don't know where to go. I can hear a grumbling bass tone of thunder, as the wind beats the boughs above. The trees are swaying, urgently, making dumb messages of panic: *Escape, Hannah.*

But how?

I am trapped in the woods. I can't get off the island, even if I had a boat, and now my pace slows, because I can't keep running this fast. Soon I will run out of places to hide.

I pause, exhale, check. The dark mass of the hotel is hidden by the thick woods between.

Think. Find a way.

'Greedy, stop.'

Hands on my knees, gasping the cruel rainy air, I halt. Take deep, stinging breaths. I think I know where I am: getting nearer the northern shore where the woods are particularly claustrophobic. The branches overhead are organically laced, forming a canopy.

It may be as dark as the devil, but I know the island well. I know her noises. I know the place with the polecats; I know where you see the glow-worms; I know the blackthorn and the sea-blite, the sea-marsh and the samphire. I know it all because I have spent six months endlessly walking these tiny paths, and the pathless woods, and maybe this is my one solitary advantage. They don't know Dawzy like me.

My breath coils in desperate, silvery clouds. I am exhausted from the running. Greedy looks up at me, loyal and bewildered. Perhaps he senses my terror. He nuzzles for attention; I crouch down, stroking his head. 'We'll be OK, Greedy.' I am lying to a dog.

The rain dangles in drops from the hawthorn twigs. The wind is trying to break into the wood. And now I can see torch beams, piercing the dark pillars. They are distant but getting nearer. Scouring the woods, seeking me out; behind the lights come the shotguns.

'Greedy, I don't know where to go. I don't know what to do.'

Now I am telling the truth. He licks my hand by way of an answer.

The bright beams of light intensify. I am stuck, para-lyzed in panic. Which way? Beyond the buffeting wind and the loud scatter of the rain, I can hear voices. They are muffled by the bruising wind, but the dark male tones are distinct.

I whisper, into the darkness, 'Help me, Kat. I need help. Tell me where to go.'

The rain hisses. Kat does not reply. I think she's maybe gone forever.

Pushing myself up, I run on, away from the lights. Into the pressing dark. I need to find somewhere that is truly out of sight. *Now*. Before they reach me. They are probably fanning out, slowly working their way across the island. Oliver is a hunter; he knows how to flush out the game. In a minute or two they will chase me from the underbrush, like a deer, and I will run into the torch beams, and they will take aim.

Torchlight slices the air directly above. Making tinsel from the rain. I fly on, faster, heart painful, pushing slimy wet branches away from my face as damp brambles snake around my ankles, tripping me up. This is no good. The woods are no good. Make for the beach. But there I am exposed. So, I wait, in the rain, in the trees, paralyzed again. Working it out.

Will they really shoot me? Why would they bother? Why risk the blood everywhere? They will just take me. Grab me, tie me up, drag me onto a boat and throw me in the river in the anonymous dark. At the Stumble. In the Drowning Hour. And I will be swept away like my sister, in the turbulent waters, down past Jaywick and Dengie, out into the North Sea, to be shredded into ribbons by the propellors of the container ships.

Movement. Men. Coming towards me.

79

I look around. I know a place.

Another voice. Words precise, close.

'Try over there!'

It's Oliver. Commanding the other men, obviously in charge. I have seconds left.

The north shore. It has an overhang.

Grabbing Greedy's collar, I steer him urgently away from the probing lights. *Go go go.* I crouch as we run, trying not to rattle the leaf litter. The roaring storm, the rolling booms of thunder, they are disguising everything.

Lightning flashes. It must capture me, sprinting, yet frozen, like a photograph flash, an escaping criminal. Did they see? Where are they? I know they are all around me.

The voices rattle from tree to tree. Hunters, hunting. The thrill of the chase. There she is, take aim. Through the rain.

Bang.

'Greedy. Go!'

Keep running. We break out of the trees, reaching the shingle. Glancing back, I see the woods behind me sway, in the gale, like a sad congregation, lifting their arms. Ahead, the beach of tiny pebbles gleams in the wet and the starlight. The beating rain is like a punishment.

Another lightning flash. It shows me the overhang.

The beach is so steep here it is more of a cliff. No one will see me under there.

The rain sizzles down, pelting my face. We have to hide.

'Down the slope – yes, boy, good boy.'

The rain has turned the shandy shingle to slides of mud. We slip; I almost go flying, onto barnacled rocks. Another torch beam pierces the veils of rain overhead. They are *close*.

I tug Greedy under the overhang, force him to sit. We can wait here. For what, I don't know. For Kat to tell me how to escape? To go in the water like the crayfish on the card? The final clue?

'The bitch must be there!'

Alistair, right above me. Five yards away.

I shudder, crouch down into myself, wanting to be absorbed by the mud and the rocks.

'Corner her, yes, over there!'

He's right above me. I can sense his rubber boots in the sodden grass right over my head. Pressing into my head. Pressing my face into jagged rocks, crushing my skull. Blood squirting. Eyes popping.

I wait, clamping Greedy's muzzle shut. This is it. I wait, body rigid. Maybe this is the last thing I will ever see. The northern view across the rainswept blackness of the Blackwater, to the lonely coast. Gore Saltings. The Bowstead Brook.

Time drags to a halt. The rain pelts, the thunder grumbles – and Alistair's voice comes again, but more distant.

'Through here, must be . . .'

They haven't seen me. They're moving on. I can picture them crossing beams, and puzzled words: she's disappeared, let's try this way; you do the beach.

All is dark. The birds rouse out there, disturbed by something. The water is silent in the rain. And black as its name, even as the wind scours away. Silence and storm. Rain and thunder.

'Hannah.'

A torch beam dazzles me. Direct in my face. I lift my hand, to shield my eyes.

The torch beam is angled away.

Oliver stands in silhouette against the night sky – tall, confident, gun broken over his arm.

And he says, 'Run for it.'

80

What?

I cower into the darkness.

Oliver speaks quickly. 'I persuaded them to wait, Hannah. They wanted to come sooner, but I saw this weather rolling in. And I saw a chance, for you.'

Bewildering. He wants me to escape?

'What chance? You've come here to kill me.'

'They have. But don't let them.'

'Why are you doing this?'

'I'm not in charge Hannah. You don't get it, but there isn't time to explain. You have a minute or two before they realize.'

'What?'

The wind moans. He almost shouts. 'The Strood! I've seen it. I've *checked*.'

The Strood. I turn from him, look out at the rain, the sky cracking with lightning, the cold, hard wind from the north. And that low, low tide I've been expecting for weeks.

The Strood.

'Go.'

I am gone. Up the scrambling slope, Greedy following. Torch beams glow down the shoreline, and they are turning, the others, they've caught me, out in the open.

'Down here!'

The men are running towards me; they are surely much faster than me. But I can see a bike. One of the bony Stanhope bikes, lying in the mud. Forgotten. Left by the last guest. Pulling up the bike, I step, hard, on the slippery pedal and cycle into the night, flying in the rain. Greedy gallops beside me.

A gunshot thuds, muffled in the night but unmistakable. Aimed at me.

Leon shouts; Freddy shouts.

I must escape them. I race around the corner, seeking my fate.

The Strood is up.

Her cobbles glisten in the starlight, leading out into the mud. She has emerged. The miracle has happened. This is my chance. Hurling the bike to the ground, I run along the Strood's serpentine curves, the miracle road that swings, across the mudflats and the saltings, heading for the Essex bullrushes, and freedom.

I turn as I run. They must be coming after me.

They have not. The men have stopped, all four of them. I see them. Leon, Alistair, Oliver, Freddy Nix. They wait on the little cliff, where the Strood begins. They are not following. Their torch beams pick me out on the Strood, yet they just stand, surveying, as I run. I do not understand. Greedy and I are getting away, racing along the Roman stones, to freedom.

Or maybe we are going to die.

Water rushes, all around me, as I run.

I look down, in horror.

The tide is coming in, that infamous tide that races, faster than a man can run. I must not let this water near me. My heart is already thumping, in agony. Yet I can't go back, to the island – they will find some other way to kill me.

I gaze down, in further horror. The Strood really is disappearing. She never meant to rise entirely: and now she is dying, in the rain and the night. Already the water is up: around my ankles, reaching for my knees, filling my mouth with the taste of vomit, scraping my nerves with pain, and I am probably a mile from the mainland, the lights of Heybridge, all too far away.

'Greedy?'

He has gone. The tide has taken my dog. The Strood has reclaimed what it gave to me, my beautiful dog. Drowning now, out there, I cannot see him.

My panic is so intense it reaches a kind of constancy. A sustained shriek, as the waters get higher and nearer and deadlier. I get it all now. Too late. But I get it. Oliver lied. They wanted me to do this. To run down the Strood. They knew it would not properly resurface. What are the odds? They have made me run towards my own death, like a madwoman, like a suicide, like my sister.

A perfect murder.

I cannot run any more. The salty water is too strong; I am wading into depths; the horrible water is claiming me. Soon it will be ten foot deep. And I will be lost beneath it, sunk under the freezing waves. A lifeless body, sent past Goldhanger, tumbling towards the North Sea. Seen by no one. Gone forever.

I am beyond panic. I am accepting. The sadness is consoling, and wicked.

The water laps at my arms, a desperately cold embrace. Like steel bindings around me. Making me gasp. Like I have no space to breathe. I can taste the water now, vinegary, in my mouth. Another wave glops over my head, like a cruel slap.

This is how Kat died, I suppose. She wanted to die

here, in this rushing tide. But she did it willingly, on a perfect summer night, under a voluptuous moon, and I am dying in the dark of December as the river spits in my face.

I stop. I am too cold, and it is too hard. My phobia is becoming pointless. Its job is redundant; it is gone. Because I am drowning anyway. I am dying anyway. It doesn't matter if my heart bursts in my chest. Let the river do the job instead. Let her take me. I can feel my feet floating free. I am out of my depth. I am dead.

I hear a bark.

Greedygut?

I kick against the water; I gaze across the choppy wet. Is it? Can it be? How?

It is him. My dog. My magical beast. My familiar. My imp. He is standing on a grey little beach in the gloom, barking furiously. The shore must be the mainland, and it must be close. He must have made it across the water. Guiding me. Saving me as I saved him.

'Greedy!'

Another bark. Then a voice. A man I do not recognize. The voice says: 'Swim!'

Swim?

Why? Why not? I can. So, I will. Yes. So, I swim.

Plunging forward, I fight the brutal cold waves, the hungry tide. It is not far, but it is hard.

Too hard. Fifty yards, less, I cannot make it. The waters are winning, even though I can see Greedy, barking in a frenzy.

I swim, but only yards: the river is too fierce and way too frigid. I can feel the cramp seizing my muscles. I am being taken again, towed away by my fate. I try once more, and as I flail at the waves, and yield to the end. I sense that I am seized, but not by the river this time. This is different; these are strong human hands, pulling me, hard and determined. Saving me? Hauling me to the shore.

I surrender to the rescue. I let this man pull me, then carry me, then gently lower me. Now I have hard earth, under my knees; I crawl up the beach, spitting dirty river water, choking on pebbles. Vomiting dirty cold water. Gasping, gasping. And wetness.

Greedy is licking my face, just as he did when *I saved him.*

'Oh, oh, Greedy.'

I turn. That voice again?

'That was close, Hannah. My God.'

I look up, squinting; shocked and bewildered.

Logan Mackinlay.

81

Hannah, Now

Logan leans close, stroking my faintly sunburned arm.

'Cold beer?'

'Oooh, yes please.'

'Alpha or Mythos?'

Tugging my sunglasses down my nose, I look at my new fiancé. I see he is also a little sunburned, and his nose is peeling. Pink Scottish skin in the strong Aegean sun is not an ideal mix. But I like the tanned cheffy muscles. He will soon be brown.

Lying back on the sunbed, I sigh contentedly. 'Alpha, please. And maybe some menus?'

'OK.'

He reaches for his wallet on the tiny table, by the sun cream and the novels.

Eyes half-shut, I say, 'Don't know why I bother, though. The menus will still be the same.' I gaze his way. Lazily. 'I think that's one reason I love Greece. Every day the same. Greek salad and grilled fish, that's your lot. It's perfect.'

'Don't forget the moussaka. There's always moussaka.'
I chuckle. 'And hummus.'
'Back in a few minutes.'

He disappears up the warm stone steps to the quaint little bar, of our quaint little resort. Lifting myself, I look out at the sun-dazzled sea, the blue Pagasetic Gulf, which is surrounded by serene blue mountains off the Pelion Peninsula. When Logan and I were choosing our Greek holiday we havered over islands – Crete, Skyros, Poros – but then I decided I'd had *enough islands*, at least for a while. So, we went for a peninsula. Pelion. Almost an island, but not quite.

'He seems nice, Hannybobs.'

I pull down my sunglasses again, look left. At my sister, stretched out on her sunbed, her tanned legs glistening with sun oil, her chic pink bikini just the right side of too skimpy. Her white teeth shine. Her ankle bracelet is made of tiny shells and silver bells. The coils of her blonde hair are still damp from a dip in the sea. The tiny delicate hairs on her shining skin have been bleached to white gold by the sun. It is as if she has an aura of silver, as if she isn't there. I say, 'He is. Really nice.'

'So how the actual fuck did that happen? You and the Mackster? Wasn't he part of the criminal master-plan?'

'He was blackmailed by them. He joined quite inno-cently, but they filmed him, just having normal, consensual sex with a girl, but enough to humiliate him, trap him, especially linked with the other videos.'

'And he rescued you! Weapons-grade hero.'

'He guessed I would try the Strood. My only choice.'

'Who knew, huh? Logan and Hannah!' My sister stretches out a languid, golden arm, picks up a clear plastic goblet of Frappuccino, and sucks so loud she

386

frightens a lizard, which skitters away, towards the nice Greek family with the inflatable dolphin.

'He's got immunity,' I add. 'He's agreed to testify against them. All of them. They were all in it together, Oliver as well.' I hesitate, but go on, 'And the Kreefts. That young guy that you spoke with. All of them.'

She eyes me.

'That's brilleeeunt!' She sucks more Frappuccino, wipes her full, red lips with a delicate hand. I can smell the sweet oil on her soft, burning skin. 'It's all good. All good! You're happy. Who doesn't love a happy ending?'

I gaze at her, sensing the tremble of a tear. 'Not so happy, Kat.' She offers me a sarcastic glance. I say, 'I mean. No one knows that, sometimes, I still talk to you.'

'So? What's the prob? We can still talk, surely?'

I shake my head. 'Oh, Kat. Darling. I don't think so.'

She pouts, sulkily. There is a tiny white smear of sun cream on her perfect unageing forehead. 'What does *that* mean?'

'It means . . . Well, it means I have to let you go. Finally. We have to stop talking, for now.' A pause. 'Maybe forever.' Another pause. 'Probably forever.'

Her frown deepens, to proper sadness. 'Really?'

She says this so quietly she is almost drowned out by the breeze in the bougainvillea, in the drowsing sunflowers, the breeze that riffles the blue silk waters of the Pagasetic Gulf.

I stifle my own sadness. 'Yes. I'm sorry.'

She says nothing; she turns, averts her face, hides, says nothing. Then she gives me a forced smile. 'You know it was *you* who worked out the card.'

'What?'

'The dogs, the lights – that wasn't me. I never saw that. It was all in *your* head.'

'It was?'

'Yeah, sillybobs. Bit of actual proper genius actually.' Her teeth sparkle in the sun as she laughs bittersweetly. 'Mum would be proud! Go, Tarot Lady.'

I laugh, and it is sad, and not-so-sad, at the same time. I don't want this moment to ever stop: me, here, laughing, with my sister, laughing together for the very last time.

She is speaking. 'I guess I'd better be going then, huh. Maybe a swim or something. Go and see Mum; maybe, baby.'

'OK, darling. I'm sorry. I am so sorry. But you know: I'll always love you.' The tears are back, behind my eyes.

She nods, sadly, with half a sob. 'And I will always love you, stupid. And I will always be somewhere in *here*.' She stretches and taps me on the head, and once again she is the little girl in Promenade Park, stealing Toffee the Bear, for a joke, teasing me, making me laugh.

I must not cry. I am on holiday; people will look.

Quickly and unexpectedly, Kat leans in and hugs me, tightly. Her warm, bare arms embrace me. I can feel the blood beneath her skin, smell the fine summer sweat and the coconut oil. And then she stands, and turns, and I watch her go, weaving barefoot between the sunbeds and the playing children, sashaying away away away, her ankle bracelet jingling, all along the sandy Greek beach. And then she climbs a grey rock at the end of the beach, and she is gone.

For a long while I lie here, saying nothing. Logan brings me my Alpha. I drink the cold beer and it is good. Then he hands me the menus.

They are those multiple language menus: English, Dutch, German, French. The choice is the usual: salads, souvlaki, fish, crayfish.

Scanning the menu, a word catches my eye in the Dutch column.

Kreeft.

So, it means crayfish? Of course it does. The very final clue in the card. I sigh, for a moment. But I resist the tears. No more tears. Put down the menu.

Logan notices. 'You all right, darling?'

'Yes. Just thinking. Memories. But I'm OK.'

'Grand.'

He returns to his novel. Then he says, 'Spoke to your dad, by the way. Just now.'

'And?

'He says Greedy is doing fine. Pining for you a bit but chasing all the pigeons in Maldon.'

I chuckle. Take another hit of beer. Then I rise, and adjust my emerald bikini, feeling the glorious sun on my bare shoulders.

And now I race down the sandy beach, and I leap. And I dive, into the beautiful water.

THE MOON.

She's in your house.
She controls your life.
Now she's going to destroy it.

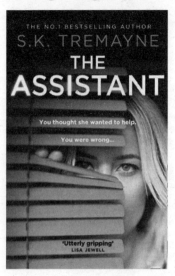

She watches you constantly.

Newly divorced Jo is delighted to move into her best friend's spare room almost rent-free. The high-tech luxury Camden flat is managed by a meticulous Home Assistant, called Electra, that takes care of the heating, the lights – and sometimes Jo even turns to her for company.

She knows all your secrets.

Until, late one night, Electra says one sentence that rips Jo's fragile world in two: 'I know what you did.' And Jo is horrified. Because in her past she did do something terrible. Something unforgivable.

Now she wants to destroy you.

Only two other people in the whole world know Jo's secret. And they would never tell anyone. Would they? As a fierce winter brings London to a standstill, Jo begins to understand that the Assistant on the shelf doesn't just want to control Jo; it wants to destroy her.